'Clarkin has created a wonderfully diverse group of characters with rooted backstories that make them altogether relatable and each one of them unique. She has a real talent for building tension from one chapter to the next, making it next to impossible to put this book down.' *Irish Examiner*

'Deliciously creepy debut YA title ... An eerie abandoned mansion, a malevolent spirit, family secrets, paranormal investigators, secrets revealed ... gorgeous, gothic & utterly gripping. If you liked *Wednesday*, you'll love it!' @TheBookaneer808

'My goodness *What Walks These Halls* by @AmyClarkin is good!' Sarah Webb, author of *Be Inspired! Young Irish People Changing the World*

'There is a creeping dread in *What Walks These Halls* by @AmyClarkin that builds with each page, absolutely loving it, very sharp YA for your shelves.' Lucas Maxwell, former UK SLA Librarian of the Year

'*What Walks These Halls* will warm your heart while chilling you to the bone. A thoroughly gripping story, of ghosts, legacy and chosen family. I adored it.' Deirdre Sullivan, author of *Savage Her Reply*

AMY CLARKIN is a writer from Dublin. Her non-fiction writing is often on the theme of chronic illness and identity, and has been featured in *Sonder* literary magazine, *Rogue* and *Dear Damsels*. *What Walks These Halls* is her debut novel. She can generally be found by the sea, drinking coffee, talking about her dog or asking people what their favourite ghost story is.

 @AmyClarkin

 amyclarkinwrites

They had trespassed.

And a voice whispered to her that

there would be a price to pay.

Amy Clarkin

THE O'BRIEN PRESS
DUBLIN

For my parents – for everything

First published 2023 by
The O'Brien Press Ltd,
12 Terenure Road East, Rathgar,
Dublin 6, D06 HD27, Ireland.
Tel: +353 1 4923333; Fax: +353 1 4922777
E-mail: books@obrien.ie
Website: obrien.ie
The O'Brien Press is a member of Publishing Ireland.

ISBN: 978-1-78849-373-4

1 3 5 7 8 6 4 2
23 25 27 26 24

Printed and bound by Norhaven Paperback A/S, Denmark.

MIX
Paper from
responsible sources
FSC
www.fsc.org
FSC® C104608

What Walks These Halls receives funding from the Arts Council.

the arts council
chomhairle ealaíon

funding literature

Published in

DUBLIN
UNESCO
City of Literature

Great Irish books
O'BRIEN
obrien.ie

PROLOGUE

SHADOWS IN THE HYACINTH ESTATE often seemed to move on even the stillest of nights, so a casual observer could be forgiven for thinking the dark figure moving stealthily across the lawn was another part of the house's long and eerie history. A closer inspection, if one were brave enough (or foolish enough, depending on who you asked) to do so, would have revealed a young man, twenty or so years of age, moving across the grounds towards the house. The observer could also be forgiven for thinking that he was talking to himself, until the light of the torch he clicked on revealed he was holding his phone in front of him and whispering enthusiastically to it.

'Hyacinth House might sound sweet, but this is one of the most haunted places in Ireland – a place so terrifying it's not even listed in the most-haunted guides, because it's not somewhere they want people to go.' He paused, clicking the screen to turn the phone's camera to face the house looming over him as he made his way towards it. 'It's only forty minutes' drive away from Dublin, near Kilcarrig in the Wicklow Mountains, but no one ever talks about it. All we know is it's said to be cursed, haunted by a spirit known only as "The Lady". Locals won't pass by after dark, and five years ago someone even *died* investigating the legends around it. And I'm going to spend the night here, on my own, tonight. This is going to be my scariest video yet!'

He stopped, the light of his screen just illuminating his frowning face as he lowered the camera. He raised it back up and clicked a button on the screen.

'This is going to be the most intense investigation I've ever done – so make sure to like, subscribe and check out my channel tomorrow evening to find out how I get on ... and if I make it out!' He grinned, replaying the footage before taking his phone and tapping a few buttons. He raised it to his ear.

'Hey, yeah, I've just uploaded the teaser now.'

He paced across the grass, then let out a delighted hoot. 'That many? Already? That's class! Yeah, I'm going in now. I'll check in with you in two hours. I still think you're being ridiculous about this ...' He cocked his head, listening to the voice on the other end of the line.

'Yeah, OK, OK. This place really is creepy, in fairness. I'll talk to you soon.'

He hung up and walked to the front of the house. The large oak doors were padlocked, and the windows, covered by thick boards nailed firmly into place, seemed to stare down disapprovingly at the trespasser. The argument could – and had – been made that perhaps the intention was not just to keep people out, but to keep someone, *something*, in. That the barricade was not a fortress, but a cage. If he had done as so many others before him had, arriving buoyed up by confidence and bravado only to feel the creeping dread that accompanied the house's gaze, the looming malice that seemed to ooze from the bricks, and decide, actually, he suddenly had somewhere else he really needed to be that evening, the night might have ended a lot differently for him.

But he did not.

Instead, he stepped up to a window on the left-hand side of the doorway that hadn't quite been boarded up tightly enough. He jimmied a thick plank off and shoved his backpack in through the gap before heaving himself up onto the window ledge and squeezing through the opening, disappearing into the oily darkness that almost seemed to reach out of the house towards him.

Had the casual observer lingered until now, they would not have detected any movement through the gap he'd created in the window once the house had swallowed him.

There was only silence.

CHAPTER ONE

'IRELAND IS A HAUNTED COUNTRY. It has seen its share of pain and upheaval, violence and trauma. These things seep into the landscape, the buildings, the people. They have a way of lingering long after the event. This creates an ideal environment for the paranormal.'

Raven's heart lurched at the familiar voice on the radio, even though she'd known it was coming: the presenter had announced his guest before the ad break. She hadn't turned it off. She never did.

'The Famine, the Civil War, the Magdalene Laundries … Ireland has a history of pain leading right up to the present day.'

'So all ghosts are miserable then?'

Raven could hear the discomfort in the presenter's voice as he joked, trying to steer the conversation towards a safer subject. Her mother had strayed too close to the political and, even worse, the contemporary. She smirked, turning old Fiat Panda into the driveway of her apartment building. People got uncomfortable when it got too close to home. They wanted their ghosts to come from the horrors of the past so they could distance themselves from it all. Shake their heads at the atrocities of history, and feel relieved that those things would never happen *now*.

Gravel crunched under the tyres as she parked. On the radio the conversation had steered towards the practical matters of ghost hunting, or 'paranormal surveyance' as her parents had always called it. She swallowed, forcing the rising pain back down.

'Your new book, *Finding the Veil*, talks about several cases that you haven't discussed before,' the interviewer was saying. 'Was it difficult to delve back into the records from your days working with your team, which included your late husband?' His 'sympathetic' tone was clearly feigned, setting Raven's nerves screaming. It was clear where he was aiming his questions: her father, his death, the case … Her mother had never spoken publicly about it beyond the key phrases: 'a shock, a loss,' etc., etc. Every interviewer wanted to be the person to crack Emily Rose O'Sullivan's composed facade.

Raven could have told him before the interview even started that he would not be the one.

'I have many pleasant memories from those days. Our work meant a lot to Pádraig. It felt fitting to honour his memory in the book, and to write more in depth about the investigation methods we developed together.' Her voice was cool but pleasant, ever the polite interviewee. 'Each case includes a detailed analysis of the different scientific methods and equipment that we used in investigations, things like Electronic Voice Phenomenon sessions, and EMF readers to measure electromagnetic fields, which spirits alter when they manifest, infrared cameras, heat-sensing technology and other equipment we used to create a strict set of protocols that ruled out any possibility of trickery.'

'And can you give listeners a hint of any particular cases they can look forward to reading about?'

Raven rolled her eyes. Not only did he not have the courage to come out and ask directly, he hadn't even bothered to read the book before the interview.

'Is there a particular case you're thinking of?' Emily's tone was neutral but Raven could sense the challenge in it. She could imagine her mother perfectly: her laser gaze skewering the unfortunate interviewer, blue eyes narrowed, blond hair pulled back into a tight bun as she leaned forward, arms folded onto the desk between them. Raven reached for the key in the ignition, then hesitated. She would wait and hear how this played out.

'Well, Hyacinth House is receiving plenty of attention since it was released back onto the market, especially after the incident with Jack Gallagher, the YouTuber who broke into the property last week,' the interviewer said. 'Everyone wants to know the story of what happened to you there – will this book be the time we finally get to find out?'

Raven's breath hissed out. The media always brought it up, hungry for the gory details. There was a pause, just long enough to be uncomfortable on the radio.

'No.'

Her mother did not embellish and Raven felt a rush of pride. She would be staring him in the eye, daring him to push further. There were few who could withstand the ferocity of her steely gaze.

'Would you like to talk about one of the cases that *will* be featured?' The presenter's voice was forcibly jovial. Emily had rattled him. Raven loved her for it.

'Of course. One of my personal favourites is the case of a small hotel in west Cork …' Emily's voice was smooth, the consummate professional. Raven turned the key in the ignition, shutting off the radio, and sat in the echoing silence. It always hurt to hear her mother's voice. She took a deep breath, picked her bag up from the passenger seat and swung herself out of the car. Now was not the time to be lost in past hurts.

Red and gold from the setting sun streaked the sky, casting everything in a hazy glow as Raven trudged up the steps to the one-bedroom apartment she rented on the top floor. Her mother's voice rang in her head as the key turned in the lock with a click. She shouldered the door open before collapsing on her small two-seater couch. Part of her wanted to message Emily, to congratulate her on shutting down the interviewer's prying.

Of course, she's always been great at closing conversations down, hasn't she? a bitter voice remarked in her head.

So have you, another voice countered.

She threw her phone onto the other end of the couch, curling her legs up underneath her, savouring the joy of a rare evening off work. The apartment was small, cramped even, but she didn't have a lot of things and, at five foot two, didn't need a lot of space. One bedroom, a narrow bathroom and a tiny sitting room-cum-kitchen were all she had and all she needed. Besides, even renting from an old family friend who charged her a considerably lower rent than everyone else in the area, this was all she could afford.

A few obligatory photos lined the windowsill: a couple of her fellow staff members at Origin, the artfully run-down bar where she worked serving pints of craft beer and a frighteningly large variety of whiskeys to hipsters in their twenties and early thirties. Behind them stood a photo of her and her brother, arms around each other on the beach in Tramore. She was fifteen, silvery-blond hair in a plait and a big grin on her face. Beside her stood

Archer, eighteen months younger and already four inches taller than her, freckles dappling his sun-kissed skin. It had been a rare hot summer in Ireland that year. The summer everything changed. Guilt tightened her throat. When had she last checked in with Archer? Besides the perfunctory likes or comments on Instagram under big life updates, like him celebrating finishing his Leaving Cert or showcasing how he'd redecorated his room in their family home – innocuous interactions that she could pretend constituted contact but didn't actually investigate how he *was*.

She sat watching the shadows grow across the walls until her stomach rumbled. Turning the oven on to preheat, she settled on her couch and reached for the TV remote. Her phone rang shrilly, making her jump and almost send a half-drunk cup of coffee from earlier that day flying off the coffee table. Swearing, she scrambled to pick up the phone.

It was Emily.

'Mum? Is everything OK?'

They spoke on birthdays, Christmas, important anniversaries – and emergencies. Since it wasn't any of the first three, she jumped to the panicked conclusion that it was the last.

'Can't a mother check in with her daughter without there being an emergency?' Emily's voice was crisp.

Raven sighed, stretching one arm overhead as she leaned back in her chair. '*A* mother can. *My* mother generally doesn't.'

Emily's *hmph* of disapproval echoed down the phone line. Silence.

'I heard you on the radio,' Raven said, as a peace offering.

'Oh, you listened?' Emily's surprise was evident.

It stung. Raven always listened. She just never told her mother she did.

'You handled him well.'

'Odious man.'

Raven could picture Emily rolling her eyes.

'Fishing for the grim details. Are ghostly tragedies not interesting enough without bringing up personal ones?'

Raven stayed silent. Emily did not require an answer.

'How is the bar work going?' she continued.

Raven filled her in on the latest about Origin: how they'd run out of a specific craft beer everyone was currently obsessed with, meaning that she'd had to placate cranky hipsters all week, all the while wondering when her mother would address the real reason for phoning. Emily did a good job of feigning interest until Raven eventually said, 'Why did you really call, Mum?'

'I need your help.'

'Did I mishear that?' Raven winced even as the words left her mouth.

'No. Believe it or not, I do know how to ask for help when I need it,' Emily's clipped voice fired back. She paused. 'It's your brother.'

'Is he OK?'

'He's starting a business. Or, to be more accurate, *restarting* a business. The family business.'

Raven swore. For once her mother didn't admonish her, something she still did constantly despite the fact that Raven was nineteen, almost twenty, and hadn't lived with her for almost two years.

'I agree,' Emily said.

'I'm surprised,' Raven said. 'I mean, you have no problem writing books and giving talks about it.' She couldn't stop the bitterness seeping into her voice.

'I don't actively investigate any more, you know that.' She paused again. 'Raven … I'm worried about him. He refused to even consider college. He's determined to restart PSI. I can't … I can't take a repeat of five years ago.'

'Neither can I,' Raven said quietly. She could almost feel Emily's worry seeping down the phone. It made her heart hurt. It was easy to blame her mother for closing up after Pádraig's death. For joining Raven in her silence, for letting grief come between them. She was the parent, after all. But any time her mother had reached out, Raven had pushed her away. Raven was too afraid of seeing what she suspected: that at least part of Emily blamed her for what happened five years ago.

'I want you to keep an eye on him,' Emily said, when the silence dragged on. 'If you can't convince him to end this, maybe you can stop him from doing anything dangerous.'

'What can I do, though? You know how stubborn he is.'

'He's more likely to listen to you than to me,' Emily said. 'He's always listened to you. You've always been able to get through to him when no one else can.' She paused, guilt creeping into her voice. 'I'm going to be out of the country for three months.'

The book tour, followed by an extended visit to her sister in California. Of course.

'I would feel better knowing that you were keeping an eye on him. If you're involved, you could temper some of his more … impetuous traits.'

Emily was worried. Though if she were truly worried, wouldn't she stay? Even if Archer wouldn't listen to her. Part of Raven wanted to refuse, to remind her mother that they had both created the distance between them, that she couldn't just call her out of the blue and start to make demands. But this was Archer. The only real thread that held their family together.

'I'll go see him tomorrow,' she sighed, as a heavy weight settled in the pit of her stomach.

CHAPTER TWO

ARCHER O'SULLIVAN WAS having an existential crisis.

That was the problem with ghost hunts. Too much time to think. Though PSI – Paranormal Surveyance Ireland – preferred to call them 'paranormal surveys' rather than 'ghost hunts'. Fionn still complained about that, arguing that it sounded like they were going up to spirits with a clipboard and pen, asking their preferences and opinions about the afterlife.

But that was what his parents had called it when they ran PSI, and since Archer was relaunching the family business, he wanted to stay true to that. Fionn had stopped complaining once he'd reminded him. You couldn't really argue with 'I'm honouring my dead dad's legacy.'

Not that it currently felt like he was honouring it, really. This was only their third job so far and, once again, it looked like there was going to be a completely mundane reason behind the fears of paranormal activity. He knew from growing up with his parents that this was often what happened. In fact, those cases added weight to their evidence when they *did* find something paranormal – it was much easier to be credible when you didn't announce ghosts at every single investigation. His parents had always managed to find good cases amongst the mundane, word of them spreading across the country and abroad too. PSI had been the go-to company for anything paranormal.

And here he was, perched on the branch of a sycamore tree just after dusk in late September to make sure the camera Fionn had placed there earlier that evening didn't fall out. And the only remotely spooky thing that had happened was the crow that flew far too close to his head for his liking. He had almost fallen out of the tree, taking the camera with him, but thankfully he'd managed not to. Fionn had had to leave after setting up the equipment, so if anything happened to it, Archer wasn't sure he'd be able to put it back again as well as Fionn had. Not to mention that Fionn wouldn't be happy if anything happened to the state-of-the-art camera he'd saved up months for, using his employee discount at the camera shop he worked in to afford it.

Focus, Archer.

Now was not the time to get distracted, even if his instincts were shouting that this was a waste of time. He couldn't let his attention get diverted from the survey, even if he was bored and uncomfortable. The air was warmer than it normally was at this time of year, but there was a branch digging into his back where he leaned against the tree trunk, and his legs were starting to cramp.

He missed the old days. At eighteen, was he allowed to use the phrase 'old days'? That felt reserved for people in their forties reminiscing about college. But it felt accurate. Him and Raven, always sneaking out of whatever room they were supposed to be staying in to go and investigate. Raven pretending she was a responsible older sister while immediately agreeing to whatever mischief he suggested. Then, once their parents let them start helping out, the two of them together waiting in the darkness, hoping to capture some evidence that would make their parents proud. Learning how to do Electronic Voice Phenomenon, or EVP, sessions, where they recorded themselves speaking out loud and asking questions during investigations in the hope of capturing a response from a spirit as evidence, learning the difference between thermal imagery and EMF readings and which was more beneficial and when, how to structure an investigation and shadowing their parents as they talked to clients. Always, no matter what, the two of them, together.

That was before, though.

Before Dad died. Before Raven withdrew. Before she closed up, cut him out of her life completely.

Now it was just him alone in the darkness.

'Arch?'

Not alone, he reminded himself.

'Still up here,' he called back. A figure came into view from the porch at the back of the B&B. Davis, the other member of his small team, strode down the steps and to the base of the tree. Archer shone his torch down at him.

'Nothing on the infrared or EMF meter inside,' Davis said, tilting his head and shielding his eyes.

'Nothing but a mildly aggressive crow out here,' Archer sighed. 'I think this is going to be another dud.'

'We still need an explanation,' Davis said, brow furrowing. He paced under the tree as he thought, sinking into his science space. Davis took the meticulous protocol he learned from his lab work in UCD, where he was in his final year of a science degree, into PSI. It could be incredibly helpful or extremely frustrating, depending on what they were trying to achieve. But that was what Davis did: he poured cool, rational logic over everything, the foil to Archer's emotional instincts.

'We're never going to find an actual case,' Archer said, rubbing an eyebrow in frustration. No wonder his mum had pushed so hard for him to go to college after the Leaving Cert instead of setting up PSI straight away. She knew he couldn't do it: not without her, not without his dad. And especially not without Raven.

Davis's response was level but reassuring. 'We will. It just takes time. You know that.'

Archer wanted to let it all spill out: how desperately he wanted this, how much he missed his family, how, deep down, he hoped Raven would come back, join the team, be herself again. How he was so afraid of failing, of spoiling everything.

Instead, he grinned, making his voice light. 'You're right. Just a slight moment of crisis there. Let's go back over the facts.'

Davis enthusiastically began reeling off what they'd gleaned from the client interviews.

'They hear shrieks at night, rattling on the windows, and scratching in the walls, like something's trying to get in. Their dog starts barking frantically to get out but when they open the door, he stares out into the darkness, hackles up, completely frozen.'

'It sounds like there should be a supernatural explanation, but my gut is telling me there isn't,' Archer said.

'And the scientific equipment,' Davis added drily.

There was a long scream from the bottom of the garden.

Archer swore loudly, nearly falling out of the tree again and barely managing to grip the branch in time. Davis spun around, his torch spreading a wide arc of light over a garden filled with thick hedges and bushes.

'I don't see anything,' he said, his voice calm, the hunch of his shoulders betraying his tension.

'The camera was pointing in that direction, the infrared too,' Archer said, starting to climb down from the tree. 'Fionn set it up perfectly. Hopefully one of them will have caught something.'

As Archer reached the ground there was another protracted scream, this time to the left of the garden. Another emerged from the original spot, almost in answer.

Wait.

He knew that sound.

He looked at Davis in exasperation.

'Foxes,' they said in unison. It wasn't mating season, which was why they hadn't thought of it before, but male foxes often screamed at each other to mark territory. A quick review of the infrared footage showed the figure of a fox, in the bushes. Even the outline on the screen showed the fierce, defensive way it was standing.

'The dog must be scared of it,' Davis said, shaking his head with a smile.

A slight rustle of movement caught their attention and the meanest fox Archer had ever seen slunk out of the bushes. It stopped for a moment, glaring at them, a slight snarl exposing its teeth, before it dipped back into the undergrowth.

'I don't blame him,' Archer said.

One aspect solved. It took them just a little longer to figure out the rest. A small number of mouse droppings by a crack in one of the skirting boards in the house explained the scratching in the walls, while a rotten wooden frame on the outside of the downstairs window meant that even the slightest breeze made the window shake.

Their clients were grateful, if embarrassed, when they explained. Archer did his best to reassure them, leaving them laughing and promising him a glowing testimonial for PSI's website. Archer felt a rush of joy at their delight. This was just as important as finding actual supernatural encounters, he reminded himself: the people. The *living* people. He was proud of his small team and the skills they each brought: he was the people person, Fionn the tech whiz, and Davis brought his keen, analytical mind to everything. They'd worked well together this evening. They were growing. That should be enough for him.

But it wasn't.

He wanted a proper case. And he had no idea how to find one. In an ideal world, he mused, a wry half-smile crossing his face, the team would have a human ghost detector too.

CHAPTER THREE

ÉABHA McLOUGHLIN STIFLED a yawn as she walked through the gates of Kilmainham Gaol. She cast an anxious glance at her mother, hoping she hadn't noticed. It wouldn't matter to her mother that it was early and that Éabha had been up late the night before reading to get a head start – at her father's pointed suggestion – on some of her course work: yawning in public was rude, in Brigid McLoughlin's opinion. And she did not tolerate anything but perfectly composed politeness at all times. They put on their face masks, though hardly anyone bothered these days, and dutifully sanitised their hands at the station by the door before Éabha showed the guide the tickets she had saved to her phone.

They lingered in the lobby, waiting for their tour to start, a few other people trickling in to join them. Moving to the front of the group to make sure she could hear the guide clearly, Éabha turned up the volume on her hearing aids on the app on her phone, a tight ball of nerves forming in her stomach. She'd be starting first year of Arts in UCD next week and she'd read in the course outline that she'd need to visit the gaol as part of one of her history modules. Her mother had asked to join her, a request that was more of a demand. 'I'd like to see the kind of things we'll be paying for you to study,' she'd said pointedly. Éabha couldn't say no then. Now, even as she tried to pay attention to the guide's opening spiel, all she could think was, *Please don't let it happen today. Not while she's here.*

The group moved towards what the guide referred to as the West Wing, a long corridor built from thick stone. It was freezing, the walls dark and gloomy while electric lights burned overhead. Their light was harsh and stung her eyes, reflecting off the steel doors to the cells that lined the corridor.

'Built in 1796 …' the guide was saying, his voice echoing around the corridor. A small man with close-cropped brown hair and a big smile, his voice boomed in the confined space of the gaol. As she stood listening, Éabha felt a creeping sensation trickling across her neck and down her spine. She closed her eyes for a moment, silently entreating her brain not to let it happen.

Not now not now not now.

It was foolish of her to come. Especially with her mother. But she'd had to, and part of her had hoped that it wouldn't happen. That maybe it was gone.

She'd wished that for years now. It hadn't ever disappeared, but she couldn't help hoping, all the same. She tried to focus on the guide's voice, shutting out the escalating panic sweeping through her.

'Victims of the famine who were caught stealing food were imprisoned here: men, women and children of all ages …'

Suddenly, Éabha was ravenous, despite the big bowl of porridge she'd eaten earlier. It was an overwhelming, agonising hunger that felt like her stomach was turning itself inside out. An aching despair crept over her, and all she wanted to do was weep. Her legs felt weak and for a moment she thought she'd pass out.

These weren't her feelings. She knew it instinctively, a sense she had never understood but that had been with her since birth. She was *experiencing* them, but they weren't coming from within her. They were invading her.

Swallowing hard, she trailed after the group when they stepped into one of the cells. Éabha hovered by the door, barely stepping over the threshold. She wanted to turn, to sprint down the corridor and away from the emotions – despair, isolation, fear and, above all, that desperate, painful hunger – that made her heart feel like it was being crushed in an iron fist. Instead she focused her gaze on the rough and uneven ground, on the slabs of stone lined by deep cracks, silently counting in her mind as she breathed slowly in, then out, as though focusing on her breath and her vision would build an invisible shield from whatever she was feeling right now. The shield was punctured by a thought she knew was all her own. One she had had countless times over the years.

I'm going mad, amn't I?

Though if that *was* the case, she had lost her mind a long time ago.

The wave of emotion started to ebb and her breathing came more easily as she cast an anxious glance to where her mother stood at the front of the group. She hadn't noticed anything. Éabha took a step over the threshold into the room.

Something tugged on her coat. She started, her bag hitting against the metal door with a low clang as she moved. A few of the people nearest to her cast glances at her and she smiled sheepishly at them before remembering she was wearing a face mask and shrugging apologetically instead. Her heart was pounding. She must have imagined it this time.

Please let her have imagined it.

Then, slowly, she felt a pressure on her right hand, as though someone was holding it. With the sensation came an overwhelming sense of fear, a craving for reassurance. It was a child. She couldn't explain it, couldn't understand it, but she *knew*. It was a child seeking comfort, and they were holding her hand, and there was no one beside her. The cell – the whole block, really – was freezing, but a sweat broke out on her forehead. She wanted to tear her hand away. She wanted to laugh and dismiss it as a flight of fancy, or her mind playing tricks. But more than anything, she could feel the childlike longing for security consuming her. She couldn't bring herself to pull away. Squeezing her hand tentatively, she tried to convey some semblance of reassurance, even though she thought she would either pass out or throw up. The small invisible hand in hers faded.

'*AY-va.*' From the way her mother sighed her name, it wasn't the first time she'd said it. She turned to face her mum, who had come to stand beside her and was scrutinising her as the rest of the tour group filed out. 'You look very pale.'

'I'm grand,' she lied. 'It's probably just the terrible lighting.'

Her mother's eyes narrowed slightly at her words and Éabha looked innocently at her over the top of her mask. She had learned long ago to hide these 'episodes', as her parents called them.

'Come on, Mum. We'll fall behind,' she said, shaking her frozen limbs into motion as they followed the guide down the corridor.

The next part of the tour went by peacefully enough. Éabha kept sensing waves of emotion, though these were faint ones lapping at her edges, not the giant ones that threatened to drown her completely. She distracted herself by examining it logically. This degree of intensity was unusual: normally she needed to touch an object or surface for one of her episodes to be triggered. This was a whole new level. Her brain kept working through it: this was a place so filled with history that it seemed to have leached from the stones into the air itself. Maybe that played a part? *Or,* the rational part of her piped up, *this is all in your head.* She'd always had an active imagination, after all. That's what her parents said. 'Éabha loves making up stories. She's so creative. The things she comes up with as well!' This last sentence had often been accompanied by a disapproving set of the lips. There were strict rules about what was acceptable in her home.

She did the breathing exercises the child psychiatrist had taught her, trying to ignore the sensations flooding through her. Everything was fine until they reached the Stonebreakers' Yard. The moment she stepped in, exhaustion overwhelmed her. Her muscles ached and she sagged under an invisible weight. Her hands throbbed and she looked down, almost expecting to see blisters forming across the soft pads at the base of her fingers. They looked the same as always – a silver ring on her right-hand ring finger, pale skin, oval nails with baby-pink shellac neatly applied.

'The yard was used for hard labour …' the guide was saying from the centre of the square. Éabha's arm muscles were burning, shoulders aching as she tried to focus on the guide's words. 'Often it was breaking rocks, repetitive hard labour that took a great physical toll on the prisoners here.' He led the group towards the monument at the back of the yard. 'And here is where the leaders of the 1916 Rising were executed.' He began to list their names.

Pain shot through Éabha's chest and she dropped to the ground. The people beside her whirled around, her mother just managing to catch her before she hit the stones, lowering her gently down. Éabha clutched at her chest, her fingers finding the navy scarf looped around her neck.

'Éabha!' Her mother's shrill voice cut through the guide's speech.

The pain receded as suddenly as it had arrived and Éabha was able to open her eyes. Her mother was leaning over her, so close she felt smothered. Éabha's chest rose and fell in deep, frantic gulps as she struggled to speak.

'I'm OK,' she croaked.

She could feel the blood rushing to her cheeks as the tour guide hovered beside her mother, the rest of the tour group standing in a loose, anxious circle around her.

'I must have fainted. I think I'm just a little light-headed.' She could feel the concern, the confusion, radiating from them.

That was new.

The guide looked worried. 'We can call you an ambulance?'

'No!' Éabha exclaimed. She tried to smile, struggling into an upright position. 'I mean, thank you, but honestly I think it was just … low blood sugar.'

Her mother smiled approvingly at Éabha and pulled her to her feet, wrapping an arm around her waist. 'We'll go and find somewhere to sit down, and get you some food too,' she said.

Éabha nodded. She thanked the guide again before leaving with her mother, still mortified that she had created such a fuss. Her mother hated a scene. Hopefully she wouldn't be too angry with her. As they walked out of the gaol, her mother gripping her arm with an almost painfully tight grasp to support her, Éabha's mind raced. What had happened? She had never felt pain like that before.

If Éabha didn't know better, she would say it felt like she'd been shot.

CHAPTER FOUR

ÉABHA COULDN'T UNWIND THAT NIGHT. It had been easy to brush off the experiences in the gaol when she was with her mother, focusing on keeping up the illusion of normality. It was harder when she was alone in her room. Her parents were out having dinner with friends and the silent house was filled with her own thoughts. She put on an old, comforting episode of *Gossip Girl* in a bid to distract herself but gave up when, after about fifteen minutes, she realised she had lost the thread of what she was watching. Sighing, she pulled her computer towards her instead, switching into private browsing mode. It was time for her semi-regular Google search, the one she did after an episode in the hope that *this* time she'd find something to make it go away. Wasn't the definition of insanity doing the same thing over and over and expecting a different result?

Though the whole 'seeing and feeling things that aren't there' thing probably fell pretty firmly into that category too.

The usual results popped up, as always, and she started to scroll, skimming the page in the hope of *finally* spotting the thing that would make all of this OK.

There were a surprising number of paranormal investigators in Ireland. She sometimes fantasised about reaching out to them, of them explaining to her what was happening. How to control it. Reassuring her that these episodes were, in fact, what so many websites claimed they were: gifts.

'It's not real, Éabha.' She could hear her father's voice in her head. 'Stop making up stories.' The face of the child psychiatrist swam up from the depths of her memory, the one her parents had sent her to when she insisted one time too many that what she felt was real. Another memory surfaced, making her cringe. Her mother's face, contorted not in the disbelief and concern of her father, but in disgust. Even now, remembering how her mother had snapped at her, mouth compressed in a thin line, eyes flashing with fury, made her recoil. Seven-year-old Éabha had apologised, agreeing it might have been a dream, and her mother had softened, wrapping her arms around her and kissing her on the forehead.

'Good girl, Éabha,' she'd said. 'It's wrong to lie, but apologising is the first step to forgiveness. Make sure to tell Father Benedict about this in confession.'

Éabha had done so, dutifully saying her ten Hail Marys as penance, her parents watching approvingly as she knelt on the worn leather pew, head bent.

She stopped trying to tell them after that. She learned how to – for the most part – hide her 'episodes', sat straight and attentive in church, got over 500 points in the Leaving, would be starting at UCD next week. She was the perfect daughter with her immaculately styled hair and perfectly polished nails, her carefully applied make-up that was never 'too much', the fashionable but modest clothes her mother bought her when they shopped. She was always quiet and amiable and helpful and –

It made her want to scream.

Tears slid down her cheeks, rising uncontrollably from the deep well of hollowness inside her. Brushing the tears from her eyes, she blinked to focus on the screen in front of her. There was a result she hadn't seen before. She'd done this search so many times that she knew them all by heart. This was a new website, with links to social media pages, for an organisation called Paranormal Surveyance Ireland, or PSI.

It was an old family business with over twenty years' experience in 'paranormal surveyance', the 'About Us' page explained. Previously run by Emily and Pádraig O'Sullivan, Emily had stepped back to write her bestselling books about her career. Pádraig had passed away in 2017. Their son, Archer, was relaunching the business, which was based about forty minutes outside Dublin in Kilcarrig. She read through the website, perusing all the information available. They applied strict scientific practices and protocols to investigate the paranormal and defined themselves as an evidence-based organisation. A photo of Archer smiled out at her from the 'Meet the Team' page. He was around her age with kind eyes. Looking at him, she felt a click in her mind like when you remember the answer to something you'd been struggling to recall. Before she could talk herself out of it, she filled in the 'Contact Us' form, with just her first name, her email address and a quick message. She typed and retyped it several times.

'Hi my name is Éabha. I see and feel things other people don't, and if I don't get answers about whether or not I've lost my mind I might have a complete breakdown. Please help?'

She laughed, a bitter sound, as she re-read the message, then furiously backspaced.

'Hi, you're going to think I'm mad, to be honest most of the time I

think I am, but a little part of me thinks that things I see and feel are real, things other people don't, so if you could confirm if they are or not, that would be fab.'

She backspaced again, closing her eyes and thinking. If she wanted to convince them to help her, she would need to act like all this didn't terrify her. That she didn't doubt herself as much as they probably would. She had to make it worth their while.

'Hi, my name is Éabha. I'm eighteen, and I've had some abilities since childhood that allow me to sense the emotions and experiences of people from old buildings they once inhabited or objects they touched. I think I could be of interest – or even helpful – to your team. I would love to meet with you to discuss this, if you're interested. Best wishes, Éabha.'

She pressed send before she could convince herself not to. For a moment she felt relieved. She'd taken control for once. Then a sinking dread swept over her. What had she done?

She had told someone.

Taking deep breaths, she shut down her laptop and shoved it away from her. She'd only given her first name and the email address she used for newsletters and marketing emails. They'd probably just ignore her message anyway, dismissing her as some prankster. It would be fine.

When she woke up the next morning there was a response waiting in her inbox.

CHAPTER FIVE

RAVEN WALKED UP THE FAMILIAR footpath to her childhood home, past the willow tree that filled the front garden, and stopped. She looked up at the two-storey house, the walls still painted the cheerful buttery yellow of her youth, then to the sky-blue front door, and hesitated. Should she just let herself in? Or ring the doorbell? Ringing the doorbell felt too formal. This was her house too, after all, even if she didn't live here any more. Her mum had told her Archer was using the front room as a base for PSI until they got enough business to afford a proper office, so she'd driven out to the house for the first time since last Christmas. She'd stayed only for Christmas Day, telling them she'd been assigned the St Stephen's Day shift in Origin. She'd left out the part where she'd requested it. At one point, she'd contemplated telling them she'd tested positive for Covid-19 so she had an excuse to avoid the celebrations altogether, but that had felt like a step too far.

Taking a deep breath, Raven took out her keys, her hand hovering just in front of the lock. She hadn't told Archer she was coming. She told herself it was to surprise him, but really it was to give herself the option of backing out at the very last minute. Tiredness dulled her brain and made her limbs heavy. What little sleep she'd gotten the night before had been perforated with dreams that felt like memories trying to push their way to the surface. Even thinking about them now was like the sensation of someone calling you from so far away you're unsure whether or not you imagined it.

She shook her head to try and clear the mental fog, tendrils of hair escaping from under her grey beanie. It was mild for late September. The autumn sun shone in the bright blue sky overhead, its warmth tempered slightly by a cool breeze, but her oversized leather jacket didn't feel warm enough. She wore it when she needed strength and today felt like an occasion when it would be called for.

It wasn't seeing Archer she dreaded. It was the questions he was sure to ask.

She opened the front door and stepped inside, closing it softly behind her and turning to a door immediately on the left-hand side. Low voices murmured on the other side. Steeling herself, she rolled her shoulders back and inhaled deeply before knocking in the rat-a-tat pattern they'd used since childhood. She opened the door without waiting for a response. The three boys inside stopped talking immediately, spinning around in their chairs to look at her, their faces showing varying degrees of shock.

'Hello, Little Brother,' she said, fixing her eyes on the person with the strongest expression of surprise on his face.

'Raven!' Archer exclaimed, leaping out of his seat and bounding over to wrap her in a hug. He lifted her off her feet, due to his enthusiasm and the fact that, at five foot ten, he stood a good eight inches taller than her. She wrapped her arms around him, hugging him back tightly. Guilt pricked at her and she stepped back from the hug, greeting the other two: Fionn, surrounded by his usual jumble of cameras and cables, his serious blue eyes, framed by dark-rimmed glasses, darting anxiously to Archer; Davis, tall and lean, lounging back with his long legs propped on the desk in front of him, twirling a pen in his hand. His tightly coiled black hair was tied into a bun at the nape of his neck, a sign that he was in the middle of discussing one of his academic theories.

'Well look, it's our first actual ghost,' he said with a grin before getting up to give her a hug. Raven huffed as he continued. 'To what do we owe this honour?'

'I was in the area. Thought I'd pop in,' she said, shrugging.

Davis raised an eyebrow.

'I brought biscuits,' she said, holding up a purple packet. 'And I wanted to have a word with my baby brother.'

'I'm only eighteen months younger than you,' Archer said, rolling his eyes as he took the biscuits and crossed over to sit behind a desk. The armchairs had been pushed to the edges of the room to make way for the three desks clustered in the centre. Hanging in between the family photos that still lined the walls were corkboards filled with newspaper articles, lists and other things in each of the boys' handwriting that she couldn't quite make out from a distance.

'Precisely,' she paused, then looked at him seriously. 'Mum called me.'

Davis stepped away and sat back down at his desk.

'Oh wow, she's really serious about this, isn't she?' Archer said, stretching.

'I can see it's really cutting you up inside.'

'She spent our childhood training us to do this. She can't act surprised when one of us actually wants to continue it.'

'You've met our mother, right?'

Archer laughed, running his hand through his blond hair. It was longer than she remembered, another reminder of how much time had passed since the last time she had seen him.

'Can we talk? Please?' Raven said, casting a look at Fionn and Davis. Fionn was scrutinising a camera manual on the desk in front of him, despite the fact that it was clearly upside down, while Davis was cheerfully – and blatantly – watching the exchange. She raised an eyebrow at him and he winked back.

'Let's go to the cafe,' Archer said, picking up the leather jacket hanging on the back of his chair. 'I have a shift in an hour but we can grab some coffee and pie first.'

Forest Fair, the cafe where Archer had worked part-time since transition year, was renowned for its apple pies and crumbles. The owner, Angela, guarded the spice mix recipe like precious treasure, and for good reason. Raven's mouth watered just thinking about it.

'See you later, guys,' she said, smiling at Davis and Fionn. Fionn lifted a hand in farewell, still determinedly engrossed in his upside-down manual.

'See you soon, Raven,' Davis said. He glanced at Archer, who was stuffing his phone and keys into his pockets, before giving her a stern look.

She could practically hear his words in her head: 'Go easy on him.' Davis's parents had been part of the original PSI team and the three of them had basically grown up together. Davis was essentially the third O'Sullivan sibling, a big brother to them both. They were the ones who'd supported Archer when he first came out as bi, who helped him through his first broken heart, who, whenever he got into trouble, were always right there beside him. Raven nodded, then followed Archer out of the office and down the stairs. The cafe was just a short walk away – everything was in this town, really. If she was going to have to talk about all the things she was dreading, at least she could do it while eating some pie.

The smell of crumble hit her the moment they stepped through the door, followed by the sight of the homemade cakes lined up in the glass display by the counter. Mismatched tables were scattered in welcoming chaos around the room, some surrounded by clusters of wooden chairs, others with deep, worn but clean and well-loved armchairs beside them. While Archer ducked behind the counter, Raven settled at a two-person table in the corner of the cafe, where they could speak openly without worrying about anyone around them overhearing. Years of being the 'ghost girl' had gotten Raven used to being stared at and gossiped about by curious people, but that didn't mean she needed to make it any easier for them.

Archer set two enormous slabs of apple pie on the table, followed by two coffees. Hers was black, as always, while he had still taken the time to do an ornate latte art of a feather on his. That was Archer: he loved to bend the rules but he never cut corners.

Raven forked a big bite of pie into her mouth, closing her eyes in delight. It was the perfect temperature, the apples caramelised, the spices dancing over her tongue.

'Oh, I've missed this,' she sighed.

'You know, if you visited more, you could have pie whenever you wanted,' Archer said lightly.

She could feel the hurt under the words. 'I know. I'm sorry, Arch. I've been pretty terrible recently, haven't I?'

'Recently?' Archer asked. 'Raven, you've always been terrible.'

She glared over another mouthful of pie and he laughed, holding up his hands.

'I'm sorry, I couldn't resist.'

'I'll let it go, but just this once.'

A red-hot stab of guilt seared her stomach even as she kept her tone light. He was joking, but she'd been an awful sister to him for five years. They both knew it. Archer was just too kind to say it.

'Fair. So, what did Mother Dearest say to get you galloping all the way down from the Big Smoke?' Archer asked, taking a long sip of his coffee.

'That you're restarting PSI,' Raven said. She dragged her fork through the remains of the pie in front of her. 'She's worried. As am I.'

'Yes, so worried she's taking off on a two-month book tour and extended holiday.'

'You know Mum. She delegates the emotional labour. I mean, usually it's to you, but seeing as this time you're the problem child, I guess she had no other choice. I assume she already tried Davis?'

Archer laughed. 'Yes. It went about as well as trying to stop Davis from doing something he has his mind set on usually goes.'

'I wish I'd seen that.'

'It was entertaining, to say the least.'

There was a pause, just long enough to become awkward. They both knew where this conversation was going.

'Does this have anything to do with Hyacinth House?' she asked softly. Archer looked down at the plate in front of him.

'Yes and no. I'd be interested in investigating it if I had the opportunity, but that's not the reason I've set PSI back up.'

'Why would you want to go back there?'

'Because no one else in this family will answer my questions, so maybe I'll find what I need to know there.'

'Maybe we won't answer them because we don't know what the answers are, Arch.'

'I know there's more than you've told me. And deep down, you know it too.'

He looked up, brown eyes tinged with ice, and she recoiled. It took a lot to make Archer angry – he was the peacekeeper, the middleman, always defusing the tension between Raven and her mother.

'I don't remember. You know that, Arch.'

'You don't want to, either.'

'That's not fair!'

'Neither is leaving me in the dark, Raven. I … I should have been there. Not off in Irish college doing water sports and dancing in bloody céilís. Can you blame me for wanting answers?' The anger had faded and now he just looked sad.

'No. But is it worth it? Archer, Dad *died* in that house. And you want to go back there?'

'It's better than being afraid of shadows for the rest of my life.' There was a silence, then he sighed before picking up his fork again and taking a mouthful of pie. 'This entire conversation is probably pointless anyway. I'd have to be invited. I just wanted to get back to doing what we used to love. Don't you miss it, Raven? Investigating?'

She did. It surprised her, but she did. She'd loved the long nights spent in the darkness, voice recorder in hand, Archer beside her with a camera. The approving smile her father would give when they found an EVP in analysis, the slight nod her mother gave when they made a good scientific point. But the thought of going into that house again …

'I miss it. But not enough to go back there.'

'Aside from Hyacinth, though. You'd be such an asset to the team. Four means we can split into teams of two, cover more ground.'

'I don't know …'

'Look, will you at least think about it?' He paused, then looked beseechingly at her. 'I could really use your help, Raven. Please.'

Suddenly the broad-shouldered eighteen-year-old sitting opposite her was just her kid brother, reaching out his hand to her in a hotel room, asking her to go exploring with him because he didn't want to go alone.

The brother she had abandoned the moment she'd finished school and found a job. She'd been desperate to get away from the family home, from the conversations she avoided and the things left unsaid. Even when they still lived together, after Pádraig died, she'd done everything she could to put distance between them – hiding in her room, spending long hours in the school library to avoid the house, lashing out at Archer when he tried to get close to her again. She hadn't been able to deal with it, with not remembering what happened. The fear of what she'd find out if she did. The constant terror that she would hurt another member of her family. The knowledge that every time she pushed Archer away, she did hurt him. But she'd been protecting him, really.

And yourself, a little voice countered.

She wavered.

Then there was a memory of shadows creeping across a floor towards her, slowly merging to form a figure … she tried to shake the image from her brain.

'I guess I shouldn't be surprised,' he said, taking the gesture as a dismissal.

'That's not fair,' she said again, pleadingly this time.

'Isn't it?' He stopped, then sighed. 'I'm sorry Raven.' Ever the peacemaker, never able to leave a conversation on an edge. 'I'm glad you came, it means a lot. And just … think about it, OK? You don't have to commit to investigating the house. I don't even know if we'll *get* to. But if you wanted to join us for the other investigations, that would be so great.' He looked at his phone, checking the time. 'My shift is due to start. I'd better get ready. I can put the rest of the pie in a box for you, if you'd like?'

That was his peace offering. He was, in so many ways, a better person than she was. She was all sharp spikes and closed doors, while he was soft edges and an open heart.

'Thanks, Arch,' she smiled, getting up from the table.

He fetched a box and brought it back, deftly sliding the pie in and sealing it. As he handed it to her, she reached out to rest a hand on his arm.

'I'll think about it, OK?' she said quietly. That was the most she could offer him right now. The way his face lit up you'd think she had promised him the stars.

'Thanks, Big Sis,' he said, kissing the top of her head and bounding back behind the counter, chatting amicably to the girl at the till. Raven watched him for a moment, then left to walk back to her car, silently praying no one would let him investigate that damned house.

CHAPTER SIX

RAVEN FOUND HERSELF BACK IN Kilcarrig the next day. The temptation to investigate with – and keep an eye on – Archer had led to another night of tossing and turning as she tried to decide what to do. It had resulted in her driving down for the day before her evening shift in Origin. She opened the front door and stopped abruptly. There was a girl with perfect porcelain skin, a subtle hint of blush on her cheeks, sitting on a chair outside the front-room door. She sat straight-backed, her manicured hands folded in her lap and her face poised.

Raven could make out a loud voice coming from the office. Her lips twitched, as she recognised it instantly. Davis had always been one for an impassioned rant. She made out snatches of sentences as she approached – 'supposed to be scientific', and 'not needing someone that sees visions and portents in the clouds discrediting everything we've worked for'. The girl smiled when Raven stepped up beside her.

'Hi,' the girl said tentatively.

'Sorry for bursting in on you,' Raven said, leaning against the wall opposite the girl. 'Are you here to see Archer too?'

'I am. He asked if I could wait here for a minute.' The girl frowned as Davis's voice cut off and Archer's came, low but firm through the door. 'I'm not sure how well it's going to go though.' Her accent was south Dublin, not quite as pronounced as others Raven had heard in Origin, but still distinctive.

'Davis can have that effect on people,' Raven said with a wry smile.

'Do you work with them?'

'Worse. I'm related to them. Well, Archer anyway. But Davis may as well be related to us too.'

'My condolences.' The pale girl gave a wan smile.

Raven let out a bark of laughter.

'Sorry,' the girl added quickly, flushing red. 'That was rude.'

'It was funny though,' Raven said. She studied the girl as she smiled back at her. She was wearing a silky slip dress under a chunky beige jumper, thick tights and neat ankle boots. A silver Celtic cross hung at her neck, and her light-brown hair fell in perfect loose curls below her shoulders. The kind of curls that looked effortless but required large amounts of practice to perfect. Both her lipstick and her nails were a pale pink, the nails immaculately shaped and painted. Raven glanced down at her own hands, at the deep-purple nail varnish she had applied at three in the morning to distract herself. It was already starting to chip from her short nails.

Archer and Davis's voices had quietened enough that she couldn't make out what they were saying. She looked at her watch, then at the girl.

'How long have you been waiting out here?'

'A while,' she replied in a noncommittal way, but her polite smile indicated it had, in fact, been quite a while.

Raven let out an exasperated sigh. 'Typical. Wait here. They'll argue rings around themselves if no one intervenes.' She crossed the corridor and, without knocking, turned the handle and stepped into the room.

Éabha continued to wait outside the door after the girl disappeared through it. She raised her fingers to her mouth, beginning to chew on a nail before immediately pulling her hand back into her lap, interlacing her fingers tightly and frowning down at them. She hadn't bitten her fingernails in years. Her mother used to admonish her every time she spotted her doing it. 'People notice your nails when you shake hands, Éabha,' she would say. 'You always need to make a good impression.'

She twined her fingers anxiously in her lap, then clasped her hands tightly, forcing herself to be still even as her mind continued to race. What would her parents say if they knew she was here?

Why was she even asking herself that question? She knew what they'd say. After all, she had lived a version of these conversations before.

'There is nothing healthy about those daydreams, Éabha,' her father's stern voice told her. 'These are figments of your imagination. You cannot indulge them.'

And yet here she was, sitting in the corridor of the building belonging to 'paranormal surveyors', about to not only tell them about her gifts, but ask them to examine them.

Even referring to them as 'gifts' felt like a major rebellion. That was how the websites she spent long hours perusing described them. She'd always called them 'episodes'. 'Gift' felt like a perverse way to describe these things that haunted her. How could something that worried her father and disgusted her mother be a *gift*?

She could still leave. They'd assume she'd gotten fed up waiting. They didn't have her number. She could disappear, fade into the evening like the ghosts they searched for. Standing up, she reached down for her bag, jumping as the door beside her opened.

'I'm so sorry to keep you waiting this long, Éabha,' said the boy in the doorway.

She recognised Archer from the website, though his blond hair was longer than in his photo, falling over his eyes in messy waves. The photo also hadn't captured the warmth of his smile, the way it made your lips curve up in response automatically. He ushered her in, waving a hand with fingernails coated in indigo nail varnish, and she stepped over the threshold feeling as though she had leapt off a cliff.

The girl with the silvery-blond plait was settled in a chair to the left of a desk cluttered with folders and files, a slim laptop open in the middle. She sat with one black biker boot crossed over her knee while her leather jacket was now hanging on the back of the chair. Her white shirt was open to her chest, revealing a black sleeveless T-shirt layered underneath. She shot Éabha a conspiratorial smile. Éabha felt her shoulders relax a little as she sat in the chair nearest the door, turning it so that she could easily see all three people in the room at once. Her hearing aids worked well, well enough for her to have picked up snatches of the boys' argument, but being able to see people's mouths as they spoke helped.

'I'm Archer,' said the boy, leaning against the front of the desk. 'This is my sister, Raven …' The girl in the corner saluted her in greeting. '… and the man lurking in the corner is Davis.'

Davis was tall and lean, with brown skin and tightly coiled

black hair that fell to just above his shoulders. He stepped forward smoothly to shake her hand. He was a little older than the others and was trying – *failing* – to conceal a frown. She'd caught enough of the conversation to know he was not enamoured with the idea of her or what she was here to discuss. Returning to his seat, he glanced over at Archer, who clapped his hands together and smiled warmly at her.

'To begin, why don't you give us an idea of why you want to be involved?'

Éabha winced, remembering the throwaway remark she'd made in her email.

'I know you told us a little in your email, but I'd love everyone to hear it from you now,' Archer continued.

'Before that,' Davis interjected, shifting forward in his seat, 'I want to ask something.'

Archer sighed, folding his arms and shooting Davis an exasperated look, which Davis ignored.

'Are you a journalist, or a blogger, or any kind of media person looking for a story?'

Éabha gaped at him, mouth open. Of all the questions he could have asked, this was the last one she had expected.

'What? No!'

Davis stared firmly at her as confusion spread across her face.

'Why would I be a journalist?'

'Davis is a little paranoid,' Archer said.

'Davis is asking sensible questions,' Davis countered. He leaned back in his chair, apparently placated by Éabha's utter bewilderment.

'Anyway, now that Davis is convinced you're not a media spy,'

Archer said, shooting Davis a warning look before continuing in an encouraging voice, 'if you'd like to tell us why you're here ...?'

Éabha swallowed, looking around the room. This was the last chance she'd have. She could back out, apologise for wasting their time and retreat back to her safe, small life.

But ... she wanted answers. And something was telling her, that gut instinct she so often tried to ignore, that this was the place she needed to be. She just needed to convince them it was worth their while.

'All my life I've had ... experiences I can't explain,' she started. Archer nodded encouragingly and Raven shifted forward in her chair. 'I walk into buildings I've never been in before and I know who lived there, how they felt, without any prior knowledge of the history. I pick up objects and ... sense ... who held them before me.'

She looked around at all of them, deliberately holding Davis's gaze. Scepticism was rolling off him in waves. Archer, however, was curious. Just like with the people in the gaol, she could *feel* their emotions. Was it happening with the living now too? She'd always been able to pick up on the mood in a room, ever since she was a child, but this was stronger than ever before. It was like she was *experiencing* their emotions.

She'd worry about that later.

She took a deep breath. 'And ... I've seen things. People that other people don't. I know things they're trying to tell me. I don't understand how. It's getting stronger, and more frequent, but I don't know how to control it. I contacted you because ...' She hesitated. If she told them how much she doubted what she experienced was real, would that stop them helping her? She could already feel

Davis's scepticism. It crept into her, bolstering her own doubts until the line between her feelings and his started to blur. Why would they want to help some random girl who was very possibly mad? Unless they thought there was something in it for them.

'I think I could help you. With what you do. And maybe, at the same time, you could help me. Figure this out, I mean.' She held her breath, waiting for their answer.

'You have feelings you can't explain,' Davis said flatly.

Éabha bristled. 'You *investigate* things people can't explain.'

'We're an *evidence-based* scientific research team into the paranormal. We need facts, irrefutable data, to provide concrete information about the unknown. We can't add "dreams and feelings" to an evidence list. Especially if you don't even know where they're coming from yourself.'

'Yes. It's true I don't know much about it,' Éabha said. She sat up even straighter in her chair, staring firmly at Davis. 'That's why I'm here. You say you're all about scientific evidence and discovery? And here I come, a prime opportunity to study the unknown, and you turn me away because of … academic snobbery?'

Davis flinched. 'That's not –' He was cut off by Archer's low laugh.

'I like you,' said Archer, grinning at her. 'I like her,' he said again, turning to Raven, who was hiding a smile behind her hand.

Éabha tried to keep her breathing steady, hoping the tremor in her fingers would go unnoticed. She had no idea where the words had come from. They'd been unlocked from somewhere deep inside her, where she kept everything she had wanted to say to her parents when they dismissed or admonished her. They'd come from that secret part of her, the one that hoped there was something more to these episodes. The one that read the word 'gift' and slowly unfurled with hope.

'She has a point, Davis,' Raven said thoughtfully.

Davis opened and shut his mouth a few times, before holding his hands up in defeat. 'If it's two against one, I'll accept that. I don't think Fionn will object so I know when I'm outnumbered.' He picked up a folder resting by his chair and stood up. 'I have labs this afternoon. I have to get going.' He walked towards the door and nodded at Éabha, attempting a polite smile. 'I'll see you soon then, Éabha.'

She smiled back, the courteousness her parents had trained into her taking over. He opened the door, paused as though he was about to speak, then shook his head and left.

'I'm sorry about him,' Archer said. 'I swear he's actually really sound. Davis just …'

'It's fine,' Éabha said quickly. The moment of assertiveness had passed and she was back to anxiety with a side of nausea. Had she been rude to Davis? Did he hate her now?

'Right,' said Archer, jumping off the desk and rubbing his hands together. 'How about a tour of the office aka my mother's front room?' He gestured around at the room, which crammed with three desks straight from an IKEA catalogue. Boxes overflowing with folders and papers were piled under two of them, while the third held a mess of cables on top of it and a large quantity of complicated-looking technology underneath it. A whiteboard leaned against the back wall in between some armchairs that had been pushed out of the way, while corkboards hung on the walls between what looked like family photos. 'This is it,' he said cheerfully.

'On the plus side, being based here means that there's also a kitchen,' Raven added helpfully. 'With coffee. And hopefully some of those biscuits I brought yesterday and *should still be there*.' She gave Archer a pointed look.

'Which is my cue to go boil the kettle,' Archer said, loping towards the door. 'We banned Raven from beverage duty years ago, because when she makes coffee it's so bitter it's practically undrinkable.'

'It is not,' Raven said, tossing her plait over her shoulder. 'You're just a coffee snob. He weighs each shot of coffee,' she added conspiratorially to Éabha.

'Appreciating the art of a fine cup of coffee is nothing to be ashamed about,' Archer huffed. 'Back in a few, then we can have a proper chat.' He dipped out the door into the corridor, leaving Éabha alone with Raven.

CHAPTER SEVEN

'SO, YOU'RE ... PSYCHIC?' Raven asked. She probably should have thought of a more subtle way to say it, but she had never mastered that particular art.

Éabha winced. 'It sounds ridiculous, hearing it out loud.'

'We investigate ghosts. It's not that ridiculous.'

Éabha smiled and glanced around the room. She looked as though she was trying to take up the least space possible, her hands clasped in front of her, twining her fingers together. Her baggy jumper engulfed her frame and even though her face was poised, there was something about her that screamed 'handle with care'.

'It's weird saying it out loud,' she said softly, crossing over to one of the corkboards and studying its contents. Raven recognised Hyacinth House in the photo and looked away as Éabha continued. 'No one knows about it. No one but you now. I always thought ... that people would think I was strange, I guess.'

There was something else. Raven could tell, almost feel the words catching at the back of Éabha's throat. Something she was holding back.

'I grew up as the weird ghost girl,' she offered. 'I understand why you'd be afraid to talk about it.'

Éabha turned back to her, eyes soft. 'People aren't great with things they don't understand, are they?'

The door crashed open behind them as Archer shouldered his way into the room holding a tray laden with coffee, a jug of milk, sugar and a plate of chocolate-coated biscuits laid out in a neat pattern.

'They've trained you well in Forest Fair, Little Brother,' Raven said approvingly, taking one of the mugs and settling into a chair behind a desk. She ignored the milk and sugar, taking a deep gulp out of the mug, waiting for the caffeine to jolt her awake.

'I work at the Forest Fair cafe on Main Street,' Archer explained to Éabha as she stirred a spoonful of sugar into her coffee. 'We all have day jobs while the business is getting off the ground. It would be great to make it full time, but … we're a bit of a way off from that. Raven works in a bar, Davis is in final-year science in UCD and Fionn works in a camera shop, which is coincidentally extremely handy for us, equipment-wise.'

'What kind of equipment do you use?' Éabha asked.

Raven sat back in her chair, nibbling the chocolate off the top of a biscuit as she listened to Archer explain the different processes for an investigation.

'Personal experiences are great, but we need evidence to show to the client, otherwise there's no way to back up our findings,' he finished.

Éabha frowned. 'I can see why Davis is so opposed to me then. You can't really back up my impressions.'

'That doesn't mean they can't help us,' Archer said. 'And some research says that spirits are drawn to people with medium-like qualities. You may even be able to pick up on things that will help us get the evidence we need.' He grinned at her. 'Rule One of investigating the paranormal: you have to look for explanations while being open to the unexplainable.'

'I'm guessing I fall into the latter category.' Éabha sounded sad, even though she smiled as she said it.

'For the moment,' Raven said lightly.

'I should mention I'm studying history in college, and I'm very good at research,' Éabha said. 'You know, to help back up the weird impressions I get when I touch things.'

Archer leaned forward in his seat. 'Could I ask you for a demonstration?' he asked. Raven was genuinely impressed he'd waited this long. He'd clearly been bursting to ask from the moment Éabha walked into the room.

'I can try,' Éabha said tentatively. 'Are there any objects I could hold? Ideally one that has a lot of meaning to either of you, that you would have on your person a lot?'

Archer frowned, then rolled up his sleeve and unbuckled the thick brown leather strap of his watch. 'Here,' he said, offering it to Éabha.

She took it, cradling it in her lap, then closed her eyes. Her forehead wrinkled and she bit her lower lip, white teeth sinking into the pink gloss.

Raven and Archer sat in silence. Archer took an A4 pad of paper off his desk, a pen poised in his hand, ready to take notes. He met Raven's eyes and raised an eyebrow.

'I feel like I'm somewhere busy,' Éabha said. Her voice was even softer than earlier, with a dreamy quality that hadn't been there before. 'There's laughter and conversation that I can't make out, a feeling of busyness that ebbs and flows. I can smell coffee, and …'

She faltered for a moment. 'I taste cinnamon, and cooked apple?'

Archer nodded as he wrote down her words. It was interesting, but a quick search of social media would have given her that information about him, even if Raven hadn't mentioned it earlier. Rave reviews of the apple crumble were the first thing that came up about Forest Fair when you looked it up.

'There's a deeper layer,' Éabha said. Her words were slower now, the way someone speaks when they're woken suddenly in the middle of the night and are still moving between dreams and reality.

'A man who likes books,' she said. 'Ink-stained fingers from writing in a journal. I feel like this is a ritual, something he does habitually.' She hesitated. 'Peppermint?'

Raven froze, almost dropping her mug of coffee. Their father had drunk peppermint tea every night while writing in his journal before bed. It was a habit that had never been spoken about in media interviews. She opened her mouth to speak and Archer waved a frantic arm to silence her. She snapped her mouth closed again.

'This feels like another layer down … I sense a different man. Stern. Precise. My right hip hurts.'

Éabha's voice was so soft now that Raven had to lean all the way forward to catch it. Éabha tilted her head the side, as though listening intently. Her eyebrows furrowed.

'There's a clicking sound. It's very faint. A rhythmic clacking that I can't quite place … A typewriter maybe?' Her head drooped almost onto her chest, then snapped up, her eyes opening. She looked from Raven to Archer, settling back into her chair and picking up her cup of coffee.

'How did I do?' she asked nervously. Archer's face broke into a wide grin.

'I can't wait to tell Davis about this.'

Archer refilled their coffees and they related to Éabha what she'd said. She remembered parts of it, especially at the beginning, but it seemed as though she had been so lost in the layers of what she was experiencing she didn't remember the details. Raven could see Archer making mental notes to himself on things to examine. She caught herself doing the same.

What Éabha had described first was Archer's daily routine, his life in the coffee shop where he worked. The second person was clearly their father, who had owned the watch before Archer. The final man was their grandfather, the original owner. He had been a stern man of few words, who had liked things to be just so. He had worked as a clerk in a bank, spending his days totting up figures on loud, clicking calculators – the rhythmic clacking Éabha had described. He'd had arthritis in his right hip.

Raven let out a long exhale. 'Even with extensive research, it's highly unlikely you'd be able to find out those details in advance – not to mention you couldn't have known what object would be given to you or by whom.'

'Even if you could have guessed from how old the watch looked that it belonged to other people before me, knowing about our grandfather, being able to describe him … that's seriously impressive,' Archer added.

'This is what I'm best at,' Éabha said. 'Apparently it's called psychometry: picking up psychic impressions from objects. It's less intimidating than the other things I've experienced.'

'How do you sense it?' Raven asked.

'Impressions mostly. Like sensations,' Éabha said. She handed Archer his watch back and he strapped it onto his wrist. 'Then smells, then images. Sound is the hardest for me. I'm hard of hearing, and apparently that translates into psychic stuff too.'

'A link between the psychic mind and the physical body? Davis will be fascinated by that,' said Raven.

'This is class,' Archer said.

Éabha smiled sadly. 'I'm glad you think so.' She took a long sip of her coffee, cradling it in her hands.

'I take it not everyone does?' Archer asked.

Éabha's face clouded over and she looked down into her mug as though searching in the liquid for the right words.

'I learned a long time ago to keep it to myself.' She paused. 'You're the first people I've told in years. There were times when I didn't believe that what I was experiencing was real myself.'

'That sounds tough.'

Éabha shrugged. 'I got used to it.'

There was something else there. Raven didn't want to pry though. She knew from experience how awful intrusive questions could be. Archer, however, was looking at Éabha with the mix of curiosity and compassion she had seen on his face so many times before. She tensed, wishing she could telepathically order him not to start asking another person questions they weren't ready to answer.

Archer glanced at his watch and swore.

'I have a meeting with a potential client in forty minutes,' he said. 'Sorry, I'm going to have to run.'

'I'll have to head myself anyway,' Éabha said, pulling out her phone to check the time. 'The next bus back to Dublin is in fifteen minutes. If I leave now I can catch it.' They quickly swapped numbers, then Éabha and Archer rushed out together, Raven promising to stay behind and lock up since she didn't have to be at Origin for her shift until eight. Timekeeping had never been a strong point for Archer. It was a good thing he had boundless energy, because he inevitably ended up running from place to place, having lost track of time. Their father had been the same: always late, but charming enough that no one ever held it against him.

Raven checked that the plugs and computers were switched off, then brought the empty coffee mugs back to the kitchen, cleaning them methodically, going over the events of the afternoon. She hadn't expected someone like Éabha to be here when she arrived. It was uncanny, what she could do. And it seemed as though that was only scratching the surface of her abilities. Even *Éabha* didn't seem to know a whole lot about them or how they worked.

Her father would have loved the chance to work with someone like that. The loss hit her like burning needles stabbing into her chest, and she bent over the sink, almost winded by the sudden feeling of grief. This was too much: Archer setting up a new team. The photos of Hyacinth House on a corkboard in the office. Why were they there? Archer had said this wasn't about the house. She couldn't shake the feeling that she was slowly being dragged back towards it and the shadows that would be waiting for her there.

CHAPTER EIGHT

CORDELIA CASSIDY CUEVAS DROVE slowly down a road in the countryside, eyes scanning the foliage for the entrance to the Hyacinth estate. Thick hedges lined the left-hand side of the road as though they were a barrier to keep prying eyes from looking at whatever they were guarding. Or to stop what was inside looking out. She shivered slightly, then rolled her eyes and laughed at herself. She'd been surprised when none of the other agents at Rafferty and Co. Estate Agents wanted to take on this property. They'd wasted no time dumping all the least desirable properties from their portfolios onto her when she'd joined the firm a month ago. The commission on Hyacinth House would be considerable, the bragging rights even more so, yet when John Rafferty, one of the owners, had asked who wanted it, an embarrassed silence had filled the room. Until she had spoken. She couldn't understand why they had let her have it after deliberately keeping her from any of the good properties. Then Richard, the golden boy of Rafferty and Co., had put on a good show of stopping by her desk, acting concerned for her.

He'd hovered beside her before sitting on the edge of her desk and leaning towards her. He was completely in her personal space, but she refused to move back. It would have felt like a concession.

'Can I help you?' she asked him, still looking at her screen.

'Have you been to Hyacinth House?'

'No. I only heard of it when I started here.'

'Well, I have. I went with John and the proprietor when we took on the property. That place,' he paused and swallowed. 'It feels wrong. No one is going to walk in there and think it's a home.'

'It *feels* wrong?' Cordelia repeated. She felt her lips curve up in amusement. 'I didn't have you down as easily spooked, Richard.'

'I'm not,' he snapped. 'Look, I'm just warning you. You don't know what you've gotten into with that house. They say it's haunted. The locals don't go near it. I'm trying to do you a favour here.' He sounded so earnest that for a moment she almost believed him. Then the memory rose in her mind of his constant jibes, his patronising smiles, his raised eyebrows and pointed comments about her manicured nails and high heels, as though being interested in fashion and being intelligent were mutually exclusive traits. How she had heard him and the other estate agents joking that she was a 'diversity hire', saying hiring a twenty-one-year-old woman straight out of college was a PR stunt from an agency that had been getting pointed comments about its all-male staff.

'I'll consider myself warned,' she'd said coolly. She'd stared at him until he stood up from her desk, going back over to his own before picking up his jacket and briefcase and leaving. The smell of his cologne had hung in the air long after he'd gone.

She'd gotten to read only an article or two before she was sidetracked by John asking her to 'help out' with some filing he never would have asked the other two – male – agents to do. She hadn't gotten to dig into the YouTuber incident last month, or the O'Sullivan tragedy from five years ago. There had to be rational explanations for both, though. Cordelia had never been one for ghost stories and the supernatural. There was enough in real life to be frightened by: the man who walked too closely behind you on a dark street; how she had been taught in school to keep her house keys between her fingers, just in case. There was no need to fabricate monsters.

She spotted a large opening in the hedge ahead and flicked on her indicator, steering the car into a wide driveway barred by wrought-iron gates. They were sealed by a large padlock, and rose over ten feet into the air, ending in sharp spikes that loomed threateningly over the car. The metal shimmered in the dull afternoon light as the world around her seemed to darken. It was just because the house sat in a steep-sided glen that added a permanent shadow, she told herself. Plus, a quick glance out the windscreen showed rainclouds approaching, adding an extra layer of gloom to the surroundings.

'I'll need to think of a good way to sell the lack of sunlight,' she thought to herself, making a mental note to research possible advantages of that. Maybe she could pitch it as being nice and sheltered from any storms. She was lost in thought when a sharp rap at the passenger window made her jump violently. Looking over, she saw a man with short grey hair and stern features glaring at her.

'You'd be the estate agent person?' he barked when she rolled down the window.

'Yes, I'm Cordelia Cassidy Cuevas,' she said, extending a hand for him to shake. He ignored it.

'I'll open the gates. Drive up to the front of the house and I'll meet you there.'

'Do you want a lift …' she began, but he'd already turned away.

Shrugging, she turned the engine back on and carefully drove through the gates as he opened them. Large, neatly kept lawns flanked the straight driveway bringing her to the house. It towered over its surroundings, its shadow seeming to extend far further across the grass than it should have for the time of day. She parked at the stone steps leading to the solid oak door, got out and leaned against the car, craning her neck back to take in every aspect of the house. The brickwork was in good repair, though ivy had begun to cling to sections of it, especially the large stone tower on the right-hand side of the building. A set of brand-new boards sealing a downstairs window stood out next to the other, more weathered barricades. Probably where the YouTuber Jack Gallagher had broken in. Tyres crunching on gravel made her turn and the man from the gates got out of his car. He was all sharp angles and pursed lips and looked at her like he had smelt something foul.

'You must be Mr Morris,' she said pleasantly. She did not extend her hand again.

He nodded. 'Yes, I'm the unlucky sod that ended up responsible for the keys to this place,' he said. He kept his gaze angled away from the house as though he was trying to avoid looking directly at it.

'Thank you for meeting me here. I'm happy to take possession of the keys to the house on behalf of –'

'Take them,' he said, almost flinging two sets of keys on hefty iron rings towards her. 'I've had the cursed things in my house for long enough.'

'Are these the only sets?'

'Yes.'

She placed one set in her bag and cradled the other, the cold metal of the many keys heavy in her hands.

'Thank you for your assistance,' she said, dismissing him. She began to walk up the stone steps, her heels clicking on the thick stone.

'You're not going in there now?' Mr Morris said sharply.

'I am.' She turned to face him. 'It's a fair drive from Dublin, I might as well get started while I'm here.'

'You can't go in on your own,' he said. The concern in his words was tainted by the hostility in his voice.

'If you'd like to show me around, I'd appreciate the input of someone familiar with the property.'

His face clouded over even more. 'I don't want to set foot in that place ever again, and neither should you.'

'I can't sell a property I haven't seen.'

'It's not selling it they should be doing, it's burning it to the ground,' he spat.

Cordelia's eyebrows shot up. She was suddenly relieved that the set of keys included the keys to the gates.

'Would you care to elaborate on that, or …'

'No,' he said shortly. He started to get into his car, hesitated, then turned back, waving an arm towards the house he still refused to look at directly. 'Don't go in there alone.'

'Thank you for your advice,' Cordelia said, summoning the 'polite with a side of f– you' smile she had perfected during summer holidays from school spent working in her parents' restaurant. She turned back and walked to the house, searching through the heavy keys for the one labelled 'front door'. A mutter of something about 'hard-headed Dubliners', followed by the sound of a car door slamming and tyres speeding down the driveway, trailed her. She placed an unusually curved and oddly hefty bronze key into the lock in the door and turned it, surprised by how easily it pivoted. Part of her had expected the house to resist.

The heavy door opened to reveal an entrance corridor wreathed in shadows. Squaring her shoulders, she stepped over the threshold, switching on the torch she had brought with her. She left the door behind her as wide open as possible: just for added light, since the electricity had long been switched off, she told herself.

Cordelia walked down the long, narrow hallway, heading towards a large room at the back of the house that her floor plans informed her was the ballroom. It was too dark to make out details, but her heels echoed on the wooden floors and the roof arched over her, the places on the walls where lamps should have protruded gaping like gouged flesh.

Maybe don't put that description in the advertisement, Cordelia, she told herself. Stepping in through the open door, she surveyed the wide space edged by large, boarded-up windows. She put her bag down by the door and lingered near the threshold. There was a jagged hole in the floor a short distance from the door, the small 'caution' sign haphazardly placed in front of it the only nod to health and safety measures. It must have been where Jack Gallagher had fallen and injured himself. She'd read about that in the few minutes she'd had to examine the accident report for what she'd dubbed 'the YouTuber incident' a few weeks ago.

Suddenly, she wanted to turn and go back out into the weak

sunlight. Any faint heat was better than the chill in this room. Everything felt stale here, a stagnant sensation that logic said was due to the lack of ventilation from the boarded-up windows. The shadows stretched up the walls, flickering in the wavering beam of her torch. She tried to steady the hand that gripped it, her stomach clenching with fear. It looked like the shadows were reaching out to her, long grasping fingers trying to wrap themselves around her, to …

Shadows and a grumpy caretaker were not going to intimidate her. She took a deep breath. *They're just shadows, that's all.* Straightening her spine and rising to her full height, shoulders back, she stepped further into the room. She had a job to do. If Richard found out she'd been too scared to spend more than five minutes in the house … She could imagine it now, the superior tone, the smug smile. The whispers of how she was too young for the job. As she walked carefully past the hole in the floor, a glint just underneath the floorboard caught her eye. Crouching down, she could see something down there. Her hand trembled as she reached towards the hole.

Her fingers closed around cool metal and she carefully pulled out a long golden chain with a locket hanging on it. It was solid and heavy in her hand, the small emerald embedded in the front glinting in the torchlight. She frowned at it. What was it doing under the floorboards of the ballroom? Surely the YouTuber couldn't have dropped it? It seemed an odd thing for him to carry around with him. Making a mental note to record it in the house file, she tucked it into the inside pocket of her coat, a secure pocket she rarely used.

Rooting around in her bag, she took out a measuring tape to double-check the floor size and looked around the room again. Tiny slivers of light managed to pierce through minute gaps in the boards on the window, and there were a few pieces of furniture draped in sheets that had once been white. Now they were covered in a layer of dust so thick that when she briefly set the measuring tape down on what looked like a piano a cloud rose up, coating her nose and throat and making her cough violently. The torch moved wildly, casting frenzied shadows dancing around the room. She pulled her phone out and began to circle the room, heels clicking on the wooden floor, recording her thoughts as she scrutinised every element.

'Large hole in the floor needs to be repaired. No obvious signs of mould or rot. Square footage is …' she turned back to the piano where she'd left her measuring tape. It was gone. Frowning, she slid her phone into her pocket and went to the piano, circling it to see if the tape measure had fallen off. There was nothing there, the dust on both the floor and piano undisturbed by anything other than her own footprints.

A prickling sensation grew on the back of her neck, spreading up her scalp. It was the feeling of being watched. She whirled to face the doorway, but it was empty. The shadows in the hallway beyond were still illuminated by the dim light coming through the front door, still and undisturbed. She turned back to the piano and took a deep breath. Crouching down, she went to pull up the sheet covering it to check if the tape measure had somehow slid under there.

Without making a sound.

Completely plausible.

'Just look, Cordelia,' she muttered to herself before reaching out to pull up the sheet. As she started to raise it, a loud slamming noise behind her made her topple over with a shriek. Panicking, she clambered to her feet, barely registering the grey dust that now coated her fitted black suit trousers. The door had shut. She bolted to it, snatching her bag up with one hand and turning the doorknob with her other. The door refused to open. She twisted the doorknob harder, her heart thudding so intensely she could feel it reverberating through her body. Then she became aware of another sound joining the thumping of her heart. She paused her frantic attempts to escape, listening intently. A low tapping was coming from the back corner of the room. Her breath started to come in loud, ragged gasps that made her second-guess for a moment whether she was actually hearing anything besides herself.

Then the tapping became louder.

Not louder.

Closer.

It was moving along the wall. A slow, creeping approach as though whatever was making the noise was inside the wall itself. Coming towards her. That realisation jolted her out of her frozen state. For a moment she thought she felt a soft, almost encouraging, nudge on her shoulder as, cursing loudly, she yanked at the door handle again, letting out a faint sob of relief as it finally turned and the door opened, allowing her to half-run, half-fall out of the room. She sprinted out the front door which was, mercifully, still gaping wide.

Emerging into the rapidly failing sunlight, she had one foot in the car before she remembered she had to lock the front door.

Slowly she turned back to face the entrance. The hallway beyond was completely dark.

'Just lock it,' she muttered to herself. She selected the front-door key from the ring, then crept up the steps, locking the door and turning the handle just once to make sure the lock was secure. An icy cold shot up her arm as though she had plunged it into a stream in the depths of winter. She let go of the handle, clattered back down the steps, and wheeled her car around so quickly that gravel sprayed across the lawn as she made her escape.

The house watched her leave.

CHAPTER NINE

CORDELIA STILL FELT INTERNALLY chilled when she arrived back at her office in Dublin 2, which she firmly told herself was due to the sun starting to set and nothing else. She already felt silly for bolting from the house so quickly, imagining Mr Morris pulled in on the side of the road, laughing at her as she sped past. Pulling into the car park, she brushed the worst of the dust off her trousers before making her way inside. Her suit was crumpled and some of the dust still clung determinedly to her, making her feel dishevelled and on edge. The ease with which the house had unsettled her scared her almost as much as what she had … experienced. *It was just a draught blowing a door shut and you let your imagination take over*. She'd let Richard get to her, and that eccentric Mr Morris.

Frowning, she made her way into the office, hoping that most of the other estate agents would be out or have already left for the day. She couldn't handle their usual patronising comments or pointed references to her age. She was rattled. She hated that. And she couldn't bear the thought of them realising it.

Thankfully, she found the office empty. Settling herself at her desk, she switched on the computer and took a deep, slow breath. Here, in the bright lights of the office, with the familiar hum of the printer and the copier, she felt foolish. It was easy now to doubt what she had heard. The problem was, she mused to herself, that, loath as she was to admit it, Richard was right: no one would walk into that house and think it was a home.

She needed a solution. Too much rested on her selling this property. There was a reason they'd let her have it, despite the sizeable commission: they wanted her to fail. They wanted an excuse to keep her on the lower rungs, pointing at her as a way of showcasing their steps towards equality – 'look, a woman!' – without actually giving her any support or credit.

She tapped her long, manicured nails on the mouse as she thought. Richard had mentioned the rumours around the property's supposed 'curse' and the ghost that was said to walk the halls. Local legend called her 'The Lady'. The fact that someone had died there five years ago would be distressing to a lot of people, though she hadn't had a chance to read the full details about that yet. Then that boy who broke in a few weeks ago – Jack Gallagher, who ended up in hospital with no memory of how he'd got injured, but terrified out of his mind – hadn't helped matters. People were superstitious. She needed to reassure them that these were nothing but stories.

But what if they weren't?

Were there people who wanted to live in a haunted house?

A quick Google search assured her that yes, in fact, there were. There was a whole industry around it: ghost tourism.

She leaned back in her chair and stretched, a plan slowly forming in her mind. There were two options here: either find a way to prove to nervous potential buyers there was nothing to fear, or prove that there *was* something in the house, and convince some person with a macabre fascination with the afterlife and too much money that this was an ideal selling point. Loftus Hall had made lots of money from being a haunted house. Leap Castle, Charleville Castle, Kinnitty Castle: the longer she searched, the more examples she found. And that was just in Ireland. The results from Scotland, England, the USA, had been overwhelming.

This could actually work, she thought, a grin spreading across her face.

All she needed was to find someone who could tell her that definitively yes, this place was haunted, or reassure the buyers it was nothing but old stories. It was standard in the industry to have a surveyor check a property before signing the contracts. Was there a supernatural equivalent? Not one to give her a structural assessment but a paranormal one.

She turned back to her computer, laughing in half-exasperation, half-amusement to herself as she typed. This was not something she'd expected her career to involve.

She definitely didn't expect the first search result to literally be 'Paranormal Surveyors Ireland'.

Before she could talk herself out of it, she rang the number on the website.

CHAPTER TEN

CAN I CALL YOU?

The message flashed up on Raven's screen, making her heart stop.

Nothing's wrong. I just want to fill you in on something.

At least Archer knew to warn her in advance. Emily's unexpected phone call had maxed out her capacity for being ambushed by family phone calls for the year.

Go for it.

She replied before she let herself think of a reason to avoid it. Her phone rang a moment later.

'Hey, Baby Brother.'

'Hey, Ancient Sister.'

She sighed in mock-exasperation. 'Remind me why I put up with you again?'

'We're related. You have to.'

She laughed. There was a long pause, the kind of pause that characteristically meant Archer was about to propose something she wouldn't be happy about.

'So, I got a call today …' He paused again.

'They have something they want you to investigate?'

'Yes. A property. She – the woman I talked to – is an estate agent and wants my professional opinion on a site she's trying to sell.'

Raven's stomach sank. 'She's selling Hyacinth House,' she said flatly.

'Yep.'

The silence stretched as inwardly she cursed loudly and effusively. Did some cosmic force out there *hate* her?

'We're meeting next Thursday,' Archer said eventually. 'I'm going to suggest the team investigates Hyacinth. And I'd really like if you'd come to the meeting.'

Raven didn't say anything.

'You don't have to commit to investigating it with us or anything. I'd just really like for you to sit in. Please, Raven, it would mean a lot to me.'

Once again, she could see Archer standing in front of her, hand stretched out in a dark hallway, asking her to come and explore with him. Before Hyacinth, she had never once turned away.

'I don't know, Arch,' she said softly.

His breath huffed out in a slow exhale. 'That's not an outright no, anyway,' he said cheerfully. 'Will you think about it, at least?'

'I'll think about it. No promises.'

'Yes, thank you! I'll text you the meeting time. It's in the office. I'll bring you a piece of crumble!'

'If I do this, and I mean *if,* Archer, you're going to have to bring more than a piece.'

He laughed. 'Fair enough. I'll see you in a few days, Raven.'

'I didn't say I'd co–'

The dial tone cut her off. She stared down at her phone, not sure whether she wanted to cry or scream.

CHAPTER ELEVEN

ÉABHA ARRIVED AT THE PSI OFFICE on Saturday morning accompanied by all of the nerves from her first visit. Her mind kept alternating between excitement and 'what am I doing?', and too often the latter won. When she knocked on the front door, a voice she didn't recognise yelled, 'Come in, Éabha, it's unlocked.' She went inside and into the office, looking around the room. It was empty except for a pale, stocky boy with dark red hair sitting at a desk, a mass of cables in front of him and an expensive-looking camera in his hands.

'How did you know it was me? I thought I was the psychic one,' she joked awkwardly.

'You're the only one that would knock,' the boy said, looking up and grinning at her.

She laughed.

'I'm Fionn, by the way,' he continued.

'Éabha, but I guess you knew that.'

'Imagine if it had been the postman or something,' Fionn said. 'That would've been embarrassing.'

Éabha laughed again, hovering in the centre of the room. There was a fourth desk packed into the room now, already stacked precariously with files and newspapers, but she didn't want to assume it was meant for her.

'That's yours,' Fionn said, following her gaze to the desk. He winced. 'And I was definitely supposed to clear it off before you arrived, but then I got distracted working out if I could enhance the night mode on this camera to make it detect smaller motions and ...' He trailed off. 'Sorry.'

'It's no problem,' Éabha said. She crossed over to the desk – *her* desk – and began to sort through the piles. 'I can work on this while we wait for the others. Are they here?'

'Archer nipped out to grab some snacks and Davis is upstairs. Arch said he'd be back by ten,' Fionn said. He looked at the clock hanging over the door, its hands already pointing to five past. 'Which, in Archer speak, means ten fifteen at the earliest. Punctuality is not a strong point for him. Davis generally has to herd him out of the house like an irritable border collie.'

'They live together?' Éabha asked.

'Yeah. Archer's mum is away most of the time, the office is here, and Davis is basically family to them anyway, so he moved in. I end up crashing here a lot too. One of the guest rooms is unofficially mine, but I have to help my parents out with the farm a lot so I can't really move out permanently.'

A little wave of sadness washed over Éabha as he spoke. The farm made him sad. Or maybe it was his friends living together without him? The little instinct in her gut was urging her to ask more, to help ease that gentle, lingering melancholy wafting from him. The rational part of her brain was yelling at her not to be nosy. It was a constant, exhausting battle, trying to keep these new sensations under control so she didn't say or do the wrong thing. The door burst open, saving her.

'Only ten minutes late, that's practically early,' Fionn said, leaning back in his chair and grinning at Archer as he came in holding a bag of pastries, closely followed by Davis.

'Look, we all have our flaws. I can't be brilliant AND punctual,' Archer said.

'I am,' Davis smirked.

'It's your modesty that really shines, though,' said Fionn.

'At least I'm not the one who manages to be late to meetings *in his own home.*'

'OK, can we focus, please?' Archer said, leaning against the front of his desk and facing the others. 'I'd like Éabha to think we're professionals for at least an hour or so before the illusion is shattered.'

'There was an illusion?' Fionn asked. Archer shot him an exasperated look and Fionn held up his hands with a contrite expression. 'Sorry. Will keep my witty comments to a minimum.'

'How kind of you,' Davis said drily.

'Anyway,' Archer said, shifting to look directly at Éabha. 'Good morning,' he grinned, his brown eyes glowing.

'Morning,' she smiled back.

'We've been hired to investigate a residential home on Tuesday night. Our usual method is that we meet, go through the account of events the clients gave us, identify areas of activity that we want to concentrate on, equipment we need, and potential non-paranormal causes to check out.'

'More often than not there's a completely mundane explanation for events that are perceived to be paranormal,' Davis chimed in.

It felt pointed.

'People think we go in to prove that there is a ghost, when

76

ninety-nine per cent of what we do is actually telling people why there *isn't*,' Archer continued. 'But that work is just as important. It means when we do find a genuine paranormal occurrence, it's clear we're not spoofers pretending every creaky floorboard is something ghostly.'

'And when we find that one per cent, it means we can really get stuck into the science of it,' Davis added. His eyes lit up as he spoke, enthusiasm rolling off him so strongly it flooded over Éabha.

'Davis loves the science part,' Fionn added conspiratorially.

'We all do,' Davis said.

'I prefer to think of myself as a tech enthusiast, actually. Far less equations,' Fionn countered.

'Is Raven joining us for this one?' Davis asked, ignoring Fionn.

'No, she has work,' Archer said quietly. 'But hopefully she'll be free for the next one,' he added cheerfully. 'How about we go through the client interview I did, and we can decide what to focus on from there?'

Éabha was out of her depth. The others fell into their roles easily, bouncing ideas off each other. She sat quietly as they talked, listening and jotting things in a notebook she carried everywhere. They moved between scientific theories and past experiences, and it was clear the three of them were used to working together. Why was she here? She didn't know how to work any camera more complicated than an iPhone. She was a words person, not a numbers one, so she was no help when it came to the science either. The house was a relatively new build and there wasn't a whole lot of history to dig into about it, so the one thing she had thought she could contribute wasn't relevant. Even though the different possibilities they discussed were fascinating, as the morning went on, the voice in her head that yelled she was an imposter got louder and louder.

'I need a coffee,' Archer yawned, stretching. He looked over at her. 'Éabha, will you help me?'

She followed him out of the room, down the hall and into the kitchen. It was a bright room, autumnal sunlight streaming through the windows onto the countertops and the dark walnut cupboards on either side of the hob. A steel oven nestled underneath the hob, flanked by drawers in the same deep, warm wood.

'By the way, I wasn't asking you because you're a girl and I expect women to make the sandwiches and whatnot,' he said awkwardly. 'I just wanted to check how you were doing, without putting you on the spot in front of everyone.'

'I hadn't interpreted it that way, but thank you for your efforts towards ensuring gender equality in the workplace.'

Archer laughed, flicked on the kettle and turned to her again, his face serious.

'How are you doing though? This must be a lot to take in at once.'

She hesitated. What if she told him how she was feeling and he agreed? *'Yeah, you're right, Éabha, you don't have anything to offer, off you pop.'*

'It's really interesting,' she said, turning to take some mugs out of a cupboard and setting them onto a tray on the countertop. 'I feel like I'm learning a lot about your processes.'

78

'OK, good,' Archer said, relief settling over his features. 'I was worried we'd scare you off, between the info dump and Fionn and Davis bickering every two minutes.'

'I like learning new things, and their bickering is sweet,' Éabha said.

Archer's eyebrows raised. 'Most people describe it as "irritating as hell".'

'Nah, you can feel the affection beneath it.' *Well, I can.* 'You all seem really close.'

'We are. Davis and I grew up together, and Fionn's been one of us since secondary school. We've been through a lot together.'

'That sounds nice. Having people who know all of you.'

The words escaped without her thinking. She caught Archer looking at her curiously, his mouth opening to speak when the hissing of the kettle cut him off. He turned back to where he was weighing ground coffee on a little weighing scales.

'Raven wasn't kidding about the coffee,' Éabha said.

'Raven sees coffee as a means of caffeination and nothing more. I firmly believe that life is too short to drink bad coffee.'

'A good philosophy to have.'

'Thank you,' he grinned, bowing slightly. 'Can you grab some biscuits out of that cupboard?' He pointed, his nails painted a rich purple today, then placed an elaborate apparatus, which was slowly filtering coffee into a glass container, onto the tray beside the mugs. She took a packet of biscuits out of the cupboard he'd indicated and followed him back down the corridor to the office.

'Quick snack break, then on to round two,' he announced. 'I said I'd help Nessa out and cover some of her shift in the cafe while she goes to an emergency dental appointment, so I'll have to disappear for a while. I'll be back straight after.'

'I have to leave around two. I told my parents I'd help move a fallen tree that's blocking one of the bridle paths,' Fionn said.

'I'll be back before then,' Archer assured him.

Éabha felt a wash of relief. She wasn't sure she was ready to be left alone with Davis. He'd been nothing but cordial to her all morning, but she knew he didn't like her – she could feel it. An annoying thing about this new 'gift' was that she knew when it wasn't just in her head.

Archer wasn't back when Fionn announced he was leaving. Despite all the warnings about Archer's timekeeping abilities, she'd hoped he would be back. Her stomach sank. Fionn bade them a cheerful goodbye, throwing on a flannel coat and leaving a tangle of wires and cables on his desk with firm instructions not to touch them. Then it was just her and Davis, and suddenly the room felt a lot smaller than it had when there'd been three of them in it.

They worked quietly, heads bent over their desks. With Fionn there, the silence had felt companionable but now the air was heavy with unspoken words. A few times she sensed the weight of his gaze on her, but when she glanced up, his head was down, brows furrowed as he studied the pages in front of him. She plunged into the documents on her desk. Archer had asked her to sort through some of the requests they'd gotten and see which she thought might be the most viable and if any seemed like time wasters. He'd taken the time to go through a few with her, and when he'd laughed at a joke she'd tentatively made, the joy she'd felt lingered until he left. It was a stark contrast to the squirming discomfort in her stomach at Davis's presence, which she was determinedly trying to tune out. She was so successful that when he spoke, she jumped, knocking a pile of paper off the desk onto the floor. Diving to the ground, she started gathering it up, feeling her face burn. Davis got up and knelt opposite her, handing sheets of paper back to her. They both stood up. She looked at him, painfully aware of the vivid crimson hue that must have spread across her face.

'Sorry, what did you say earlier? I missed it in all the flailing.'

He smiled at that, before his face settled back into its usual serious expression. 'I said that I owe you an explanation. I think we may have got off on the wrong foot.'

'OK,' Éabha said warily, sitting back down in her chair.

Davis leaned against the end of the desk adjacent to her. 'After Hyacinth, and especially after Emily refused to do interviews about it, a lot of journalists started to target Raven and Archer to get the stories. Which was so messed up, like. They were grieving teenagers. But the press wouldn't leave them alone. And even now, every time Emily does an interview it comes up. Even though she's made it clear she'll never speak about it. People are desperate for the grisly details.' His mouth curled in disgust. 'There have been times before where people have tried to get close to Archer just to find out what happened. I was worried you were doing the same, especially after that incident at the house a few weeks ago.'

Éabha listened, questions racing through her mind as he spoke. Who was Emily? What was Hyacinth and what had happened a few weeks ago? The name sounded familiar, but she couldn't place it. She could feel the emotions associated with them flowing from Davis: grief and anger and concern, but she couldn't tell which emotion belonged to which person or event he was describing.

'And, though I know that isn't the case, I'm still worried. I'm in final year of science at UCD and I want to make this my career, to make parapsychology a respected field of study across academia. To say people can be disparaging about it as a legitimate field of research is an understatement. It's so important to make sure that our findings are irrefutable, and while I don't doubt you believe what you experience is real …'

'I *believe* that it's real?' Éabha folded her arms across her chest, fixing him with a firm gaze. 'It's not a question of belief, Davis. I *know* it's real.'

At least I think it is. I need it to be. Even if I wish it wasn't.

'I know you think –'

'Did Archer tell you about his watch? Do you really think I could have faked that?'

That was what she told herself. Every time she doubted herself, she tried to turn back to the facts. How else could she have known? It was real. It had to be. Davis's eyes bored into hers. Inwardly, she was wilting. She tried to force the rising doubts back down as she stared back at him, hoping the uncertainty in his eyes wasn't reflected in hers.

'Sorry I'm late – oh, who left the two of you unsupervised?' Archer bounded into the room, pausing with his mouth comically open as he took in the scene.

'Fionn had to go help his parents clear that tree, remember?' Davis said, settling himself back behind his desk.

82

'He definitely mentioned that about three times this morning, didn't he?' Archer winced.

'Excellent time-management skills as always, Arch.'

'There's a reason I'm not in charge of the shift schedule in the café.' Archer shrugged off his coat, hanging it up on the ornate wooden coat stand by the door and sitting at his desk. He leaned back in his chair and stretched, his cobalt jumper rising up as he did, revealing a flash of pale skin. Éabha quickly looked away.

'So, any updates on the research?'

'I've found a few possibilities,' Éabha began, sorting through the pile on the desk to find the exact section she was looking for. Even if Davis didn't believe in her gifts, maybe he would see that she was an asset in other ways.

CHAPTER TWELVE

IT LOOKED LIKE A NORMAL HOUSE. Éabha hadn't known what to expect, really. A large dark cloud hanging over it? A ghost painted on the door to warn people that the occupants thought it was haunted? It was just a house, the same as every other one in the cul-de-sac. Redbrick, two storeys, semi-detached. A cement driveway bordered by neat squares of freshly cut grass. A silver Peugeot 206 in the driveway. The picture of generic suburban life.

The drawn, nervous faces of the owners when they opened the door were more unusual. The feeling of sadness that swept over her as she stepped into the house even more so. This house was filled with grief. It oozed from the bricks, clung to the walls, dripped from the light fixtures. It took everything in her to breathe through it, to smile, giving a little wave instead of shaking hands as Archer introduced her and the others to their clients, Natalie and Oscar. Her mother would have admonished her for being rude, for not stepping forward, hand outstretched politely. She wouldn't have understood.

'Does the activity still usually begin around seven p.m.?' Archer asked.

Natalie nodded. 'That was his bedtime,' she said, her voice catching.

Oscar rested his hand on Natalie's shoulder and continued. 'It's the same every night. The footsteps, like he's running around the edge of the room.'

'We had to chase him to get him into bed. It was a game to him.'

'We hear him every night, like he wants us to chase him, but we can't.' Oscar turned away. 'Excuse me,' he said, and left the room.

Natalie looked after him for a long moment. 'He struggles to talk about him. He was there when … He was there.'

Archer nodded, eyes soft. 'I understand. We have all the information we need from you for the investigation. If you'd like to head off now, that's fine.'

Natalie mustered a weak smile. 'Yes. We'll be gone until about ten o'clock. That's enough time for you, right?'

'Absolutely. From your accounts, the activity seems to be at its strongest between seven and eight p.m. We'll only need a couple hours to run all the tests we have to do.'

Oscar reappeared, holding Natalie's coat out to her. 'That's great, Archer, thank you,' he said.

Natalie slipped her coat on and picked up her bag. She took Archer's hand in her own again and squeezed it. 'Thank you.'

Éabha almost doubled over with the pain of it. Natalie's hope, her fear, her grief. A tangled web of emotions reaching out to pull her into its centre. Oscar tried to smile goodbye, managing only a tight grimace.

As he walked past Éabha in the narrow hallway, he brushed against her sleeve and she barely contained the gasp in her throat. The force of his sense of guilt made her want to vomit. The door closed behind them and she stood in the hall, shaking. Davis and Fionn emerged from the living room, carrying the equipment to set up upstairs. There was only one room where the clients had reported the paranormal activity: their son's bedroom.

Their dead son's bedroom.

'Are you OK, Éabhs?' Fionn asked.

Archer looked at her. 'You're very pale,' he said, his voice laced with concern.

'I'm grand.' Her voice sounded weak even to her.

'You don't look it.' Davis gave her a searching look.

She took a deep breath and slid on the mask she had perfected over the years of hiding episodes from her parents.

'I'm grand,' she repeated. She looked at her watch. 'It's twenty to seven. Shouldn't we finish getting the equipment ready?'

'That's my line,' Archer said, giving her a friendly nudge with his elbow. He turned to Davis and Fionn. 'It's twenty to seven. We should finish getting the equipment ready.'

Davis rolled his eyes and Fionn picked up the two bulky camera bags. 'Aye aye, Cap'n,' he said, walking towards the stairs, Davis behind him, more equipment in his arms. When Éabha went to follow them, Archer reached out and took her arm, holding her in place.

'You sure you're OK?' he asked.

She looked up at him. All she could sense from him was concern, genuine concern, for her. For a moment she hesitated, wondering how he would react if she told him. That she'd held parts of herself back when she'd told him about herself.

A memory emerged, of chanting voices and pointed fingers, faces contorted in scorn.

'I'm fine, really,' she said, easing her arm from his grasp and going upstairs. He fell into step behind her.

Éabha was not fine. She'd thought it would get easier once the couple were out of the house, but it hadn't. Their sadness was everywhere. It lingered in the air, seeped from the ceilings, clogged the thick carpets. She could feel it closing in around her, the aching grief of parents who had lost a child in a tragic accident.

Two months ago, their son, Charlie, had been playing outside the house. His ball had rolled into the road and he'd darted after it.

The driver didn't have time to brake.

Oscar had been cutting the grass, keeping an eye on his son while he played. He didn't make it to him in time, and he blamed himself for Charlie's death. That last part wasn't in the report, but she had felt it when he brushed past her. He was being crushed under a weight of self-loathing.

She hovered on the threshold of Charlie's room. If the rest of the house had stolen her breath, the grief in here was suffocating. How were the other three moving around? Did they not feel it? It was like she was in a pit, dirt being piled on until she was buried alive.

Outside the window the sky had darkened and the clouds looked like they were about to burst. The three boys chatted quietly as they rigged everything up efficiently. They moved like a unit, always sure of what they were doing, never in each other's way.

'No, the angle needs to be adjusted or we'll have a blind spot,' Fionn told Davis, pointing at the camera he had just set on a tripod.

Davis immediately stepped back over and began to adjust it, looking to Fionn for guidance. 'Say when.'

'Now. That's perfect.'

It was strange seeing Davis and Archer defer to him, but the quiet authority in his voice made it clear this was his field of expertise. Would they ever accept her experiences in the same unquestioning way? It was hard to imagine.

'Five to seven,' Archer said, looking at his watch. 'We good to go here?'

Davis and Fionn agreed. Archer had suggested that Éabha watch and learn how they used the different technological tools, as well as keeping herself open to any sensations she might pick up. It was a good plan, even if she felt a bit useless just hovering in the doorway.

Charlie's room was exactly how it had been before he died. Toys lined the shelves, while his bed was dressed with a duvet cover that had stars and planets on it.

'Éabha, do you want to set yourself up in that corner?' Fionn said, pointing to the far corner of the room.

She took a deep breath, bracing her shoulders as she stepped inside.

'The "footsteps" start here,' Archer was saying to Davis as she squeezed past them, 'then move around the edge towards the bed. They said it sounds like a child running.'

Davis frowned, scanning the room. His eyes settled on one wall. 'I have a theory,' he said with a triumphant smile. 'I'll tell you after we've done all the checks.'

Any other time, she would have been curious about what had made his eyes light up like that. But now all Éabha could do was lean against the wall to stay upright, trying not to fold under the overwhelming crush of grief. They stood in silence, waiting.

At exactly seven o'clock, the footsteps started.

Éabha jumped, though none of the others did. Fionn tracked them with the camera, Archer had the sound equipment. Davis covered the room from another angle with an infrared device. It sounded exactly like someone was pattering on light little feet around the edge of the room. After a moment, she remembered that she had a role to play too. Closing her eyes, she took deep breaths, trying to block out the sadness in the room and feel if there was anything else there. It felt dangerous, trying to reach out deliberately. Like there was a shoddily built wall in her mind that she had spent years trying to construct and now she was taking a wrecking ball to it in one go.

If the grief had been strong before, it was unbearable now that she was actively opening herself to it. She doubled over, clutching her stomach, tears starting to roll down her cheeks.

'Éabha?' She heard Archer's concerned voice like a call echoing through an abyss, not from three metres away in the same room. 'Éabha?'

She crouched down, her hands in her hair, feeling the emotion blasting through and around her, filling her, choking her. She heard a far-off whimper and realised it was her.

She could sense Archer standing beside her, Davis and Fionn hovering, unsure what to do. A gentle touch on her shoulder made her flinch and the hand withdrew immediately.

She had to leave. To get away from the sorrow and heartbreak and what she knew unquestioningly with no proof: the only thing haunting this house was tragedy. And hope: that somehow the child they'd lost so cruelly was communicating with them.

PSI would rip that hope away with the facts. And it would break them.

And she would feel all of it.

That was the thought that gave her the strength to push herself to her feet and stumble to the door.

She staggered down the stairs and out the front door. The autumn rain had started in earnest, soaking her the moment she stepped into it. She'd left her coat inside and her dress and jumper were sodden almost instantly.

'Éabha!'

She froze halfway down the path, turning slowly. Archer was stepping out of the house, slow careful movements as though he was afraid she would turn and bolt.

She wanted to. Her muscles were shaking from more than cold now.

'Are you OK?'

'No.'

The recklessness of that word. One word, one admission she had never made before.

'I know your first encounter with a potential paranormal experience can be intense ...'

'You don't understand,' she said, cutting him off. Tears streamed down her face, mixing with the rain. 'It's not the ghost. There is no ghost. I'm sure you'll find evidence to show that. That's the problem.' She took a deep, shaky breath and let it all pour out. 'I feel *everything*. I didn't tell you before because I was afraid of what you'd think. But I feel emotions too. The emotions of the living, I mean. It only started recently, but it's getting stronger and I can't – make – it – stop.' She shook her head, then pointed at the house. 'Those people in there, they're not haunted: they're grieving, and it hurts so much I don't know how they can stand up under the weight of it. They're being torn apart and I can *feel* it. And Davis's suspicion, and your hope, and Fionn's curiosity, and it's just too much. I feel like I'm losing my mind. Sometimes I think I am. I hoped you would have answers for me and that maybe I could help you and then this horrible curse would have some kind of purpose, but it doesn't. I'm just messing things up. And I'm sorry. I'm so sorry, Archer.'

He stood staring at her. She was gasping with the exertion of finally speaking it out loud. He was far enough away that she couldn't feel his emotions, and her own – her fear, her exhaustion – were too strong anyway. The weight and lightness of the truth of her being out in the world.

The wind whipped her hair across her face, damp tendrils sticking to her skin. The cold wetness woke her up.

She'd revealed everything. Archer was staring silently at her through the sheets of rain, the water making it too hard to read his expression. There was just the sound of raindrops hammering onto the cement they stood on.

It had been a long time since she had let someone in this deep. She should have learned from the last time. Archer finally opened his mouth to speak. She turned into the storm and fled.

CHAPTER THIRTEEN

ARCHER LEANED AGAINST the wall opposite Theatre L in the UCD Arts Block, Éabha's coat folded over his arm, trying not to give in to the instinct telling him to run away immediately. Éabha had dodged all his calls since last night, sending just one 'home safe' message. She'd told him yesterday that she had a two o'clock lecture in Theatre L, remarking on how strange it felt to be in a room that could seat five hundred people, after years of home schooling and lockdowns. By half past one today, he'd been so worried about not hearing from her that he'd driven up to UCD to check on her. He hadn't been able to sleep last night, replaying the image of her face, despair and heartbreak clear even through the rain, and the agony in her voice as she'd explained the extent of her powers. How it had cracked as she apologised. Why did she feel the need to apologise? Did she think he was that judgemental?

She'd probably think he was a stalker now too.

The lecture hall doors opened and students started to pour out. This was his last chance to leave, to not let her know he'd come all this way to find her.

She hadn't answered the phone. Maybe she didn't want to see him?

Had he overstepped by coming here? He couldn't help thinking of all the times he'd knocked on Raven's door just for her to scream at him to go away. She'd wanted to be left alone, so much so that at the first chance, she'd disappeared out the door in a flurry of black clothing and stomping boots, a few belongings stuffed into duffel bags.

He just wanted to let Éabha know she wasn't alone, but maybe she didn't want – or need – that reassurance from him.

But her wide blue eyes streaming with tears, her long hair slicked to her head, wouldn't leave his mind.

Just as he was about to turn and leave, he saw her. She was walking out of the hall, tucking her notebook into her bag, when she looked up and saw him. She stopped in her tracks, her lips, coated in their usual pale pink, parting in an almost comical 'O'.

He smiled, trying to act casual, even though from what she said last night she could probably sense how nervous he was.

'Hi,' he said.

'Hey.'

'I, um, brought you your coat,' he said, holding out the coat – and the flimsy excuse he had for being there.

She hugged it to her like it was a shield.

'I'm sorry for low-key stalking you,' he continued, rubbing the back of his neck and shifting from foot to foot. 'I was worried, and I couldn't get through to you ...'

'I'm sorry. I didn't mean to worry you. I just ... needed some time. To prepare.'

'Prepare for what?'

'For you to tell me to leave the team.'

'Leave the team?' He heard his voice echo around the now-empty Arts Block. 'You think we'd kick you out?'

She thought so little of them? Of him? He felt like she'd grabbed his heart and started to squeeze.

'I wasn't exactly fully honest with you. Then I had a complete meltdown mid-investigation. And we both know Davis doesn't think I should be there at all.' Her eyes were downcast, her voice soft and resigned.

'He doesn't think that,' Archer said. 'He just needs more time to learn about your gifts.'

She gave him a sardonic look. 'There's a reason I've spent my whole life hiding them, Archer. My parents … let's just say any mention of the paranormal would have my mum calling for a priest and my dad for a psychiatrist.'

'They must love you joining PSI then.'

'I'd have to tell them first.'

She moved to a nearby bench in the hallway and sat down. Archer sat beside her. He tried to wait patiently for her to continue, but his mind was racing. What other secrets was she keeping? And would she even want to share them with him?

She took a shaky breath, then started to speak.

'The first time I remember seeing a spirit, I was about four. It's all a bit hazy, but I remember telling my parents about "the woman in the corner". They dismissed it as the fabrications of an imaginative child. Then I started to tell them things she said and they began to get concerned. They told me to stop making things up, to tell the truth. When I insisted it was real, my mum yelled at me and locked me in my room.' She took another deep, shuddering breath.

Archer made himself stay quiet, even though a burning outrage flamed through him. Her mother *locked her in her room*?

'When I was seven, we went on a school tour to a castle. We were in one of the bedrooms and all I could feel was this aching dread. I saw a man there, a man with a leering grin who just radiated menace. He was looking right at me. I was so scared, I started crying and shaking. I told my best friend what I could see, and she laughed. Told everyone what I'd said. The teacher called my parents. Mum was furious. Later that night, I overheard them talking about sending me for psychiatric treatment. Dad made me go for a few sessions. Between that and the way the other kids reacted to me in school … I learned to stop telling people when I saw or felt things after that.'

Archer let out a low exhale. 'That sounds incredibly hard.'

Way to understate, Archer.

Éabha shrugged, the resignation in that gesture making him want to reach out and hug her.

'I got used to it. My parents moved me to a different school. I kept to myself when I got there, in case I had another episode and someone found out. I pretended to my parents that it had all gone away. I thought if I just ignored it, it would. But the older I get, the harder it is to keep it in. Or out, really. It's getting stronger, more overwhelming. That's why I came to you. I wanted to find people who would believe me. Maybe be able to figure out what's wrong with me, so I can stop it.'

'Nothing's *wrong* with you, Éabha,' Archer said earnestly.

She snorted, her eyes trained on the tiled floor in front of them, her hands twining in her lap. Archer put his hand on her chin and gently turned it towards him.

'I mean it,' he said. 'I'm sorry for everything you've been through, but there is *nothing* wrong with you. We'll help you figure this out. You're part of the team now.'

Her eyes started to well up and a single sob escaped from her. As though that one soft, broken sound had snapped the thread keeping her emotions back, she started to cry, deep, wrenching sobs.

Archer wrapped his arms around her, murmuring comforting words into her hair. She stiffened for a moment and he prepared himself to pull back, to give her space if she wasn't comfortable. But almost immediately she relaxed, clinging to him as she cried. Eventually the sobs shaking her body eased and she pulled back with an awkward laugh, wiping her face.

'Sorry about that.'

'Honestly, it's refreshing to see someone actually express their emotions,' Archer said. He could feel the sadness welling up in him, and shoved it back down. This wasn't about him.

She smiled tentatively at that. 'Did Davis find the evidence you needed yesterday?'

'Yeah, his theory was right. It was the heating. The pipes were expanding under the floorboards when the heating came on, making the floorboards creak like footsteps as the heating spread through the room.'

'That makes sense,' she said. She looked down at her hands. 'I almost wish I had been wrong, though. For them. I hope they're OK.'

She was a kind person. He could see it, how deeply she felt for those people she barely knew. He felt a rush of affection for her, at how, despite everything she was going through, she wanted to check on other people.

'When do you finish? I'm meeting Fionn and Davis for a coffee, if you're up for it?'

She hesitated and he readied himself for her to decline.

'A coffee sounds great.'

He hoped she couldn't tell that seeing her smile made his heart skip a beat.

CHAPTER FOURTEEN

RAVEN WASN'T SURE SHE WAS ACTUALLY going until she got in the car. Archer had texted her the finalised details of the meeting the night before, and she'd spent the next few hours sitting in bed, watching old episodes of *Pretty Little Liars* on her laptop and worrying at her fingernails with her teeth.

This was so typical of Archer, she seethed to herself as she turned the key in the ignition. Since they were kids, he'd always pushed to do the thing they knew they shouldn't do, and then she'd *have* go along to protect him.

And because you wanted to do it too, a sly voice sidled into her head. Because if her only motivation to do things she didn't want to do was to protect Archer, she wouldn't have left him, would she? Guilt clawed at her as she swung the car out of her apartment block.

She'd let him down for years. The least she could do was turn up to the meeting. Hopefully, she could convince him for once to do what *she* thought they should do: turn their back on that house and walk away for good.

She walked into the office at five to eleven and Archer's face lit up.

'You came,' he said, bounding over and wrapping her in a huge hug.

'Just to talk you out of this,' she replied, her voice muffled.

'You mean try.'

She stepped back, shooing him away. 'At least tell me there are snacks.'

'I was just getting them now,' Archer said, disappearing out the door to the kitchen. 'Come help me carry.'

She trailed him to the kitchen where he picked up a tray that carried three mugs, milk, sugar, some spoons and his beloved V60, the cone dutifully filtering large amounts of coffee into a glass jug. Archer maintained that it 'brought the best notes out of the coffee'. Raven didn't care how coffee was made once it was caffeinated, but it seemed to make her brother happy. A separate tray beside it was laden with a large plate of pastries from Forest Fair, surrounded by ceramic pots of butter and jam. A set of delicate plates was stacked beside them.

Raven picked one up. 'Are these ...'

'The ones from Dad's office? Yes.'

Her eyes filled for a second and she blinked hard. 'He'd be really happy.'

Archer's shoulders relaxed. They were a set of plates with different herbs drawn artfully onto them, their folkloric properties written underneath in beautiful cursive. Raven picked one up, looking at the delicate drawing of lavender in the centre. Every Sunday morning, they would have what their father called elevenses, consisting of some sort of baked treat and, when they were old enough, tea or coffee, in his office. He'd always served them on those plates. She could recite the meanings of the herbs off by heart now: lavender for sleep, rosemary for memory, sage for wisdom, peppermint for clarity ...

'I miss him,' she said softly, putting the plate back on the tray.

'Me too,' Archer said.

He paused and Raven hurriedly picked up the tray, not ready to hear whatever he was about to say. As she carried it back into the office, she realised there had already been three mugs set out when she came into the kitchen.

They'd just set the trays down when an efficient knock came at the front door.

Archer went to open it, returning with a woman a year or two older than Raven. She smiled and for a moment Raven forgot how to breathe. The woman was tall – as tall as Archer – and striking, authoritative in a red shirt under her immaculately tailored black suit. Her dark hair was cut in a sharp bob that hung between her chin and her shoulders and she filled the space in the door unapologetically. This was not who Raven had been expecting when Archer said he'd met an estate agent.

'Cordelia,' Archer said, getting to his feet and shaking her hand. 'It's lovely to meet you. This is my sister, Raven.'

Cordelia stepped over to shake her hand and Raven smiled mutely. She could smell Cordelia's perfume now, a faint musky scent that wafted over her.

Cordelia settled into the seat Archer offered her and the two made polite small talk as he poured the coffee. Raven took her cup gratefully, taking a deep sip in the hope it would kick her back into coherent functionality after Cordelia's arrival had momentarily shut her brain down. She helped herself to a croissant, inwardly wincing as flakes of pastry went everywhere when she cut into it. She hadn't been this instantly nervous around another person since her first shift at Origin, when a gorgeous girl with a nose ring and long brown hair had sat at the bar with a friend. Raven had almost dropped an entire bottle of vodka when the girl smiled at her.

Cordelia heaped several teaspoons of sugar into her coffee before taking a pain au chocolat off the plate Archer proffered, thanking him as she did so. She exuded composure, but there was a tightness in her eyes and the way the teaspoon clattered against the side of her cup made her seem on edge. Raven racked her brains for something interesting to say.

'So,' Archer said before she could think of anything, leaning back in his chair and taking a sip of his coffee. 'You wanted to talk about Hyacinth House?'

Raven tried not to shudder.

Cordelia nodded. 'My estate agency is selling the property, and it's in my portfolio. The sellers are anxious to shift it as quickly as possible, but between the house's tragic history and the business with Jack Gallagher last month, tensions are high.'

Raven's stomach clenched. Was she going to bring up Pádraig?

'Jack Gallagher?' Raven asked quickly, before Cordelia could continue speaking.

'You didn't hear?' Cordelia asked, eyebrows rising in surprise. 'Some college student, a wannabe YouTuber, broke into Hyacinth House a month ago to make a video along the lines of "my night in a haunted house". He ended up in hospital. I'm surprised you didn't know.'

Raven bristled. She'd known there had been an incident, but

she hadn't looked up the details. She felt a spasm of fury at Cordelia's comment.

'I try to avoid any reference to that place,' Raven said stiffly.

Cordelia's face fell and Archer cut in, smiling lightly.

'Raven's more of an Instagram fan. So, things aren't great, selling-wise?'

'No,' Cordelia said. 'We're starting viewings in a month, but with all the rumours resurfacing about it, it's going to be a hard sell.'

'So where do we come in?'

'Well, I was trying to construct the best sales strategy, and I realised there's a whole *industry* in hauntings. People pay money to stay somewhere they might see a ghost. Or, if you're superstitious, knowing that a place is definitely *not* haunted would put you at ease. Especially if a professional assured you of that.'

'You want us to investigate Hyacinth House,' Raven said flatly.

'Yes. And say definitively if it is haunted, in which case I'll market it as such and sell it as an opportunity to capitalise on ghost tourism, or I can soothe any concerns by assuring buyers that it's not.' She beamed at them, clearly pleased with her strategy.

Raven felt sick. Cordelia was treating the events of the house, the history of it, like some kind of commodity.

'Hotel owners or businesses often got our parents to investigate so they could reassure staff or guests that they were safe,' Archer said thoughtfully. 'It's a good plan.'

'Oh, your parents do this too?' Cordelia asked.

'They did.'

'Between that and the fact that you're local and grew up with the legends, you'd be perfect to investigate the house. I've already asked the owners and they'll agree to anything once it helps them get rid of it.'

'Did they say why they wanted to sell?' Raven asked. She was trying to keep a lid on her bubbling anger, though she could feel the tension in every word she managed to push out through her gritted teeth.

'No. Only that they were keen to get it sold as soon as possible. They bought it a few years ago, but I guess their renovation plans didn't go as they'd hoped. Especially since there's a conservation order on the property. It's possible they hadn't looked into that properly before buying, or had been hoping to get it changed. Either way, they weren't able to make it work.'

'They rarely can in Hyacinth,' Raven said.

Cordelia's dark eyes were gleaming with delight at her plan, though Raven thought she could detect a faint shakiness under her confidence. Beside her, Archer was practically bouncing in his seat, but all Raven could focus on was the sense of dread creeping over her. This, all of this, was so familiar. And she knew how it had ended the last time. The sound of sobs she'd taken too long to realise were her own, a coffin and a grave. She tried to focus on what Archer was saying now, but her vision narrowed. Dark spots formed in front of her eyes and her heart was beating so violently her chest hurt.

'Excuse me,' she blurted, getting up and almost running to the door, wrenching it open and rushing outside. Bending over, hands on her thighs, she took gulping breaths of cold air. When her lungs began to fill easily again, she sank back onto the doorstep. She rested her head on her knees, wrapping her arms tightly around them, hoping to stop the violent shaking of her limbs.

Cordelia watched Raven disappear through the door, her long plait whipping out behind her. For a moment, she had an overwhelming urge to chase after her.

'Did I say something?' she asked Archer, who was looking out the door after his sister with a pensive frown.

He smiled gently and shook his head, a lock of hair falling into his eyes. 'It's not you,' he said.

He hesitated, leaning forward to refill his coffee cup and raising his eyebrows at her cup. She held it out and he filled it slowly. She added milk and sugar and stirred it methodically, giving him time as he searched for the right words to say. An uneasy feeling was starting to creep over her. There was something she was missing here. It felt like she had accidentally kicked a wasps' nest on a forest walk.

'My parents' team investigated Hyacinth five years ago.' He looked down at the cup cradled in his hands, his elbows resting on denim-clad knees. 'My dad died during the investigation.'

Cordelia swore. 'I am so sorry, Archer. I didn't realise those were your parents, I never would have asked you if –'

'It's OK, Cordelia. I'm glad you asked.' He sighed, still staring down at his coffee. 'I wasn't there,' he continued in a strained voice. 'I don't know what happened. No one will give me any details. I need to know if anything is in that house. If it was investigating it that –' He cut off, then looked up at her, his brown eyes filled with shadows. 'I need to know.'

'What about …?' She looked over at the door, Raven's departure still fresh.

'I don't know. She doesn't talk about it. She was there. She says she doesn't remember, but I think it's more that she doesn't want to.' Archer's brow furrowed. 'She tends to hold onto things.' Then he looked up, sunny smile back, eyes light. It was as though a cloud that had briefly blocked the sun had shifted.

'That's enough of our tragic backstory,' he grinned. 'Even if Raven doesn't want to investigate, the rest of the team will be up for it. There's three others. Fionn is our tech manager, he sources and sets up our equipment. Davis has really structured our analytic processes to make sure we can verify and back up with evidence as many of the things we experience as possible. Then Éabha is what we call a sensitive. She's got clairvoyant abilities. She's new to the team, but a really exciting addition.'

Cordelia shook her head. 'No offence, but I can't believe you said all that with a straight face.'

Archer laughed. 'I grew up with this. To me, it's as regular a career as accountancy.'

'Slightly more terrifying a concept though.'

'You haven't seen me do maths.'

Cordelia laughed. 'So, what do you need me to do at my end?'

Raven slipped back into the office a while later. 'Sorry, the heat got to me. I needed some fresh air.'

The lie sounded weak even to her ears. Cordelia smiled, kindly pretending to believe her, while Archer shot her a 'you OK?' look. They'd always been able to communicate by minute expressions and gestures. So much time as kids spent trying to sneak into places they shouldn't be had allowed them to create their own silent language. Raven nodded back, forcing a smile onto her face.

'We're going to go to the house after this,' Archer said.

Raven stiffened.

'Cordelia has the keys and needs to take a few measurements, so I said I'd go with her to get a look at the place and see if I can figure out what kind of equipment we'll need. Ideally, Fionn would be here too, but he's working weekdays this week so it probably makes more sense for me just to go now.' He was babbling, trying to placate her in case she freaked out.

'I got a little creeped out last time I was there on my own,' Cordelia said sheepishly.

'I'll tidy up here so you can go now before it gets dark.'

'Thanks, Raven,' Archer said.

'Give me a text when you're done,' she said breezily. She wanted to say 'Let me know you're OK'. But of course she couldn't just say that. Why couldn't she tell her own brother that she worried about him?

Cordelia stood up and Raven waved away her offer to help with the dishes. Archer shrugged on a thick camel coat, wrapping a burgundy scarf around his neck.

'It was lovely to meet you, Raven,' Cordelia said politely. She couldn't quite meet her eyes, which meant one of two things: either Archer had filled her in on the family history and she felt awkward, or she thought Raven was weird. Raven didn't know which she'd prefer.

'You too, Cordelia.'

They left, and Raven sank back into her chair, staring at Cordelia's abandoned cup and the red impression of her lips on the rim.

CHAPTER FIFTEEN

THE SUN WAS SETTING BY THE TIME Raven let herself out of the house, carefully locking the door behind her. Archer wasn't back yet, but he had texted to say he and Cordelia had left Hyacinth House. He hadn't given any more details than that, and honestly, she didn't want any. All she needed – and wanted – to know was that he was safe. The growing chill in the air pinched at any exposed skin, and she hunched her shoulders as she hurried to the car. She turned up the heat the moment the engine purred to life, closing her eyes with relief as the air around her began to warm. The radio played one of the latest chart toppers as she turned the wheel, heading back onto the road to Dublin.

Just a few kilometres before the road connected to the motor-way, her headlights caught a car up ahead by the side of the road. Its hazard lights flashed with vivid brightness, seeming more of a beacon than a warning. Her heart began to beat a little faster when she spotted the figure leaning despondently against the car. A figure in high heels and a black suit, red shirt gleaming in the headlights. Without thinking, she flicked on her indicator and pulled over behind the car.

Cordelia looked over warily, her expression melting into relief when she saw Raven get out.

'Car trouble?' Raven asked.

'The engine cut out about fifteen minutes ago. A tow truck

is coming to take it back to the garage in Kilcarrig.' She sighed, folding her arms. 'Honestly, it's the last thing I need right now.'

'How are you getting back to Dublin?' Raven asked.

'Bus, I guess,' Cordelia shrugged.

'I'm driving back there. I can give you a lift if you'd like,' she said, the words out of her mouth before she could stop herself.

Cordelia's face brightened. 'Are you sure? Honestly, that would be such a help.'

'It's no problem.' Inside she was already panicking. What would they talk about on the drive back?

Cordelia turned to scan the road behind them for a sign of the tow truck, clapping her hands in delight as she saw it approach. 'You must be a good-luck charm.'

Raven's stomach leaped at the warm, intimate smile Cordelia gave her. Once the car was safely in the hands of the mechanic, they both got into Raven's car. They'd barely closed the doors when a deluge started, thick raindrops splattering off the windscreen.

Cordelia let out a delighted laugh. 'I'm telling you, you're a good-luck charm!'

'I'll add it to my CV.'

They spent most of the journey talking about innocuous things, warily circling the topic neither of them wanted to broach. The shadow of Hyacinth House had extended all the way to the car, though Raven appreciated the fact that Cordelia didn't mention it, or try to talk about her and Archer's visit to the house that afternoon. They arrived back to the city just in time to catch the last dregs of rush-hour traffic and, as they slowed to a crawl, Cordelia let out a sigh.

'I can't wait to eat.' She cocked her head thoughtfully. 'I've just had an idea. Would you like to have dinner with me? My treat, as a thank-you for coming to my rescue.'

'Oh, you don't have to do that.'

'Please, I want to,' Cordelia said earnestly. 'Honestly, I'd still be on a bus back to Dublin right now if you hadn't pulled over.'

'If you're sure,' Raven said. Why was she saying yes? This person was the reason Hyacinth House was back in their lives. She should be doing everything possible to push her away. Not drive her around, and chat about music and TV shows and notice how beautiful she was when the streetlights shone through the windscreen, illuminating her face.

'I know the perfect place.'

Raven nodded and Cordelia directed her to a restaurant just outside the city centre. They managed to find somewhere to park easily, though it took Raven's heart the entire walk to the restaurant to calm down after the stress of trying to parallel park. She struggled with it at the best of times, and with Cordelia beside her, her perfume filling the car and her gaze on her, her hands suddenly seemed to have forgotten how to turn a steering wheel.

'*Get it together,*' she chided herself, trying to focus on the facts: that Cordelia was trying to get Archer to investigate Hyacinth House. That she had only asked her to have dinner as a thank-you. That this could all just be some ploy to get her onside.

The restaurant was busy enough for a Thursday evening, packed full of small groups of friends, and couples out for a midweek dinner. The buzz of chatter and low background music filled the room, and they settled at a table for two in an alcove. A small tea light flickered on the table between them, and the waiter handed them menus before bustling off.

Raven studied the menu, almost as much to avoid the faintly mischievous glint in Cordelia's eyes as to decide what to eat. It all felt like too much. They were seated too close, near enough to see her eyes dancing in the candlelight and the curve of her lips when she smiled, red lipstick still immaculate despite her long day and roadside adventure. Beside this polished woman, Raven felt like a chipped teacup. Her hair was escaping from its plait and her nails were even more ragged than earlier. No amount of concealer had succeeded in covering up the dark rings that circled her eyes.

Then there was the fact that she was furious with Cordelia. Whenever she thought about Hyacinth House, resentment seethed inside her. But then Cordelia would laugh or roll her eyes dramatically as she told a story, and Raven couldn't take her eyes off her.

You're being a creep. You don't even know her.

Maybe if she finally looked up from the menu she could find out more. She raised her eyes. A small smile hovered at the corners of Cordelia's mouth, a slight quirk of her lip that made Raven worry she knew exactly what thoughts were running circles in her mind.

The waiter appeared again, setting two glasses and a carafe of water on the table. He quickly took their order.

'I'm so excited for this,' Cordelia said. 'This is one of my favourite restaurants – besides my parents', of course.'

'They own a restaurant?' Raven asked. What would that have been like? Late shifts in a busy restaurant packed with life, instead of long hours in the darkness trying to contact the dead.

'Yeah, a Mexican one in town. They met working in the restaurant on a cruise ship, fell in love, and moved back here. Mum's a chef and Dad runs front of house. Mum said since she was moving to Ireland for Dad, she should get to choose the cuisine, so of course she went with her own heritage. I know I'm biased, but her food is amazing. Anyway, they opened the restaurant right around the time they had me. It's basically their second child.'

'Do you like cooking too?' Raven asked.

'God, no,' Cordelia laughed. 'I appreciate good food, but I am a mediocre cook at best, much to my parents' chagrin. I know they're disappointed I didn't want to go into hospitality, but honestly, I don't have the creativity to be a good chef or the patience to be good at front of house,' Cordelia sighed. 'It was hard to tell them, though: I mean, no parent wants to hear their child say that the thing they've been training them to do all their lives isn't for them.'

Raven felt a sharp pain in her stomach. It must have shown on her face, because Cordelia paled and swore emphatically.

'I'm sorry, Raven. That was such an insensitive thing to say.'

Archer had filled her in on the family history, then. Before she could respond, the waiter appeared beside them, setting down a juicy steak with a side of hand-cut chunky chips for Cordelia and a large bowl of freshly made pasta with a thick tomato sauce and an extremely generous helping of parmesan cheese for Raven. They spent the rest of the meal talking about favourite foods, arguing over the perfect pizza toppings, and swapping restaurant recommendations. Raven made sure to keep the conversation as far away from her family as possible, her only stumbling block being her effusive praise of Angela's apple crumble in Forest Fair.

She kicked herself even as she said it, not wanting to bring Archer into this. He was at the centre of everything she wanted to avoid.

'Archer mentioned he's working there while he gets the business back off the ground,' Cordelia said. She laughed. 'I have to say, when I arrived, I wasn't expecting the person I'd spoken to on the phone to look like him.'

Raven felt herself stiffen. *Of course* Archer would have had that effect: with his easy charm and his warm smile, he'd had a steady stream of eager boys and girls hoping to date him since they were old enough to be interested in that.

'Not expecting a handsome, young paranormal surveyor?' Raven tried to joke, hoping her voice sounded light. 'I can imagine that would throw you.'

'I mean, people underestimate me for my age too, so I wouldn't doubt him for it,' Cordelia said. She paused, before carefully saying, 'And the handsomeness isn't really a distraction for me.'

'Too blond?' Raven said lightly.

'Too male,' Cordelia said casually.

Raven took a long sip of her water to hide the hopeful smile that was threatening to break across her face.

There was a pause.

'About earlier,' Cordelia said tentatively.

Raven stiffened, keeping her eyes firmly on the piece of penne she was picking up with her fork.

'I know now that Hyacinth House is a sensitive topic for you and your family. I saw your face when Archer told you we were going back there today too. I'm sorry I barged in without knowing the details.'

'It's fine,' Raven said, staring down at her plate.

'It doesn't feel fine,' Cordelia said.

'Cordelia,' Raven said quietly. 'I'm having a really lovely dinner. Can we not spoil it?' She glanced across at her.

Cordelia pressed her lips together as she nodded. 'OK,' she said. Then her lips curved up in a smile that felt to Raven like a challenge. 'For now.'

The rest of the meal passed in a blur. Raven dropped Cordelia off at her apartment before heading home herself. She let herself in, dumping her bag on the couch and starting to get ready for bed. Her thoughts swirled as she tried to process everything that had happened that day. If only Cordelia had been less … funny. And smart. And captivating. Then she could just hate her for stampeding into their lives and bringing up all the things she wanted to forget.

Maybe Cordelia would change her mind about getting PSI involved, and Raven could just keep getting to know her without the shadow of Hyacinth House hanging over them. She fell asleep with that foolish hope warming her heart.

CHAPTER SIXTEEN

CORDELIA WOKE SHIVERING. She turned over to check the time on her phone, snatching her arm back under the blankets the moment the screen lit up. Two fifty-eight. Groaning, she rolled onto her back to stare up at the ceiling. The light from the hallway illuminated the room just enough for her to see the breath clouding in front of her. She frowned and blinked. It was probably tiredness merging with the remnants of sleep playing tricks on her. It had been a long day, after all, between the meeting and going back to the house, her car breaking down and the surprising – and wonderful – dinner with Raven. All she wanted to do was sleep, but a quiet instinct whispered to her not to close her eyes.

Teeth chattering, she sat up against the headboard, wrapping a blanket around her shoulders. She reached out to click on her lamp, then froze. She was not alone in the room.

A figure was standing in front of the door. A woman in a black dress, with a long veil covering her face. Cordelia opened her mouth to scream, but the cold in the room surged down her throat, freezing her lungs. She tried to move, but something unseen was holding her firmly in place. The figure stood completely motionless, watching her. Cordelia stared back, unable to do anything else. Everything was still for a moment. Then the figure's head tilted. The veil she wore mimicked the movement but didn't ripple the way it should, as though it were immune to the laws of physics. Everything about it screamed of Otherness. Of a predator studying her prey. A strangled gasp broke from Cordelia's throat, a tiny piece of air managing to wriggle free from her immobilised lungs. The sound hovered in the air in front of her for a single, agonising moment.

The noise spurred the figure into movement. It dropped to the floor and crawled towards her with the rapid disjointed speed of a spider, limbs jutting out in sharp angles no body should make. When it reached the foot of the bed it disappeared from Cordelia's line of sight. There was an excruciating pause, accompanied by an oppressive silence.

Cordelia stared at the end of her bed, horrified and still frozen in place. She tried desperately to scream, or move, or do *something* other than wait.

One heartbeat passed.

Two.

Three.

A pair of pale white hands appeared, spindly fingers grasping at the bed frame as the figure climbed up, slithering onto the bed and up the covers towards her. She pressed back even closer to the headboard, lungs screaming for air, fingers clutching her blanket to her. Just when the figure reached her, it disappeared.

Suddenly she could breathe again. Taking a deep, shuddering breath, she leapt out of bed, grabbing her keys and phone from the bedside table and bolting from the room. Cordelia was already in the stairwell of her apartment building, blanket trailing behind her as she tore down the stairs two at a time, her phone pressed to her ear, when *she* answered. A sleepy, confused voice greeted her.

'I need your help,' Cordelia gasped.

CHAPTER SEVENTEEN

RAVEN WAS WOKEN BY THE SOUND of her phone ringing. She fumbled it from the floor beside her bed, bleary eyes registering the time – three a.m. – and the caller.

'Hello?'

'I need your help.' Cordelia's voice was shaking, and from her frantic breathing it sounded like she was running.

'Cordelia, are you OK?' She sat bolt upright in her bed, instantly awake.

'Something was here, in my room, and I couldn't move and I was cold and …' She let out a fractured sob. 'I know I shouldn't call you with this, but you're the only person I can think of that's nearby and won't think I'm crazy and …'

'Cordelia,' Raven said, cutting across her. 'I'll be there in ten.'

'Thank you,' Cordelia whispered.

Raven threw on the first clothes she found. She went to her wardrobe, hesitating just a moment before pulling down a box from the top shelf. She rifled through its contents before picking out a few different things, shoving them in her bag and running out the door. The roads were empty and she sped along, hoping she wouldn't stumble on a late-night speed check.

'Well, Garda, it was an emergency. My friend was attacked by a ghost.' That would go down well in court.

She turned the corner onto Cordelia's street and saw a figure on the side of the road, framed by the headlights, a blanket wrapped around her shoulders. She pulled up and was out of the car before she had even fully turned the engine off.

'Raven … I … thank you,' Cordelia stammered. She was shaking, her long legs covered in goosebumps, while her white-knuckled fingers clutched the blanket.

'Have you been out here the whole time?'

Cordelia nodded. 'I couldn't go back in there,' she whispered.

'I'm here,' Raven said.

She swallowed as she looked up at the building, trying to create an air of reassurance. Cordelia had called her for help. She couldn't leave her like this: alone, scared, on the side of the road. Even if she wanted to run away and never look back.

It was probably just a bad dream, Raven thought to herself, feet growing heavier with each step as they walked up the path towards the building. *She just needs you to reassure her there's nothing there. It couldn't be* her. *Not here.*

Though She had left the house before.

Cordelia unlocked the doors to the building with a fob on her keychain. Neither of them spoke as they stepped into the lift.

'Do you want to tell me what happened?' Raven said gently, breaking the silence. *Please tell me I'm wrong.*

'Can we check the apartment first?' Cordelia asked.

'Of course.' She knew what Cordelia would say anyway.

Cordelia unlocked her door, the key shaking so vigorously in her hand that it took her several attempts to fit it into the lock. Raven put a hand on her arm to steady her.

'I'll go first,' she said.

Cordelia shot her a grateful glance and Raven tried to let that buoy her up as she stepped over the threshold.

'My bedroom is to the left,' Cordelia breathed behind her.

Raven nodded and went towards it, Cordelia on her heels. She had expected her to stay by the door. That's what Raven would have done. A rush of shame shot through her. Cordelia Cassidy Cuevas had a streak of iron in her.

Raven snapped on the light. The room *felt* fine. It was the same temperature as the living room, and considerably warmer than outside. The bedclothes were askew and a lamp was on the floor beside the bedside table but, besides that, nothing looked amiss. She turned to look at Cordelia.

'It didn't feel like this,' she said, looking embarrassed. 'It was so cold. And I couldn't move, and ...'

'Cordelia,' Raven said, laying a hand on her arm. 'I believe you.'
I wish I didn't.

'I'm going to do some EMF readings. That's electromagnetic fields. Ghosts disrupt them, so it's a good way of finding paranormal activity. I won't be surprised if it all comes up normal though. These things only register during a manifestation, and it seems like whatever you saw is long gone.'

Cordelia's shoulders dropped in relief. 'I was standing on the road convincing myself it was all a dream and I was making a fool of myself,' she said.

The corner of Raven's mouth turned up in a wry smile. 'I know that feeling.'

Raven took out her EMF meter. Her father had given it to her

118

for her fifteenth birthday and, despite everything, she kept it close. The readings all came back as normal. If Raven concentrated, she could almost feel something, some lingering sense of malice … She shook herself. It was her mind playing tricks. The readings were all normal. She turned to where Cordelia stood beside her, still trembling, clutching her blanket to her.

'We need to get you warmed up,' Raven said. 'You're frozen.'

'I'm scared of being alone,' Cordelia whispered. She looked at the ground, avoiding Raven's eyes. Each word dragged from her throat as though it physically hurt her to speak them. 'I'm afraid I'll be in the shower and she'll appear at the door again or …'

'I'll sit outside,' Raven said. 'Right outside the door. You can leave it ajar, and we can talk the entire time. Then we'll have some tea and you can tell me what happened.'

'Why are you so kind?' Cordelia said, her brown eyes soft.

Raven tried to think of a clever reply, but all that came out was a weird half grunt. She followed Cordelia back out of the room, cringing.

After Cordelia had dried off and changed into cosy flannel pyjamas, Raven brewed some chamomile tea and they settled onto the couch. Cordelia couldn't deal with how, even pulled out of bed at three in the morning, Raven managed to look cool: her silvery hair pulled back in a low ponytail, black ripped jeans, a black sleeveless T-shirt and a checked red flannel shirt. Cordelia, on the other hand, had been a shaking mess on the side of the road in a pair of pyjama shorts. The moment they'd stepped back into the apartment and everything felt normal, she'd wanted to curl up in a ball and die. But Raven had been kind, sitting and chatting from outside the bathroom, her low laugh weaving through the steam. Now she was holding a mug of tea in her hands and looking at her with compassionate eyes as she waited for her to tell her what happened.

'I woke up, and it was freezing. Like, end of *Titanic* when Jack is in the water freezing. I was so tired and I just wanted to sleep, but there was this little voice screaming at me that ... that I wasn't alone.'

She took a deep breath and continued. When she described how the figure had crawled across the room, she stopped again, taking a long sip of the tea and closing her eyes, trying to focus on the warmth spreading down her throat, into her stomach, chasing away the last remnants of the cold that had invaded her bones. The images came fast as she spoke, her hands gripping the mug to try and stop their trembling. When she finished with how the figure had disappeared, she looked desperately at Raven, searching her face for some sign of scepticism.

'I could move again, and I just ran. Before I knew what I was doing I was halfway down the stairs and you were answering the phone.'

Raven watched her calmly for a moment, waiting to see if she had anything else to add.

'That's it,' she said awkwardly, shrugging.

'OK. Well, thank you for telling me while it was all fresh in your mind,' Raven said. 'I believe you. I ...' She hesitated. 'I think I know who you saw.'

Cordelia's head snapped up.

'She's the one from the stories about the house, isn't she?'

'The Lady,' Raven confirmed.

She'd been completely composed the entire time Cordelia had spoken, as though she was just telling her about her day and not an apparition that had appeared in her room at three in the morning. But now there was a tightness in the line of her shoulders, light creases forming around her eyes.

'Is there something you haven't told me?' Cordelia asked.

Raven opened her mouth, then shut it again. She tilted her head, chewing thoughtfully on her lower lip. 'I think it might be worth asking Éabha to come over later. She's the sensitive Archer mentioned before. We could see if she picks up anything on a different level than what I would notice. I think Archer would want that.'

Cordelia shrugged. 'Sure,' she laughed, trying to sound casual despite the slightly high pitch betraying her. 'This whole thing can't get much weirder.'

She pretended not to notice that Raven had deliberately avoided the question. She owed her that.

Raven took her phone out of her bag and tapped out a message. 'I'll send her the address now so she sees it first thing and ask her if she can come over. Hopefully she's an early riser.'

Her phone beeped with a response almost immediately.

'Or an insomniac,' she said, brow furrowed. She smiled reassuringly at Cordelia. 'She'll be here at eight.'

'Great,' Cordelia said weakly. She stifled a yawn. Now that the adrenaline had worn off she felt exhausted, like every muscle in her body was dissolving into the couch.

Raven looked down at her watch, a chunky silver-faced one

with a thick black leather strap. 'You could get a few hours' sleep before Éabha arrives?' she suggested.

Cordelia hesitated, looking longingly towards her bedroom door. Then she looked down at her lap. 'I'm afraid to go in there.' She could feel her cheeks heating with shame. Raven had done this sort of thing when she was a *child* and Cordelia couldn't even handle going back into an empty room.

'OK, just a sec,' said Raven. She went into the bedroom and returned carrying Cordelia's duvet as well as some spare blankets she kept stacked by her bed.

'We'll sleep here,' she said, offering the duvet to Cordelia. She flushed, then said in a rush, 'I mean, if you want me to stay?'

'Please,' Cordelia blurted out, reaching out to take her hand. 'Please stay,' she said softly.

'Of course.' Raven settled herself at one end of the couch while Cordelia took the other, her duvet around her and her head propped up on cushions. She never slept like this: her height made it difficult, and seeing Raven curled up neatly at the other end made her painfully aware of her own broad frame. Raven must have spotted her frown, though she definitely misinterpreted its cause, because she leaned forward to squeeze her hand.

'It'll be OK,' she said. 'I'll be right here.'

Cordelia squeezed her hand back, and drifted off into a dreamless sleep.

CHAPTER EIGHTEEN

RAVEN WOKE UP WITH A CRICK in her neck. She felt a warmth down her side and looked down to see Cordelia lying pressed against her, her head somehow on Raven's shoulder despite their height difference, duvet wrapped tightly around her. She tried to rotate her arm to see her watch without waking her, but the moment she moved, Cordelia's eyes snapped open. She sat bolt upright and turned to face Raven.

'I'm so sorry, Raven,' she said, cupping a hand over her mouth.

'Don't worry about it,' Raven said. Her side felt cold from where Cordelia had moved away. 'Éabha will be here in about half an hour.'

'I should get dressed,' Cordelia said, looking down at her pyjamas and brushing her hand through her hair. 'I feel like such a mess.'

'You were woken up in the middle of the night by a ghost and got about three hours' sleep. I'd say you're looking pretty good.'

'That is a low bar,' Cordelia laughed. 'How about I make us some coffee first? I think today will be one of those "all the caffeine" days.'

'Sounds like every day in my life.'

At precisely eight o'clock, the buzzer sounded. Raven opened the door to find Éabha, her cheeks flushed from the cycle over in the crisp morning air, but her hair still falling in perfect waves around her shoulders. She stepped into the apartment, a light-brown Michael Kors backpack slung over one shoulder and a pink helmet hanging from her hand. She looked as poised as ever, but Raven could feel an apprehensiveness surrounding her.

'Hi,' Éabha said, waving awkwardly.

'Éabha, this is Cordelia,' Raven said, waving a hand towards her. 'Cordelia, Éabha.'

'Hi,' Éabha said again, shaking Cordelia's hand. She sucked in a sharp breath as their hands touched, though Cordelia didn't seem to notice.

'Thanks for coming. Should we fill you in?' Cordelia asked.

'No,' Éabha said firmly, cutting across Raven before she could answer. Éabha quickly continued, her voice shaking as though her assertiveness had taken her by surprise. 'It's better if I don't know anything. It means no one can say that what I pick up on was suggested to me.'

'Makes sense,' Raven nodded.

'Davis suggested it,' Éabha said, her voice strained. 'Am I OK to wander around?'

Cordelia nodded and Éabha came further into the living room. She closed her eyes, taking a few deep breaths, then turned sharply and walked straight into the bedroom. Raven and Cordelia trailed after her.

'This is where it happened,' Éabha said. Her voice was soft, the way someone speaks when they're half-listening to something else. She shivered. 'It was cold.' She hesitated, then stood just over the threshold, exactly where Cordelia had seen the figure the night before.

'Someone very angry stood here, filled with hatred. It's faded, though. As though it's an impression that they left.'

Cordelia looked at Raven, who had taken out her phone and was recording everything Éabha said. Éabha walked slowly over to the bed, to the left-hand side, the side Cordelia slept on. Her fingers reached out to touch the headboard. Her eyes snapped open.

'Oh, you poor thing,' she said, her voice warm with sympathy. 'You were so scared.'

Then, as though all the energy had drained from her, her legs began to tremble. Raven moved quickly, taking her by the arm and leading her out into the living room where she sank gratefully into the armchair. Cordelia grabbed a packet of chocolate-coated biscuits from a cupboard and offered them to her. Raven mouthed 'water' to Cordelia, watching Éabha carefully as she bit down gratefully on a biscuit, crumbs falling onto her lap. Her face was white and her arms were covered in gooseflesh. Cordelia handed her a glass of water and she drank it down, then took a deep breath. Raven's curiosity grew as it became clear Éabha was OK. She'd never met a psychic before.

'May I take another biscuit?' Éabha asked politely.

'You can eat the whole packet if you want,' Cordelia said.

Éabha took another, pulling a blanket draped over the back of the armchair from behind her and wrapping it around her. 'Sometimes the sensations take a few minutes to ease,' she explained.

Raven and Cordelia waited as she munched on the biscuit in silence.

'What do we do now?' Cordelia asked after the silence had dragged on.

'We should to talk to Arch,' Raven sighed. She hated this. He'd gone to the house *once* with Cordelia and already it was starting again. 'He needs to know what happened. And the rest of the team too.' She turned to Éabha. 'What are your schedules like today?'

'I have lectures, but I can skip them. I just need to be home for dinner so my parents don't know I cut class. They think I'm already on my way to college. They have my timetable.'

Éabha's parents kept constant track of her whereabouts? She didn't seem to find it strange, saying it matter-of-factly.

'I'll call the office, tell them I'm driving down to do some stuff on the Hyacinth property,' Cordelia said. 'I mean, technically that's true,' she added with a wry smile.

'I'll drive,' Raven said briskly, slinging on her leather jacket.

'May I bring the biscuits?' Éabha asked.

CHAPTER NINETEEN

ÉABHA AND THE OTHERS FOUND Archer at the cafe, where he was working the morning shift. His expression grew increasingly surprised when first Éabha and then Cordelia trailed through the door after Raven. Éabha could see him take in the dark circles under Cordelia's eyes, the tense way she was holding herself, and watched his surprise morph into concern.

'I have a break at half ten,' he told them. 'Round up the others.'

They ordered breakfast while they waited, eggs accompanied by stacks of freshly baked bread alongside yet more coffee. The café was warm and bustling, filled with mismatched furniture, the air permeated with the scent of spices Éabha recognised from her psychometry experiment with Archer and Raven. Davis arrived just before half-past ten, as the breakfast rush subsided and the early morning customers left in almost unison. He swung into the free chair beside Éabha, settling in. Fionn rushed in just after Archer had joined them with a latte and a scone, the six of them clustering around the table. The rest of the cafe was completely quiet now and Archer's co-worker was in the back. Raven filled them in on the events quickly. Her voice was matter-of-fact, as though she was giving a report on the weather, but under the table Éabha could see her hands were curled into tight fists. Davis shifted slightly in his chair as she spoke, and Éabha caught him studying her out of the corner of his eye while Raven outlined her involvement.

Éabha stared determinedly ahead, trying to keep her face impassive. She'd spent the whole car journey down trying to act naturally, but she didn't know whether she wanted to laugh or vomit. She'd thought trying to learn about her 'gifts' would help her to suppress them: instead, the more she opened up to them, the stronger they got. She'd felt everything Cordelia had experienced. Even the faint remnants that lingered had been potent.

'I've never heard of The Lady being seen anywhere other than the house,' Archer said.

Raven looked down at her lap, and Éabha felt a needle-prick of guilt from her as she did. Beside her, Davis stared out the window.

Cordelia bristled. 'I know what I saw.'

'I'm not doubting that,' Archer said. 'It's just … unprecedented.'

The guilt at the table intensified.

'We need to document this,' Davis said thoughtfully, drumming his fingers on the table. 'So next time she appears, we have scientific back-up for the personal experiences.'

'A "personal experience" is what we call experiences like yours,' Fionn explained to Cordelia. 'The equipment we use can help capture things like temperature changes, noises you hear, so next time we have irrefutable evidence of what's happening.'

Cordelia nodded, then her eyes opened in alarm. 'You think there's going to be a next time?'

'We don't know,' Archer said. 'But it's good to be prepared.'

Fionn whipped a notebook out of his leather satchel and began to write, muttering to himself.

'Thermometers … infrared … video …'

'Video?' Cordelia said. 'You do remember this is my bedroom?'

Fionn blushed. 'Sorry, it's just normally with a full-bodied apparition, we … yeah, sorry.'

'We can talk through the particulars later,' Davis said, raising an eyebrow at Fionn.

'It could be worth going to Hyacinth again,' Archer mused.

Raven stiffened.

She was a difficult one to read, Éabha thought. Her emotions didn't spill out of her the way the others' did, but she could sense them roiling, as though trapped behind a glass panel, screaming to get out.

Glass was so fragile too.

If she concentrated, she might be able to pick up on some of it. Fear, worry, frustration … a tendril of emotion she couldn't place … She stopped, shame flooding through her. It was invasive to probe someone's emotions without their knowledge or permission. She looked down at her hands, where she had unconsciously started worrying at her cuticles, and stilled the motion. *Back straight, head up, hands still.*

She looked back up. The conversation had continued, but she could see Davis again watching her out of the corner of his eye.

'It makes sense,' Archer was saying. 'If Éabha goes to the house, she can see if she picks up anything and if it feels similar to what she experienced at the apartment. Cordelia too.'

'Going to the house is probably what got The Lady's attention in the first place,' Raven argued. 'Going back and bringing more people is dangerous. She'll see it as interfering in her house.'

'We can't investigate the house without going inside.'

'Maybe we shouldn't be investigating it then.'

'I'm not walking away just because you're scared, Raven!'

'And I'm not risking myself or others just because you can't let this go!'

Silence. The emotions spun and eddied around the table so intensely that Éabha had to shut her eyes. She could feel them, spiralling in a whirlwind that made it hard to figure out which were attached to whom. Fear, shame, discomfort, frustration, grief, guilt all swirled together, picking her up in a tornado and sending her flailing out of control. She took deep breaths, her nails digging into her hands. A sudden warmth landed on her arm, soothing her with a gentle touch, bringing her back down from the tornado and into her body. She half-opened her eyes. A hand was resting on her arm. She looked up and Davis tilted his head, asking a silent question. She nodded and he took his hand away, turning back to the table as though nothing had happened. No one else had noticed. Fionn was staring down at his notebook as though he could dive into the pages and escape. Cordelia's eyebrows were knotted together as she looked between Raven and Archer. Archer was leaning forward, determined but hurt, while Raven bristled like an angry cat. Then she deflated.

'I don't suppose you could just ... not sell the house?' she asked Cordelia jokingly.

'I wish. I'm starting to understand why the guys were so fine with me taking it,' she said. She looked around the table. 'Look, I need this for my career. I have a lot to prove. But I completely understand if you want to step away. I didn't know what I was asking when I asked you to get involved.'

'We knew when we took it, though,' Archer said.

Davis shifted in his seat at that.

'I'll go with you to the house,' Cordelia said. She pushed her shoulders back, sitting upright. 'If I already have The Lady's attention, I might as well figure this out.'

Archer grinned. 'I finish at two, we could go straight after?'

'I'll come,' Éabha blurted out. The others at the table turned to her. 'If you want me to, I mean,' she said.

She was terrified. The lingering chill, the malice she'd felt in the apartment, had been only an echo. But if Cordelia could experience what she had last night and still walk back into that house, how could she refuse? She'd spent most of her life afraid: of what she experienced, of someone finding out about it, of thinking she was going mad. She was so tired of always being afraid.

'I have a shift in the shop at one,' Fionn said apologetically.

'I'll handle the equipment,' Davis offered. He turned to Fionn. 'We can go back to the office now and figure it all out. I'm not expected in labs today.'

'I'm not going to the house,' Raven said firmly. She took a deep breath and continued. 'But I can do more digging into the history of the estate. I've been thinking. Emily wouldn't have destroyed the file. I bet she's hidden it somewhere.'

'Éabha and I can help you look while we wait for Archer, if you'd like?' Cordelia offered. Éabha nodded her agreement.

'Thank you,' Raven said with a warm smile. She and Cordelia looked at each other just a moment longer than usual before looking away.

Éabha had a sneaking suspicion that both Raven and Cordelia would prefer if it was just them going to the look for the files. You didn't need to be clairvoyant to see that.

CHAPTER TWENTY

RAVEN LET THEM INTO THE house, ushering them into the hall. Davis and Fionn dipped off into the office, while Cordelia and Éabha followed Raven.

'I guess we start with Mum's study, then go from there,' Raven said. 'Heads up, there's a lot of files in here.'

She wasn't exaggerating. Her mother's office was on the ground floor, in a large room lined on three sides from floor to ceiling with bookshelves. One wall of them was filled with neat, identical folders, all labelled with case names and dates. A beautifully carved oak desk faced out a large bay window, an empty laptop stand sitting in the middle of it, a silver photo frame to its left. Éabha stepped over to examine it more closely. A young Raven and Archer beamed out from the silver casing, sitting on concrete steps leading down to a beach. Behind them, a tall woman with silvery-blond hair pulled back in a bun and a shorter man with kind eyes and a big smile had their arms around each other. The two teenagers were leaning back against their parents' legs. They looked happy.

'That was the summer before,' Raven said softly, stepping beside her and looking down at the photo.

Éabha didn't need to ask 'before what'.

'I'll take the desk,' Raven said, clearing her throat and gesturing at the deep drawers underneath it. 'Will you two start going through the files? There's a chance she may have hidden the Hyacinth one inside another, or labelled it under a code name, so we're going to have to go through them file by file.' She winced. 'Sorry, I know it's tedious'

'It's grand,' Cordelia assured her. She rested a hand on Raven's shoulder briefly as she crossed to the bookshelf of files. 'I'll start from the top if you start from the bottom, Éabha?'

'Sounds good.' Éabha settled herself on the floor and pulled the first folder from the shelf.

'Cliff Abbey, 1993' was written in beautiful cursive on labels across the front and on the spine of the folder. She flipped it open, pulling out sheets and beginning to read. The file was meticulously organised, compiling the interviews with the client, the thoughts the team had in advance, the equipment they used and their findings. Any extra information – media coverage, historical reports, etc. – was also included, neatly clipped and carefully organised. After a few minutes, she forced herself to put it back. No matter how fascinating the case files were, she couldn't just sit here reading them all. She worked faster, skimming each file to make sure they were about the case they claimed to be.

Despite all her intentions, when she opened a file labelled 'Beachside Hotel, 2010', she was completely absorbed within moments, fascinated by the tale of the young girl who was said to haunt the hotel and the testimonies from the owners, both previous and at the time. When she got to the findings, she gasped. There was an image, a still from a video camera, that showed two children who could only be a young Archer and Raven peering through the banisters, both wearing pyjamas. Beside them was an outline of a figure. It was small and seemed to be wearing a dress. Attached to the photo was a neat explanation of all the possible logical reasons this could have occurred: shadows, equipment malfunction, lighting issues, etc., and why they had been ruled out. The conclusion was that there was an image of a small child kneeling beside Archer and Raven. This, accompanied by the two children's accounts of being lured from their beds without any knowledge of what phenomenon their parents were investigating, led to their official conclusion that the hotel was haunted by a benign, if somewhat mischievous, child.

Cordelia looked over her shoulder, letting out a low whistle. 'Oh wow.'

'Did you find something?' Raven asked. She sounded almost worried.

'No, sorry. Just looking at your friend from the Beachside Hotel,' Cordelia said.

Raven laughed, her face softening as she came over and looked at it. 'That was our first real encounter. I'm so glad that camera caught the ghost or our parents would have murdered us for being out of bed during an investigation.'

'I love how chill you are about this,' Éabha said. 'Oh, here's a childhood photo of me and my brother and a GHOST.'

Raven tilted her head thoughtfully. 'I guess when you grow up with it, it doesn't seem overly weird, or scary. It's just what we did.'

'My parents just dragged me to mass every Sunday,' Éabha huffed. 'This is way more interesting.'

The other two girls laughed and she felt a rush of warmth. It was still strange to her, being able to relax around people. A twinge of fear crackled through her. What if they decided they didn't have any need for her after all? Would she lose this? She shoved that thought deep down, locking it away, and turned back to the files.

Raven sighed, leaning back in her mother's desk chair and stretching before checking her watch. Archer would be here in half an hour, and they'd had no luck finding the Hyacinth files. She felt a moment of guilt for rifling through her mother's desk, though if Emily had just *let* them have the file, they wouldn't have had to do this.

Not that she was entirely sure she wanted to find it. She knew the history could help, but the thought of reading her parents' version of what had happened to their family in that house made her stomach churn. There were so many gaps in her memory, and the bits she did remember … A part of her whispered that, if she found the file, she didn't have to give it *all* to the others. After all, she had promised them the backstory of the house. What had happened to her was practically the present. It felt like it was, anyway. She could go through it herself first, and see if there was anything worth passing on. She tried to ignore that sneaky voice as she leaned down to open the bottom drawer of the desk. Despite pulling firmly on the handle, it stayed solidly shut. It was the only drawer that was locked.

'That's interesting,' she murmured. She searched the rest of the desk for a key, but couldn't find one anywhere. Frustrated, she yanked on the drawer again, creating a thud that made Cordelia jump and Éabha let out a startled yelp, scattering the pages of the file she was holding.

'Sorry,' Raven said. She pushed her chair back from the desk and gestured exasperatedly at the drawer. 'I don't suppose either of you know how to pick a lock?'

Éabha shook her head but Cordelia gave a slow, mischievous smile. 'I do, actually. Do either of you have a hair pin?'

Raven pulled one from her plait and Cordelia took it, crouching down beside the desk. 'I had a childhood obsession with *Veronica Mars*,' she explained with an embarrassed chuckle. She fiddled with the lock for a few minutes, letting out a delighted 'ha' when she heard a click. 'I can't believe that actually worked!'

'Thank you, Veronica,' Raven said.

Cordelia moved aside and Raven slid to the floor, pulling out the contents of the drawer piece by piece. She sifted through bank documents, old driver's licences and birth certificates. Her breath caught slightly when she found a folder containing a will, quickly placing it to one side. Éabha stopped reading the file she'd been focused on to hover nervously behind them, fiddling with a lock of her hair.

All too soon, the drawer was empty. There was no file. Raven sat back on her heels, letting out a disappointed sigh.

'Any ideas, Veronica?' she asked hopelessly.

Cordelia shook her head.

'If this was a film,' sighed Éabha, sinking back to the ground and picking up the file she'd abandoned, 'there'd be a false bottom to that drawer.'

Raven and Cordelia looked at each other. Cordelia reached into the empty drawer, her fingers prodding and searching for any catches or grooves in the base. As her fingers worked down the left side of the drawer, she stopped.

'Hang on,' she breathed. She dug her finger into an indentation in the wood and with a pop the bottom of the drawer released. Underneath it was a thick white folder. There was no label on it. Raven reached in with shaking hands and pulled it out. She opened it, staring down at the first page: a newspaper clipping from 1950. About Hyacinth House.

'OK, was that a psychic thing or just an Éabha-being-a-genius thing?' she asked.

Éabha smiled and shrugged. 'Probably more of a "pure luck" thing.'

'I can't believe we actually found it,' Cordelia said. She glanced ruefully at her hands; releasing the false bottom had chipped her shellac. 'At least that was worth destroying my nails for.'

'I'll buy you a manicure myself,' Raven said.

'We're just in time,' Éabha said, looking at her phone. 'Archer should be here in five minutes.'

'I'll bring the file to the office and work through it there while you're gone,' Raven said. 'When you're done with the house, we can compare notes.'

'Sounds like a plan.' Cordelia looked around the room. 'Should we fix the mess before we go?'

'Nah, Archer and I can handle that later,' Raven said. 'Mum won't be back for weeks.'

'Anxiety--wise, do you think having another coffee before going to a haunted house is a bad idea?' Cordelia asked, yawning as they made their way to the office room.

'Personally, I never turn down a coffee,' Raven replied.

'I've witnessed your frightening levels of caffeine consumption first-hand, so I don't know how much I should be taking your advice.'

'I work in a bar and grew up doing all-night ghost hunts. It's practically mandatory to have an unhealthy relationship with caffeine.'

Cordelia laughed, the sound racing across the hallway ahead of them. Raven would do anything to hear that laugh again.

They joined Davis in the office space, and Raven excused herself under the pretence of getting the coffees. Really she just needed a few minutes to pull herself together. They had found the file. Was she ready to face whatever was inside? To answer the question she was afraid to even think, never mind ask?

No. She knew that anyway.

The kettle was boiling when Davis stepped in behind her.

'Hey,' she said, standing on tiptoe, trying to reach a mug on the top shelf. *Of course* Davis and Archer would keep everything high up. They used to do it all the time when they were younger, just to mess with her.

Davis reached around her and took down two mugs, handing one to her.

'Sorry,' he grinned, reading her thoughts. 'Looks like the habit stuck.'

'I'd be flattered if it wasn't so annoying.'

'Well, I guess we haven't had to worry about accommodating the short one for a while,' Davis said lightly.

She could feel the barb behind his words and grimaced. She'd known this was coming: it was a surprise it had taken him this long to talk to her about it. Davis never held back on a strong opinion and, while he loved her, he'd always protected Archer with a fierceness that only increased after Pádraig died. Archer was always everyone's favourite.

A traitorous voice pointed out that maybe he would have protected her too, if she hadn't shoved him, and everyone else, away.

The kettle clicked off. Raven picked it up and began to add boiling water to her mug. 'Can I at least drink my coffee before you have a go at me?'

'I'm not going to have a go at you,' Davis said.

She raised an eyebrow at him.

'I may have a strong word with you, though, as the oldest and wisest of us.'

She snorted, filling up a second mug and silently offering it to him as he smiled teasingly at her. Davis's face turned serious again.

'We should tell him that wasn't the first time She's appeared outside of the house.'

Raven shook her head. 'He doesn't need to know. It doesn't change anything.'

'It doesn't feel right, though.'

'Davis,' she could hear the sharpness in her voice and tried to soften it. 'Please. It'll just make him ask questions. And I can't … I can't answer them.'

Davis looked at her for a long moment. She could see the conflict in his eyes. Whatever he saw in hers must have been enough to convince him, though. He nodded once, and she felt the tension start to ease from her body.

'He's thrilled you're back, you know that, right?'

'I do,' Raven replied quietly.

'He's really missed you. We all have.'

'I missed you too.'

'Not enough to call, or visit, or stay in touch beyond the odd message.'

She opened her mouth to retort, snapping it shut again. She wanted to defend herself against his statement, but she had nothing to say. Nothing that justified it.

'I'm here now.'

'And I'm glad. But you can't just float in and out of our lives when it suits you, Raven.'

She twitched at the hurt in his voice, before a rush of anger replaced the guilt. She'd left to protect them. She'd been doing them a *favour*.

'We all want you back. But just, if you're here, it needs to be to stay.'

Part of her wanted to hug him, to tell him everything. She didn't even know what it was she needed to tell him, though. She opened her mouth, then closed it again. She could see the disappointment in his eyes. He sighed, reaching out to squeeze her shoulder gently.

'I really am glad you're back, Raven,' he said softly. He took his mug and strode out of the kitchen.

She stared after him, taking a deep breath before following. She wondered how long he would feel that way.

CHAPTER TWENTY-ONE

ÉABHA HAD SEEN PICTURES OF Hyacinth House, but she still wasn't sure exactly how to envisage it before it came into view. From what she had gleaned from skimming the corkboards in the office, it had taken several forms over the years: a nobleman's estate, a hotel, a school. Each form had come to a quick and tragic end, shrouded by a veil of secrecy and rumour. Only the barest outlines of the accidents that seemed to plague the inhabitants were described in official records and, over the years, the local legends had grown enough that it was hard to figure out what was rooted in fact and what simply made a good ghost story.

'My mum's family is from near enough to here, but I'd never even heard of Hyacinth House,' Éabha said, as Davis steered the car up the drive. 'I mean, Mum is not a fan of anything paranormal, so I'm not surprised, really, but it's strange that the name never even came up in passing.'

'You're from around here too?' Archer asked, turning in the passenger seat to look back at her.

'Just my mum's family. Dad's from Dublin and I grew up there. Once my grandparents passed away, we didn't come down here much.'

'Is your mum an only child?'

'No. She has a sister. I think she lives nearby actually. They don't speak.'

'Oh, I'm sorry.'

'It's fine,' Éabha shrugged. She hesitated, then said, 'Actually, it's because of things like this. My aunt does psychic readings and stuff, I think. I don't know a lot about her. Mum doesn't approve of her.'

Davis glanced at her in the rear-view mirror. 'It sounds like a tough environment for someone like you,' he said.

Éabha met his eyes in the mirror. 'I manage.'

She turned to look out the window at the house that was beginning to loom in the distance. In the back seat beside her, Cordelia looked oblivious to the fact that anyone had been speaking. Her eyes were fixed on the house ahead, fear oozing from her in a steady stream. Éabha wanted to offer her some sort of comfort, but she was afraid to reach out. Cordelia was so pulled together with her crisply tailored suits, her sharp haircut, her precise, immaculate make-up. She'd been terrorised in her own home less than twelve hours ago and now she was walking back into the place that had triggered it. What support could she, Éabha, provide, really? She already felt afraid and they weren't even inside yet.

The bricks felt cold, even from a distance, and the upper windows that hadn't been boarded up gaped like empty eye sockets. Grasping tendrils of ivy and green foliage had dug into the cracks in the walls, though in some trick of the cloudy afternoon light, the vines gleamed black like poisoned veins creeping across the body of the house.

Davis pulled up outside and they got out. Éabha's door slammed shut behind her, making her wince. This felt like a place to try to go as quietly as possible and hope nothing in the shadows noticed you.

'The last time we were here,' Archer said to Cordelia, 'was there anywhere in particular that you felt anything? Either sensations, or anywhere you felt particularly unwelcome or uncomfortable?'

Cordelia hesitated.

'Nothing is too small or "silly",' Davis said reassuringly.

'Upstairs,' Cordelia said quietly. 'Yesterday, when we were in one of the bedrooms beside the tower, I felt like someone was watching me. Something that didn't want me there. I was too embarrassed to say.' She tilted her head, dark eyebrows furrowing tightly into almost a single line as she spoke.

'Then the first time, the time I told you about, was in the old ballroom. It felt cold, but only in certain parts, and the windows are really securely boarded up. I thought it was just my brain playing tricks, because that's where they found Jack Gallagher. Then the knocking started.'

'The ballroom?' Davis asked. His voice sounded slightly strangled.

Cordelia nodded.

'OK, when we go in, Cordelia and I will head to the ballroom,' Archer said, handing them each a torch. 'Davis, can you and Éabha take the bedroom? Then we'll swap. Make sure to stay together at all times.'

Éabha swallowed as they walked up the stone steps. Cordelia turned the key in the lock and gently eased the heavy front door open. The inside was shrouded in shadow, the pathetic beams of sunlight that worked their way through the boarded-up windows weak and fractured. Davis attempted a smile to Archer and Cordelia that formed more of a grimace, and began to make his way up the

143

sweeping staircase, Éabha trailing behind him. His long legs took the steps two at a time and she rushed to keep up, instinctively trying to move as quietly as possible. He turned right at the top of the stairs, down a long corridor strewn with shadows that their torches barely managed to push back. The paint was faded in spots where paintings and portraits must have previously hung, giving the impression of pale wounds that had been covered by a bandage for too long and not given access to the air to heal. The paint, a once-burgundy shade that now, in the faint light, resembled flakes of dried blood, peeled off the walls. Davis strode down the corridor and Éabha suddenly realised what was bothering her about his speed: he knew his way around.

'You've been here before,' she whispered to him.

He nodded tersely. 'When Raven and her parents were doing the investigation. My parents were helping out doing EVP work – the Electronic Voice Phenomenon sessions – and stuff.'

'I feel like I'm the only one who didn't grow up with this,' she said with a shaky laugh.

His lips curved up. 'We didn't grow up with clairvoyant gifts, so I guess we're even.'

She smiled back, trying to quash the voice that whispered that, clairvoyant or not, she didn't have his easy confidence, his fearlessness. Her heart was pounding so hard she could feel it reverberating down through the soles of her feet and into the structure of the house. She hated that. She didn't want this place to have any part of her.

They reached a door at the end of the corridor, to the left of a large bay window that hadn't been boarded up, too high for anyone to reach from the ground. Sunlight was straining to get through, barely making a dent in the gloom of the hallway, but the brief kiss of warmth on Éabha's face as she followed Davis into the room infused her with a spark of courage.

The lingering heat was chased away the moment she stepped over the threshold.

'Do you feel that too?' she asked Davis.

He'd clicked on his voice recorder as they'd entered the room, and he nodded down at it. 'Describe what you feel first,' he said.

'The cold. It's icy in here,' Éabha said. She wrapped her arms around herself, holding her cropped beige jacket close to her body.

Davis stepped across to the window on the far side of the room, moving his hands to its edges. 'The window seems pretty solid,' he said, half to her and half to the recorder. 'There's no noticeable gaps in the frame, so the low temperature isn't likely to be caused by a draught. It'll be worth using a thermal-imaging system to double-check that, though. There's a similar amount of sunlight in here as in the hall, or perhaps even more, so it's not a change in natural light contributing to the noticeable drop in temperature.' He turned to Éabha. 'Do you want to do your thing?'

She didn't. She wanted to turn and run: from this house, from the cold and from the growing feeling that was humming through her veins screaming, *Run, go, this is not your home and you are not welcome in it. Leave before she finds you.*

You are being hunted.

But she had already run once and she couldn't do it again. More than she was afraid, she wanted to prove that she belonged.

She sat down on the rough wooden floorboards, crossing her

legs and sitting upright. Davis took out a handheld video camera and nodded encouragingly when she looked at him to see if she should begin. Something had shifted in him. Earlier, the faintly sardonic note that usually was in his voice when he spoke about clairvoyance wasn't there. Maybe Archer had spoken to him. She cringed at that thought.

Focus, Éabha.

She shut her eyes, took a few deep breaths. First, she brought her attention to her body, how her chest rose and fell, feeling the steady movement of blood through her veins. Then she turned her awareness outside of herself, probing gently. She could feel Davis hovering near her, a sense of protectiveness emanating from him.

She wanted to linger there, with his warmth. The cold in the room made her shrink away, but she forced herself to examine it instead.

'It's like the room is … pulsing,' she murmured. Archer had told her to speak whatever came into her head, no matter how trivial or strange she thought it was. 'The walls, they're watching. It's like … the house knows we're here. Or not the house. The thing in the house, but it's part of the house, and we have its attention.' She could feel it now, slipping through the shadows, stalking the hallways towards them to see who had dared trespass.

'It's coming. It's not happy we're here. It's …' She tried to control the terror rising as the presence drew closer. Panic gripped her as an overwhelming sense of vitriol swept into the room. Her eyes snapped open and she looked behind Davis.

There was a woman standing there. A figure in a long black dress, a veil covering her face. Even though her eyes were covered, Éabha knew she was glaring at them. The word 'glare' didn't do justice to the seething hatred pulsating from her, an onslaught she had no idea how to defend herself against. Éabha recoiled, leaping to her feet. Davis turned, following her gaze, before looking back to her.

'What is it?'

'She's here,' Éabha said. The figure was already fading, barely visible now. Éabha could just make out the unnatural tilt of her head, looking up at the ceiling. Some instinct told her the figure had spoken, though she hadn't heard what she said. She wanted to follow The Lady's gaze but she was frozen to the spot by the aura of malice she was emitting. Suddenly it eased, as though a shield had been dropped in front of her to protect her from The Lady's fury. *Did I do that?* It wouldn't be the first time she'd done something new without realising. But it didn't *feel* like her. Now wasn't the time to think about it anyway; the important thing was that she could move again. Her gaze snapped to the ceiling.

To see the timbers crack directly over Davis's head.

She dived forward with a scream, knocking him backwards and to the floor, landing on him with a thump. They stayed there for a moment, winded, her head buried in his chest. Slowly she raised it to look at him. His eyes were wide as he first met her gaze, then looked past her to a jagged plank of wood now lying directly where he had been standing. Éabha jumped to her feet, frantically scanning the now-empty room. The dense sense of hatred that had filled the room like an oil slick had faded somewhat, but an acidic taste of bile still lurked at the back of her throat.

'Are you OK?' she asked shakily. She barely registered the way her jacket now hung at an awkward angle, a large tear down one side making it gape. All her focus was on the dust-covered person in front of her, staring at her with wide eyes.

'Thanks to you,' Davis said. He sat up, wincing slightly.

'We need to find the others,' she said. She held out her hand to pull him to his feet and he took it. She swayed slightly on her feet, almost pitching forward. The exhaustion and light-headedness that came with intense episodes washed over her. She felt drained, as though all of her energy had rushed out of her like water down a sink. Davis put his other hand on her shoulder, looking at her with concern.

'I'm fine,' she said softly. 'We need to get the others.'

Davis nodded and, still holding her hand, pulled her from the room. The two of them walked down the corridor to the stairs, feet light on the thick carpets. She wanted to run but some instinct told her not to.

Predators loved to chase.

CHAPTER TWENTY-TWO

RAVEN WAS AFRAID. The file sat on the desk, watching her as she put off opening it for as long as possible. Eventually the weight of its presence in the room – and the knowledge that the others would be back soon and curious about its contents – made her reach for it. She started from the beginning, partly as a way of delaying the inevitable and partly because her parents had always emphasised the importance of being methodical. Their training was instinctive now. She sorted through the old newspaper stories, neatly cut out and stored, from the openings and closings of the house's various lives: announcements of a school opening, then closing, a new hotel that shut just one season in. She focused on making sure they were in chronological order and putting any accompanying resources – interviews, eyewitness accounts, recordings of old local tales about that time – into the corresponding pile.

There were two USB keys affixed to the back of the folder. One contained the audio files of interviews with people her parents had managed to get to talk about the house and digital copies of both anecdotal folklore from the area and slightly more reliable sources. The other made her freeze: *Hyacinth Investigation, 2017*: *Audio and Video Records* was written in neat, tiny handwriting that she recognised instantly as her mother's. She plucked it out, staring down at the small black key as it rested in her palm. What was in here? What would it tell them about the time she couldn't remember? The doctors had said it was temporary amnesia caused by a head injury, but even though she sometimes had flashes, she still couldn't remember. She woke up from nightmares, sweat-soaked and panting, afraid that what she had seen wasn't a dream but a memory. The threads were there, glimpses of images and snatches of conversations, but she couldn't bring herself to pull on them. Could she remember if she tried? Was she using amnesia like a shield?

There was only one way to find out.

She turned to the computer and plugged in the key. The mouse hovered over the file. All she had to do was click, and the answers that Archer so desperately wanted would be clear.

Did she want to know?

She thought about what she remembered from the days leading up to Pádraig's death. What she'd done. The mistakes she'd made. The things Archer didn't know about. If she clicked on this, she'd know whether what she had been afraid of all these years was true. They'd all know.

Her hand quivered, sending the cursor flying over the screen. She shut her eyes, the memory of bony hands reaching for her in the darkness swimming to the forefront of her mind, her breath coming in short gasps. Her eyes snapped open.

In one swift movement, she pulled the flash drive from the computer and slid it into a side pocket of her bag. The moment it was out of sight the fear that engulfed her ebbed away. It was replaced by a searing guilt.

She wouldn't hide it forever. She'd go through it in a day or two, when she was ready, then pass it on. They had all the previous research into the history of the house, that was the most important part. This could wait a few days.

If she told herself that often enough, she might even begin to believe it herself.

She had just placed a newspaper article on the desk, studying the accompanying photo of a man and a woman with two young girls standing in front of the looming property, when the door to the office swung open.

'That was quick,' she said, looking up as they filed in.

Cordelia's face was grim, while Davis was covered in dust and Éabha was bleeding from a jagged cut on her leg. Her jacket was torn, her tights ripped and her hair wild. Archer was last through the door, his expression unreadable.

'Yeah, we called it a day after I nearly got brained by a chunk of wood,' Davis said casually, throwing his coat over his chair and frowning at the dust on it.

'You left out the part where a ghost dropped it on you,' Éabha said quietly. She sank into Fionn's chair, Cordelia taking the chair between her and Raven.

'Yeah, you still need to fill us in on that part,' Cordelia said.

'You should take care of that cut first,' Raven interjected, pointing at Éabha's leg. She could barely contain her anger. She'd *known* this would happen.

Éabha looked down slowly, blinking in confusion as she saw the wound.

'Oh. I didn't even notice.' Her brow furrowed. 'I hope I didn't leave blood in the house,' she said, almost to herself.

'There's a first-aid kit in the kitchen,' Archer volunteered, starting to move towards the door.

Davis jumped to his feet, cutting in front of him.

'Come on, Éabha,' he said. 'I'll help you.'

Éabha got to her feet shakily and followed him out the door. Archer stared after them for a moment before turning away.

'It seems to take a toll on her,' Cordelia said quietly.

'Like an energetic workout or something,' Archer agreed. He dropped into his own chair, spinning it to face Cordelia and Raven.

'What happened?' Raven asked. She tried to keep her voice neutral, when all she wanted to do was scream 'I warned you!' and shake him.

'We're not sure yet.' Cordelia answered. 'We – Archer and I – were in the ballroom, Éabha and Davis had gone to a room upstairs, when all of a sudden they came rushing in, Éabha was bleeding, Davis was shaken, and they said they'd had a near miss with a block of wood coming from the ceiling.'

'What room upstairs?'

'A bedroom, in the back beside the –'

'Tower.'

The cold seeped into her, memories of darkness and whispers and knocks that came from unseen hands. She shuddered.

'You know it?' Cordelia asked.

Archer watched her curiously.

'That was my room when … that's where I stayed,' Raven said. She looked around the room, then down, anywhere other than at Archer. She could feel the hidden flash drive throbbing in her bag. Could they feel it too? Silence thickened the air in the room until she felt like she might choke on it.

'Anything interesting so far?' Cordelia asked, pointing at the file on the desk.

Raven shot her a grateful smile. 'I haven't gotten too far into it. This article is from when a family tried to renovate it as a hotel: they only lasted one season there before they put it on the market and left.'

She spun the article around on the desk to face them, and Cordelia leaned across her to take a better look. Her hair almost brushed Raven's face, and the faint scent of sandalwood filled her nostrils. She swallowed hard.

Davis and Éabha came back and Cordelia retreated from the desk. Éabha's legs were bare now, a large plaster with a Disney princess on it covering the cut. She sat on the desk beside Raven, nibbling on some biscuits, her legs swinging.

'I like your taste in plasters,' Éabha said, grinning at Archer.

He laughed. 'Plain ones are just so boring.'

'I can't believe all the Belle ones were gone.'

'She's my favourite.'

'Can someone *please* tell us what happened?' Cordelia asked.

Éabha and Davis looked at each other, then, haltingly, Éabha filled them in on what she had felt before and during the incident.

'It was intentional,' she said, shivering. 'She would have killed him if she could.'

Archer turned to Davis, one eyebrow raised.

'I didn't see anything,' Davis said. 'I felt the temperature change, and like I was being watched, but I'd need evidence on the equipment to back it up. I'll get Fionn to go through the audio and visual files, he's the best at it. But for now I can't say anything

153

other than it was a personal experience.'

Éabha's face fell.

Davis looked at her, his expression softening as he continued. 'I'm not saying I don't believe what Éabha's saying. Just that I can't back it up scientifically. But I looked up at the beam that wood fell from when we first went in and it seemed fine. There was no sign that there was any danger.'

'According to this article, all the structural foundations were checked and improved in any way that the conservation order allowed,' Raven said, picking it up from the desk. 'And that was twenty-nine years ago. Not to mention each new buyer would get all that stuff checked. And the last person only bought it three years ago.'

'I can see if I have any records of previous surveys in the company files,' Cordelia suggested. 'They may have had one done before putting it on the market.'

'Good idea,' Davis said, nodding. 'It'll help to know the exact details.'

Éabha idly picked up the article Raven had placed back on the desk beside her. She looked down at the photo and let out a startled gasp, her fingers tightening and crumpling the edges of the paper.

'Oh my god,' she breathed. She put it back down on the desk, smoothing it out carefully then leaning in again as though she wanted to be completely sure. She pointed a shaking finger at the photograph. 'That's my mum.'

CHAPTER TWENTY-THREE

ÉABHA LET HERSELF IN THE front door just as her mother was placing dinner on the table. She rushed down the hallway, apologising for her lateness as she washed her hands at the sink.

'It's good of you to join us,' her father said pointedly. 'You've barely been home recently.'

Éabha sat at the table, keeping her voice neutral as she picked up her fork and skewered a piece of potato.

'I know, I'm sorry. I have a mountain of coursework.'

Technically, it wasn't a lie. She *did* have a lot of coursework. Which she'd been neglecting, to spend time with the team and researching. Though when she thought of the growing pile of reading she needed to tackle at some point before the next week's tutorials, she felt queasy. Maybe she needed to set aside a little more time for college work? Or just accept that she wouldn't be sleeping for the next while.

'It's good you're working so hard. If you want a first in your degree you need to start working now.'

That was Éabha's father. It wasn't enough to do well, you needed to be the best.

'I'm working as hard as I can,' Éabha said. *And first year doesn't even count,* she added silently.

'I'm sure that's more than enough to get a first,' Brigid said.

Éabha smiled weakly at her. Even her mother's encouragement

felt like a threat. Would they ever accept her for who she actually was, not the projection she put forward to them? If her best was a 2.1 and not a first, would they still love her? If she didn't follow their pre-approved set plan for her life, what would they do?

She couldn't imagine being Archer or Raven, being able to tell their mum they weren't going to college, that they wanted to choose their own path. She longed to move out, to get away from her parents' watchful gazes and pointed comments, which had only gotten more suffocating during all the Covid lockdowns and home schooling, and the constant feeling that she needed to do *more* to be worthy of them.

She imagined herself spending a Sunday morning lying on the couch watching TV in her pyjamas without judgement instead of having to kneel in a church and pray to a god she didn't believe in. What it would be like not having to always be perfectly groomed and polite and quiet, no longer feeling the weight of their relentless standards crushing every atom of her into the ground?

But she was eighteen, her college was nearby and rent prices were unaffordably high. She couldn't justify it. She didn't have a job; they had never let her get one, telling her to focus on her studies. 'Why would you need one when you live with us?' they'd said. 'We'll pay your college expenses. We'll buy your clothes.'

She was lucky. That's what she told herself. Other people didn't have that option. Yes, all her clothes were items her mother approved of. Yes, they wanted to know everything she spent her money on. But they gave so much to her. Was she ungrateful for wanting to get away from them? For not wanting to follow the path they had worked so hard to lay out for her?

Even if it wasn't who she was. Even if they didn't want to know who she truly was. Even if their financial support felt more like a leash than a gift.

She swallowed hard. If they knew she was now actively working to explore her episodes, not suppress them, how would they react?

She stayed quiet for most of dinner, listening to her parents' conversation and asking the correct questions in the appropriate places. Every time her mother spoke, the article about Hyacinth House flashed in front of her eyes. Was that house why her mother hated anything supernatural? Or had she been oblivious to its past when she was there? They had stayed only a year, after all.

'Have you ever heard of Hyacinth House?' she asked, trying to sound casual during a lull in the conversation, her heart thudding against her chest.

Her mother stiffened.

'Why?' her father said.

'Some people were talking about it at college today. I know it's near where you grew up, Mum. I was curious.'

'Well, don't be,' her mother said.

Normally, that would have been enough to stop Éabha. Instead, she took a deep breath and continued. 'They said it's haunted.'

The atmosphere went cold. Her father sat up even straighter, his face stern.

'Now, Éabha, you know how we feel about that nonsense.'

'I was just curious whether –'

'No,' her mother snapped. 'I don't know anything about that house other than that people who play with what they shouldn't, get what they deserve.'

'What do you mean?'

'That. Is. Enough!' The icy fury in her mother's voice made Éabha shrink back into her chair. Her mother took a deep breath before a placid smile spread over her face, a blank mask more terrifying than her anger just a moment before. 'Now, tell us about your lectures.'

The tone was gentle, but the words were an order. Dutifully, Éabha began to speak. When dinner was finished, she did the dishes before retreating to her room. She heard the television come on in the sitting room. Her parents always watched the same shows each night, a familiar routine that she could time to the minute. She would stay undisturbed for the duration. Waiting until she heard the TV in full flow, she crept out of her room and down the hallway into her parents' room. Hands shaking, she rifled through the chest of drawers on her mother's side of the bed until she found her address book.

Her mum hadn't seen her sister in years, but she was meticulous in keeping records of names, phone numbers and addresses. She opened the book at the 'O's and found her: Lizzie O'Brien. She took a photo of the details and hastily replaced the address book, rushing back to her room. Sitting at her desk, she stared blankly at the textbook in front of her.

She felt sick. Her mother hadn't spoken to her sister in years. Reaching out to her would be a betrayal. And her aunt might not even want to hear from Éabha. But the team needed answers.

She needed answers.

She needed to talk to Aunt Lizzie.

CHAPTER TWENTY-FOUR

ÉABHA'S NAUSEA GREW AS THE BUS GOT closer and closer to the town. Archer had offered to come and visit Lizzie with her. 'To explain what the team did,' he'd said, but she knew he wanted to support her. He'd even managed to wangle a much-coveted Saturday off from the café – they'd had to wait nearly two weeks, but the relief of not being alone had made enduring her growing anxiety worth it. A text popped up on her phone: her mother asking her if she'd be home for dinner. She dashed off a breezy response about how the library was nice and quiet, ignoring the guilt gnawing at her. It seemed all she did was lie to her mother now. Had it only been three weeks since she'd met Archer and the others? It felt like stepping through the office door that day had set her on a path she couldn't turn from even if she'd wanted to, and she was going further and further away from who she had been until then.

She rested her head against the window, watching the fields that bordered the motorway blur past. A dim memory floated into her mind. Her fifth birthday, sixth maybe. Her aunt on the threshold, Éabha peering around the corner at the top of the stairs. She'd been sent up to her room the moment her mother saw who was on the doorstep. A woman with long, dark-brown hair, a present in her hand. She remembered her mother's voice hissing that the woman was not welcome. They spoke too low for Éabha to hear, her hearing aids not nearly as effective then as they were now. She knew it ended with a slammed door, a figure silhouetted in the frosted glass for several long seconds before turning and disappearing down the driveway. Éabha's mother hadn't seen her crouched at the top of the stairs. She'd scurried back into her room to await the call to come and blow out her candles. She'd waited over an hour.

Her aunt never tried to visit again.

She saw Archer waiting at the bus stop, two take-away cups in his hands, as she alighted. He had a grey beanie on his head, tufts of his blond fringe poking out under it, and his long camel trench coat hung open to reveal a forest-green jumper and grey jeans. The wool of his jumper looked expensive – cashmere, most likely.

'You dressed up,' Éabha smiled, taking the proffered cup.

'I always dress well,' Archer huffed.

Éabha rolled her eyes at him. 'Thanks for the coffee. I'm impressed you already know my order.'

'It's one of the perks of having a friend who is also a barista,' he winked.

'I knew there was a reason I liked you.'

'Besides my dazzling charm and good looks, of course.'

'Of course.'

Éabha took a sip of her coffee as they began to walk towards the small car park off Kilcarrig's main street. The skies overhead were grey, the clouds heavy as though they could burst open to release a deluge at any time. She studied Archer out of the corner of her eye. In some ways, he was the hardest to get a read on. He was always smiling, always affable and light. He'd been so quick to check on her, support her, but whenever she went to ask him how *he* was doing he managed to sidestep the question. Sometimes she saw him looking at Raven sadly, hurt surrounding him like a fog. They all had their secrets, but Archer seemed determined to pretend he had none at all.

Or maybe he just didn't want to confide in the girl he'd met only a couple of weeks ago, even if she'd promptly dumped all of her baggage on him.

He caught her studying him. She looked away quickly, feeling her cheeks warm, and took another sip of her coffee. Her pink lipstick was already smudged onto the rim.

'So, you and Davis live together, right?' she asked, looking for a topic of conversation that didn't revolve around ghosts, clairvoyance or the meeting she was about to have.

'We do,' Archer said. 'Davis's parents and mine were really close, so we were always in and out of each other's houses. His parents worked a lot of night shifts at the hospital, so the guest room in our house was basically his anyway, then Raven and I would stay with his family if Mum and Dad had an overseas case or one they didn't want to bring us to. When Raven moved out and Mum was touring constantly giving lectures and book tours, it made sense for him to move in permanently.'

There was more, she could feel it. A deep loneliness that made her heart ache and pulse in recognition. She could learn more if she delved deeper, reached out with the empathic power that seemed to grow stronger every day. But that would be invasive, unfair. He deserved to confide in her when, *if,* he wanted to, not have her probe his feelings uninvited. They walked to a red Volkswagen Polo, Éabha crossing behind it to the passenger side.

'It's OK to tell people when you're hurting,' she blurted out.

Archer stopped, startled, his key hovering beside the lock.

'I'm sorry,' she said. 'I don't want to overstep. But I'm a good listener. Even without the whole empathic clairvoyance thing, I can tell you spend most of your time looking after everyone else.'

He stared at her for a long moment, and she thought she might crumple into a ball. Then he let out a low whistle, shaking his head admiringly.

'You are really something, Éabha McLoughlin.'

'I'm going to take that as a compliment.'

'It is.' He opened the door, sliding into the driver's seat. 'And thank you.'

The journey to her aunt's house in a town twenty minutes away went all too quickly. They chatted about innocuous things on the way: music and books, and bonding over a love of *Avatar: The Last Airbender*. She couldn't believe how free she felt around him. Now that she didn't have to worry about hiding so many parts of herself, she could just be herself. A Taylor Swift song came on the radio and she started singing along without thinking, blushing when she caught Archer looking at her with amusement. She felt a delighted smile spread across her face when he started – enthusiastically and off-key – to sing along too. He laughed hard as Éabha swung her arms dramatically at the crescendo of the chorus, and for once she was having too much fun to feel self-conscious.

The maps app on her phone led them down a quiet residential road lined with redbrick houses and they pulled up outside number seven. Archer turned off the engine, the two of them sitting in the sudden silence.

'Are you ready?'

'No.' She turned to look at him and forced a smile. 'But I don't think I'll ever be, so now is as good a time as any.'

'You don't have to do this if you don't want to. None of the team would hold it against you.'

'There's no way I can ask my mother about Hyacinth again, and my grandparents are dead. Lizzie is the only person we can get information from.'

Archer pushed his hand through his hair and turned in his seat, fixing his eyes on her. 'I want you to go in there because *you* want to, not because you're doing it for the investigation.'

'I want to help the team,' Éabha said. She looked down at her hands, fingers twisting in her lap, then stilled them and glanced back at him. 'But I want to do this for me too. She might be able to give us answers about more than the house.'

The silence stretched between them before she whispered, 'I need to know the truth, Archer.'

His face softened. 'I can understand that,' he said, serious for once. He smiled at her. 'You're not walking in here alone.'

'I think that's the only reason I haven't run away yet,' she said, trying to smile back. 'I'm not particularly brave.'

Archer snorted. 'That's the only ridiculous thing I've ever heard you say, Éabha.'

'I turned up in your office and told you I was psychic.'

'Exactly.' He leaned over her, opening her door. 'Come on. Let's go talk to Lizzie.'

Éabha pressed the doorbell and the door opened immediately. A woman with lightly freckled skin and dark brown hair pulled back into a sleek bun, wearing a white silk shirt and grey suit trousers, opened the door.

'Éabha!' she said, beaming and opening her arms out wide, enveloping her in a hug. 'It's so good to see you.' She turned to Archer. 'And this must be your friend –'

'Archer,' he said, holding out his hand.

She gave him an appraising look as they shook hands, then smiled easily. 'Come on in.' She stepped back and waved them over the threshold. She headed down the hallway, beckoning them to follow. A black cat appeared and wound its way between Éabha's legs, before trotting down the hallway after them.

'A black cat feels a bit on the nose,' she murmured to Archer.

He laughed softly, gesturing for her to go first. They stepped into a spotless kitchen with a marble island in the middle. Small pots of herbs lined the windowsills, and the few beams of sunlight that had broken through the clouds shone in through skylights over the window.

'Tea?' Lizzie asked, snapping the kettle on. 'I infused it myself. It's chamomile and rose. Good for nerves,' she winked.

'Sounds great,' Éabha said. She stood awkwardly beside Archer, racking her brains for something normal to say.

'I like your kitchen,' she said.

'Thank you,' Lizzie replied, pulling mugs out of a cupboard. 'I don't get to spend nearly enough time in it during the week but I love spending the weekends cooking. I have a herb garden out the back too, if you're interested in that sort of thing.'

'I've started to grow sage, lavender and rosemary,' Archer said. 'I can barely keep them alive. How do you manage an entire garden?'

Lizzie laughed. 'I've had some rough patches over the years. I'm a lawyer and I find it helps after a day in court. It also helps after intense healing sessions: getting my fingers into the earth, grounding myself. Of course, you know all about grounding yourself.' She directed the last part at Éabha. She didn't say it like a question.

'I've read a bit about it,' Éabha said. 'Are you in court a lot?'

'A fair bit, unfortunately,' Lizzie said. 'I work pro bono with domestic abuse charities alongside my regular divorce clients and sadly they never seem to run out of cases for me.' She set the mugs on the kitchen island, and then a plate of brownies and a novelty teapot in the shape of a cat.

'Please, sit, make yourselves at home,' she said, gesturing at the high stools surrounding the island.

They duly sat, and Éabha found herself suddenly wishing she could reach for Archer's hand.

Lizzie poured the tea, offering them the plate of brownies, then leaned her elbows on the countertop, scrutinising them. 'I was delighted when you called, Éabha. I'm not sure what you know about me, but I've wanted to reach out to you for a very long time.'

'I have too,' Éabha said quietly. She took a sip of her tea, surprised by how comforting the aroma of the freshly stewed leaves was. The warmth flooded through her, helping her relax. Her fingers still trembled slightly. She wasn't sure what she was more afraid of: not getting answers, or what the answers might be.

'I don't know a lot about you,' she admitted. 'All mum would say is that you turned from God in more ways than one.' She winced. 'I'm sorry if that's painful for you to hear.'

'It's nothing that hasn't been said to my face,' Lizzie said, studying Éabha's expression. 'I'm assuming she isn't aware of your gifts?'

'I learned not to mention them pretty quickly.'

'I'm sorry,' Lizzie said, leaning over to squeeze her hand. 'I wish I could have guided you. I tried to reach out, but your mother returned any cards or letters unopened. Eventually I realised I'd have to wait for you to come to me.'

'I didn't know you wrote to me!'

'Every year,' Lizzie said with a wistful smile.

Éabha cleared her throat, glancing at Archer, who smiled encouragingly at her.

'That's kind of why we're here. I mean, I wanted to see you and there's so much I want to talk to you about, but Archer's here too because ...' she looked pleadingly at him to explain.

'I'm part of a paranormal research team. We both are, actually. Éabha reached out to us a few weeks ago, to see if we could help her understand her gifts. We were researching a case we've been asked to investigate, and we found this.' He pulled out the article with Lizzie and Brigid's picture in it and pushed it across the table.

Lizzie looked down at the page. Her faced blanched.

'You're investigating Hyacinth House?' Her voice was tight.

'We are.'

'You know about the house, its history.'

It felt more like a statement than a question to Éabha, but Archer answered anyway.

'We do. I have some history with it myself. But we're trying to find out more. And we were hoping you could help us.'

166

Lizzie smiled sadly at him. 'You really are Emily and Pádraig's son.'

'You know them?' he asked, startled.

'I used to help them with the spiritual aspects of investigations. I never met you or your sister; the cases they needed me for were generally the ones they didn't bring you along to. They told me they were investigating Hyacinth. I advised them not to go.' She looked down at her cup, her fingers cradling the edges, her face sad. 'Your father was a good friend. I'm sorry he's no longer with us.'

Archer swallowed hard. 'Why did you tell them not to?'

Lizzie paused.

'Because of that,' she said, nodding down at the article in front of them. Her words were careful, as though she was trying to figure out what to say. How *much* to say. 'Because of what happened to us in that house, and what it did to my family. It tore us apart. And none of us, in our own way, was ever whole again.'

'Will you tell us?' Éabha asked.

Lizzie hesitated.

'You may not like what you hear.'

'I know. But it's better than never knowing.'

Lizzie studied her carefully, then sighed. 'All right then.'

Archer took a voice recorder out of his bag, raising his eyebrows at Lizzie to ask permission. His entire body was tight, excitement humming from him like the buzzing of hundreds of bees.

Lizzie nodded her consent, and he clicked it on as she began to tell her story. Éabha listened intently, clutching her tea for comfort while beside her, Archer leaned forward, drinking in Lizzie's words like a parched flower in a rainstorm.

CHAPTER TWENTY-FIVE

'I HATED HYACINTH HOUSE FROM the moment I set foot in it,' Lizzie said. Her eyes were distant, as though she was walking back through its halls once again. 'My parents said it was just my imagination. That's what they always said about the things I sensed: that they were just stories. Even when I was proved right, they shrugged it off. Brigid was the only one who ever believed me.'

Éabha started slightly at that. Her mother had always reacted so dismissively, so angrily, whenever Éabha had tried to tell her the things she'd seen.

Lizzie smiled sadly at her surprise. 'I know it's hard to believe now. But at the time, it was always myself and Brigid. We knew everything about each other. We trusted each other with our secrets.' Her face darkened. 'Until Hyacinth.'

'What changed you?' Archer asked. Lizzie tilted her head thoughtfully.

'It started with the tower. I didn't want to go in, but Brigid convinced me; she was always good at persuading me to do the things she wanted to do. I was ever the younger sister idolising her older sibling.' Her mouth formed a tight, bitter smile. 'Of course, afterwards, Brigid would never admit it was her idea. I think she knew it was what started it all, and she was afraid of what that meant. But there was no way I would have set foot in that tower without her cajoling me.'

'Why was that?' Archer asked.

He was good at this, Éabha thought: gentle, open questions to get details without interrogating her aunt.

'It felt twisted to me, unwelcoming. It was like the air thickened to try to push you away. I had flashes of those feelings all over the house. I often felt like I was being watched, but it always got worse the closer you got to the tower. Our bedroom was right beside it, and whenever I walked down the corridor to it on my own it felt like I was being stalked by a predator I couldn't see.' Lizzie took a deep breath. 'But that wasn't enough to stop me when Brigid wanted to explore the tower. I wanted to run the moment we got there. Half the boxes and furniture were shrouded in grey, dusty sheets. There was a chair Brigid uncovered, a faded red armchair with deep cushions, that had a stain on it that looked like dried blood. After a while, the air in the tower became freezing. My hands were shaking, my teeth chattering. I was so distracted by trying to keep myself together I didn't see her take it.'

'Take what?' Éabha asked, her voice low and breathless.

'The locket. It was a fancy, ornate thing, hanging on a gold chain, a green emerald set into it. She'd found it in an old chest or something. And The Lady … she didn't like that. She sees the whole place as hers, and everything in it. It marked us. We had trespassed, and there would be a price to pay.

'That night, the haunting began properly. I woke up in the middle of the night with the firm conviction that there was someone – something – in our room. They, It, She, whatever you want to call it, at the foot of our beds, directly between them.'

Lizzie shuddered, then gave a rueful laugh. 'Look at me – thirty years later and it feels as real, as terrifying, as it did then.'

'What did the figure look like?' Éabha asked.

'I don't know,' Lizzie answered. 'I curled up into a ball under the covers, barely breathing, and kept my eyes shut until I sensed it disappear. I was always surprised at how quickly I fell asleep afterwards, until I learned that spirits can drain a clairvoyant's energy. She was using me to manifest.'

'You say "always",' Archer said carefully. 'This happened more than once?'

'Every night. And each time it felt like the figure was that bit closer to the head of our beds.' Lizzie shuddered. 'I've never felt anything like it: that unadulterated malice, all directed at us. It was worst at night, but even during the day I could feel her, watching from the shadows, stalking me down the corridors. Sometimes I'd even feel a shove on my back that made me stumble, but when I'd turn around, there was no one there.'

'What did Mum say?' Éabha asked quietly. She felt nauseous; she knew she wouldn't like the answer.

'She said I was crazy at first. That I was making up stories, that she'd only ever pretended to believe me. She denied noticing or experiencing anything for the first while. Then, as time went on, she turned it on me.'

'How? Why?' Éabha blurted. She could see Archer watching her and flushed. He'd told her it was best to stay neutral when someone was telling their story. But she couldn't help it. This was her mother – and it might explain why she'd always been so furious when Éabha had tried to tell her things as a child.

'I found a shop in Wicklow town, a spiritual one that sold tarot cards, crystals, herbs and books. The owners were so helpful. One of them was like us – a sensitive, a clairvoyant, whatever you want to call it – and picked up on my abilities straight away.'

Lizzie smiled, her eyes distant. 'It was such a relief. To have someone believe me, to confirm that what I experienced was not only real, but a gift.'

Éabha looked at Archer, a wave of warmth flooding through her. That was who Archer had been for her – the first person to not only believe in her gifts, but be excited about them. He noticed her looking at him and curved a corner of his lip up, his eyes soft. She could feel herself starting to go red and quickly tore her gaze from his, focusing back on Lizzie.

It was taking everything in her not to reach for his hand.

'They advised me on crystals and ways of protecting us from The Lady's attention, gave me reading material to learn more about myself. I owe them so much. But Brigid was always a snoop, even before all of this. She rejected the crystals I offered her, laughed at me for thinking some rocks could help against an "imaginary enemy", but that didn't stop some of my crystals going missing, and I definitely saw them under her pillow later.'

Lizzie's voice was measured. Éabha couldn't feel any emotions from her either, even though it was surely incredibly painful to revisit this. It felt almost like an invisible shield hovered between her and her aunt. A sudden thought jolted her. Could people like them do that? Block their emotions from others? She felt her heart lift. Did this mean she could learn to stop herself from feeling everyone else's feelings too? *Pay attention, Éabha.* This was no time to get distracted – she needed to focus on Lizzie's words.

It wasn't a surprise that her mother had always been someone to rifle through another's belongings. Éabha had lost count of the number of times her mother had 'just been tidying up' Éabha's room and 'happened to notice' things. She hadn't had anything to hide, with no friends, followed by the years of lockdown when she barely left the house, but she was always aware that she was being monitored. It was why her diary was hidden in the air vent, why she cleared her browsing history any time she Googled anything to do with her gifts. Part of her had always felt disloyal to her mother for it, but it was clear now that it had been the right decision.

'It protected us. But I hadn't thought ... I hadn't realised that would make The Lady turn her attention to the people around us instead.' Now sorrow filled Lizzie's eyes as she looked from Archer to Éabha. 'It started with the feeling of dread spreading through the house. It affected business. I could see that many of the guests were uncomfortable, on edge for their whole stay. Lots of them never walked down certain hallways alone. The business started struggling, and I kept walking in on my parents having hushed conversations over spreadsheets and piles of bills.' She laced her fingers together, wringing her hands before taking a deep breath and releasing them again, her calm court face slipping back into place.

'Then the accidents started.'

Archer leaned forwards slightly at that, a tension in his body that hadn't been there before. Éabha could feel his emotions rising in a whirlpool of conflicting sensations: dread, curiosity, excitement, fear.

'It started with George. He fell from a ladder when he was

172

washing the windows, broke a leg, and narrowly missed being impaled on a statue. Everyone said it was an accident, but I managed to persuade Sinead, one of the maids, to tell me what he'd told her: that he fell because a figure appeared on the other side of the window. A woman, dressed in black, with a veil over her face. Brigid and I were at school at the time and the only guests were in the living room. All the staff were elsewhere. *There was no one in that room.*'

Lizzie swallowed, steeling herself to continue.

'Then Sinead fell down the stairs. She was carrying some bedclothes, tripped, and broke her neck. She died instantly.'

Éabha's hand flew to her mouth.

'I don't want to sound like I'm doubting you, but I have to ask: what makes you think that it was supernatural? If she was carrying bedclothes, wouldn't it be easy for her to simply trip?' Archer's tone was gentle.

Lizzie nodded approvingly. 'Asked like your mother's son. I know for two reasons: one, before I got the crystals, I'd lost count of the number of times I'd been on those stairs or in the hallway to my bedroom and felt a sharp shove on my back that sent me stumbling. I'd only managed to avoid falling because I had my arms free to steady myself. And two, I was in the hallway nearby, and felt all of my energy drain from me. I'd just got out of the shower. I remember sinking to the floor, wrapped in my towel, my legs shaking too much for me to stand. At the exact same time as my energy was taken, I heard Sinead scream.'

'You wouldn't have had your crystals if you were in the shower, would you?' Éabha asked.

'No,' Lizzie said quietly. 'And Sinead paid the price. Our parents decided to sell after that. We were already struggling, and Sinead's death was just too much. They were devastated. When they'd found a place they could actually afford to turn into a hotel, they thought it was their dream coming true. It ended up being a nightmare.'

'How did Mum react to it all?' Éabha asked.

Lizzie stopped to take a sip of tea, her brow furrowed in thought. She appeared to be measuring her next words carefully.

'Badly. It all came to a head when I noticed she was wearing the locket, right as we were packing to leave. I was furious with her for taking it. I knew it was why The Lady had focused on us. And then, when she couldn't get to us, she turned her attention to the people around us. I think it was the first time I'd ever stood up to Brigid. She ... did not take it well.' She took another sip of tea, fortifying herself. 'I told her the locket was the cause of all the things that were happening. But she said she'd read the books and knew that spirits were drawn to people like me. That they used our energy. She told me that if I hadn't been *unnatural*, Sinead would still be alive.'

Tears pricked at Éabha's eyes, both because her mother could think that, and because of how Lizzie must have felt. 'How could she say that?' she whispered.

Lizzie's eyes were warm with sympathy. 'I think she was afraid. That I was right, and she had set off the chain of events by taking the locket. It was easier to blame me and my gifts than truly examine the idea that she might have played a part in it.'

'But to cut you out of her life completely ...' Éabha felt panic rising. Would her mother do the same to her if she found out about PSI? Especially now that they were investigating Hyacinth?

Anxiety churned in her stomach and for a moment she thought she might throw up.

Lizzie stood up from the table, flicking on the kettle and selecting a tea from among the neatly labelled jars on a shelf over the hob. She poured the water into a mug, then placed it in front of Éabha. 'This helps with anxiety and nausea,' she said.

Éabha took it automatically, not even questioning how Lizzie knew. She took a long sip of the drink, her mind racing.

Archer cleared his throat. 'I might go have a look around your herb garden if that's all right with you, Lizzie?'

'Of course.'

He stood up and ambled out the back door, his hands in his pockets.

'He's a tactful boy,' Lizzie said, smiling.

'He's a good person. I've only known him a few weeks actually.' Éabha quickly filled her aunt in on how she had come to meet the team. She started with just the bare facts, but once she started speaking, it all came tumbling out: the feelings, how they were becoming overwhelming, her fear and anxiety. 'I think I'm going mad sometimes,' she said, staring down at her cup. A bitter laugh wormed its way from her throat. 'Sometimes I wish I was. I think Mum and Dad would be more accepting of that.'

'People have many ways of dealing with fear. Sometimes it means pushing people away so that they don't have to face it.'

'Mum volunteers with three different charities, she visits anyone who's ill to help out and keep them company. She's so kind. But then she can just cut you out of her life? Stop you seeing me? I never got *one* of your cards.'

'We all have our blind spots.'

'You're her *sister*.' Éabha looked down at her hands, still gripping the mug in front of her. Her knuckles were white. 'I'm scared, Lizzie. I don't want this: to be able to feel and sense these things. I tried to be normal, but –'

'Éabha,' Lizzie reached across the island, prising one of her hands off the mug and clasping it tightly. 'There is nothing wrong with you. You have a gift.'

'It doesn't feel like one.'

'They don't always do.'

Éabha tried not to shake. 'She blamed your gifts for what happened in that house. She obviously still does.'

'People can do cruel things out of fear.'

'How are you so calm about this?'

'Many years of therapy.'

They both laughed. Lizzie paused, then began to speak again, weighing her words carefully. 'I don't want to encourage you to go behind your mother's back. But you're an adult. If you want help with your gifts, I can guide you.'

Éabha's eyes filled with tears and she blinked fiercely. 'I'd like that.'

She squeezed her aunt's hand and they smiled at each other. Lizzie glanced out the window to where Archer was crouched down, closely examining a plant.

'Should we summon your friend back in from the garden? I think he has some questions he'd like to ask.'

Éabha went to the window and waved. Archer looked up and smiled, striding quickly back into the kitchen.

'The lavender plants smell amazing, even at this time of year,' he said.

'I have an extra one over there. You're welcome to take it, if you'd like?' Lizzie pointed at a lavender plant in a small pot on the windowsill.

'That would be great, thank you,' he grinned, his eyes lighting up as he settled back down on his stool beside Éabha at the island.

Lizzie offered them more tea and when she turned to boil the kettle, he leaned in close to Éabha, squeezing her arm.

'You OK?' His warm breath brushed her ear and she turned slightly to smile at him, nodding.

'Thank you,' she whispered back, briefly covering his hand with her own. She felt a tingle of electricity when her skin met his, little sparks that danced through her, making her come alive.

Lizzie brought the refilled mugs to the table, and Éabha excused herself to go to the bathroom. Lizzie directed her down the hall. She meandered along, taking a few minutes to steady her racing heart, studying the pictures on the walls and trying to focus on the meeting, rather than the sensation of Archer's hand in hers. There were photos of Lizzie with friends, a framed newspaper article of her and three people in front of a newly opened centre for victims of domestic abuse, and, at the base of the stairs, an old photo of a family. She recognised her grandparents immediately. Lizzie and her mum were a similar age to the photo from the newspaper article when their parents had bought Hyacinth. Lizzie and Brigid were laughing, arms wound tightly around each other, as a breeze blew strands of their hair across their faces. It reminded her of the photo she had seen on Emily O'Sullivan's desk, the one Raven had described as being taken 'just before'.

Archer and Lizzie were chuckling together when she came back into the kitchen. The growing dread she had felt the past few days lifted as they turned to smile at her.

'Archer was just telling me about some of his more colourful investigations.'

'He has some good stories all right.' Éabha settled herself back at the table.

'So,' Lizzie said. 'Hyacinth.'

The atmosphere in the room changed instantly. It was as though one of the shadows from Hyacinth had slipped into the room though the crack in the window, wrapping itself around them.

'My advice to you, as your aunt, as an old friend of your parents, is to drop it. Leave whatever walks those halls to claim them.' She eyed first Archer, then Éabha.

Éabha shifted in her seat but Archer stared back resolutely, his jaw set.

Lizzie sighed. 'I can see you won't do that. So, my advice to you as a professional is to go quietly. Get your evidence. Take nothing. Don't use any of the more confrontational methods I know your parents sometimes used. This is not a spirit whose attention you want.'

Archer twitched slightly at that. 'And if someone already had the spirit's attention?' he asked.

'What do you mean?' The sharpness in Lizzie's tone was softened by concern.

Archer quickly recapped Cordelia's experience, Éabha chiming in to explain what she had felt in the apartment. By unspoken agreement, they didn't mention Davis and Éabha's encounter with the ceiling timber. They needed Lizzie onside, and it was clear that the moment it seemed like Éabha could be at risk, she would stop giving them advice. Lizzie's emotions didn't spill out of her the same way other people's did, but Éabha didn't need empathic abilities to predict how she would react. Lizzie closed her eyes for a moment, taking a deep breath.

'You'll want to cleanse the space,' she said. She talked them through a few ways: salt in bowls and crystals to place beside the bed and keep on her person, a mix of herbs to burn to cleanse the air. Éabha pulled her notebook from her bag and took it all down. Lizzie's face was neutral, but the hard line of her shoulders and the coiled way she sat from the moment they mentioned Cordelia's experience made Éabha start to wonder whether Raven had been right to push for them to abandon Hyacinth altogether.

CHAPTER TWENTY-SIX

'WELL, THAT WAS A LOT OF INFORMATION,' Archer said, sliding into the driver's seat of the car.

Éabha smiled wanly at him. 'You have a gift for understatement, do you know that?'

'It's one of my most cherished attributes,' Archer said solemnly. He looked over at her and laughed, his face lighting up as she laughed with him.

The worry that had been gnawing at her heart started to ease. She looked down at the book on her lap, one that Lizzie had pressed into her hands just before they left. The vibrant red of the cover was faded and the pages worn from time and use. She could feel a small smile tugging at her lips, unsure whether the rush of warmth came from the book itself or the sense of connection that had come with Lizzie's words as she gave it to her.

'I was given this book when I started learning about my gifts. I was told I'd know when to pass it on. I think it's time,' she'd said kindly.

It felt like a delicate chain linking her to a long line of people who had each been gifted this book in turn. Just looking at it made her feel less alone.

Éabha's bag contained a selection of crystals and herbs now too, and her wrist sported a chunky bracelet of black crystal. Lizzie said that tourmaline, the crystal it was made from, would help shield her from others' emotions until she learned how to do it for herself. Archer had placed the lavender plant in its small ceramic pot on the back seat, and Éabha'd had to hide her smile when he carefully tied a seatbelt around it like he was securing a small child. As he started the drive back to Kilcarrig, Éabha stared out the window at the growing darkness. She was still trying to process everything: what had happened to her mum in Hyacinth, how she'd turned on Lizzie and lied about her for years. Éabha had always been told her aunt's 'interest in the occult' had hurt people. In truth, it had been her mother who had made mistakes, and Lizzie's 'dangerous, sinful interests' were the gifts Éabha had struggled to understand all her life. How could the mother who tucked her into bed when she was young, who made her soup when she was sick and told her she loved her be the same person as the one who let her daughter think she was hallucinating, that she had a mental illness, when in fact Brigid had known all along that Éabha's gifts were real?

For a moment hot anger burned through her. How *could* she?

Cold fear quenched it. What would her mother do if she found out?

She would have to hide the book very well.

She sat lost in thought until she caught Archer eyeing her. He looked back at the road quickly, and she realised they had been driving for fifteen minutes without her saying a word.

'I'm sorry, I'm being terrible company,' she said.

'Yes, I always judge my friends for their entertainment value right after meeting estranged family members for the first time.'

She snorted.

'Éabha! That is the most unladylike thing I've ever seen you do.'

'What can I say? I have hidden depths.'

He looked over at her, brown eyes glowing in the headlights of an oncoming car. 'I believe that.'

'I was messing.'

'I wasn't.'

She met his eyes for a moment before he turned his attention back to the road.

'So, what next?' she asked lightly, adding hastily, 'For the investigation, I mean.'

'We'll need to fill in the rest of the team on Lizzie's interview. I'll transcribe it and send it around, so everyone can have a look at it. Obviously they need to know the facts, but you can read it first and let me know if there's anything too personal that you want removed.'

'Thank you,' Éabha said. She thought for a long moment, then sighed. 'But it's OK. Print it as is. I've had enough of keeping secrets.'

Archer glanced over at her again, and for a moment she thought his eyes were shining.

'No more secrets,' he said, nodding. 'I like that.'

'I'll arrange to go to Cordelia's as well and try the things Lizzie suggested,' Éabha said. She bit her lip pensively. 'The sooner I do that the better really, even just for her peace of mind.' She half raised a hand to her mouth to chew on a nail before lowering it down, clasping her hands together to stop herself. 'I just can't help but feel like I don't know what I'm doing.'

'You know more than you think,' Archer said. 'Hidden depths, remember?' The corner of his lip curved up.

'So hidden even I can't find them.'

'You have us to help you. And Lizzie now too. You're going back next Saturday, right?'

Lizzie had made them promise not to go back to the house until she could teach Éabha more about her abilities. Part of Éabha was grateful that Lizzie had been so insistent, so she had a reason to delay going back to the house. Archer had seemed amicable to the agreement, but then he always gave that impression of affable ease. Underneath, she wondered if he felt exasperated by her not knowing more about her own gifts. Did he see her as deadweight, slowing the team down? A pity project more than an actual asset?

Archer turned onto the road that would take them down Main Street. Most of the businesses were closed now, rows of dark buildings lining the way. Light spilled from the pub, where groups of smokers were clustered in tight groups, shoulders hunched against the October chill, grey smoke rising in clouds over their heads. The windows were filled with Halloween decorations, pumpkins and witches and – she didn't know whether to smile or shudder – ghosts. For a moment, Éabha wished she were a different person, one on an evening out with friends, complaining about coursework, blissfully unaware of spirits and clairvoyant abilities.

But she had wished for her gifts to go away for years. It was time to stop running from who she was. She just hoped it didn't come at too high a price.

CHAPTER TWENTY-SEVEN

'SO, WHILE WE WAIT FOR FIONN, where are we at with Emily's files?' Archer asked, drawing the meeting to order. He, Éabha, Davis and Raven had gathered in the office on Sunday morning, to fill the others in on Lizzie's account and catch up on research. Every time Raven walked through the door, a tightness in his chest eased. Part of him spent the lead-up to every meeting expecting this to be the one where Raven changed her mind without warning or explanation and simply didn't turn up. It felt disloyal to think it, but she'd shut him out of her life without warning once before, and he couldn't fully shake the fear that she would do it again.

'I saw something that could help us nail down what happened to the original owner's descendants. Apparently the records from what happened in the house are in their care,' Éabha said. She bit her lip as she sorted through a big pile of documents on her desk, her long loose curls framing her face. 'I haven't had a chance to look at it thoroughly yet but ... OK, according to this family tree, The Lady's brother inherited the house but he immediately sold it, though he kept the records. His daughter married Jack Maguire, they had two children, Mary and Sheila. Mary married and had one daughter, Annie, who married and had a son ...' Éabha's voice trailed off.

'The suspense is killing us here,' Davis said drily.

'John ... O'Shea. Whose son Óisín married –'

'Olive. And they had one child. Me.' Fionn's voice was quiet, weaving its way across the room from where he stood in the open doorway.

Archer froze.

Davis swore emphatically.

'And were you planning on mentioning this?' Davis asked when the silence stretched too long.

'If it was necessary,' Fionn said.

'Of course it's necessary!' Davis exploded. He took a deep breath when Fionn flinched. 'Every bit of information we have about this house that our parents didn't is crucial. We know from the file that the ancestor that has all the family records around her death refused to share them. Now we know who that is – your grandfather. This could change everything.'

'You've met my grandfather, right? If he didn't help Emily and Pádraig, he isn't going to help us. He hates that I'm involved in PSI.'

'We'll convince him,' Davis said. He paced around the room, burning with purpose. 'There has to be something we can do.'

'Archer?' Fionn asked quietly.

Archer was still sitting at the table, trying to get his head around what he had heard. He looked around the room, hoping someone would give him a sign that he had hallucinated that last conversation. Raven was looking from him to Fionn, her face pale with concern, eyes tight.

'Why didn't you tell us?' His voice was flat and emotionless. He didn't sound like himself at all.

'Because I was ashamed,' Fionn said. 'Because that ghost is my ancestor, and my grandfather refused to help your parents, and … I feel like that makes what happened my bloodline's fault.'

'We're not our families, Fionn,' Davis said.

Éabha nodded vehemently in agreement.

'I know. I just …' Fionn paused, gazing down helplessly at his shoelaces. His voice was shaking. Normally Archer would be the first to offer him comfort, but he had none to give just now. He didn't have anything. He just felt empty.

'I'll make this right,' said Fionn, looking from Davis to Archer. 'I promise.' He stood up abruptly and left, leaving the rest of them sitting in silence.

'OK, if anyone else has more startling revelations, now would be the time,' Davis said, looking around the room. His tone was light, but underneath was a tension that revealed just how shocked he was.

Éabha gave Davis a tight, awkward smile but Raven kept her gaze firmly down at her thick biker boots. Archer felt like he'd been punched in the stomach. He was reeling, winded, his mind somehow both racing and completely unable to process anything.

'I'm going to get some air, I'll be back in a second,' he said quietly.

Davis nodded and Archer left the room, going down the hallway, through the kitchen and out the back door. He sat on the low concrete steps that led into the garden, staring out at it blankly, trying to pull the pieces of himself back together.

After a minute or two he heard soft footsteps approaching.

'You OK?' Éabha asked, perching beside him.

'Not really,' Archer said, the corner of his lip turning up in a wry half smile.

'You want to talk about it?'

He hesitated. Did she actually want to know? Or was she just doing the thing where someone feels like the polite thing to do is to ask but they're actually hoping you'll just say 'it's fine'? He turned to look at her. Her wide blue eyes were filled with earnest sympathy, and she nodded encouragingly.

It was so rare to be around someone who actually wanted to listen to how he felt. He looked back over the garden, trying to find the words.

'It's just … I feel like everyone around me is keeping things from me. Something is up with Raven, though what's new there? My own mother barely returns my calls. I've always been able to count on Fionn to be honest with me and yet he hid this massive thing.' He huffed a sigh. 'I feel like I'm chained down by other people's secrets and they're suffocating me.'

Éabha slipped her hand into the crook of his arm, squeezing it gently. He covered her hand with his and tilted his gaze to meet hers again.

'I wish I was like you. Knowing exactly how everyone feels all the time.'

'You really don't,' she said, shaking her head.

She was always so poised, the mask firmly in place, it was hard to tell how she felt, but there was a sadness in the corner of her lips. With a jolt, he realised he would do anything to ease that sadness.

Focus, Archer.

'I just want the truth.'

'OK,' she said, taking a deep breath. She always seemed to do that whenever she was about to express an opinion, as though she was waiting for someone to tell her she was wrong or to be quiet. 'Well, here's the truth. I've been trying my best to shut off my empath abilities, with the grounding exercises and the crystals, because I don't want to invade people's privacy. I don't think it's fair, you know? I want people to tell me how they feel because *they* want to.' She looked down at her lap, the fingers of the hand not nestled in Archer's arm anxiously crumpling the material of her skirt. 'But when things are heightened, emotions slip past my shield. I know Fionn feels terrible for not telling you. I know he kept quiet out of shame. He didn't hide this because he wanted to keep something from you, Archer. He hid it because he had things to work through himself. And while it's fair that you're hurt and confused, please don't take his feelings about himself as an indication of how he feels about you.'

'Honesty means everything to me, Éabha,' Archer said. 'Fionn knows that.'

'He messed up,' Éabha said gently. 'Tell him what you've just told me. Hear him out. And then go from there.'

'You make it sound so simple,' Archer said with a rueful half-smile.

'It's easier when you're the outside perspective,' Éabha said, shrugging. She hesitated. 'If you want to chat about anything … I'm here. As evidenced by right now, I probably won't have any solutions, but I can listen.'

She had no idea how much those words meant to him, had she? She said them so simply, like it was no big deal. Like she had no idea of the gift she was offering him.

He squeezed the hand that was still tucked into his arm again and smiled at her.

'Thank you.'

'It's nothing.'

'No, it isn't,' he said. Her eyes held his and he couldn't tear himself away. Then his phone buzzed in his pocket, jolting him out of the moment, and he dragged his gaze from hers, looking down at the screen.

'What fresh hell?' he muttered, opening a message. It was a panicked message from Angela about someone calling in sick at the last minute. Part of him resented the interruption, but the sensible part of him thought maybe it was for the best. Maybe Éabha was just being kind, and he didn't want to cross a line. They worked together, to start with, and sometimes he wondered if Davis was interested in her from more than a scientific perspective. He didn't want to make things weird for anyone. Even though he couldn't stop himself gravitating towards her, finding reasons to spend time with her. Not just because she was kind and thoughtful, but because day by day he could see her relax around them. See how she was starting to ease into the others' affectionate teasing, how she occasionally allowed herself to drop that perfectly poised mask and act a little silly. How she'd immediately read *The Night Circus* on his recommendation and then arrived, eyes shining with delight, to enthusiastically discuss the intricacies of the plot with him. He wanted to learn more about the parts of her she'd been too afraid to show people until now. What she liked and disliked, her favourite foods, what TV shows she'd binged on during lockdown. Everything.

But there was enough going on now, with PSI floundering, the Hyacinth House investigation, Raven's return and now this revelation from Fionn. He shouldn't complicate this any more. He sighed, looking back at her from his phone screen. 'I need to cover a shift at Forest Fair. But thank you.'

He couldn't stop himself from squeezing her hand one more time before he let it go, then stood up, running a hand through his hair. 'Will you tell the others where I've gone?'

She nodded.

'Thanks, Éabhs.'

He hoped she knew exactly how much he was thanking her for.

CHAPTER TWENTY-EIGHT

CAN I GIVE YOU A CALL?

Raven did a double take at the name on screen. It wasn't that she didn't like Fionn, but they weren't close. They didn't really interact one on one without the buffer of Davis or Archer. Fionn had only become good friends with them the year before Pádraig had died, and Raven had immediately pulled away from them after his death.

Sure.

Her phone rang immediately.

'I need your help, but I thought it was better not to put it in writing,' Fionn's voice was low and hushed as he spoke.

'Oh god, are you planning a murder? Hello, by the way.'

'Sorry, yes, hi. And I promise, no murder. More of a light felony.'

'Okaaaaay.'

'I need your help to rob my grandfather.'

Raven's bark of surprised laughter reverberated down the line.

'Well, is it actual robbery if you intend to give it back? I need your help to *borrow* some items from my grandfather without his knowledge or consent.'

'I don't know if I should be flattered or concerned that you came to me.'

'Well, I remember you being very good at finding your way into abandoned buildings a few years ago.' He paused. 'Look, I know it's a lot to ask. But I need to get the information about my relatives, and there's no way he'll give it to me.' His voice quietened. 'I messed up, keeping this from Archer. I need to make it up to him.'

She glanced over at her bag, where the USB key was still sitting in the pocket, guilt flooding through her. How would Archer react to that? She'd give it to him eventually. She just needed to know what was on it first. Which required her finding the courage to look at it. Which she would.

Soon.

She hoped.

Fionn was still speaking, his voice speeding up in earnest anxiety as he explained. 'I can't ask Archer, because I'm doing this for him, and Davis is about as sneaky as a tornado. While I like Éabha a lot, she definitely gives off too much of a wholesome vibe for me to casually ring her up and say "hey, want to rob a pensioner?", you know?'

'I don't know. It's always the quiet ones that are secretly miscreants,' Raven mused. She paused, staring at her bag, then sighed. 'I'll help you. But you need to come up with a good plan to make sure we don't get caught, because your granddad would happily have me carted off to jail.'

'Thank you, Raven,' Fionn said, the relief clear in his voice. 'I have it all worked out …'

It went surprisingly smoothly. Once a month, Mr O'Shea gathered his relatives for lunch in his house. Attendance was mandatory. Mr O'Shea had a tongue like a whip and a glare that could peel the skin from your bones, and he used them both liberally and effectively. It was, the rest of the family had agreed in secret, hushed conversations, easier to placate him than weather his wrath. He was an astute judge of people's weaknesses and skilled at knowing exactly what buttons to press; challenging him only made him focus on you more. So on the second Sunday of every month, they gathered at his house for lunch. He did not cook the meal or clean up afterwards: that had been done on rotation by the other members of the family ever since Fionn's grandmother died a few years ago. He provided the venue; they did the rest.

It was the perfect time, Fionn said. He wouldn't be able to slip away unnoticed long enough to search for what they needed, but he could open a window for her. The noise from the chatter of voices and clatter of cutlery would conceal any sounds Raven made while she searched. His grandfather's attention would be firmly fixed on bestowing favour and criticism on whichever members of the family he had selected for attention that day.

So, at half-past three, Raven found herself crouched at the back of Mr O'Shea's house, waiting for Fionn to open the window overhead and wondering how her life had come to this. The October air was cool against her face, and she knew that, as always, her nose was slowly turning red from the cold. The window opened and Fionn leaned out, looking down to where she squatted in the dirt and raising a finger to his lips. She gave him a sardonic look. As if she needed the reminder. She braced her gloved hands on the windowsill and boosted herself up, landing lightly on the floor inside, grateful for the sudden warmth of the house. A rucksack with a few choice supplies was secured tightly against her back.

'They just put out the starters,' Fionn whispered. 'I'd say we have an hour before people start moving around the house.'

Raven nodded, checking her watch. 'I'll be quick,' she said.

Fionn's eyes were wide and his face pale. 'If he catches us –'

He swallowed deeply.

'He won't.'

'– I'll take the blame,' he continued. He looked at her, blue eyes frightened but determined. 'This was my idea. You just get out of here as quickly as possible, OK?'

She nodded, then reached out and squeezed his shoulder.

'It'll be fine,' she said in a low voice.

They crept to the doorway. The murmur of polite conversation floated towards them as Fionn pointed down the hall to the set of stairs that led to the upper rooms. There were two places the files were likely to be: the attic or his grandfather's bedroom. Raven had to dart down the corridor to the right to get to the stairs. To the left of the room they were in, at the opposite end of the corridor, was the dining room where the family were gathered. All it would take was one person leaving at an inopportune time for it all to go horribly wrong.

But Raven had grown up sneaking around houses without permission, Archer alongside her. She knew how to move soundlessly, how to make herself small and inconspicuous. Despite everything, she felt a little thrill rush through her. She winked at Fionn before stepping lightly down the hall and up the stairs. She sensed, rather than saw, him wait for her to safely disappear out of sight before he returned to the dining room and the voices within.

Knowing how fiercely Mr O'Shea guarded them, Raven had expected the files to be hidden in a slightly fancier receptacle, but no, they were just in a cardboard box, wedged into a far corner of the attic. It took her longer to find them than she'd hoped. As she came back down the stairs, she could hear movement and the sound of voices coming towards the dining-room door. She swore internally, darting into a room to the left of the stairs, disappearing from sight just as Mr O'Shea stepped into the hallway. She looked around, her heart pounding at the close call. She was in a guest bedroom decorated with plain white wallpaper and an alarmingly graphic crucifix on the wall. She eased the window open and looked out.

They'd prepared for this. Taking a length of rope out of her backpack, she tied it securely around the box before texting Fionn to check she could make it down the driveway unnoticed. When he responded with the all-clear, she lowered the box down, letting the rope escape from her hands and join the box on the ground.

She climbed up on the windowsill and started to edge herself out. Loud voices directly outside the door startled her, and rather than lightly easing herself down she fell forward, thudding to the ground and landing in the damp earth of the garden below. Her leg ached underneath her, but she could stand. Getting up, she quickly grabbed the box and rope, and half-ran, half-limped, around the side of the house in a low crouch. She put the box on the passenger seat and climbed into the driver's seat, leaning her head back against the headrest, eyes shut, heart pounding. She took a few long breaths before opening her eyes. When she looked at the box on the seat beside her, a giggle escaped from her lips.

She had done it.

Adrenaline still coursing through her, she turned on the ignition and drove around the corner to wait for Fionn to meet her as soon as the lunch ended.

CHAPTER TWENTY-NINE

ÉABHA HAD JUST FINISHED RUNNING THROUGH some clairvoyance exercises with Davis, Archer quietly taking notes, when Raven limped through the door, followed by Fionn. Éabha took in Raven's mud-splattered jacket and jeans, and the cardboard box in Fionn's arms, with wide eyes. His expression was triumphant, and Raven's eyes had a mischievous sparkle that Éabha had never seen before.

'What were you two up to?' Davis asked, folding his arms.

Raven and Fionn looked at each other nonchalantly.

'Why do you just assume we were up to something?' Fionn asked.

'Because Raven is covered in dirt and you're carrying a giant box.'

'OK, that's fair.'

'Fionn here coaxed me into some light breaking and entering,' Raven said, brushing earth off her sleeve and onto the floor. Davis glared pointedly at it and she winced. 'Sorry. Anyway, he has a gift.'

'What's the gift?' Éabha asked eagerly.

'Where did you break into?' Davis said at the same time.

'Technically, we didn't *break* into Granddad's house. Just entered.' Fionn said.

A slow smile started to spread over Davis's face as he pointed at the box. 'Is that –'

'All of Mr O'Shea's records to do with Hyacinth House?' Raven said casually, examining her fingernails before looking up with a wicked grin. 'Why yes, yes it is.'

It was fun, seeing this playful side of Raven. Normally, even when she joked around with the others or explained something to Éabha, there was an air of tension around her.

'You legends,' Archer said, wrapping first Fionn, then Raven in a massive hug. 'I had no idea.'

'Fionn wanted it to be a surprise,' Raven said.

'Who doesn't want a big box of historical records that may or may not actually be useful?' Fionn joked. He shifted from foot to foot awkwardly, looking up at Archer.

'Well I, for one, feel like Christmas has come early,' Archer grinned. He started to walk to the desk where Fionn had placed the box, stopping to squeeze him on his shoulder. 'Thank you. I know what you risked getting these.'

Fionn grinned at him.

'I mean, I committed a felony and jumped out a window, but OK,' Raven said. Her tone was sardonic, but she smiled as she spoke.

'As always, Big Sis, I am grateful for your assistance,' Archer said. He opened the box and started to pull out piles of paper. 'Let's get stuck in, then.'

It took hours, even with the five of them.

'There's definitely something dodgy here,' Davis said. 'The reports around her death don't match up.'

'We're supposed to believe that she tripped and impaled herself on a letter opener?' Raven asked, shaking her head.

'When she and her stepson were having a legal battle about the house,' Davis added.

'Nothing suspicious there at all,' Fionn said drily.

'We need more information,' Archer said, frustrated. 'I feel like we have more questions now than answers. Was it an accident? Or was it –'

'Murder?' Davis said.

'I'm leaning towards that option to be honest,' Archer agreed.

'I see why the family wanted to hide this,' Raven said thoughtfully. 'It doesn't exactly shine the best light on them.'

Fionn winced at that, and Archer patted his shoulder reassuringly before picking up a faded newspaper clipping.

'I wonder if the chair they talk about is the one Lizzie mentioned? The one with the weird stain that looked like blood,' Archer said, looking at Éabha.

'The creepy tower does sound like a perfect place to store a Murder Chair,' Fionn agreed.

'I think I should touch it,' Éabha said quietly.

Everyone turned to look at her.

'You want to TOUCH the Murder Chair?' Fionn asked, aghast.

'Psychometry is my strongest skill,' Éabha reminded him. 'This is the best way to find out the truth.'

'It makes sense,' Archer said, his brows furrowed. 'Apart from the fact that it involves going into a haunted house with an angry ghost who gets mad at people for taking her things, and touching a Murder Chair.'

'Technically, we don't know if it is a Murder Chair yet,' Davis pointed out helpfully.

'Oh please, it's definitely a Murder Chair,' Fionn said.

'We don't have the evidence to support that hypothesis yet,' Davis reminded him.

'I can get evidence if I touch the Murd –' Éabha paused, '– Hypothesised Murder Chair.'

Davis laughed.

'Is it safe, though?' Raven asked. She hesitated. 'I've been in that tower. When I … before … ' She stopped, then took a deep breath and continued. 'It feels like trespassing.' Archer stared at her hopefully, waiting for her to continue. Eventually the silence stretched too long as Raven looked around the room, at everything and everyone besides her brother.

'It's the best way to get answers,' Éabha said to break the silence.

'I think we should do it,' Davis said. 'Besides, it's a good opportunity for us to test Éabha's powers in a new way.'

'You don't have to come, Raven,' Archer said. 'You were clear about not going back there.'

'Thanks,' Raven said.

A sense of hollow grief swept from her to Éabha, strong enough to slip past her shield. It happened the most with Raven. She either couldn't sense her at all, or her emotions were overwhelming. Éabha couldn't quite figure out why.

'– Cordelia to get the keys,' Archer was saying, all action now. 'Then we'll decide who goes with Éabhs.'

'We should make it quick and quiet,' Davis said. 'Get in and get out without anything noticing.'

'Agreed,' Éabha said, shivering slightly despite the heat in the office.

CHAPTER THIRTY

ÉABHA WAS ONCE AGAIN STANDING OUTSIDE Hyacinth House, craning her neck back to look up at the tower. Beside her, Archer popped the boot as Davis unfolded himself from the car. Cordelia had given them the keys, looking nothing but relieved when Archer asked if she would mind not accompanying them. The Lady hadn't appeared to her again – the crystals and herbs Éabha had given her for her apartment and to carry with her seemed to be working – but Archer hadn't wanted to take the chance of The Lady being more aware of Cordelia's presence. This would be a quick visit, staying just long enough for Éabha to get her reading.

She tried to comfort herself with that: that the intention was speed and stealth. It didn't stop her remembering the menacing sensation prowling through the hallways towards her. She'd left her tourmaline bracelet at the office in case it interfered with her psychometry skills, so there was no shield between her and the dread she felt pulsing from the house.

But this was why she had joined the team: to help. So she followed Davis and Archer up the steps, Archer unlocking the door and easing it open. One by one, they slipped into the darkness beyond.

She knew exactly what Raven and Lizzie meant about the tower. It felt *wrong*, like it was actively pushing her away. Her heart was pounding so hard she thought her ribs might crack, and she felt herself hunch over slightly, as though trying to make herself a smaller target. Archer touched her back gently, his torch beam illuminating the concern on his face.

'You OK?' he whispered.

She nodded, then started to follow Davis up the stairs. The sensation eased slightly as she climbed, as though a protective bubble had formed around them. It was weak, so delicate she wasn't sure if she was imagining it. Was she doing this? Or was it the guys' protectiveness that she felt? She took a deep breath, and caught a faint scent, too light to place. It was something fresh, comforting: a brief respite from the oppressive gloom that surrounded them in the staircase.

They reached the top quickly. The room was exactly how Lizzie had described it all those years before: sheets that looked like shrouds covering various items of furniture, precariously stacked boxes that looked like they had been abandoned as quickly as possible by their bearers. A portrait of a man, handsome and kind-eyed, leaning against the curved wall of the tower. And beside it, a burgundy armchair, a sheet crumpled in a pile on the floor to one side.

'I think that's the Murder Chair,' Archer said, pointing his torch beam at a stain on the cushion.

It really did look like blood.

If it was the chair from the autopsy report, it was.

'OK, Éabha,' Davis said, taking out a voice recorder as Archer took a video camera from his bag and turned it on. 'Whenever you're ready. We'll be here the whole time: any time you want to stop, or if you start to feel unsafe, just let us know.'

'OK,' she said. Her voice was mercifully steady, despite the fact that all her nerves were on fire. She could feel the armchair simultaneously calling to her and pushing her away. It was like when you wanted to touch a flame but knew it would burn you when you did.

'Here goes nothing.'

She reached out a hand and rested it on the chair.

The strength of the images would have knocked her back if her hand wasn't glued to the chair. She couldn't have pulled away if she'd wanted to.

Normally the messages from objects came in faint images, smells or sensations. Occasionally sounds too, though those were always the hardest for her to pick up on. This time, she was *there*.

She was in the ballroom. It took her a moment to realise it, because bright sunlight shone through the wide windows, the buttercup paint was fresh on the walls, and the wooden floors gleamed with varnish. Beside the fireplace were two comfy armchairs – her hand was still resting on one that she instantly recognised as the Murder Chair, despite the fabric being soft and bright under her hand. A noise from behind made her turn. A young couple walked through the door, arm in arm. The woman was beautiful, with long, black curling hair, high cheekbones and sparkling eyes. She was wearing a yellow dress and beaming at the man beside her, a handsome man with brown hair and eyes and a wide smile. The man from the portrait, Éabha realised with a start.

'This is where we'll host our friends, and where our children will play,' he said.

His voice echoed around the room, loud enough for Éabha to hear. They walked directly towards her and she stiffened, almost expecting one of them to yell 'what are you doing here?' at her. But they continued past her, the woman's dress almost brushing her feet. They couldn't see her. She was a ghost to them in this moment.

The man swung the woman into his arms, holding her close. Éabha could feel love and joy radiating from them.

'This is my favourite room, besides our bedroom, of course,' the woman said, a playful smile on her lips. Her face dropped into sadness. 'I just wish I wasn't spending the next nights alone in them.'

The man put his fingers to her chin, gently raising it so her eyes met his.

'When I get home, we will truly begin our life together.'

'I wish you didn't have to go,' the woman said, her voice quivering slightly. 'We're just married. We have lived here only a week and it's the happiest I have ever been in my life.'

The man stroked her cheek gently. 'I wish I didn't either, my love. But I'll be back soon, and then we have the rest of our lives to be happy together in this house.'

She closed her eyes, leaning in to his touch. 'I don't know how I came to be this lucky,' she said, reaching up to clasp one of his hands in hers. 'It feels like a dream.'

'It is not,' he said. 'And I have something to remind you of that every day I'm away.' Reaching into his pocket, he pulled out a velvet box. The woman reluctantly released his hand to open it, her eyes shining as she pulled out the object from within.

A golden locket, inset with a single emerald.

Éabha was looking at The Lady.

Everything went fuzzy around her, the figures blurring, and suddenly it was evening time, the summer light now an autumnal haze, the ballroom lit by a chandelier hanging from the ceiling. The woman was standing in front of the fireplace, a piece of paper in her hands, shoulders heaving.

'My lady?' a man in a soldier's uniform asked tentatively.

The woman whirled to face him, her expression contorted with rage and grief.

'This has to be a mistake,' she cried.

'It is not, my lady,' he replied.

The woman let out such a wail of despair that Éabha thought her heart would shatter from the sound of it. The soldier and Éabha watched as the woman reached out to the table between the two armchairs and picked up a teacup, smashing it to the floor. Then she picked up another, and another, each item shattering loudly. The china teapot joined them, before she finally hurled the tray into the wall with a clang, and sank into the burgundy armchair, tears streaming down her face.

'Get out,' she said.

The woman was thinner now, her features pinched and gaunt. The light through the windows was faint, just illuminating the grief that lined her face, her beauty tinged with sorrow. She still wore mourning black, and she was sitting in the burgundy armchair, a piece of embroidery in her lap. Across from her was an older man, stocky and earnest, speaking entreatingly to her.

'I know you cannot love me as you loved him, but three years have passed and I know your finances are dwindling rapidly. You can't keep this house on your own for much longer. Won't you even consider marrying me? I could make you happy, if you gave me the chance.'

'I cannot leave this house,' the woman said, her fingers reaching for the locket around her neck.

'I wouldn't ask you to. My son and I, we'd live here. Won't you try?'

Éabha moved around to stand in front of the fireplace. The Lady stared through her, her mind clearly working.

'Yes, I'll marry you,' she said, turning back to look at the man. Her voice was even, but the wave of grief that pulsed from her nearly sent Éabha to her knees.

'You don't even care that he's dead.' A man in his thirties was standing, bristling with anger, before where the woman sat with a cup of tea in hand. Her black hair was streaked with grey now, and her eyes had a hardness that hadn't been there in earlier scenes. She wore a long black mourning dress, the hand not holding her teacup playing with the locket around her neck. The younger man's eyes narrowed as he looked at it.

'All he ever wanted was for you to try and love him, but you never did.'

'I fail to see what this has to do with you trying to take my house.'

'I'm in trouble. I invested in the wrong place, and now they're coming for money I don't have. Selling this house would solve that.'

206

'It's my home.'

'It should have been mine too, but you never let it be.' The younger man's voice cracked slightly. 'You never made me feel welcome, never made me feel like your son.'

'You are not my son.' The woman's voice was matter-of-fact, the indifference making Éabha take a sharp inhale. The man's face hardened, his voice going cold.

'Even if I'm not, this house will still be mine one day. Maybe I'll sell it. Or maybe I'll tear it to the ground first.' He got up and left the room. The woman's grip on her teacup tightened so much it broke in her hand, one of the shards cutting into her palm, bright beads of blood dripping onto her. She didn't even notice.

'I was surprised you agreed to talk.' The scene had changed again. It seemed like only a little time had passed, the leaves on the trees outside still golden, the woman still in mourning black. Her veil was pushed back over her head, allowing Éabha to see her face. She smiled, a brittle expression, as she poured boiling water over a collection of herbs in a strainer over the teapot. A collection of letters and a long, silver letter opener rested on the table beside the tea set.

'No reason we can't settle this like adults,' she said.

'Thank you, Mother,' the man said.

The woman flinched slightly at the title. There was a long silence as she poured out the tea, handing him a cup.

'It's a new infusion I've created from the herbs I've been growing,' she said. 'Drink up and let me know what you think.'

The man took a long sip, grimacing slightly. 'It's rather bitter.'

'Oh, that fades as you drink, or at least I think so,' the woman said, picking up her own cup. 'I'd appreciate a second opinion though.'

Her eyes didn't move from him as he look another long sip, the faintest of smiles playing at the edge of her lips. Éabha looked between the two, a sudden urge to knock the teacup from his hands sweeping over her.

'So, we could sell the house and split the proceeds. I'll set you up in a lovely, more manageable property, with a monthly allowance, and …' The young man's voice cut off. He reached his hand to his chest, his face paling. His breathing was ragged.

'Are you all right, dear?' the woman asked casually, stirring her tea. She still hadn't taken a sip. The younger man's eyes fell on her full cup.

'What did you …' he asked hoarsely, stopping again as he gripped his chest over his heart, fingers digging in. Each breath he took came with jagged edges.

'I haven't been keeping the garden as tidy as I'd like,' the woman said, feigning concern. 'I hope I didn't pick the foxglove by accident. It can cause heart failure in large doses.'

Rage flickered over the younger man's face. 'You'd kill me over a house?'

The woman glared at him, emitting an icy fury that raised goosebumps on Éabha's flesh.

'It is not just a house.'

The younger man let out a roar of fury and staggered to his feet, grabbing the letter opener from the table and, lurching forwards, stabbed it straight into her chest in a vicious strike. Éabha let out a long scream as the woman's expression changed from fury to shock. He pulled the letter opener out of her ribcage and stepped back, as blood poured from the wound, over her dress, onto the chair. She fell forwards to the ground, looking up at him, trying to speak. He backed away, still clutching at his chest, as she started to crawl towards him, dragging her limbs at awkward, skewed angles through the pool of blood she left behind her.

He crouched down just out of reach as she collapsed, going deathly still.

'You didn't use enough foxglove,' he said. 'I win, *Mother*.' He waited a few beats until her breathing stopped, then turned towards the door to yell. 'Help, help, Mother has fallen and injured herself!'

A maid came running in as he stood there calling for help, the picture of distress. She gasped at the scene.

'Quick, call for the doctor,' he urged her.

'I'll get Dr Murphy immediately,' she said.

'No!' the man cried. He recovered himself. 'Get Dr Phelan. He's a close family friend.'

As the scene started to fade once more, Éabha saw a figure appear behind him, radiating the cold malice she recognised so well. The veil covered her face now, but she knew it was *her*. Her hands reached out like claws, and the younger man clutched at his chest again, taking deep breaths to steady himself. Éabha knew, without a doubt, he would not survive long in that house.

'I knew it was a Murder Chair!' Fionn said triumphantly.

They were back in the O'Sullivan house, spread out on different pieces of furniture and holding assorted hot beverages. When Éabha had snapped back into herself and the temperature in the room had dropped, their breath condensing in small clouds in front of them, they'd made the executive decision to get the hell out immediately. Éabha felt watched all the way, a calculating gaze burning into her. There was no knocking, no sudden shoves or falling beams this time, at least. It was like The Lady knew what she had seen. Wanted to see how they would react to the truth of it.

'Yes, we're all very proud,' Davis said with an exasperated but affectionate smile.

Éabha shut her eyes, clutching her mug of herbal tea, another of Lizzie's calming infusions. She went to take a sip, then paused, remembering The Lady pouring poisoned tea so calmly. She kept seeing the letter opener plunge into the woman's body, the blood pooling around her. Her hand shook and she narrowly avoided sloshing tea down her front.

'What does this mean?' Cordelia asked.

'Well, I think we can say our main theory is that it's haunted by the ghost of its murdered former owner,' Archer said, tapping his pen against his notebook thoughtfully.

'Who seems to have become rather murderous herself,' Fionn added.

'Well, she was pretty murderous beforehand too,' Davis said.

'She was so sad,' Éabha said softly.

Everyone turned to look at her, and she flushed. 'I don't mean what she did was OK!' she protested. 'I just … feeling her grief. That house was the one place she was happy, and he wanted to take it away from her.'

'Still not exactly an OK reason to *kill* him,' Fionn said.

'Or any of the other people who came into that house,' Davis added harshly.

Raven and Archer stayed silent, their faces drawn in identical expressions of grief.

'I know!' Éabha exclaimed. 'I just … I felt it. All of it. And I can't get it out of me.' She shuddered and Davis softened.

'I know, Éabha. I'm sorry. I know you experience this differently to the rest of us.' He rested a hand on her shoulder.

Éabha saw Archer staring at Davis's hand, before he turned away.

'The stepson died a week later from heart failure. The doctor ruled it was cardiac arrest, possibly from ingesting a toxin. So either the foxglove weakened him enough that he passed …'

'Or The Lady's ghost helped him along?' Fionn finished.

Éabha thought of the clawed hands reaching for his chest. 'Both very likely possibilities,' she said quietly.

'That is not the answer I'd been hoping for,' Cordelia frowned.

'We just need to do more research on how to safely conduct an official investigation,' Archer said confidently.

Cordelia eyed him sceptically and he smiled sunnily back at her. 'It's going to be fine.'

Éabha almost believed him.

CHAPTER THIRTY-ONE

WHEN RAVEN ARRIVED, Davis, Fionn and Éabha were all in the office. She was exhausted from the long days of working on the case and the night shifts in Origin. She hadn't seen them all week, though they'd kept in touch over WhatsApp in the group chat Fionn had named 'Messages from the Beyond'. The USB drive that was still nestled in the side pocket of her bag haunted her. The guilt of hiding it from Archer and the others was constantly wrestling with her fear of seeing what was on it.

Davis and Fionn were both at their computers, headphones on. Éabha was perched cross-legged in the centre of her desk. Her eyes were closed and her face serene. Raven hesitated, not wanting to make any noise that might disrupt her. She looked at Davis, who was acting as though it was completely normal for someone to be meditating in the middle of the office, and tried not to laugh. It was a big change to the guy who had been yelling about scientific evidence and Éabha being a journalist plant or a prankster just a few weeks ago. That was Davis, though. He was passionate and extremely stubborn, but he would always admit when he was wrong. Science, he often said, was all about identifying your mistakes so you could fix things and improve. It was an approach that he took to all aspects of his life.

Raven leaned against the wall beside the door, watching Éabha take three deep breaths before blinking open her eyes.

'Hi, Raven,' she smiled, swinging her legs over the side of the desk and scooting forward to sit on the edge of it, her legs swinging as she slipped a chunky black bracelet onto her wrist. She was wearing black leggings with a loose-fitting caramel tunic over them, a pair of brown knee-high boots neatly placed on the floor beside her. She seemed completely at home in the office now compared to the tentative way she had moved when she first joined them. It had been as though she was constantly expecting someone to tell her to leave.

Fionn and Davis both slid their headphones off, Fionn hanging his around his neck while Davis placed his on the desk in front of him.

'I found something you're all going to be very interested in,' Fionn said, his eyes bright with excitement.

Davis wheeled his chair over to him, leaning forward eagerly to look at his screen.

'We should probably wait for Archer,' Éabha pointed out.

'Why did we let someone responsible join the team?' Davis grumbled jokingly.

She threw a paperclip at him and he caught it, laughing.

'I'm responsible,' Fionn protested.

'Yeah, but you're a pushover.'

'I'm amiable, there's a difference.'

The door beside Raven opened and Archer strode in, pulling off his hat and scarf with one hand and balancing a tray of take-away coffees with the other as he said, 'I know I'm late, but I brought coffee!'

'At least there's coffee,' Raven said, taking a cup.

'Just in time, Arch. Éabha was all for steaming ahead with whatever exciting footage Fionn's found,' Davis said, stretching his long arms over his head languorously.

Éabha let out an indignant squawk. Archer handed her a coffee as he grinned teasingly at her. 'I would have expected better of you, Éabhs.'

Éabha glared with feigned annoyance at Davis as she took a sip of her coffee.

'Is Éabha the one we mock now? Because I could use a break,' Fionn said.

'Oh Fionn, we could never replace you,' Archer said, patting him on the shoulder. He finished handing out the coffees and came to hover behind Fionn's computer expectantly.

'Now what's this about evidence Éabha was bullying you into showing before I arrived?' Archer asked.

Éabha swatted him playfully as she stood beside him.

Raven noticed her brother shift slightly closer to Éabha. She'd seen him with enough crushes – including a memorable one on Fionn – to know when he liked someone. Archer always seemed easy-going, but the truth was, when he fell, he fell hard.

Maybe she should have a little word with Éabha, she mused, as she crossed over to stand on the other side of Archer, behind Davis.

'I've been going over the footage from Hyacinth from when Éabha and Davis were in the upstairs bedroom,' Fionn said, pushing his glasses further up his nose and clicking on a file on the computer. 'I've found two anomalies on the tapes that I think you should take a look at.'

Raven's heart started to beat faster as she leant in over Davis's shoulder. She could see how she felt mirrored in Archer's face – an eagerness, a hunger for answers. This was the most exciting part of paranormal investigation: capturing actual evidence.

Then she remembered what the footage was investigating, and anticipation faded into dread.

'I've isolated some footage from when Éabha saw the apparition. Tell me if you notice anything.' Fionn pressed play.

Éabha was sitting on the floor in the middle of the empty bedroom, her eyes closed.

'It's like the room is pulsing,' she murmured. Her face was slack, dreamy, as though she was not entirely present. 'The walls, they're watching. It's like ... the house knows we're here. Or not the house. The thing in the house, but it's part of the house. And we have its attention.'

Raven felt herself go cold, remembering that sense of being hunted through the hallways by something invisible.

'It's coming. It's not happy we're here. It's ...'

The screen flashed black for a moment, then the image reappeared to show Éabha scrambling to her feet, staring past the camera, her face ashen with horror. The camera turned, showing an empty corner.

'What is it?' Davis's voice came from behind the camera. The camera turned back to Éabha.

'She's here,' Éabha said, still staring at the empty space. Her eyes were panicked and her gaze lifted as though following an arrow traced through the air, to look at the ceiling over Davis. The screen went black again, the image reappearing as Éabha dived towards the camera. The view tilted to the ceiling as Éabha knocked Davis to the ground, accompanied by a large thud that Raven guessed was the lump of wood she had saved him from. The clip ended there.

'Oh wow, that looked as painful as it felt,' Davis winced, rubbing his elbow at the memory.

'I look mad,' Éabha said quietly.

Everyone turned to look at her. Her eyes were downcast and she was paler than usual. 'Is that what I sound like? No wonder ...' she trailed off.

'You don't,' Archer said gently.

'Besides, there's evidence here that proves you're not,' Fionn added helpfully.

'There's nothing there, though.'

'I'll play it again,' Fionn said, clicking the mouse. 'It took me a couple of passes to notice it too.'

Raven watched the footage carefully, then let out a low gasp. 'Of course.'

Fionn beamed at her. Archer let out a delighted 'Aha.'

'I'm still lost,' Éabha said, looking around at the others.

'It's not what's there, it's what isn't,' Archer said.

Éabha stared at him blankly.

Davis sighed. 'Enough of the theatrics, Sherlock, put her out of her misery.'

'The screen goes black,' Raven said, cutting in. She loved Archer, but he couldn't resist using five hundred words to explain something when five would do, and Éabha looked close to a breakdown.

'A theory in paranormal investigation and parapsychology is

that entities draw on energies around them to manifest. So, camera batteries, phones and other equipment can often go dead mid-investigation even though fresh batteries were just put in or it was charged recently,' Fionn added. 'The screen flickering black is the camera's resources being drained. If you look at the battery percentage in the top right-hand corner of the camera screen, it drops significantly after both times the camera goes black – which coincides precisely with you seeing the entity, and with the wood falling from the ceiling.'

Éabha's eyes widened.

'My hearing-aid batteries died when we were in there. I had to replace them in the car on the way back to the office. I'd only put fresh ones in that morning.'

'Ah, so the murderous ghost is also ableist,' Fionn said.

Éabha laughed.

'So, the battery drop is proof of a ghost?' she asked.

'Well, we can reasonably hypothesise that the camera malfunctions are a result of an entity manifesting,' Davis said. 'Though on its own it's not enough to definitively say that's the case.'

'Which leads me perfectly on to my next clip,' Fionn said with the enthusiasm of a magician producing a rabbit from a hat.

'I thought Archer was the dramatic one,' Raven said.

'I have an audio file from the same time. It's faint, but I've isolated it and raised the volume as best I can. I'll play the original first though.' Fionn clicked on it.

'What is it?' Davis's voice asked, booming from the computer.

'She's here,' Éabha's said.

The fear in her voice made Raven's heart clench.

Then, right after Éabha spoke, there was a low, venomous hiss Raven couldn't quite make out. It was followed by a thud that was Davis hitting the floor. She looked at Archer, who was leaning in so close he was nearly lying across Fionn's shoulder. Éabha's face hadn't changed at all.

'OK, did you hear that?'

Everyone but Éabha nodded.

'I'll play you the isolated clip now. I've looped it so we can hear it a few times.' He clicked play.

'She's here,' Éabha's voice said.

'*Get out,*' a menacing voice hissed.

Thud.

Raven's mouth went dry, adrenaline coursing through her. Every instinct was screaming at her to run from the room.

'She's here.'

'*Get out.*'

Thud.

Her heart hammered painfully in her chest.

'She's here.'

'*Get out.*'

Thud.

'We get it,' Raven snapped.

Fionn paused it, and Raven stepped away to sink into an empty chair, taking shaky breaths, pricked by guilt at how Fionn had flinched at her tone. She should apologise. She couldn't, though; her whole body was on edge, every instinct screaming at her to run, while her legs felt like they would collapse under her if she tried to stand again. In the far corners of her memory, a dark space she didn't want to step into, something was crying out with familiarity. It recognised that voice, and the more it was repeated the more it was hauled to the surface of her mind, like a shipwreck being raised up from the depths of the ocean.

Archer came over and, resting a comforting hand on her arm, crouched beside her.

'Raven?'

'I'm fine. Sorry … it brought some stuff up.'

'You remembered something?'

She could hear the eagerness in his voice and felt a spike of rage. Of course he would be excited. It wasn't *his* darkest memories that were being dredged up, *his* fears and guilt and pain mined for explanations.

'No.'

He recoiled at the snap in her words, as though she had sunk her teeth into him. He stood up and went back to his desk. The others were conferring in low voices, pretending not to have heard their exchange, though she saw Éabha cast a worried glance at her and Archer.

'We need to go back for a longer investigation,' Fionn was saying. He looked at Éabha and Davis. 'Safely, I mean.'

'I wish our parents' records had been in that file,' Archer said, running a hand through his hair in frustration. 'It's so unlike them to have all the pre-investigation evidence on file, but none of their own notes.'

'Would your mum have deleted them?' Éabha asked gently. 'It's a painful subject for you all.'

'No,' Archer said, shaking his head. 'She's too meticulous. She'd never look at the files, but she wouldn't destroy them either.'

Davis leaned back in his chair, crossing one long leg to rest a foot on his knee. 'Should we just ask Emily outright?'

Raven blanched. If they rang her and she told them there was a USB drive with the file, it wouldn't be long before all roads led to her being branded a traitor.

'No,' Archer said. 'She'd be so furious at us for breaking into her desk that even if she'd tell us, she'd hold back for a few weeks just to teach us a lesson.'

That was probably unfair on Emily, but at least it worked in her favour. Raven tried not to let the relief show on her face. A loud buzzing noise from behind made her start and she turned to see her phone vibrating furiously on the desk as it rang. Cordelia's name lit up the screen. She answered, trying to ignore the excited flutter in her stomach.

Cordelia's voice came down the line, low and urgent.

'Jack Gallagher has released a video from Hyacinth House.'

CHAPTER THIRTY-TWO

FIONN OPENED THE LINK Cordelia forwarded to them on his computer. The screen filled with a still of Jack's face, illuminated white in a dark room, one hand over his mouth, his eyes wide. Underneath was the caption 'A ghost tried to KILL ME? My NEAR DEATH supernatural experience, SCARIEST adventure yet. **Not Clickbait**'

'Catchy title,' Davis said, raising an eyebrow. 'Short. Succinct.'

Behind them, Raven slipped out of the room, speaking into her phone in low, soothing tones. Éabha wondered what this would mean. The hype had only just died down over Jack's accident in the house.

'Can you download this? Or save it somehow?' she asked urgently.

Fionn nodded, clicking a few buttons before a file appeared on the desktop.

'Good thinking, Éabha,' Archer said, squeezing her shoulders gently as he slid past her to sit on the other side of Fionn. Her shoulders tingled where he had touched her.

'The sellers are going to do their best to get this taken down as soon as possible, aren't they?' Davis mused.

'I'd put money on it,' Archer said.

The video had been up for only a few minutes, but the views, likes and comments were climbing rapidly.

'A lot of people have push notifications for his account. They'd get an alert the moment the video went up. By the time they get him to take it down, it'll already be everywhere,' Fionn said, tapping away at his keyboard as he saved the video.

'Better to be on the safe side, though,' Archer said.

Raven came back into the room, her phone still in her hand. 'That was Cordelia. She's freaking out a bit.' She shook her head. 'Understatement of the century there, but she wanted to make sure we knew the video was up so we could watch it. She's hoping we might be able to find evidence that things in it were faked.'

Archer nodded. 'Fionn and I can analyse it frame by frame and get back to her. Even the fact that it's edited and not a live stream casts doubt on the authenticity.'

'She's calling the sellers now but she wanted to get us to start analysing the footage immediately so she could tell them she's on top of it. I think she's scared they'll pull out of the sale.'

A slightly bitter note crept into her voice at the last statement.

'You all ready?' Fionn asked.

'I guess,' Raven sighed. They once again took up positions around the computer, and Éabha couldn't help but notice how Raven stood slightly back, almost as though she was afraid something would leap from the screen.

'Here we go,' Fionn said, and clicked play.

A text caption flashed up on screen: 'This footage may be distressing to some viewers. Please watch with caution.'

'Way to make sure everyone immediately wants to see this,' Archer said, sighing.

Fionn shushed him and Archer winked back. He was almost convincing at seeming completely relaxed, but his air of nonchalance was too extreme to be believable. His excitement was strong enough that it seeped through the protection Éabha's bracelet gave her, a fizzing energy different from her own.

'I'm outside Hyacinth House, a place so haunted no one even talks about it.' Jack's face lit up on the screen, standing outside the front door of the house. His voice was hushed but eager, speaking in a breathy whisper. Blond curls poked out from underneath a beanie and his eyes danced with mischief. 'It's hard to find the exact history behind the house, because no one will speak about it, but there's a legacy of tragedy and death with every owner.' He turned the camera to pan along the building, showing the boarded-up windows, the tower looming ominously on the right-hand side. 'The most recent death was in 2017, when a paranormal investigator died mid-investigation. I'm going to spend the night in here and do what he couldn't – if the ghost doesn't get me first!'

Archer's fingers formed a fist at his side, and Raven's hands tightened on the back of Fionn's chair.

'What a prick,' Davis said, his voice dripping with disgust.

The video shifted to Jack inside the house, breathing more heavily. 'I've just gotten through the window of the house. They've boarded it up, but not well enough to keep yours truly out!' He winked ostentatiously at the camera. He panned the camera around, showing a few pieces of furniture covered in sheets. It was eerie, the light from the camera the only illumination in the room and, as obnoxious as Jack was, Éabha was impressed at his bravery.

Though arrogance could often masquerade as bravery in the right circumstances, she supposed.

The time stamp in the bottom corner of the camera jumped forward a few hours. Jack was sitting on the floor, leaning against a wall, speaking in hushed tones. 'I'm upstairs now. I've been exploring and I haven't found anything of interest, but I keep feeling like I'm not alone.' He swallowed hard, then looked around. 'I thought I heard knocks on the wall that were just behind me, but when I turned around there was nothing – no one – there. I have this feeling that I'm being watched.' He looked at the camera, grinning mischievously. 'I might see if I can get them to come say hello.'

He got up, the camera shaking a little in his hand and moved out of the room. It looked like he was in the upper corridor near the tower. Raven inhaled sharply, releasing it in a slow breath when he turned to go back down the main staircase.

'Hello? Helloooo?' he called tauntingly.

Lizzie's voice telling her to 'Stay quiet and hope you don't draw the attention of whatever is in the house' echoed in Éabha's head. She held her breath.

'Would you like to do an interview for my channel?' he called, chortling to himself. His laughter, however, had a much higher pitch than earlier.

He walked down the stairs, the floor creaking beneath him. The only sounds were his voice, his footsteps, his slightly haggard breathing. It felt as though the whole house was lying in wait, a brief pause before it sprang into action. Or, Éabha realised with a chill, it was playing with him. Allowing him to explore, to act as though he was the one in control, when anyone who set foot in that house should instantly know they were not the one with the power. The shadows cast on the wall by his camera light didn't help quell the growing sense of dread. Everything seemed to be a figure looming in the corner. A few times he started, letting out a gasp before the lighting revealed just an empty corner or an abandoned item. He'd laugh and make a joke, but each time it happened, his laughter became more forced.

Beside her, Raven's eyes were trained on the screen. Every muscle looked taut, poised to run and, as they watched, Éabha couldn't blame her. Her determination to prove herself to the team was the only thing stopping her from looking away.

On screen, the camera showed a large, open room that Archer whispered was the ballroom. Éabha recognised it once he said it. Raven stiffened even more beside her. Éabha wouldn't have thought there was any more of her to tense.

Jack flipped the camera back around to show himself instead of the room.

'You know I'll always be honest with you, my stream-fam – no bullshit, only authenticity here.' His face filled most of the camera screen and his voice was ragged, fear cutting into the edges of it, his courage fraying one thread at a time.

'This is the creepiest place I've ever been, and you know some of the things I've done! I feel like –'

A loud knock from behind made him whirl around. The camera was still on his face, so they couldn't see what he was looking at, until he reached a quivering hand out to flip the camera.

'There's nothing there,' he said. 'But I heard a knock. I hope the tape caught it too.' He almost seemed to be talking to himself at this point. Or he was a very good actor.

Another bang reverberated through the room, followed by a series of light knocks. The knocks were gentle, some so faint you had to strain your ears to hear them. Éabha slid the volume up on her hearing-aid app and leaned in as close as possible to the screen without actually climbing on top of Davis.

The tension between the knocks was almost unbearable. All they could see were shadows, scored by Jack's sharp inhalations of breath. Just when the gap between sounds became achingly drawn out, another knock would echo around the room. The camera was shaking in his hand, and he must have been frozen in fear. That was the only reason she could think of for why he hadn't bolted.

The knocks were advancing towards him, along the wall to his left. The wall between him and the door.

BANG! A loud thud on the wall right beside him made him scream.

The camera image went black.

Now all they had was sound, his frantic footsteps, gasping, 'Leave me alone.' A rattling that sounded like a doorknob. He was narrating, almost on autopilot, 'I left this door open when I came in.' A rattling sound, then frantic banging.

'Let me out!' in a desperate, angry voice.

'Please let me out,' in a whimper, a soft, terrified plea.

The video ended.

It followed up with a plain text caption, scrolling along the screen.

'I was found by emergency services at three-thirty a.m. I have no recollection of the time between when this video was taken and then. I woke up in hospital, and after psychiatric assistance for stress and trauma (#ItsOKToNotBeOK), I was discharged from hospital. I wasn't sure whether to upload the footage. But I thought that you, my loyal friends who have followed me on my journey from Day One, deserved to know the truth. Make sure to subscribe for updates!'

'He almost had me until "subscribe for updates",' Davis said, leaning back with a sigh.

'You have to admire the hustle,' Fionn said.

'What do the comments say?' Raven asked quietly.

She walked away from the computer and leaned against a desk, drinking from her water bottle. She hugged her flannel shirt closely around her body as though it was a protective layer of armour.

Fionn started scrolling, calling out items of note as he skimmed through the comments. 'OK, it seems to be a combination of "wow, scariest thing ever, you're so brave" and "this is fake", conspiracy theories on how it could be faked, a few unsolicited suggestions of a "collab" and a bunch of well-wishes. And this is all within, what, twenty minutes of going up?'

'We need to interview him ourselves,' Archer said.

'He's going to be inundated with media requests, there's no way he'll talk to us,' Davis pointed out.

'Ideally we need the raw, unedited footage too,' Archer continued, as though he hadn't heard, or was just ignoring, Davis's interjection.

'Arch, I know you're used to being able to charm things out of people, but this may be too difficult, even for you.'

'I do not "charm things out of people". People just generally agree with me because I'm right,' Archer huffed.

Raven snorted.

'There has to be some way of either getting the footage or talking to him,' Fionn mused, resting his chin on his hand as he continued to scroll down the ever-mounting pile of comments.

'Cordelia!' Éabha exclaimed, pointing at Raven.

Raven started, then raised an eyebrow at her. 'No, I'm Raven.'

'I know that, but I mean Cordelia.' She looked around the room. They were all staring at her, perplexed.

'She's on a call with the sellers, right? Who I assume have contact details for Jack because they had to negotiate the legal stuff after he broke in. Why don't we ask them to put us in touch with him? It'll be quicker than waiting for him to sort through the media requests.'

'You genius, Éabha!' Archer leapt out of his chair and picked her up, spinning her around in a circle. She could feel her cheeks flushing, more from the sensation of Archer's arms around her than from the compliment.

'You're right. If we get the sellers to say that we've been hired to investigate the house and they would appreciate it if he spoke to us –'

'For free,' Davis added.

'– for free, it should help.'

'Besides, we wouldn't be publishing anything he said, and he can retain all the original footage himself,' Fionn added.

'That sounds fair,' Raven said thoughtfully. 'But I don't want him to feel pressured by the sellers to talk.'

'In fairness, the guy did just post full video footage of himself breaking and entering on the internet after the people whose property he was breaking into didn't press charges. He kinda owes them this,' Davis pointed out.

Raven glared at him, a fierce sharpness in her eyes, and he held his hands up. 'I'm just saying.'

'I know what it feels like to be put under pressure to talk when you're not ready,' Raven said. 'We're not doing that to anyone.'

Éabha could feel Archer shifting uncomfortably beside her.

Davis softened. 'I know, Raven, and we won't force him. But he did share the footage himself. It shows he's at least willing to revisit it long enough to edit it. And this could really help the investigation.'

'If he agrees, we could go together,' Archer offered tentatively. 'Then you'll know no one is forcing anyone to talk about something they don't want to address.'

Raven nodded. 'That's fair.'

A slow, delighted smile spread across Archer's face.

'I'll ring Cordelia,' he said, picking up his phone and walking out into the corridor.

CHAPTER THIRTY-THREE

JACK AGREED TO TALK TO THEM immediately. The sellers had passed on his contact details via Cordelia, and Archer arranged to meet him the next day. Raven sleepwalked through a shift in Origin the evening before, then spent most of the night tossing and turning in between nightmares that felt like memories. Or memories revealing themselves through nightmares. It was hard to tell which.

The team agreed with minimum debate that just she and Archer would go. Fionn said he'd be more disappointed if they'd asked him to go, the interview being his least favourite part of an investigation. Davis had several papers to work on that he had already neglected too long in favour of Hyacinth House, so he was relieved. Éabha was behind on coursework as well, and was more than happy to bow out too.

This was the first time Raven and Archer had been completely alone in a long while. There was a residual tension, an unspoken acknowledgement that there were things neither of them was addressing. The flash drive was still in Raven's bag, and she felt like it was giving off a traitorous signal, like a distress beacon, trying to call attention to her deceit.

Archer collected her in the family car to drive out to Jack's house together. Getting into it felt like stepping back in time, only instead of her and Archer sitting in the back seat, bickering and scheming as their parents drove them to the site of their latest investigation, it was them in the front seats, a stilted silence stretching between them. Their mother away, their father gone forever.

It was a sunny late-autumn day and the light through the windscreen shone on Archer's face. Raven squinted against it, the sun hovering at the exact height in the sky to blind her. Of course, Archer had thought to bring sunglasses and was smiling at the warmth. Beside him, she felt small and bitter, dark circles from lack of sleep ringing her eyes as she second-guessed the all-black clothing she had picked to make herself feel strong. Maybe she should have tried to dress a bit … friendlier? Should Éabha have done this interview instead? Éabha, with her soft jumpers and delicate dresses, her wide blue eyes radiating empathy. Rather than her, who had built such high walls around her heart she didn't know how to bring them down, even though she wanted to.

'It's fun,' Archer said. 'Investigating with you again.'

'It is,' she smiled back, the expression quickly fading. If only it was any other investigation.

'I've missed this.'

'I have too.' She could almost feel the thought coming from him: if she missed it, why had she avoided it – *him* – for so long? But, being Archer, he didn't say it. He simply flicked on the indicator and turned into a small housing estate.

'We're here.'

The Gallaghers' home was a detached house in the suburbs, the driveway lined with perfectly trimmed hedges. All the houses in the road had varying types of Halloween decorations in their driveways, a reminder that the holiday was fast approaching. There were carefully carved pumpkins on doorsteps, plastic decorations dangling from tree branches, dancing in the breeze. Even though the leaves had been falling thick and fast in flurries of vivid orange interspersed with brown, there wasn't a sign of them on the driveway as they walked up to the front door.

'Ready?' Archer asked.

Raven nodded and he rang the bell. Jack answered, looking as tired as Raven felt, wearing a pair of navy sweatpants and a bright blue hoodie. His curly hair exploded out around his face, and he smiled as he ushered them into the house. He was leaning on a crutch on his left-hand side.

'Tea? Coffee?' he asked as soon as they'd introduced themselves, already limping off to the kitchen before either of them could offer to help, instructing them over his shoulder to make themselves at home in the living room. Photos lined the walls, mainly of him and his parents, and trophies for various martial arts jostled for space on top of bookshelves and a glass cabinet. From a quick scan of the room, it was clear he was an only child, and a doted-on one at that.

'Yeah, this room is kinda embarrassing,' he said, coming back in pushing an old-fashioned drinks cart with a tray of coffees, teas and biscuits balanced on top of it with one hand, while the other held his crutch. 'But I can't really complain to my parents, can I? "Please stop being openly proud of me?"' He laughed. 'Help yourself to tea and coffee there. Who knew a drinks cart would come in useful? I hate not being able to do things for myself, so it's been a lifesaver.' He talked quickly, jumping from one thought to the next in a way that made it difficult to tell if it was nerves or his personality.

'Mum got the good biscuits in for your visit and everything,' he grinned, offering them the plate. They were individually wrapped biscuits, marshmallow sandwiched between two biscuits and covered in chocolate.

'Ah, the Christmas Day biscuits, we're honoured,' Archer grinned, taking one.

'Are your parents in?' Raven asked politely.

Jack shook his head. 'They're both at work. Probably for the best – they'd hover. They've been a little on edge since … all this.' He gestured awkwardly.

'How are you doing?' Archer asked, leaning forward. The concern on his face was genuine.

'Ah, grand. The leg's healing well and I only need the one crutch now.'

Raven looked at him sceptically. He met her eyes and held her gaze for a few moments before wilting. 'Well, not so OK. I've been having trouble sleeping. I keep having nightmares where I'm back in the house and … yeah. It's not fun.'

'I'm not sure how much you were told, but we're investigating the house ourselves,' Archer said.

'Yeah, they said you'd been hired to figure out what's going on. You're like, professionals at this?'

'We have some experience,' Archer said modestly.

'More than some. You're the O'Sullivans! I read about your family when I was looking stuff up about the house.'

Suddenly the twenty-year-old in front of them looked a lot younger than that. 'I'm sorry. About the intro to the video. I didn't think, you know? There's so many true crime and ghost story podcasts out there, you forget that they're not just stories. There's people connected to them who might hear you.'

'It's OK,' Archer said. 'But thanks.'

'Do you mind if we tape the interview?' Raven asked, setting her recorder out on the table between them. 'It's just for our records. No one outside of the team will hear it.'

'Go for it,' Jack said.

'Could you take us through what happened that night?' Archer asked. 'No detail is too silly or too small. Anything you heard or saw or felt – even if you just *thought* you did.'

'I'll sound weird,' Jack said, pulling his hoodie sleeves over his hands.

'Not to us,' Raven said firmly. 'I promise.'

'OK,' Jack said. Taking a shaky breath, he began.

'My girlfriend Caroline grew up near to the house, a couple of towns over, but had never actually been there. I've been doing a series on my channel where I go to creepy places at night. It's doing really well and I wanted to try somewhere new, somewhere that wasn't just one of the old favourites for hauntings. Caroline mentioned Hyacinth House in passing and I was hooked. Like this is only forty minutes or so from Dublin and no one really talks about it. It pops up when something happens and immediately disappears again. It just made me feel like there was more to it. She tried to talk me out of it, but I can be stubborn as fuck – sorry, can I swear? Oh, right, yeah, it's not for a podcast. Force of habit.

'I decided to go to the house, and she only gave in when I promised to check in with her every two hours. She wanted it to be every hour, but I was like "no, it'll ruin the flow of filming if I keep having to call."' He paused, looking down at his feet. 'She saved my life by doing that. And I was slagging her for it.'

Archer and Raven stayed silent. It was best to let the subject talk until they ran out of things to say, rather than interrupting with questions. Archer had a notebook on his knee, to scribble down anything he wanted to ask once Jack was finished speaking.

'I went into the house through one of the downstairs windows. And at first it was fine. The standard old-house-at-night kinda thing. Like obviously that's always a bit creepy, but it was nothing unusual. Then I went upstairs. I thought I heard footsteps behind me a few times, but when I turned around there was no one there. Bit weird, but I thought it was just my own footsteps echoing or my mind playing tricks on me. I wandered down this corridor, towards the side of the house where the tower is. I wanted to see if I could get into it, but I couldn't find the door so I went into the room on the left, to see if there was an entrance through there.'

Raven tried not to shudder.

'And it felt … like something didn't want me in there. I started to get freaked out, and I don't scare easily.'

Raven had to fight to keep her expression neutral at that.

'So I started to head back downstairs. I'd seen this paranormal investigation show where the investigators were talking out loud to the spirit, trying to rile them up to get them to appear, so I thought I'd try that. At least it'd look good for the video. I started calling out. And it did not like that at all. Like, before, the feeling had been "*Who are you? Get out*", but now it felt like it was actively pissed at me. I thought it was just my head playing tricks, because there's no way ghosts are actually real. Then I went to the ballroom. And. Well, you've watched the video, yeah?'

'We have,' Archer said. 'Can you tell us what you were seeing when the screen went black?'

'That's all a bit hazy,' he confessed. 'The doctors say it's probably because of the blood loss. Or the trauma. Or was it the trauma of the blood loss?' He cocked his head thoughtfully, then shrugged. 'I remember the door being locked, even though I'd left it open. And I was pushing and yelling and it just wouldn't budge.' He looked down at his feet again. 'It was embarrassing to hear myself completely freak out like that. Over a stuck door. I guess I was so panicked I didn't see the loose floorboard or else my foot cracked it or something, but I ended up tripping and impaling my leg on the jagged end. It missed my – what's that artery in your leg? The big one. Whatever that is – by millimetres. I still lost enough blood that if the ambulances hadn't arrived when they did, I would've died. I woke up in hospital the next afternoon, no memory, Caroline and my parents freaking out and some very official-looking people in suits wanting to speak to me. Not my best day.'

'I can imagine,' Archer said sympathetically. He shifted slightly in his seat before asking, 'At the end of the video you posted, the screen goes black. Was that a ... stylistic choice?'

'You mean, did I do it deliberately for the shock factor?'

'Well, yes.'

'No. It's all authentic. My camera has this quirk where, when the battery goes low, the picture goes. It records sound for a little while longer, then shuts down completely. It's strange, though. I'd just put a freshly charged battery into it. I always bring spares. I thought maybe the camera was damaged, but I got it checked and it's completely operational. Slightly dented from when I dropped it falling over, but in terms of filming and batteries and stuff, it's grand.' He looked at them perplexedly, raising his hands and shrugging. 'No idea what caused it to malfunction.'

Raven had a pretty solid idea.

She let Archer take the lead on asking questions. It was clear that Jack was comfortable talking about his experience – though he claimed not to remember certain chunks of it – and some of his descriptions felt eerily familiar to her own recollections. What she could remember anyway? Did everyone who set foot in that house end up with amnesia? Though Éabha's aunt had been able to give detailed descriptions over thirty years after her experiences there.

Archer asked their usual checklist of questions: temperature changes, physical sensations, sounds heard, atmosphere. Sometimes people didn't realise a detail was of note until they were asked. Other times they held back, embarrassed. Once it was clear they would be believed, they tended to be more forthcoming with details. In some ways, investigating the paranormal was as much about reassuring the clients themselves as it was about documenting the scientific aspects of it. Their father had always been better at the people aspect, while their mum, like Raven, had relished the science of it all. She'd liked the people too, but Pádraig – and now Archer – had that easy way with people where within moments they felt like he was an old friend. Raven always felt awkward, never really knowing what to say. She was better with a script: the experiments, the results, the data.

After an hour or so they said their goodbyes. Jack looked exhausted, 'probably from the blood loss rather than reliving the trauma,' he announced cheerfully. He was still being carefully monitored, but overall he said his health was in good condition. Physically anyway. Every now and then, a shadow would cross his face, or he would start at a noise, like the pipes creaking to life in the walls, and the scars of his experience became clearer.

He handed over the original footage he'd shot, asking only that it be returned when they were finished with it.

'To be honest, I've had a lot of people claiming I've faked it,' he said sadly. 'My whole thing is authenticity, no bullshit, you know? So it's a bit of a blow. If you guys were willing to sign off on it being authentic, that would be a huge help to me.' His eyes lit up suddenly. 'Or even, we could do a collab when you finish your investigation? Real ghost hunters talking about the house. No one would doubt me then!'

'We'd have to see what our client says but we'll keep it in mind,' Archer said gently. Raven wanted to snap at Jack, tell him that this wasn't some opportunity for sponsored content or likes. This was real life. People had died. He'd almost been one of them. Then she looked more closely at him, the way he leaned painfully hard on his crutch, the dark circles under his eyes, the almost pleading note to his voice as he'd said, 'No one would doubt me then.'

He was afraid. Not just of other people's opinions, but of himself. Of not being able to tell what was real and what were nightmares.

'If you remember anything else, or if you need to talk to someone who understands, here's my number,' she said suddenly, pulling a piece of paper from her notebook and writing it down.

Archer's eyebrows shot up, though Jack didn't seem to notice his surprise.

'Thanks, Raven.'

'Take care,' she said, already feeling awkward.

Archer shook Jack's hand and the two of them headed back to the car.

'Cake and analysis?' he asked.

'Cake and analysis,' she agreed.

CHAPTER THIRTY-FOUR

ÉABHA KNEW SOMETHING WAS WRONG the moment she walked through the door. The tension reached out and wrapped itself around her, pulling her down the hall to where her parents were sitting in the kitchen. It erased the happy cloud she'd been in, thinking about the messages she and Archer had been exchanging, debating the twists in Volume Four of *Stranger Things*. They'd both started watching it only recently, a few months after what felt like everyone else in the world, so they'd decided to watch it in tandem, messaging during each episode as though they were watching it together.

Her joy was quickly snuffed out when she saw that her mother's face was grim, her father's drawn. He looked up as she walked in and put her bag on the floor, his lips thin.

'Is everything OK?'

Silently, her mother pushed a book that was resting on the table towards her. She used just her index finger, a look of disgust on her face as though it was something repulsive.

It was the book Lizzie had given her.

'I found this.'

'You went through my room?' Éabha asked, aghast.

'You've been acting strangely.'

'I'm eighteen. You can't go through my things!'

'It's our home,' her father interjected harshly. 'We have a right to know what you are doing in it.'

'I'm not doing anything wrong.'

'Father Benedict would disagree.'

'Because the Catholic Church *really* has a leg to stand on when it comes to morality in this country?'

Her father slammed his fist on the table. Her mother gasped.

'Where did you get this book, Éabha?' she said, her voice low and angry.

'I –'

'Because I remember a book exactly like this. My sister had it, right before she started messing with all of that nonsense.'

'That nonsense saved your life, and you thanked her by cutting her out of it.'

'Of course she filled your head with lies.'

The bitterness seeping from her mother left a sour taste in Éabha's mouth.

'You went behind your mother's back to her sister, you brought this into our house,' her father spat. 'You will never see that woman again. You will destroy this and the other books. We'll get you the help you need.'

'All I need is for you to accept me for who I am.'

'You're imagining things, Éabha. It needs to stop.'

'I can't turn this off, Dad. It's a part of me.' Tears spilt over her lashes and her voice quavered. 'Lizzie's helping me to understand it. There's nothing wrong with me.' She looked at her mother pleadingly. 'It's not dangerous, or evil. I can help people. I am helping people.' Her whole body trembled as she looked from one parent to the other. Her voice cracked. 'I can't turn my back on it.'

Her father looked down, but her mother stared her straight in the eye.

'Then get out.'

Éabha's finger hovered uncertainly before pressing the doorbell of Archer's house. A small suitcase stood forlornly beside her, her backpack was slung over her shoulder and her laptop in its case banged against her hip. She hadn't known where to go at first. Her parents had given her half an hour to pack, telling her she could arrange to fetch the rest of her things at another time.

She didn't have any friends. She'd kept everyone up until the PSI team at arm's length in case they found out about her gifts. Lizzie was away in Galway for four days, so she couldn't go to her. Her phone battery had died just as she left the house. Almost automatically she had gone to the bus depot in town, buying her ticket and catching the bus she had become so familiar with. There was only one place she wanted to be right now, one group of people she wanted to see. One person, really.

It had started to rain as she got off the bus. Forest Fair was closed, the door locked. She trudged along the road to the house, the rain seeping inside her shoes and down the back of her neck, but she couldn't bring herself to care. Part of her wondered what she was doing, turning up at the home of people she had known for such a short amount of time. But that instinct, the one in her gut that Lizzie had told her to listen to, said this was the right thing to do.

The door opened and Davis stood there in a teal jumper and a pair of grey tracksuit bottoms.

'Did you forget your keys ag–' he began, then seeing who it was, exclaimed, 'Éabha!' He looked at her, eyes wide in concern, taking in her soaked hair, her mascara streaked halfway down her face from the rain.

'I'm sorry,' she said, looking up at him. 'I didn't know where else to go.'

He stepped aside. 'Come in.'

'Give me two minutes to get you some dry clothes,' he said, pointing her into the living room. 'The fire's lit, go get warm. I'll bring you a towel too.'

She did so obediently, gazing into the flames dancing in the grate, drops of water dripping from her hair and her clothes to form a puddle around her. Davis came back holding a fluffy towel, a hoodie with a GAA logo on it, and a pair of navy tracksuit bottoms.

'Put these on, you must be frozen.'

It was only when he said it that she realised she was. He pointed down the hall to the bathroom, where she stripped off her wet clothes and dried herself before putting on the outfit he'd given her. Her own clothes were in her suitcase, but the thought of explaining why she had them, or trying to root through the parts of her life she had managed to pack, made her feel ill. The hoodie was long on the arms and she had to roll the tracksuit bottoms a few times at the ends, but the soft material enveloped her like a hug. She padded barefoot back into the living room, sinking into one of the armchairs at the opposite side of the fire to Davis. He cleared his throat awkwardly, first looking around the room and then at her.

'Do you want some tea?'

'Yes, please.'

He went to the kitchen and she stayed curled up in the armchair, grateful to have her explanation delayed a little while longer. Her mind was starting to race.

Her parents had kicked her out. She had no home any more. Thoughts barged around her brain in a chorus of shrieking voices, each one a new worry. Where would she live? Would she have to leave college and get a job? Could she defer? Did 'being kicked out of the house by your parents because you're a psychic freak' count for compassionate leave?

She jumped as the front door slammed.

'Oh great, you lit the fire –' Archer cut off as he saw her sitting there, his face an almost comically perfect copy of Davis's when he'd opened the door. She would have laughed if she hadn't been completely numb. His eyes took in her clothes and he looked confused, almost hurt.

'Hey,' she said weakly, giving him an awkward little wave.

Davis came down the hall, holding two mugs, looking relieved. 'You're back. You've seen we have a visitor.'

'I have.'

'Take this, I'll get another,' Davis handed Archer one mug and Éabha the other before turning and striding back to the kitchen.

'Davis isn't great at emotions,' Archer said lightly, sitting in the armchair beside her. His eyes raked over her and she saw his confusion turn to concern. Her still-damp hair clung wetly to the back of her neck. She'd wiped off as much of her eye make-up as possible, but there were still black smudges around her eyes. She was too exhausted to care. Normally she felt everything, to the point that it was overwhelming, but now she was empty inside. A hollowed-out husk where Éabha should be sitting.

'Éabha?' Archer's voice was so gentle that tears welled up in her eyes. 'What happened?'

'They found the book. They kicked me out.' The words broke the dam, sweeping away the numbness that had protected her from breaking down until this moment. She burst into tears, deep sobs racking her body. 'I'm so sorry, but Lizzie's away and … I had nowhere else to go.'

Archer put his mug on the floor and crossed over to her chair. He squished in beside her, sliding his arms under her and lifting her onto his lap, cradling her in his arms. She cried harder, looping her arms around his neck as he held her tightly, whispering words of comfort into her hair. Eventually her sobs eased and she sniffled, dimly aware that her tears had soaked through his jumper and her nose was dripping.

He handed her a tissue from a box on a coffee table nearby and she blew into it, suddenly incredibly aware of how close they were.

'Sorry.' She winced.

His arms were still around her waist and he smiled at her. 'You have nothing to apologise for.'

'I think I just soaked through your jumper.'

'It'll dry.'

The doorbell shrilled, startling them both. Davis walked past the living room towards it and Éabha jumped out of Archer's lap. She coughed awkwardly, sitting down on the chair Archer had vacated.

'I brought pizza,' Fionn said, bouncing through the door

carrying two pizza boxes. Davis followed behind him, holding two more. From the number of pizzas to Fionn's lack of surprise at Éabha's presence, she guessed Davis had texted him.

'Excellent,' Archer said.

Davis set the pizzas on the floor. They all settled on the thick rug in front of the fire, ignoring the chairs clustered around the room. Archer was uncharacteristically quiet, and Éabha noticed him shooting a few scrutinising looks at Davis. Fionn seemed to pick up on it too, filling the silence with anecdotes from the shop that day, his quiet, dry humour perfectly skewering some of the ridiculous questions he got working in retail. Even Éabha found herself smiling.

The warmth from the fire filled the room and, as she ate, she realised how hungry she had been. The numbness had faded and now she could feel everything again, good and bad. She leaned back against the base of the armchair, knees up, Davis's clothes cocooning her. Her fingers clutched at her tourmaline bracelet. She could barely handle her own feelings right now: she couldn't deal with the others' sinking into her too. Besides, she didn't know if she wanted to know how they felt about her right now. Anything – sympathy or exasperation – would snap her like a twig underfoot.

After a while, Davis and Archer brought the boxes to the kitchen and Fionn leaned towards her conspiratorially. 'I got you these,' he said, pulling a large bag of Maltesers out of his bag. 'Don't let the others see them. They'll have half of them eaten before you've had two.'

'Thank you,' Éabha said, slipping them into her handbag.

Fionn smiled, then settled back to lie on his side as the others came back in.

She'd thought she was all cried out, but this small gesture of solidarity made her feel like she would dissolve all over again. The boys' chat washed over her as she leaned back against the chair, fullness and heat and the waning adrenaline of earlier events draining her to the point that she could barely keep her eyes open.

Archer calling her name snapped her out of the doze she'd slipped into. From the barely suppressed smile on his face, she could tell it wasn't the first time he had said it.

'Do you want me to show you to your room?'

All she wanted to do was curl up into a ball and sleep.

'I probably owe you an explanation first,' she said reluctantly.

The boys looked at each other.

Davis waved a hand. 'There's plenty of time to talk tomorrow, Éabha. Go to sleep. You look wrecked.' He caught himself. 'I mean that in a caring way.'

She laughed, heaving herself to her feet and picking up her bags. 'Thank you all, for everything. Good night.'

She followed Archer up the stairs as he pointed things out.

'The main bathroom's along here, but your room has an en suite, so you don't have to worry about sharing with messy guys,' he grinned. 'Though Davis applies lab levels of cleanliness to every aspect of his life, so you don't really need to worry. Actually, remind me to show you how he likes the dishwasher stacked, because he feels very strongly about it …'

She trailed after him until he opened a door and ushered her in.

'OK, there are fresh sheets on the bed, the en suite is in there, there's toothpaste and stuff in the cabinet too. My room is next door to the left. If you need anything, just knock.' He paused and bit his bottom lip thoughtfully. 'I think that's everything?'

'It's more than enough.' She swayed slightly on her feet, exhaustion overwhelming her and fogging her brain so much that she couldn't form the words she wanted to say: how incredibly grateful she was for how they'd all rallied around her, not pushed for answers but just accepted where she was.

'I … Archer …' Her eyes filled up again and she stopped, embarrassed. 'Thank you,' she finished, hoping he would get the meaning she put into those words. Sometimes she wished everyone could feel emotions the way she did, just so she didn't have to articulate them.

'Anytime, Éabhs,' Archer said earnestly. 'I'll see you in the morning.'

He left, closing the door behind him. She trudged into the bathroom, pulling her toothbrush from her bag and brushing her teeth quickly, resolutely ignoring her reflection in the mirror. She didn't want to see what kind of state she was in. She climbed into the bed, not even bothering to change out of Davis's hoodie and tracksuit bottoms, pulled up the duvet and switched off the lamp. She was fast asleep within seconds.

CHAPTER THIRTY-FIVE

ARCHER WAS STANDING AT THE HOB, humming along to the music playing from his phone, when he heard the kitchen door open behind him. He turned to see Éabha, in black leggings and a long grey jumper. Her hair was scraped back into a high ponytail, her eyes were framed by dark circles and the smile she was clearly forcing to her lips was weary.

'Morning' he said cheerfully. 'Did you sleep well? Do you want some breakfast? Orange juice? Coffee?'

She looked momentarily taken aback by the flurry of questions. *Maybe Éabhs isn't a morning person*, he thought, panicking at his enthusiastic onslaught of queries.

'Coffee would be great, please,' she said, sitting onto one of the sturdy wooden chairs at the table.

'We have eggs, bread for toast, or cereal too? I'll let you have some of my secret stash of Coco Pops if you promise not to tell Davis I have them.'

She laughed at that and the sound made his heart lift.

'You're very kind, but I couldn't do that to you. I'd love some toast, though.'

He bowed to her, cringing internally as he did. *Really, Archer? Bowing?* He popped two pieces of bread into the toaster, flipped a tea towel over his shoulder and turned back to the fried eggs that were spitting angrily in the frying pan. There was a pause, then Éabha's soft voice came from the table.

'I like the music.'

He turned to her and smiled. 'It's Ravel's "Boléro". One of my favourite pieces.'

'It's beautiful.' They listened in silence for a while. Archer's mind raced, searching for something to say. Should he ask her what had happened? Should he wait until she brought it up? Could she sense how much he was panicking trying to think of what to say? Before he could speak, Éabha asked, 'Have the others left for the day?'

Was she hoping Davis would be around instead? After Éabha had gone to bed in Davis's clothes last night, he'd asked him what his feelings towards her were. Davis had sworn he had no interest in her as anything other than a friend. He'd looked almost taken aback that Archer had asked, then smiled that annoyingly knowing smile when he asked why he had. But none of that would matter if Éabha liked Davis as more than just a friend. When he'd held her last night, all he'd wanted to do was to kiss her tears away, but he would never have overstepped like that, especially when she was so vulnerable.

'Davis is in the lab today, so Fionn got a lift with him to Dublin. He's going to sort equipment for the investigation this weekend.' He struggled to keep his voice neutral. The toast popped and he put the two pieces on a plate, putting two more slices into the toaster. 'Besides, I thought you might prefer to have some space today.'

He poured two cups of coffee from the V60 filter and brought them to the table, as Éabha fetched milk and butter from the fridge before joining him at the countertop.

'How do you always know the right thing to say and do?' she asked, tilting her head to look at him.

'Years of practice,' he said with a grin. He had to tear himself away from her blue eyes before he drowned in them.

The silence stretched between them. He was still bursting to ask her how she was doing, what had happened, but he was afraid of asking too much too quickly. Years of Raven shutting doors in his face, of her snapping at him when he tried to get her to open up, of seeing her close up and pull away from him, had made him hesitant in a way he had never been before. Watching Raven was like watching a slow-motion car crash he could do nothing to prevent. But maybe Éabha was waiting for him to invite her to share? It was what he himself had – still – hoped for.

Hey Archer, is there anything you'd like to talk about?

He wouldn't even know where to begin. Maybe he should stop letting the ghost of Raven's distance haunt him. He opened his mouth to speak.

Beside them, the toaster popped, shooting its contents onto the counter. Éabha jumped, letting out a startled squeal, and Archer couldn't help laughing. After a moment, she joined in, a rare, unfiltered beam of a smile that made his heart light up. Éabha smiled a lot, but it was usually a polite, contained smile, as though she was afraid of showing too much. This was an unimpeded expression. It was beautiful. She was beautiful.

Focus, Archer.

'Sorry, the toaster is kind of aggressive sometimes,' he said, taking the toast and putting it on the plate before adding his eggs to it.

'Noted,' she smiled, picking up her plate and following him to the table. She started to spread butter slowly over her toast with a focus that made it clear she was delaying the conversation. Archer munched on his toast patiently, waiting to see if she said anything. Eventually she looked up at him.

'So,' she said.

She took a bite of toast, followed by a sip of coffee.

'So,' he said, waiting.

She took a deep breath, visibly steeling herself to speak. 'My mum found the book and the crystals and stuff that Lizzie gave me. She recognised the book from when they were younger. They figured out that I'd seen Lizzie –' She swallowed hard, her voice cracking slightly. 'I tried to explain, but they wouldn't listen. They've kicked me out.'

Archer's stomach sank. Did she blame PSI – him – for this?

'I'm so sorry, Éabha,' Archer said. 'That's awful.'

Way to state the obvious, Archer.

'I'm still trying to come to terms with it,' Éabha said. She looked back down at her plate as she spoke. 'I think, deep down, I always knew that they'd react like this, but ... it's a part of me. I didn't ask for it, and I can't ignore it. And they hate me for it.' A single tear slid down her cheek and she wiped it away angrily.

All Archer wanted to do was fold her into his arms and hold her. He racked his brain for the right thing to say, wishing he could confront her parents, ask them why they needed to hurt such a kind, sweet person.

'People do strange things when they're afraid,' he said eventually. 'I'm sure they don't hate you.'

'Just this part of me.'

'If they don't see how amazing you are, with or without this gift, then they don't deserve you.'

Éabha let out a bitter laugh. 'I'm overwhelmed by everyone else's emotions and I see and sense things no one else does. I'm hardly the dream daughter.'

'No,' Archer said forcefully. He leaned over, squeezing her hand in his. 'Éabha, you've spent so long afraid of what you can do, but you're still determined to figure out how to use it so you can help others. You literally saved Davis's life, thanks to your gift. I think you're incredible.' He stopped, then hastily added, 'All the team do, I mean. We all care about you.'

She turned her hand upward, her fingers gently squeezing his. 'Thank you.'

They stayed like that for just a few heartbeats longer than normal before letting go. Clearing his throat, Archer picked up the notebook that was sitting on the table beside him.

'Raven has a shift at Origin tonight, but she said she can come down in the morning and work through the research with us. It's a good way of making sure she actually turns up to her own birthday party in the afternoon, too.' He saw the flicker of consternation in Éabha's eyes and realised he hadn't actually mentioned it was Raven's birthday. *Good job, Archer.* 'She basically only agreed to having a party if I didn't tell anyone it was for her birthday. Being the centre of attention is very much not Raven's thing.'

Éabha smiled at that.

'I'm trying to track down more students or staff from when Hyacinth was a school in the 1950s, but it's proving harder than

I'd hoped,' he continued quickly. He was babbling now, wasn't he?

'I can go through the transcripts today and see if there's anything helpful there,' Éabha offered.

Of course she was still trying to be helpful, despite everything she was going through.

'That would be great,' he said. 'Only if you're feeling up to it, though. It's OK if you need some time to process everything.'

'I think I could use the distraction, to be honest.' Her mask was back in place. The sadness lingered in her eyes, but her face wore its usual composed expression. How long had she been hiding everything she felt?

'OK, I'll be back around four. I want to bake the cake for Raven's party today so I can decorate it in the morning. Would you like to do that together? Then I'll cook us dinner.'

'Archer, are you sure this is OK?' Éabha asked. 'I don't want to overstay my welcome.'

'Éabha, you can stay here as long as you want,' Archer said. He could feel his face clouding over. 'It's because of us that you're in this situation.'

'It's not your fault,' she said, looking down at her coffee cup. 'It was my decision to come to you.'

'I know, it's just …' He caught sight of the clock behind her and leapt to his feet, swearing. 'My shift starts in ten minutes.'

She laughed and his heart soared again.

'Go get ready,' she said, shooing him out of the kitchen.

She was still at the table, pensively staring into the depths of her coffee, when he bounded back in five minutes later. He gave her frazzled instructions on the alarm code in case she needed to leave, then took himself off in a whirlwind of flustered energy, wishing he could stay with her, afraid she wouldn't want him to.

CHAPTER THIRTY-SIX

OF COURSE ARCHER HAD INSISTED on throwing her a birthday party. Just the team, he assured her. And Cordelia, since she was PSI adjacent, he claimed, the mischievous gleam in his eye telling her he knew exactly what he was doing.

Her little brother setting her up. Could her love life get any more pathetic?

Cordelia drove them down to Kilcarrig, an offer Raven accepted just that bit too eagerly, only to regret it immediately. It would be so much easier to blame Cordelia for this situation. To be angry at her for bringing the house back into her life.

Even though Cordelia hadn't made her hide the flash drive. Cordelia wasn't the one too afraid to look at it. Though she was the reason they'd had to find it. The one so determined to succeed in her career she would take on a ghost.

Why did she have to be so *hot*?

The others were all there when they arrived. Though, considering they were the only two not living there at least part-time, it was understandable. Éabha was curled up in a chair in the corner of the living room, her legs folded neatly underneath her, when they walked in. Her hair was in its usual perfect loose curls, but the shadows under her eyes told a different story as she smiled in greeting.

Raven couldn't imagine how much it must hurt. To be thrown out of the house by her family.

She had walked away from hers.

Still, here Archer was, handing her a present, in a room decked out in streamers and balloons. She could imagine him sitting on the ground, blowing them up, sticking them carefully in the perfect arrangement, despite the fact that he'd promised not to make a big deal out of the fact that it was her birthday.

'We have to do a twentieth, Raven, we missed nineteen,' he'd told her earnestly when she tried to protest.

'We missed nineteen' was a kind way to put it. She'd refused to come home for it, had lied about inflexible work shifts. Avoided his phone call, sent a brief thank-you text. How much had it hurt him? To have her go from being his closest friend to not answering his calls?

She'd run from what she couldn't face. And he'd been the collateral damage. Yet he wasn't holding it against her. He hadn't given up on her. It was that alone that had made her put a smile on her face and agree.

It wasn't long before she realised she was actually having fun. Cordelia fitted right in with the others. Éabha was already clearly part of the pack, even if she didn't seem aware of it herself. The others gravitated around her, Davis hovering like a protective parent, Fionn enthusiastically explaining whatever tech question she'd asked him. And Archer: always aware of where she was in the room, smiling when she laughed, beaming when she enthusiastically complimented his cooking. Her little brother was falling hard, and part of her wanted to make sure the landing didn't break him. Another part felt like she had lost that right.

'OK, cake time,' Archer announced gleefully.

Éabha and Davis disappeared into the kitchen, returning with a large cake.

'I couldn't find the candles,' Éabha said as she set the cake down, an elaborate sponge filled with cream and strawberries and covered with chocolate and Smarties. Smarties had always been Raven's favourite.

'I'll grab some from the cabinet,' Fionn volunteered.

As he walked to the back of the room, his foot caught in the strap of Raven's bag and yanked it off the chair it was perched on, spewing its contents all over the room. She scrambled to gather them, the others helping as Fionn profusely apologised. As she stuffed an EMF recorder back into her bag, she looked up to see Archer standing completely still, staring at something in his hand.

It was a small black USB flash drive.

Her stomach dropped. He looked down at her, a range of emotions flitting across his face in quick succession.

'Raven. What is this?' he asked quietly. It was a dangerous, low tone. It was the sound of him finally reaching the cliff edge of his almost limitless control.

'It's ...' she swallowed, eyes darting around the room.

The others were looking from her to Archer in confusion.

'I ...' She'd been so *stupid* leaving it in her bag. She hadn't had the courage to look at it, but she also couldn't bring herself to admit that part of her never wanted to reveal it, wanted to destroy it. So she'd just left it in her bag, trying to summon the courage to make a decision. And now it was in Archer's hand for everyone to see. Archer, who was looking at her with such a look of absolute betrayal her heart felt like it was splintering into a thousand tiny slivers.

'The label says it's a flash drive from our parents' investigation into Hyacinth House,' Archer continued in the same low, controlled tone. 'But it couldn't be, because that would mean you've kept it from us, from *me*.'

Raven glanced wildly around the room. Éabha had a hand over her mouth. Davis's lips were set in a grim line, while Fionn stared at his shoelaces, shoulders hunched and uncomfortable. And Cordelia … she couldn't look at her, couldn't see the disgust that must be spreading across her face.

'I couldn't look at it,' she whispered. 'I'm so sorry.'

'So you took that opportunity away from everyone? What if there's important information in here? Something that could protect us? For fuck's sake, Raven!' Archer's voice radiated fury.

Out of the corner of her eye Raven saw Éabha take a step back as though she'd been pushed, one hand reaching for the thick black bracelet she wore at all times now.

'Once again you make the decision that protects *you* without caring how it impacts on anyone else!'

'Archer,' Davis interjected.

'No!' Archer said. His face was rigid with fury. 'She needs to hear this. You're so selfish. You couldn't face what happened, so you just shut yourself off from anything that could remind you of it, even if it was your own family. I lost my father too, but you *left* me, Raven.' His voice caught and he brushed his arm angrily across his eyes. 'And not when you moved out. You left me long before then. We were in the same house, but we might as well have been on different continents.'

Raven stood silently, letting his torrent of words strike her like physical blows.

'All I could do was tiptoe around, trying to keep you and Mum together, because someone had to. I stopped asking questions, sat on it for *years*, all in the hope that maybe we could become a proper family again. When you joined the team, I finally felt hopeful after all that time. I knew you didn't want to go back to the house and I respected that, but the fact that you'd actively try to hide stuff from us ...' He trailed off. 'Why, Raven?' he asked bleakly.

'I was going to show it to you. I was just afraid.'

'That doesn't explain why.'

'Because,' she could feel the words she had been choking back for years rising and she wanted to force them back down. Once they were released, they could never be taken back. 'Because it's my fault he's dead.'

With that, she turned and fled from the room.

CHAPTER THIRTY-SEVEN

ÉABHA SAT IN THE STUNNED SILENCE. She felt like she had been physically pummelled by the force of Archer's anger. Fionn was still staring down at his shoes as though he wanted in sink into the floor, hands shoved into his pockets, trying to make himself as small as possible. Davis was, for once, without anything to say. He seemed to be reeling as much as she was. And Archer ... she looked at him and her heart broke. His anger had receded and he seemed fragile, like a vase that had been dropped and cracked. One touch in the wrong place would shatter him forever.

'I'll go after her,' Cordelia said, standing up from her chair. 'What she did isn't right, but ... I don't think she should be alone right now.'

Davis nodded and Éabha tried to muster up a smile of agreement. Archer's anger had overwhelmed her but, before that, she had felt the violent storm of emotions that engulfed Raven: fear, guilt and shame all mingled into a cocktail of self-hatred.

'Go,' she said quietly.

Cordelia nodded and crossed to the door. She hesitated, turning back to Archer, then bit her lip and firmly turned the handle.

'Archer,' Davis said gently.

Archer looked at him, opened his mouth and shut it again. He shook his head, dropping it forward so that his hair fell over his eyes and hid his expression. Éabha wrapped her hand around her tourmaline bracelet. She didn't want to invade his emotions. He looked back up at the three people still left in the room.

'I need some air,' he said, then walked out the door, his slow, deliberate pace showing just how hard he was trying to keep himself together.

It clicked shut behind him and Fionn finally looked up. 'Well, that was even more awkward than singing "Happy Birthday".'

Éabha and Davis stared at him, then Éabha let out a giggle, before Davis started laughing properly. It was laughter born more of the need to release tension than of humour.

'Should we go after him?' Éabha asked when they had calmed down.

Davis shook his head. 'I think it's better to give him some time to get his head together.'

'This has been a long time coming, I think,' Fionn added.

'Understatement of the century,' Davis muttered. He sat down at the table, the cake abandoned in the middle of it.

'What do you think is on that flash drive?' Fionn asked.

'Nothing pleasant,' Davis said grimly. He hesitated. 'I don't agree with her lying about it, but I can understand why Raven didn't want to look at it. If it includes the investigation from the night Pádraig died … I wouldn't want to hear that either.'

'Were you there?' Éabha asked.

Davis hesitated, then shook his head. 'I was visiting my grandparents in Cork for the weekend. I came back and it felt like the world had fallen apart overnight.'

'Did Raven tell you anything?'

'No. She was in hospital with a concussion when I got back. She said she couldn't remember anything. I don't know if her memory ever came back, but she never talked about it. She just … walled up. Any time someone tried to talk to her about it, she'd snarl and snap at them. She was a completely different person. Eventually, we just gave up. Well, everyone but Archer. But then, first chance she got, she was out of here. She barely even visited on holidays or birthdays.'

'That must have been tough. For everyone,' Éabha said softly.

Davis nodded.

'I know this is the worst time to mention it,' Fionn said, looking at his phone, 'but my mum just texted to remind me that we promised to help mend that fencing today.'

Davis cursed. 'I'd completely forgotten.'

'Go,' Éabha said. 'I'll be here if anyone comes back.'

'Thanks, Éabha. We'll see you later.'

Éabha waved them off, waiting five minutes before slipping the spare keys in her pocket and heading off.

She knew Davis meant well by saying to give Archer his space, but something told her that was part of the problem. All Archer had had was space. It was time someone actually talked with him.

CHAPTER THIRTY-EIGHT

RAVEN FELT PHYSICALLY SICK. As she burst out the front door, she thought she might throw up in the driveway. She staggered away, walking around the corner and sinking onto a low wall, elbows on her knees and head in her hands, trying to take deep breaths. Her mind was racing, thoughts screaming at her so loudly she couldn't focus.

She didn't know how long she had been sitting there when she sensed someone approaching. The click of heels on tarmac raised her hopes, though she couldn't bring herself to look up. The scent of sandalwood washed over her.

'Well, that was eventful,' Cordelia said, her tone light.

Raven snorted, raising her head from her arms. 'You can say that again.' She paused. 'You must think I'm a monster.'

'I think you could have handled it better,' Cordelia said bluntly. 'But I don't think you're a monster. Neither should you.'

'I know how much this means to Archer,' Raven said. 'I've hurt him so much since Dad ... I should have looked out for him.'

'Was anyone looking out for you?' Cordelia asked.

'Archer tried. But ... I wasn't ready.'

'Raven, Archer was thirteen. Did anyone offer you professional help? Trauma counselling? Grief therapy? Your dad *died* in front of you.'

'On a ghost hunt. What counsellor is going to hear that and

think anything other than "she's making things up"?'

'You never know.'

'I do. I had years of it: of being the weird ghost girl in school, of adults in the town giving us pitying looks because they thought our parents were either delusional or scam artists.'

Cordelia sighed. 'That's my point. Raven, you're beating yourself up over letting people down without ever considering that maybe you were let down too. You were trying to protect yourself. Yes, by doing that you hurt other people, but that doesn't make you an intrinsically bad person.'

Raven turned, shifting to face her. She hadn't realised how close Cordelia was sitting to her. Her knee brushed Cordelia's and she left it there, the warmth from that one small point of contact sending a tingle of heat through her whole body.

'I feel like one.'

'Well, you're wrong.'

Raven huffed and Cordelia smirked. 'Sorry, but it's true. You know what I see when I look at you? I see someone who'll face her biggest fear to protect her brother. Who'll turn up at a borderline stranger's apartment at three in the morning because they were asked for help. Who, yes, makes mistakes, but guess what? We all do! That doesn't make you awful. It makes you human.'

'I want to believe that,' Raven said softly.

'Well, let me believe it for you then. Until you can.' Cordelia rested her hand on Raven's knee, leaning towards her until there were only inches between them. Her long lashes framed her dark brown eyes, which flashed with conviction. 'Read my lips, Raven O'Sullivan – you're a good person. And nothing will convince me otherwise.'

Raven's gaze moved down to Cordelia's lips, gleaming with the sheen of their usual red coating, and swallowed. She forced her eyes back to up meet Cordelia's. She was staring at her intently, the heat from her hand burning into Raven's knee, the connection of where their legs brushed together pulsing.

She wanted to kiss her.

She wanted to run away.

The sound of a car door slamming in a driveway to their left made her jump. They sprang apart, Cordelia's hand slipping from her knee, their legs separating. The place where Cordelia's hand had been suddenly felt cold in its absence.

'I have to talk to Archer, don't I?' Raven sighed. She pulled her hair out of its plait, running her fingers through it to separate the strands before she began to re-plait it. 'Do I go tonight? Or give him the evening to cool off?'

'Maybe text him and ask if you can meet tomorrow? That way he knows you're not avoiding the conversation, but you're giving him time to process everything too.'

'How are you so good at this?'

'I've had practice.'

'You've gotten caught hiding potentially vital information pertaining to your father's death from your sibling?' Raven asked with an arched eyebrow.

Cordelia laughed. 'No, but I've gotten drunk and told my friend her boyfriend is a Grade A creep. In front of him. And all our friends. At her birthday party.'

'I'd say that went down well?'

'Extremely. I mean, I was right. But the timing and delivery resulted in much grovelling.'

Raven stood up and smoothed down her jacket. 'I guess I better head back to Dublin if I'm not going to talk to Archer until tomorrow,' she grimaced.

'Would you like to hang out at mine?' Cordelia asked. 'We could get a pizza, watch something that has nothing to do with ghosts or family conflicts …'

'That sounds amazing,' Raven grinned.

She felt a twinge of guilt. She should be sitting in the dark in her apartment, thinking about what she had done. But Cordelia was smiling at her, and she couldn't deal with anything until tomorrow anyway.

She might as well put it off until then. It was what she did best, after all.

CHAPTER THIRTY-NINE

ÉABHA HEADED INTO KILCARRIG down a shortcut along the river that the guys had shown her. The water gurgled past as she mulled over everything she had learned. More than anything, she was worried about Archer. It felt like something had broken inside him.

Rounding a bend, she saw a figure sitting on the riverbank just ahead of her. Archer was staring down at the water, knees to his chest, arms wrapped around them. His cheeks shimmered in the fading sunlight and the edges of his eyes were rimmed in red.

She walked up and sank onto the ground beside him. Gently, she wound her hand under his arm, gripping it tightly, saying nothing. After a moment, he tilted his head onto her shoulder and she rested her cheek against his hair. The ground was damp, the wet slowly soaking through her dress, but she didn't care. She would sit there as long as he needed. They silently watched the water flowing past them.

'I'm sorry for earlier,' he eventually said in a strained voice.

She squeezed his arm. 'You don't have to apologise.'

'That wasn't like me. I'm not … I don't …' he trailed off.

'You're allowed to feel angry, Archer. And frustrated. And all the emotions people tell us aren't nice. You're human.'

'I'm so mad at her. And I'm so scared of losing her. Having her back the last few weeks has been incredible. She's my *sister*.'

'And you're her brother. You know, she's probably thinking the exact same things.'

He snorted. 'I've been here the whole time. She's the one who walked away.'

'A wise person once told me people do strange things when they're afraid.'

He laughed softly at that. 'They sound smart. And handsome.'

'Modest too.'

They sat there companionably for a while. The temperature dropped as the late October sun sank lower in the sky. Archer shivered, then raised his head from Éabha's shoulder and turned to look at her in concern.

'It's freezing. We should get back to the house.'

'I am starting to lose feeling in my butt,' Éabha admitted.

Archer let out a bark of laughter, before getting to his feet and extending a hand to help Éabha up. Her legs were slightly numb and she wobbled, almost losing her balance. Archer looped an arm around her waist to steady her, pulling her close against him. One hand was still in his, the other splayed on his chest from when she stumbled forward. She looked up at him, his eyes soft as they met hers.

'Thank you, Éabhs,' he said in almost a whisper.

'There's nothing to thank me for.'

He smiled, shaking his head. 'You really have no idea how great you are.'

She bit back the joke she wanted to make, an instinctive urge to deflect any compliment she received. Instead, she raised a hand to his cheek, cupping it gently.

'I could tell you the same thing.'

Then, before she could step over a line she wasn't sure she was ready to cross – or even if he wanted her to cross it – she pulled back, taking her hand away from his face, his arm slipping from around her waist.

'Let's go home.'

He smiled at that.

'Let's go home,' he agreed, turning to walk back towards the house. He didn't let go of her hand.

CHAPTER FORTY

RAVEN RAISED HER HAND TO KNOCK on the front door. It opened just before her hand hit it, revealing Éabha standing on the other side, holding her bag and jacket. They both jumped back, startled, then laughed. Well, Éabha did. Raven just about managed to dredge up a smile.

'Archer's inside,' Éabha said.

Raven saw her hesitate, like she was going to say something else, rolling her chunky black crystal bracelet around her wrist. Then she laid a hand on Raven's shoulder and smiled reassuringly. 'It'll be OK. Just talk to him.'

Raven wanted desperately to believe her.

'Thanks. I'll see you later.'

'See you,' Éabha echoed, walking down the driveway to where her aunt's car was waiting.

Raven took a deep breath and walked inside.

Entering her childhood home still felt like walking into unknown territory. The worst part was that she knew she had created that divide. Éabha had told her about a theory that places absorbed emotions, that moments of tragedy or joy could seep into the walls, leaving imprints. It could explain why Éabha was so sensitive to historical sites, and why ghosts often repeated moments of great pain or trauma. They were apparitions playing on a loop.

What emotions would this house have soaked up? She wanted

to believe that the joy of their younger years was there, remnants of happier times preserved in the bricks and mortar. Would that mean that the later years – the ones filled with sadness, guilt, regret, isolation – had left their mark too?

She could hear faint music playing in the kitchen, following it down the hallway, and pushed the door open. Archer was sitting at the table, classical music playing from his phone, cradling a large mug of coffee. He looked as exhausted as she felt.

'Éabha let me in,' she said. She was entitled to have let herself in, but she wanted him to know she hadn't simply barged into his space.

'Do you want a coffee?' he asked, already getting up from the table to go to the kettle.

'Always,' she said, smiling tentatively at him and sitting on one of the kitchen chairs. The awkwardness hanging in the air was painful. It prickled at her skin like cheap wool, making her want to scratch. Archer quietly made her coffee, making a fresh cup for himself too. Him making her a cup felt like a peace offering, but the abrupt way he deposited it on the table in front of her before settling in his chair, waiting for her to speak, showed his hurt.

'I'm sorry,' she began, her fingers clutching the warm mug for strength.

Archer stared back impassively.

'I'm going to explain why I did it, but I need to say that first. So you know I'm not making excuses. It wasn't fair for me to hide the flash drive, and I am so sorry that I did.'

'Why did you?' he asked. The pain in his voice made her throat tighten.

'I was scared,' she said. She had to force the words out. Not just from the shame of letting fear take control of her but because of what would follow. It was time to have the conversation she had been avoiding for five years.

'I don't remember a lot about that night. The memory loss, it's not a lie. But I have dreams. I don't know if they're nightmares or memories, but they're terrifying. And whenever I try to think about the house … I don't know what's real and what's not.'

'Don't you want to find out?' Archer asked, leaning forward.

'I do,' Raven admitted. 'But I also don't.'

Archer's expression was unfathomable.

'I'm scared of what I'll find out,' she whispered. She gazed down into her coffee as though she might find the answer there, unable to meet his eyes. 'I think it's my fault, what happened. What I do remember … I made mistakes. And I'm afraid that Dad paid for them. That that's what the flash drive will show. I was going to look at it, and share it with you, I swear. But I was too afraid, and too much time went by, and then you found it and … I've just made so many mistakes.' Her eyes filled with tears and she swallowed hard. She couldn't look up, couldn't face whatever expression Archer was looking at her with.

His chair scraped back and footsteps moved beside her. She saw him crouching down out of the corner of her eye, his face heartbreakingly concerned. For her, despite everything she had just said.

'Raven,' he said softly. 'We need to look at that flash drive. I'm not just saying that because I want to know what's on it. Because not knowing will hurt you more than whatever you find out.'

She nodded once. She'd tried hiding from it, running from it, but Hyacinth House still managed to creep back into her life. There was no escaping it. Archer stood up again, biting his lip and looking away from her for a moment.

'I just … I wish you'd talked to me.'

She could feel the effort it took for him to say it. Not because, like her, he found it hard to express himself – that had always come easily to Archer. But because, once again, he was prioritising her feelings over his. As he had for the last five years. He didn't want to hurt her, even though she had hurt him more times than she could count.

'You didn't have to go through this alone,' he said.

She'd chosen to, though. And, in doing that, had left him on his own too. They had always crouched in the darkness together, but this time she had abandoned him there, lost in her own grief.

'I know,' she said. 'I wasn't ready to face it. And I'm sorry you had to pay for that too.' She took a deep, steadying breath. 'I am ready now, though. But before we watch the tapes, I'll tell you what I remember.'

He made a noise in the back of his throat. 'I don't want to pressure you.'

She tentatively reached out and took his hand. 'I want to tell you. You should know. I did some really stupid things.' She took a deep breath, squeezing his hand tightly in the hope it would convey how much she meant what she was saying. 'But I don't want to hide things from you any more. Will you listen?'

He smiled, the warm, open smile that lifted her heart higher than it had been in a long time, squeezing her hand back.

'Of course.'

The memories flooded through her as she started to speak. The images came so thick and fast that suddenly she was back there, in her awkward fifteen-year-old body, stepping into Hyacinth House for the first time.

CHAPTER FORTY-ONE

Ireland, 2017

'I THOUGHT IT WOULD BE CREEPIER,' she said, dropping her rucksack at her feet and looking around. The sweeping staircase was brightly lit, and she could see a fire crackling merrily in the lounge. Davis stepped around her, giving her a friendly nudge on the shoulder.

'Just wait until the sun starts to set.'

'I stopped being afraid of the dark when I was about three, Davis,' she retorted.

He'd grown yet again, and towered over her now. Archer did too. Davis pulled off his woolly hat and loped over to the fire in the lounge, holding his hands out to the flames. He had shorn his hair close to his scalp, and constantly complained of feeling cold now.

'Davis, you're supposed to be helping us unload the equipment,' his father, Nicholas, chided. His American accent had developed a hint of an Irish intonation that made Raven smile whenever he spoke. Looking at his watch, he frowned slightly as though the passing of time had set out to displease him personally. 'I have to be at the hospital in ninety-five minutes.'

Davis's father was a paediatrician in Crumlin Children's Hospital, while his mother, Laura, was a surgeon in the Mater Emergency Department. Nicholas had come to Ireland to study medicine, because the student fees in the US were so high. He'd originally planned to move back once he was qualified, but when he met Laura, who was in his class at UL, he changed his plans. Laura and Emily O'Sullivan had been best friends since childhood, and the two families had grown up like one big unit. Davis often spent nights with the O'Sullivans when his parents were on call. It was partially so he wasn't alone and partially because all their parents were extremely aware of the mischief they would get up to if left to their own devices.

Laura came in, carrying a large camera case. She handled the camera's unwieldy bulk with practised ease, her biceps flexing under its weight.

'You can head now if you want,' she said, kissing Nicholas on the cheek. 'We can handle the rest here. Especially once our son starts helping,' she added, pointedly raising her voice. Davis held his hands up and strolled back out of the drawing room.

'I'm coming, I'm coming,' he said good-naturedly.

'I'll take those,' Raven said, pointing at the boxes Nicholas was carrying.

'Thanks, Raven. I'll be over tomorrow evening to help your parents out.' He kissed Laura goodbye and strode back out of the house. They were a striking couple. He was a tall black man, with sharp cheekbones and kind eyes. Laura was the same height as him, pale with light brown hair and dark brown eyes. Her smile was almost a mirror image of Davis's, and both Williams parents had a razor-sharp intelligence and dry wit that Davis had inherited too, though unfortunately that was often directed at Raven.

The first night was fine. She'd been pleading for her parents to start bringing her on their more complicated investigations, and this was her trial run. They'd been invited in by the current owners to see if they could explain some of the things they'd experienced, and the stories they'd heard, after buying the house. They were from America, and had bought the house remotely – a decision they'd quickly regretted. PSI's investigation would help them decide whether to stay or to sell the house.

With Archer at the Gaeltacht, she'd been able to stay instead of being packed off to their grandparents or to stay with Davis's family. This was her chance to really prove herself to her parents, and there was no way she was letting it go.

She set out in the morning to explore the house, bringing her voice recorder, notebook and a torch with her. Her parents had a large pile of research, but she wanted to get her own impressions first, before being influenced by the stories of others. She felt a rush of pride at her own initiative. She'd crack this case and her parents would *finally* allow her to be a full member of the team. She'd still do her Leaving Cert in a few years' time, but what was the point of college? There were no degrees in parapsychology. She'd checked.

The morning passed peacefully. She'd have been despondent, but she knew that this was often how the most exciting investigations went. That statement could also be applied to the most boring of cases too, but she dismissed that thought. She was getting some fresh air in the grounds when she turned to study the house from the outside. Her eyes settled on the tower. It seemed more wreathed in shadow than the rest of the house, even at this early hour of the day. A tingle of excitement fizzed through her veins. *Of course* she needed to investigate the tower. All good ghost stories involved a tower.

She bounded past the lounge, where her father was sitting at a desk surrounded by paperwork. Her mum had gone to interview a woman about the house; Raven hadn't caught the details. Emily would have stopped her from exploring the tower on her own, distracting her with paperwork or checking equipment, but luckily Pádraig had a tendency to become so engrossed in whatever task he was currently undertaking that it was easy to slip by him unnoticed. He'd emerge at three o'clock wondering why he was tired and hungry, only to realise he'd forgotten to have lunch or take a break since breakfast.

Raven walked all the way down a narrow corridor to the right until she reached the deep curve that indicated the wall of the tower. The wooden door was tightly locked. Long gouges on the stone floor showed that the door was old, and worn enough to be pulled open at the hinges. Digging her fingers around the edge and sweating slightly with the exertion, she hauled the door open wide enough for her to slide through. Her top caught on a wooden splinter and she swore softly, examining the tear before looking up, her flashlight bouncing off the walls around her. The door led to a narrow spiral staircase. She started to climb, the air surrounding her heavy and musty. It was probably due to the lack of ventilation, a note she immediately made in her voice recorder, but the way the air weighed on her, like it was pushing her back down the staircase, put her on edge.

She stepped into the high-ceilinged round chamber at the top. There were boxes piled haphazardly to the side, as though they had been discarded in a hurry, and a few items of furniture covered in grey, dusty sheets. She pulled one back, exposing a portrait of a handsome man, a half-smile on his face and soft eyes that gazed out of the painting. She studied it for a moment before turning to pull another sheet away. It fell to the ground and she sneezed loudly as dust rushed up her nose.

She froze. Deep in her gut, a buried instinct was whispering to her that she should make as little noise as possible up here. She shook her head. That wasn't a very scientific reaction. Still, she dutifully noted it down as a 'personal experience'. She'd uncovered a deep burgundy armchair, which had a dark brown stain on it that looked almost like blood. Someone had probably spilled their coffee on it.

It really did look like blood though.

She circled the tower, her stomach growling aggressively as she finished her circuit. It was already one o'clock. Maybe she should take a break, make a sandwich and remind Pádraig to eat one too. She could start going through the files now that she had formed her own impressions. She made a point of noting that she thought the tower would have a key role in it all. It was hunger that drove her to leave the tower, she told herself. It wasn't the feeling of eyes watching her from the shadows.

Still, she took the stairs back down much more quickly than she had ascended them. When she reached the bottom step, relieved to see the light from the hallway shining through the still-open door, a glint to the side of the bottom step caught her eye. Stooping, she picked it up. It was a delicate golden chain holding a locket that was covered in intricate swirls with a small green stone set into it. She slipped it into her pocket to look at it away from the shadows of the tower and slid back through the door, closing it behind her.

She took a couple of steps, paused, then returned to push it firmly, double-checking that it was securely closed. Satisfied, she bounded back down the corridor towards the warmth of the kitchen.

Raven woke that night certain she was not alone. The moon was full, streaming in through the window with enough intensity to soften the edges of the darkness that filled her room. She kept her eyes squeezed shut for a moment, as though that would protect her from whoever – whatever – was in the room with her. It was the logic of a child – *I can't see you, so you can't see me* – and she knew in her heart it would not shield her. Cautiously, she opened her eyes. The moonlight illuminated enough for her to make out the figure standing perfectly still at the foot of her bed: a woman with a long veil hiding her face. Malice radiated from the figure. She knew instinctively that it was entirely directed at her. The air was freezing, and the breath she barely let escape from her mouth clouded in front of her. She shifted involuntarily, in the most minuscule of movements.

The figure twitched.

Never had so small a gesture filled her with such terror. The figure's head tilted ever so slightly. Its fingers flexed, long, pale digits protruding from the ends of elegant sleeves. Raven couldn't move. She wanted to, imagined herself jumping from the bed or screaming for help or any of the things she should do. Instead, she stayed pinned against the headboard by the weight of that gaze, limbs locked, eyes wide and frantic. She had never felt so powerless. All she could do was wait to see what the figure would do next.

It took one step forward.

Raven's throat constricted.

It took another.

Tears formed in her eyes.

It disappeared.

The gasp she took was half sob. Limbs shakily coming to life again, she clicked on her beside lamp before casting a wild look around the room for a weapon. The door hadn't opened. Whoever – whatever – had been in here couldn't have simply evaporated: they – it – had to be in here somewhere. She reached to her bedside table with trembling hands, picking up a heavy book, *An Introduction to Ghosts* by Hans Holzer. Slowly, agonisingly slowly, she leaned to the side to check under her bed. She was terrified of getting out of the bed only to be pulled underneath it, fingernails scrabbling at the floor to try and save herself. Steeling herself to see eyes staring at her from the gloom, grasping hands reaching for her, she looked.

Nothing.

There was only one other place they could be concealed. She studied the wardrobe from the corner of her eye; the door was closed, just as she had left it.

She leapt from the bed in a single bound and dived over to the wardrobe. Clutching the book to her chest like a weapon, she wrenched the door open. Aside from a thick coat and a few chequered shirts she had half-heartedly hung up, it was empty.

Breathing heavily, she sat on her bed, mind racing.

She hadn't heard breathing or footsteps.

The figure had disappeared from the room without opening the only door. They were two storeys up, so it hadn't jumped out of the window, which was locked anyway. The room was empty.

The few files she'd had time to skim through before her mother arrived home and roped her into helping with dinner had talked about a ghost prone to physical, sometimes violent, interactions. Thoughts whirling, she reached for the notebook she kept beside her bed at all times. Dutifully, she noted everything that had happened, all the sensations and temperature changes and anything else she could think to mention, as though she was interviewing a client, not recounting her own experience. Her fingers trembled so badly her usually neat handwriting was a scrawl like a spider scuttling across the page. She didn't sleep again that night, despite the overwhelming exhaustion that overtook her. She didn't tell her parents what had happened, either.

She woke up the next night, choking. Hands grasped her neck. Strong, bony hands that cut off her airway. Thrashing, she clawed with desperate fingers at the iron grip on her throat. The room was cloaked in complete darkness this time, the moon's light shrouded in shadow by the cloudy sky, and she couldn't see her attacker. She tried to scream, to suck in a breath. Terror overwhelmed her. She couldn't think. All she could do was tear at the skeletal fingers around her neck. Just when she thought she would black out, the hands were gone. She fumbled wildly for the lamp beside her bed, pulling the cord with shaking fingers. Light flooded the room.

It was empty, the door shut. She was shaking, her throat aching, and she panted as she drew in long, sweet gulps of air. Air that burned her lungs with cold as she inhaled it.

Part of her wanted to scream for her parents. She wasn't sure if she could produce so much as a whisper, though. Her throat felt crushed. She was exhausted, more tired than even the night before. Huddling back against the headboard, she wrapped her blankets tightly around her and waited for dawn to break.

She dozed off at some point, waking stiff and sore, still pressed against the headboard, her neck aching. For a few precious moments, she managed to convince herself that it had all been a nightmare. One glance in the mirror proved otherwise. She arrived down to breakfast wearing a thick polo neck jumper to hide the bruises already blossoming on her skin, deep purple marks that formed the perfect imprint of fingers. She knew she should tell her parents, but she was afraid of being packed off to the Williamses the moment she did. Not to mention that if they found out about the apparitions, the tower, all the things she had hidden from them, they would never let her investigate with them again.

So she stayed quiet, piled an industrial amount of concealer under her eyes to hide the dark circles, and curled up in an armchair in the corner of the lounge to go through the files yet again, hoping to find some small nugget of information that she could use to figure this all out. Preferably before night fell.

In the end, it was not something supernatural that destroyed her plan to keep things hidden. It was her own clumsiness. She was drinking a cup of tea at the kitchen table when it happened. Emily was at the sink, washing her hands.

'Laura and Nicholas are going to come to do a night session this evening. Do you want to join us?' Emily asked.

Raven's hands shook as she lifted her tea to her mouth, sending boiling liquid down her front. She yelped and her mother stepped over to pull the tea-sodden jumper off her, Raven raising her hands over her head to help.

Emily's cry of shock made her freeze.

'Raven, what happened?' Emily's eyes were wide, her hand over her mouth, as she took in the ring of bruises marking her daughter's neck.

'It's nothing,' Raven said, hastily tugging her jumper back on.

'It absolutely is not nothing,' Emily said firmly, pulling the collar of her jumper to the side again. 'Raven, these look like …'

'Fingerprints,' Pádraig said. They both turned to where he stood, pale and serious, on the threshold of the kitchen. He held a file in his hand, though his fingers were slack and pages were drifting one by one to the floor as he looked at his daughter.

Emily pointed to the kitchen table. 'Sit. Now. We need to talk.'

The conversation still haunted her. That memory had stuck as clearly as though it had happened earlier that day, even though so much of what came next was shrouded in fog. Once she had been discovered, there was no point in trying to hide anything. Underneath Emily's stern interrogation and Pádraig's dismay at her concealment were flashes of fear. When she told them of the attack, even Emily's unflappable composure cracked. They sat in silence as she finished her tale, a silence that stretched so painfully she wished they'd just scream at her instead.

'Why didn't you tell us?' Emily asked.

'Because I didn't want you to send me away,' Raven said, her eyes filling with tears. 'If I failed on the first investigation, you'd never let me try again.'

'Raven,' Pádraig said, reaching out and squeezing her hand. 'Trust and safety are two of the most important things in this business. If you'd told us what happened, we'd have known we could trust you to be honest with us. We can't have secrets on the team. It endangers everyone.'

Hot, burning shame filled her. She couldn't raise her head, couldn't look at them and see their expressions.

'Hiding things from us shows that you're not ready more than being targeted by the spirit does,' Emily said.

'I just wanted to prove myself.'

'We're a team, Raven. Going on a solo run and endangering yourself is not proving yourself.'

'I'm sorry,' she whispered. The tears began to slide down her cheeks and she swallowed hard.

Pádraig shook his head. 'It's not your nature that's in question here, Raven, it's your judgement.'

'Which you've shown an astounding lack of,' Emily interjected.

Raven sank even deeper into her chair, shoulders hunched, hair falling like a curtain in front of her face, wishing the ground would open up and swallow her. Or that the ghostly figure would turn up and throttle her again. It would be less painful.

'We need to assess what to do next. The first step is to get you out of this house. This "Lady" has clearly fixated on you for some reason,' Emily said. 'The rest of us haven't experienced anything of the magnitude that you have.'

'You've experienced things?' Raven asked, raising her head slightly.

Emily sighed. 'Yes. We didn't tell you before because we wanted to see what you experienced on your own. None of the experiences felt overly threatening, and independent correlation is important.'

'We thought you'd inform us of any experiences immediately,' Pádraig added pointedly.

Raven felt a spike of anger. She wasn't allowed to keep secrets from them, but it was fine for them to keep things from her?

She hadn't realised she was speaking out loud until the words had left her mouth. Emily's lips thinned.

'It's quite different and you know it. You deliberately hid important experiences from us, with no intention of sharing them. We didn't want to influence you in a way that could make the experiences seem like the product of suggestion or expectation. We'd have shared ours the moment you confided in us. And had our experiences in any way implied threat to anyone, we'd have told you immediately.' Pádraig's voice was uncharacteristically stern.

'Transparency is key, you know that,' Emily added. '*And* you know that we generally record experiences independently before we share them to see if they correlate.'

'Unless there is a risk to a member of the team,' Pádraig finished.

It was so much easier to go on the attack than to deal with the roiling guilt whispering to her that her parents were correct, that she should apologise. Instead, she hissed, 'That sounds like bullshit to me.'

'Language!' Emily exclaimed.

'We just explained …' Pádraig began, but Raven cut across him.

'Of course, I'm expected to be a team player, but you can keep secrets, no problem. That's completely fair. You dangle the hope of being treated like a proper investigator, but you *always* find some way to exclude me!'

'Because you are a child!' Emily said sharply. 'And the way you're behaving right now only proves that. You're still too impetuous, too irresponsible, to be involved in investigations like these.'

'Or maybe I just have to hide things because I know that if I tell you anything you'll put me back in the sandbox with the other kiddies!' Raven shouted.

'Go and pack your bags,' Emily said icily. 'You're not spending another moment in this house.'

Raven's mouth fell open in horror. 'You can't mean that.'

She looked pleadingly from Emily to Pádraig. Her father looked back with stern eyes, his mouth in a firm line.

'Your mother's right. I'll bring you to the Williams' once you're packed.'

Raven let out a frustrated shriek and went to storm off.

'Raven?' Pádraig began.

She turned, almost daring to hope.

'Be ready before sunset.'

The journey to Davis's house passed in stony silence. Raven sat, one foot on the dashboard, arms folded, her body turned away from Pádraig to look out the window. The relief of being away from the oppressive tension of the house was dampened by frustration. She could have figured this out. They should have let her stay.

You should have told them the truth, a small voice countered. But if she had, no matter what they claimed about 'trust' and 'being part of the team', they would have sent her somewhere else immediately. Pádraig pulled up outside the Williams' house and she got out, stomping to the boot. Her father came to help her with her suitcase and she shot him a fierce glare, yanking the case out by the handle.

'Raven,' Pádraig said.

She turned her back and stormed up the driveway, then half-turned to look at him.

'We're doing this to protect you, you know that, right?'

'Putting someone in a cage isn't protection,' Raven sneered.

Pádraig's gentle expression shifted. 'Recklessness isn't bravery either. We'll check in tomorrow. Stay out of trouble.'

Raven rolled her eyes and turned her back on him again. She knew she was being childish and just making herself look worse. She couldn't stop herself. Davis opened the door as she reached the doorstep, a sardonic smile on his lips.

'Your first advanced investigation is going well then.'

She shot him a withering look and he laughed. After a moment, she laughed too.

'You could say that again.'

'Mum and Dad are both on night shift and I have hot chocolate in the cupboard,' he said, stepping out of the way so that she could come in, hauling her suitcase behind her. 'Just give me a minute to make some and you can fill me in.'

'I can't believe you didn't tell me,' Davis sighed. 'Not even a *text*.'

Raven was curled up in one armchair while he lounged across another, long limbs sprawling out over the edges. Raven hugged her mug of hot chocolate to her chest, searching for comfort in the warmth.

'I didn't want to risk anyone finding out. And you'd tell Archer, and he'd do everything possible to get kicked out of Irish college or something just to get back.'

'I can keep a secret,' Davis said defensively.

'From Archer?' Raven raised an eyebrow.

Davis looked at her, then sighed. 'Fair enough.'

'I didn't want to put you in an awkward position.'

'He's going to be furious when he finds out. Well, Archer's version of furious.'

'Yeah, honestly, that conversation will be worse than the one with my parents.' She had never kept a secret from Archer before. He would either be angry or hurt; she didn't know which was worse. Raven put her mug down and dropped her head into her hands. 'He's going to make me feel *terrible.*'

'So, what's the plan now?' Davis asked, taking a sip of his drink.

Raven picked up her mug again, looking into the depths of the velvety liquid as though she could divine the answers there. 'Give them a day or two to cool off, I guess,' she shrugged. 'The conversation didn't exactly go calmly because –'

'You immediately went on the offensive and stormed out?' Davis grinned.

She threw a cushion at him that he caught easily in one hand.

'Don't get mad at me, I'm not the one who threw a tantrum.'

'It wasn't a tantrum,' Raven said defensively. She cocked her head. 'OK, maybe a small one but, in fairness, they pretended they wouldn't have sent me away the moment I told them what happened, and we all know that's bullshit. It was lose–lose for me, except now they get the moral high ground.' She sipped her drink and then sighed angrily. 'It's so frustrating.'

Davis stayed quiet, waiting for her to continue.

'I just wanted to be properly involved,' she said sadly. The hot chocolate warmed her from the inside and she could feel the exhaustion from the last few sleepless nights loosening her tongue and letting the words she'd been trying to keep in spill out. 'Everyone at school hates me because I'm the weird ghost girl, then at home I don't even get to be fully included. If I'm going to be ostracised for being weird, I should at least get to be a proper weirdo.'

'No one hates you.'

'They don't *like* me either. They think I'm strange. Archer somehow manages to avoid it, because he's good at sports and he's the world's most likeable person but … I just never fit in. And now all my family either are or will be mad at me.'

She watched Davis look at her, his face scrunching up as though he was searching for the right words to say. Archer was the feelings one of the three of them. Though if he was here, he'd be just as angry with Raven as their parents were. Or they'd be in trouble together. A pang reverberated in her heart. She missed her brother.

'*I* like you,' Davis eventually said.

She smiled grimly at him, raising her mug in a salute. 'Right now, I think you're the only one who does.'

Despite how late they stayed up talking, Davis appeared quickly when Raven started screaming in the middle of the night. She was curled up tightly with her back pressed against the wall in the top corner of her bed, knees hugged in tight, when he burst through the door. The relief of seeing him only took a small edge from the hysteria threatening to overwhelm her.

'She was here,' she gasped, staring at him with wide, frantic eyes. 'How was she here? Spirits don't move location.' Her chest rose and fell with short, panicked breaths. Davis slowly stepped towards her, hands out in front of him soothingly as though calming a wild horse.

'You're safe, Raven, it's OK.'

'How was she here?' Raven repeated. She'd never felt so scared. Usually, she strode into the darkness like she owned it. She'd gotten startled or slightly unnerved during investigations before, but she had never felt this uncontrollable, wild terror completely take her over. Davis sat down on the edge of her bed. She was still pressed against the wall, eyes flitting around the room, convinced the figure would reappear behind him.

'It wasn't a nightmare, was it?' he asked, almost hopeful.

Raven shot him a scornful look, looking pointedly at the goosebumps that had sprouted all over his arms. The room was freezing. He held up his hands pacifyingly. 'I had to ask.'

Raven's breathing was slowing now, and her arms began to loosen their grip around her knees. 'What do we do?'

'I think we call your parents.'

It was a sign of how bad things were that Raven didn't object.

They convened in the Williams' house at six o'clock the next morning. Pádraig swept Raven into a big hug and she hugged him back fiercely. When he released her, Emily clasped her shoulder tightly, peering intently into her eyes. She hated herself for it, but she was relieved to have her parents there. They would know what to do.

She'd been frightened during the experiences at Hyacinth House, but in her heart she'd always thought that she could simply leave the house to escape. The Lady appearing in Davis's house had shaken her to her core. What had she done that was so terrible that The Lady felt the need to stalk her to another house? How was that even *possible*?

She tried to hide how exhausted she was, fatigue pulling at every muscle in her body, her thoughts slow as treacle, but it was clear by the concerned way they all hovered near her that she was fooling no one. Emily was trying to stay detached, to see this as just another case. Raven could tell by the way she spoke, all facts and citing research, but her eyes were ringed with purple and her knuckles constantly gripped whatever she held at that moment that little bit too tightly. She had never seen her mother's shoulders this stiff, the skin around her eyes this taut. She was on edge. They all were.

They gathered around the table, cups of tea and coffee in hands, a plate of untouched toast in the centre. Raven talked them through the events of the night before, then Davis gave his account. They mentioned all the usual markers for investigations unprompted: observations on temperature, sounds, everything, and Emily's nod of approval made Raven's heart jump with hope.

'Have you heard of spirits travelling before?' Davis asked her parents.

Emily and Pádraig looked at each other.

'Not verified accounts,' Emily said, her mouth a thin line.

'But we know someone who may be able to advise us,' Pádraig added soothingly. 'She lives just a few towns over, so hopefully she'll meet us immediately. She has a busy schedule.'

'She'll make time for this,' Emily said.

Raven relaxed. Her parents had a plan. Everything was going to be OK.

Emily and Pádraig met their colleague the next day. They came back with serious expressions, though, as promised, they allowed Raven and Davis to join the meeting. They would perform a séance, in an attempt to help the spirit cross over to the other side. It was the least scientific thing that Raven had ever heard her parents say, yet Laura and Nicholas didn't act surprised at all. It seemed this was something they were familiar with. What happened on the investigations she and Archer weren't allowed to take part in? She saw her thoughts mirrored in the furrow of Davis's brow. It was only when Pádraig announced that he would be leading the séance that Laura and Nicholas showed any sign of confusion.

'What about ...' Laura began.

'She's not available,' Emily said. There was an edge to her voice and her eyes flicked over to the couch Davis and Raven were sitting on.

Raven's irritation at this evolved into fury when they told her that she wouldn't be at the séance. She tried logic, then yelling, then pleading, but nothing swayed them.

'It's the first time we're leading a séance ourselves, and this spirit is dangerous and already fixated on you. It's not safe,' Pádraig told her.

'The only reason you're coming back to Hyacinth House at all is that we don't want you to be here on your own,' Emily added. Davis was leaving to visit his grandparents in Cork that day. He'd begged not to go, but his parents insisted. That argument had run parallel to Raven's own.

Eventually she retreated with a baleful glance to get her still-packed suitcase. When they got to Hyacinth House, Emily directed her up to the room she and Pádraig had been staying in. Pádraig, ever the peacemaker, came with her, kissing the top of her head and telling her how impressed he was with her research and evidence gathering. She'd given them her notebooks so that they could see her records of her personal experiences. He tried to placate her with promises of 'in the future' and 'another time'. She glared icily at him in response.

It was the last conversation she'd ever had with him.

CHAPTER FORTY-TWO

RAVEN STOPPED SPEAKING, staring down at the table in front of her, dreading the moment she had to meet Archer's eyes. One scalding tear slid down her cheek, followed by another and another until they flowed freely. The silence peeled her skin from her bones one tiny sliver at a time.

'Raven.' Archer was crouching in front of her again, tears glistening on his cheeks. His voice was gentle.

It was her fault.

She didn't realise she'd said it out loud until he responded.

'Nothing you've said makes me think that this was your fault,' Archer said.

'I … I don't remember what happened next. But I know I didn't stay in the room like they told me to. That's how I got the head injury.'

'That doesn't mean it was your fault.'

'I think the flash drive is going to show that it was,' Raven whispered.

'There's only one way to find out,' Archer said. He paused, exhaling heavily. 'You don't have to watch. I can do it alone.'

He meant it. But then she would be leaving him alone, again.

'No. I need to face this,' she said. She could see his relief in the way his shoulders softened.

'Thank you.'

They went into the living room, taking their coffees with them. It was barely ten o'clock, but the sky was overcast, the gloom spreading into the room with them. Raven turned on as many lamps as possible, trying to drive back the shadows that lingered on the edges of the room. Archer set up his laptop on a coffee table, inserting the flash drive, as Raven took a blanket that was folded over the back of a chair and wrapped it tightly around her, curling up beside him. Archer opened the file, looking at her apprehensively.

'You ready?'

'No,' Raven said, her voice shaking. 'But press play anyway.'

The video showed the ballroom as her parents and the Williamses were setting up for the séance. The sound on the video was the four of them chatting as they placed candles in a circle with practised, familiar movements that made it clear this was something they were all used to.

'Did you have any idea they used to do these?' Raven asked Archer.

He shook his head. 'She's never even mentioned it in her books.'

'You're sure you're ready for this?' Emily's voice came from off camera, low and concerned.

'Absolutely,' Pádraig's voice responded. 'I've been working with –' His voice was muffled briefly by the noise of Nicholas taking some equipment out of a bag. '– it'll be fine, Emily. Don't worry.'

Raven and Archer watched as the séance began. Their parents lit the candles and added a ring of salt around them too.

'Remember, everyone: don't break the circle,' Pádraig said as he closed it.

Raven's nausea intensified. She knew how this would end, but not how it would get to the ending. She barely took in the words they were saying, her eyes glued to the screen. The video flickered, going black, the sound cutting out. Then Emily's voice, high and panicked in a way Raven had never heard before, calling her father's name, came from the speakers. The images returned to show Raven bursting through the door. As she did, one of the candles went flying and the salt circle broke.

Pádraig's hand went to his heart. The Raven on screen stopped, staring behind him at a place the camera image didn't show. The images went black again, the sound of Raven's screams reverberating around the room. The video came back again to show Pádraig crumpling to the ground, as a chandelier fell down onto Raven's head. Someone – or something – knocked the camera over, and the video ended.

Archer and Raven stayed completely still. Archer was as pale as Raven felt, his breathing ragged. Tears filled his eyes as he looked at her.

'It *was* my fault,' she said quietly.

Archer shook his head vehemently. 'He had a heart attack. It looked like it was already happening before you came in. That's what you heard that made you interrupt it. You didn't do this.'

'I broke the circle –'

'He would have died anyway.'

'But her stepson also died from his heart –'

'From the foxglove poisoning, Raven. Look, you can blame the house, blame the ghost, blame the undiagnosed congenital heart disease. But you need to stop blaming yourself.'

'If I had told them about her sooner …'

'Nothing would have changed. It hurts, losing him. It always will. But if anything, this tape proves that you were not to blame. There was clearly so much more going on than we ever knew. I bet we'll find out more in the digital copies of their journals.'

Raven hung her head, silver-blond hair falling in curtains in front of her face. 'I should have talked to them the moment I first saw her.'

Archer leaned over, putting his hand on hers. 'Everyone was keeping something from someone. These records prove that. No more secrets in this family, Raven. Please.'

His voice broke as he spoke. Suddenly she realised just how lonely it must have been, to have been left in the dark about so much for so long. Raven should have been there for him, the way they had always been there for each other. Two kids sitting at the edge of a landing, peering through the banisters.

'Never again, Archer,' she said, wrapping an arm around him and pulling him tightly to her. 'I promise.'

CHAPTER FORTY-THREE

ÉABHA WAS DISTRACTED. Her mind kept wandering during the guided meditation Lizzie led her through; then she couldn't focus on the information Lizzie gave, her pen stopping mid-word, ink smudging on the paper. The first few times, Lizzie said nothing as Éabha flushed guiltily. Lizzie was a busy woman. She didn't have to give up her time to teach her estranged niece about clairvoyancy. But all Éabha could think about was Archer and Raven, the deep wells of pain and loneliness that trapped them both. Something else kept sneaking into her mind too: Archer's hand in hers, his heart beating under her fingertips. Wondering what would have happened if she'd let her lips close the distance between them.

Would he have pulled her closer or pushed her away?

'Éabha.' From the tinge of exasperation in Lizzie's voice, Éabha knew it was not the first time she had said her name.

'Do you need a break?' her aunt asked kindly.

'Yes, please,' she said.

Lizzie got up to make tea and set biscuits out on a plate while Éabha chewed nervously on a fingernail.

'I'm sorry,' she blurted out. 'I do really appreciate that you give your time to me, I don't mean to be distracted.'

'No one can be focused all the time,' Lizzie said, handing her a mug of chamomile tea. She sat opposite her at the table. 'Is there anything you want to talk about?'

She wasn't sure if she was ready to talk about her feelings, whatever they were, for Archer. She didn't know if her relationship with Lizzie was there yet either. In many ways they were still strangers. It was easier to talk about veils between realms and methods of meditation than it was to talk about her emotions.

'Archer found a flash drive with the records from his parents' investigation in Hyacinth House,' she said. It was a half-truth, part of what was on her mind. She didn't mention Raven hiding it. It would be a betrayal to share that part before she knew why she'd done it. Whenever Raven showed a rare sliver of her feelings, she mostly seemed scared.

Lizzie's face was impassive. 'And has he opened them yet?'

'Not yet. He'll probably have looked at some of them by the time I get back.'

'OK,' Lizzie said. She looked out the window, deep in thought.

'Lizzie? Are you OK?' Éabha asked.

Lizzie turned back to her. 'I haven't told you everything.'

Lizzie sat with what Éabha imagined as her 'court face' in place – a composed facade that concealed anything she might be feeling. 'I occasionally worked with Archer's parents, Emily and Pádraig. I mentioned that before. I told you that they interviewed me when they realised my connection to the house.'

Éabha nodded.

Lizzie took a deep breath. 'What I didn't tell you is that they asked for my help with a séance. You see, there are spirits who cling to places they see as their own. They're trapped in that moment, in that emotion. The Lady was in the middle of a fierce battle to keep her home out of the clutches of her stepson.'

Éabha knew that already, of course, but she hadn't exactly told Lizzie that she and the others had gone into the tower to find a Murder Chair.

'When she died, she was frozen in that emotional state. She still sees the house as her own, a place she has to keep others out of.'

Éabha frowned. 'So she doesn't understand what's going on?'

'Partially. The Lady is stuck in a delusion that her home is under attack.'

Éabha's mind raced as she tried to process all of her thoughts. 'So if she was just going to keep attacking anyone she sees as invading her house, what did they plan to do?'

Lizzie looked down sadly. 'They wanted to do what I'd helped them achieve before. Assist her in crossing over.'

'Crossing over?'

'To wherever you go when you die and move on. Your mother would tell you it's Heaven or Hell. I am … undecided.' Lizzie smiled wryly. 'Normally, when we held a séance, I'd communicate with the ghost, explain that they're dead and guide them in crossing over. Emily asked me to help them.' Sorrow spread across her face. 'I refused.'

Éabha waited for her to continue. Questions bubbled in her brain, each fighting for a place at the forefront of the queue. Pepper, Lizzie's cat, jumped into her lap and she petted him as Lizzie took a long sip of her tea. Grief tinged every word she spoke. Éabha didn't usually pick up on Lizzie's emotions – her shield was too strong – but her armour was down today and Éabha had taken off her bracelet for their exercises. Lizzie's regret filled the room, covering them both like a heavy blanket.

'I was scared, to be honest. That house destroyed my family. I knew Pádraig and Emily were giving me a chance to make sure that never happened to anyone else, but I refused. I was too frightened.' She set her jaw. 'I've lived with that decision every day since.'

'It wasn't your fault,' Éabha said gently.

'Pádraig decided to lead the séance instead. They wanted to do it as quickly as possible, because for some reason The Lady had fixated on Raven. He'd never led a séance before. The stress of it aggravated his hidden heart condition, and he died,' said Lizzie, looking away. 'I should have helped them.'

'Then help us now.'

Lizzie turned her head sharply.

'Cordelia has to sell the house. If she doesn't, someone else will. Help us stop the cycle. Teach me how to get The Lady to cross over, so no one else ever has to experience this.'

'It's too dangerous for you,' Lizzie said. 'You're too inexperienced.'

'I have to try.'

'Not alone. I'll help you.'

Éabha's eyes widened. 'Are you sure?'

'I should have done it the first time. It's time to make amends for that.'

Éabha reached across the table, squeezing her aunt's hand. 'Thank you.'

'Don't thank me yet,' Lizzie said. 'This isn't going to be easy.'

CHAPTER FORTY-FOUR

'THAT'S WHAT WE NEED TO DO. Have a séance. Explain to her that she's dead, and that she needs to move on. It isn't her house any more.'

Archer looked around the room, at where the rest of the team were gathered, hoping he had said enough to convince them. Éabha had got back from Lizzie's even paler than usual, but with a steely glint of determination in her eyes that he hadn't seen before. He'd rung around the team and after Raven had persuaded someone to cover her evening shift, Davis had finished class and Fionn had completed his final tasks on the farm, they'd congregated in the living room. They'd been talking for hours, first Éabha explaining what Lizzie had told her, then Archer detailing what they had learned from the flash drive files, Raven pale and red-eyed beside him. He wished it wasn't these circumstances that had caused it, but having her here, feeling like the wall she'd built between them was finally starting to come down, made him feel far more cheerful than he should be, considering the news he was delivering. He pulled his gaze from his sister to Fionn, who had just started to speak.

'We just … have a polite chat? Explain that murdering people who come into your house is not, in fact, OK? This isn't Christmas dinner with my homophobic Aunt Deborah, Archer. This is a ghost that has clung to hatred and violence for decades.' Fionn's voice was sceptical as he stared at Archer, his eyebrows furrowing so hard they almost met in the middle.

'I think we need to consider the repercussions if this doesn't go right,' Davis interjected. 'This is way outside of our usual remit. We have no protocol for this.'

'We don't have a choice,' Archer said.

'We do. We could walk away.'

Davis's words were like a bucket of iced water being dunked over his head. Silence spread over the room.

'Are you serious?' he asked.

'Yes,' Davis said, drawing himself up to his full height.

They were standing in the centre of the living room. Archer could feel himself bristling, while Davis folded his arms, using his extra two inches of height to tower over him. They hadn't had a proper argument in a long time. Even the dispute over Éabha joining the team had ebbed quickly, although that had been mainly due to Éabha herself winning him over more than Davis actually listening to Archer. Davis had a tendency to think that he was always right – in fairness, a lot of the time he was, but not always. Not now.

'Archer, why are we doing this? Really. Because Cordelia already said she'd pay us for our time so far, so it's not to get the cheque. And whatever Éabha managed to do with the energy cleansing has kept The Lady away from Cordelia, so it's not to protect her. So why are we potentially risking our lives to do this?'

'Because it's the right thing to do,' Archer snapped.

'Or is it just the thing you want to do?'

It would have hurt less if he'd punched him.

'Davis,' Raven said, taking a small step forward, her voice filled with warning.

Even her defending him did nothing to alleviate the churning unease gathering in his stomach as Davis continued to speak, holding out a hand to silence Raven.

'No, Raven. He needs to think about this. I get it, Archer. I know you've hated not having answers, I know how hard the last few years were for you.' He refolded his arms and looked Archer straight in the eye. 'But you know what happened now. You can't drag the whole team on a suicide mission because of your own desire for closure.'

Archer heard Éabha take in a sharp breath.

Did Davis really think that? Did everyone else agree? Was he right?

No.

He couldn't be.

'Do you really think I'm that selfish?'

'No, I'm just asking you to consider whether anything could be clouding your judgement before we commit to this.'

'We know the true history of the house. We know the suffering it's brought on people who live there and we know how to stop that happening to anyone else. And I *know* that if I open the newspaper and read about another death in that house when we had a chance to stop it, I couldn't live with that guilt.' The words spilled from his mouth in a passionate rant. He locked his gaze on Davis's as he let the words hang there in the room, let the enormity of what they were attempting to do, what was at stake, sink in.

Davis stared back, a long pause where no one spoke. This was between them.

'OK,' Davis said. He sighed, reaching up to scoop back his hair and tie it into a low bun at the nape of his neck, a mannerism that, ever since they were kids, had signalled he meant business. 'When do we do this?'

'Halloween,' Archer said.

Fionn let out a sigh. Raven looked at Fionn and he shrugged. 'Sorry, it just feels a bit clichéd, doesn't it?'

'Lizzie said the tales about the veil being at its thinnest then are true. It'd be the easiest time to get her to cross over,' Éabha said quietly.

'Doesn't that mean it'll also be when she's at her most powerful?' Davis asked.

'It's a gamble we have to take,' Archer said. He looked around the room, at the team he had gathered, the team he trusted unwaveringly. The team he hoped trusted him too. 'Who's in?'

One by one, they all raised their hands. Éabha's went up first, Davis's last.

'I'll call Cordelia,' Raven said grimly.

CHAPTER FORTY-FIVE

ÉABHA WAS ALONE IN THE OFFICE when the cramping started. The warning signs had been there: the dull ache that had hauled her from sleep long before her alarm, the increasing throb of pain escalating throughout the morning. And now, vicious cramps that made her feel like small creatures were tugging long nails down the inside of her uterus. She let out a whimper as she thought of the prescription-level painkillers she had left in her bedside table at home. In her parents' house, that is. She didn't get to call that 'home' any more. Eventually, she slid out of her chair to the ground, crawling under the desk and rolling into a ball, pressing her fists into her abdomen. She didn't know how long she was down there, focusing intently on not throwing up all over the floor, before the office door opened and two voices came into the room.

'Where is everyone?' Raven asked, confused.

Éabha tried to answer, but all that came out was a mangled whimper. Footsteps were followed by the scent of sandalwood sweeping over her. She opened her eyes to see Cordelia crouched down beside the desk.

'Éabha! What's happened?'

Éabha felt ridiculous. They probably thought she'd been seriously injured. Though she'd broken her leg before and right now she would take that over the clawing agony of her period.

'I'm OK,' she croaked, pushing her hands into the floor and trying to sit up.

'Yes, everything about this situation says you're fine,' Raven said from where she hovered behind Cordelia.

Éabha laughed, then groaned as the movement wrenched her stomach.

'I have cramps and I don't have my painkillers. They're prescription only.'

Raven winced in solidarity, while Cordelia immediately perked up.

'For once, I can actually help one of *you*.' She went to where she'd discarded her coat. 'I also happen to require the strong stuff on a monthly basis and I'm pretty certain I have some here.'

Éabha hauled herself up by the edge of the table and sat heavily back into her desk chair.

Cordelia dug her hand into a deep pocket on the inside of her coat. 'I know they're in here,' she muttered. Letting out a triumphant 'aha', she pulled a foil packet out with a flourish. Caught up around it was a gold chain, the end still descending into the pocket.

'What …' Her eyebrows knitted together in confusion as she unwrapped the chain, pulling on it. An ornate gold locket emerged, a green emerald set in the front. Éabha gasped. Raven blanched.

'Where did you get that?' she asked in a strangled voice.

Cordelia stared at the heavy locket dangling from her fingers, confused. 'I don't … Wait! I found it. In the ballroom, the first day I visited the house. I got so freaked out by everything that I completely forgot about it. I only use this pocket for my painkillers, so I don't lose them.' She stared at the gold locket in her palm, shaking her head. 'I'm so lucky no one knew about it or I'd have gotten in so much trouble for not immediately mentioning it in work.'

'I saw that, in the Murder Chair flashbacks,' Éabha said. 'It's The Lady's.'

Cordelia paled. Raven was still staring at the locket as though it was a snake about to strike.

'Lizzie mentioned something before,' Éabha continued, trying to think around the clawing pain in her gut. 'About objects, and how they can be linked …' She doubled over, clamping her mouth shut in case more than words got expelled from it.

Cordelia pressed the painkillers into her hands. 'Take one, then we'll talk.'

Éabha put one into her mouth, followed by a long gulp of water.

'I hate having a uterus,' she moaned, looking up at Raven, who was still frozen and silent in the centre of the room. She didn't appear to have even heard Éabha speak. 'Raven?' Éabha said gently. 'Are you OK?'

Raven shuddered, but said. 'Yeah, I'm fine, it's just …'

'You've seen it before.'

'You sensed that?'

'Not in a psychic way. Just in a "people don't tend to look at inanimate objects like they're sentient nightmares unless there's a story there" kind of way.'

Raven let out a low, forced laugh. 'I found it at the door to the tower when I was there. I lost it the night … I guess I dropped it.'

'Lizzie said my mother found a locket in the tower. She left it at the foot of the tower stairs when they left,' Éabha mused. The painkillers were already starting to kick in, the ache ebbing just enough that she could begin to form coherent thoughts again.

'Your mum found a locket? That locket?'

'I think so. Could I show this to Lizzie? She'd know for certain.'

'The only place you should bring that is back to the house,' Raven said firmly.

Cordelia looked at her. 'I have to report any objects of value I find.'

'This is about more than your procedure,' Raven snapped.

Cordelia flinched and Raven's stare flickered with a moment of guilt before she drew herself up, arms folded firmly. 'That *thing* is cursed.'

'And you have a scientific protocol to determine that, do you?' Cordelia snapped back.

'Forgive me for actually trying to look out for you,' Raven snarled.

Éabha opened her mouth to interject, only for another wave of cramping – milder than before but still enough to make her double over – to pass through her. The other two kept arguing, their words thudding into her brain as she focused on breathing.

'Listen to me!' she eventually choked out when the pain subsided.

Cordelia and Raven stopped mid-sentence and turned to her, both of them looking sheepish.

'Lizzie mentioned something about objects. How spirits can have strong attachments to them. It must be how The Lady turned up in your apartment.'

Now Cordelia was pale, while understanding flickered across Raven's face.

'Let me bring it to her, see what she has to say. Then you can argue about what to do.'

Chastened, both Cordelia and Raven nodded.

'Éabha, that was almost assertive,' Cordelia said after a moment, grinning at her.

Raven laughed, a genuine laugh this time. The tension ebbed from the room as quickly as it had filled it.

Éabha giggled. 'Let's face it, it's probably a one-off.'

'You should really give yourself more credit.'

She was starting to believe that herself.

CHAPTER FORTY-SIX

LIZZIE PICKED ÉABHA UP ON HER way home from Dublin. They chatted about her day in court on the drive to the house, as though both of them wanted to be in the warm safety of Lizzie's kitchen before they broached the subject.

There was a rawness to Lizzie that Éabha had never felt before. It was as though talking about her own experiences at Hyacinth House and her involvement with Emily and Pádraig had worn away some of the armour that protected her wounds from that time. Everything was shimmering close to the surface.

'I'm sorry I've brought this back into your life,' Éabha said quietly. She was settled at the kitchen island, a mug of herbal tea – another of Lizzie's infusions – in her hands. Lizzie sat down and sighed as Pepper wove between her legs, his tail upright, as though supporting her.

'It's not your fault, Éabha. These things always come back. You can only hide from them for so long.'

'But still, I just –'

'Éabha. I could have said no at any point. I've chosen to face this now,' Lizzie's voice was gentle, but firm. 'You're not responsible for the feelings of everyone around you, even if you can sense them.'

Like the tap of a hammer, these words cracked the layers of obligation and guilt she had carried around with her for so long. She hadn't realised the weight of it until it started to lift.

'Thank you,' she said in a whisper.

'You're welcome,' Lizzie said, squeezing her hand.

Éabha hesitated, not wanting to add more pain to her aunt. But she needed to ask a question that had been formulating in the back of her mind whenever she replayed the events of the times she had been in the house.

'Lizzie?' she said eventually.

Lizzie looked at her enquiringly.

'Can more than one spirit be in a house?'

'Yes,' Lizzie said. 'It's possible. Sometimes stronger spirits use the others to help themselves manifest.'

Éabha's heart sank.

'Why?'

She could see the realisation dawning in Lizzie's eyes, hated that she would have to be the one to voice this. 'When I've been in the house, I've sometimes felt something I can't quite place. Like there's something trying to warn me, to shield me. Or someone,' she paused, then continued softly. 'And the last time I was there, when that happened ... I could have sworn I smelt the faintest hint of peppermint.'

'You think Pádraig could be in the house.' Lizzie's face was white, a sickly sheen spreading over it, devastation in her eyes.

'I don't know for sure. I didn't want to say anything to the team until I'm certain. But I wanted to check if it's possible.'

'It is. And it's likely. Pádraig would have stayed to try to protect people from The Lady, even if it meant her feeding from him. It was his nature.' Lizzie dropped her head into her hands. It was the most vulnerable Éabha had ever seen her aunt. When she raised

314

her head again, agony was etched into her features.

'This is all my fault.'

'You can't keep punishing yourself for this,' Éabha argued. 'He made his own choices. But we can free him, right? If we get The Lady to cross over?'

'We can,' Lizzie said. 'We will.' She took a deep breath, sitting up straight.

'Now, you've something to show me?'

Éabha took the locket out of her pocket where it rested, securely wrapped in a thick piece of cloth. She hadn't wanted to touch it before talking to Lizzie, in case her psychometry powers dug into something before Lizzie had a chance to face it.

Part of her was afraid of what she would sense, too. Her mother had worn it when her relationship with Lizzie began to warp and splinter into fear and disgust. She didn't know if she could handle being immersed in that perspective. Not when she was currently on the receiving end of it herself.

She held the cloth parcel out to Lizzie, who delicately placed it on the marble countertop and carefully unwrapped it. She stared down at the locket, gleaming under the kitchen lights, for a long moment while Éabha held her breath. Part of her didn't want to be right.

'This is it,' Lizzie said. She stared at it sadly. 'It's been over thirty years, but I'd recognise it anywhere. I can feel it.'

'What do we do?'

Lizzie hesitated. 'I'd like to hold on to this for a day or two, if that's OK.'

'I'm sure it'll be grand,' Éabha lied. She could imagine Cordelia having a slightly stronger reaction, but she would come around. Especially now that the theory was pretty much confirmed: The Lady was linked to the locket, and bringing it to other locations helped her gain access to them – and the people in them. 'Is it safe for you to have it?'

Lizzie smiled. 'Of course. I'll use some crystals and herbs, keep it protected.'

'Like I did for Cordelia?' Éabha asked.

Lizzie nodded. 'Exactly. I'll drop you back to Kilcarrig after dinner, then call you in a few days with some updates.'

'Thanks, Lizzie.' She hated how much she'd missed the reliable solidity of an adult. She was eighteen, technically an adult herself. But for a long time she'd felt like she was drowning: it was a relief to have someone say they would take this on for her, even if part of her was ashamed for it.

They chatted easily over dinner, and Lizzie drove her back to the O'Sullivan house later that night. They didn't speak of Pádraig or the locket again, dancing around it as they discussed everything else it was possible to discuss. Before Éabha got out of the car, Lizzie gave her a tight, comforting hug.

'Don't tell the team yet. Give me a chance to think this through,' she said, before giving Éabha a reassuring smile. 'Everything's going to be OK.'

In that moment, Éabha believed her.

The next morning, she was woken by a call from the hospital.

Éabha hovered in the waiting room for hours before she was allowed to see Lizzie. Archer stayed with her the entire time. Any attempt to convince him that he should leave, that she was fine, was met with a steady gaze and a smiling shake of the head. Eventually, the third or fourth time she said it, he crouched in front of the chair she was sitting in, looking at her intently.

'If you tell me you don't want me to stay with you, I'll leave. But if you want me to be here and are just worried about inconveniencing me, I'm not going anywhere. I choose to be here. I want to stay with you.'

She opened her mouth to lie. Then she deflated, shoulders slumping.

'I want you to stay with me,' she said quietly.

He smiled. 'That wasn't so hard, was it?'

He had no idea what it had taken for her to wrench those words from her heart, force them from her throat. Yet, as his comforting solidity settled beside her and he reached out an arm to pull her close to him, she nodded.

When the nurse finally gave her the all-clear to see Lizzie, it took all her self-restraint not to sprint down the corridor. It was family only, so Archer stayed in his hard plastic seat in the waiting room.

'Take your time,' he said. 'I'll be here when you get back.'

She smiled, and he hesitated, as though gauging her reaction, then added, 'If it's what we think it was … can you record the conversation? If Lizzie's OK with it? It could be important.'

She felt a pang of dismay. Had he only stayed in the hope of talking to Lizzie himself? She arranged her face into schooled neutrality and nodded, spinning on her heel to follow the nurse as he led the way to Lizzie's room. The antiseptic smell of the hospital that had seeped into her nostrils all day only got stronger as she moved towards the ward.

'She's weak, so keep it short,' the nurse told her.

She nodded obediently, casting a worried glance at the door.

He smiled reassuringly at her. 'She's doing well, she'll only need to stay a few days.'

'Thank you,' she said, and the nurse hurried away.

She took a deep breath, bracing herself to have her fears confirmed, and pushed the door open. The weak afternoon sunlight streamed through the windows. Lizzie was sitting upright, leaning against a pile of pillows, a hospital gown on. Her hair was dishevelled and her eyes rimmed with purple, but she smiled when she saw Éabha. Hers was the only bed in the room.

'The benefits of private healthcare,' Lizzie said cheerfully, as though she could read Éabha's mind.

Éabha sank into a chair beside the bed. She leaned forward and took Lizzie's hand.

'Are you OK?' she asked. 'The nurse didn't tell me many details.'

'Fractured ribs and a concussion,' Lizzie said, wincing. 'I've had an MRI and should get the results soon. They want to monitor me for a few days, but I'll be fine. I lost some blood too, from a wound in my side, but nothing a blood transfusion couldn't fix.'

Éabha made a mental note to donate a pint as soon as possible as she studied Lizzie, searching for the truths she had omitted or underplayed. Her aunt's breathing was ragged, as though every inhalation caused her pain. Her face was gaunt and lined. She'd aged twenty years overnight. Although she was smiling, there was a haunted look on her face.

'What happened?' Éabha asked in a low voice.

Lizzie's hand slackened in hers. 'I made a mistake. I didn't wait for you.'

Éabha sat back in her chair. 'You said we'd do this together.'

'I didn't want to put you in danger.'

'So you risked yourself? I should never have brought this to you. This is my fault,' Éabha's voice was shrill with guilt. She swallowed hard, trying to shove it down before it clogged her throat and rendered her speechless.

'This isn't your fault,' Lizzie said. 'I ignored everything I said to you – not to do this alone, not to do it when you're emotional. That's on me, and no one else.'

Éabha opened her mouth and closed it again, shaking her head. She peered at Lizzie through the curtain of brown waves that had fallen in front of her face, then pushed it back to look her in the eye.

'I need you to tell me what happened,' she said steadily. A petty part of her wanted to refuse Archer's request, but she wasn't experienced enough to know the important details of Lizzie's story. The recording would help them. 'Can I record it? For the team? Only if it's OK with you.'

'It's fine,' Lizzie sighed. 'Your team should know.'

CHAPTER FORTY-SEVEN

'I MADE THE MOST FUNDAMENTAL mistake someone like us can make. I let my emotions take over. You know how I've been teaching you how to block sensations coming to you without your intent? There are multiple reasons for that. Firstly, of course, is because it was causing you a lot of distress. But secondly, it's because if you're going to do our work, you need to know how to keep your own self protected from what's around you.

'I broke every rule. I saw the locket, and I desperately wanted this to be over before *she* could do any more harm. Even though your mother and I made our own choices in life and maybe this all would have happened anyway, *she* was the catalyst. I didn't take the proper precautions. My emotions were high. And when you're in that state, you're vulnerable. She didn't just appear in the room when I called her. She came into me.'

'Do you mean … she possessed you?' Éabha asked. Her voice croaked as she spoke.

Lizzie nodded, a deep shadow falling over her face. 'It's happened to me twice before, and it never gets easier.'

'What happened?' Éabha imagined the aura of malice that stalked through Hyacinth seeping into her aunt and shuddered.

'It was a contest of wills that I barely won. Her rage brought the bookshelf crashing onto me. When I came to, I was in a pool of my own blood. I barely managed to call an ambulance before

I passed out again.'

'You could've died,' Éabha whispered, aghast.

Lizzie nodded. Éabha wished she had denied it instead. She could feel the panic rising up. What if she came for someone else on the team?

'Can she possess people without our gifts?' she asked urgently.

Lizzie thought, wincing as she did. 'I think it would take too much energy for her to do so. It's easier for her to manifest when she can siphon off someone's energy easily, someone like us. She fed on me when I was there, then when Raven was there it must have been Pádraig. The person she draws from doesn't need to be the person she's targeting.'

'Pádraig was like us?'

'Not as strongly. He had some gifts. I hadn't trained him enough before …'

They were interrupted by the nurse coming into the room.

'I'm sorry, but it's important Lizzie rests. It's best to keep visits short,' he said pleasantly, holding the door open with an expectant look.

'Of course,' Éabha said, clicking off the recorder.

'I just want to give Éabha a list of some things I need,' Lizzie said firmly.

The nurse nodded. 'I'll wait outside to show you back to the waiting room.'

Lizzie reeled off some of the items she needed. 'And please feed Pepper and let him know I'll be home soon,' she added. 'He's very independent, so he'll be fine, but just let him know, for my sake.'

'Of course,' Éabha said.

Lizzie leaned forward with sudden vigour, clutching Éabha's hand with a fierce grip.

'Promise me you won't go near that house until I'm home,' she said, her voice urgent.

Éabha hesitated. The viewings were due to start any day now. It was almost Halloween. Pádraig was trapped there and, besides Lizzie, she was the only one who knew.

'Éabha, I mean it. Don't risk yourself. Promise me.'

Éabha swallowed. 'I promise,' she said.

Lizzie sank back against the pillows with relief.

It was a sign of how unwell she was that she didn't sense the lie in Éabha's words, or the guilt that spilled from her as she left the room.

CHAPTER FORTY-EIGHT

RAVEN STARED AT THE RECORDER like it was a bomb about to explode. Éabha and Archer had just arrived back from the hospital, playing the recording of Lizzie's interview for the others the moment they got home. Davis leaned back in his chair and stretched, his too-casual body language showing just how hard he was trying to appear nonchalant.

Fionn broke the silence with a single expletive.

'My thoughts exactly,' Raven said, turning to look at Archer and Éabha. 'This changes things.'

'What do you mean?' Éabha asked.

'Lizzie was supposed to lead the séance. Without her …' Raven paused, hoping Éabha would fill in the rest so she didn't have to.

Éabha folded her arms. 'We still have me.'

'With all due respect, Éabha, you're very new to this. Do you even know *how* to conduct a séance?'

'I know the basics,' Éabha said. 'And Lizzie has more detailed books in her house.'

'This is not the case to do a test run on.' Raven could feel herself squaring her shoulders, straightening up as though to make herself seem taller. It was what she had always done when she argued with Davis or Archer growing up, once the two of them had shot up like weeds, teasing her constantly about how they towered over her now.

'I don't think we have a choice.' Éabha's voice had a quiet determination in it. It was so different from the tentative way she used to speak, as though she was apologising for having an opinion. Normally Raven would have been happy to see the other girl being more assertive. But really, *this* was the battle she chose?

'There's always a choice,' she said firmly.

The boys were watching them, their heads turning back and forth between them as though they were watching a tennis match.

'Not this time.' Éabha took a deep breath, her eyes sad as she looked away from Raven to Archer, before looking Raven in the eye again. 'There's something else you need to know.'

Raven could feel the tension in the room reach out and wrap itself around her. It was like being wrapped in cling film, a suffocating layer that choked her.

'The Lady isn't the only ghost in that house.' Éabha took another deep inhale, her voice shaking slightly. 'Pádraig is there too.'

Raven's vision narrowed. She could see the others were talking, but the sound was muffled, like her ears had been filled with cotton wool. She stumbled backwards into a chair, her shaking legs giving out underneath her.

Her dad was trapped in that house, with that thing. Had been for five years. Because of her. No, not because of her. Archer said so. But what if Archer was wrong?

Her brain was filled with thousands of buzzing bees, her eyes only able to focus on a spot in the carpet in front of her. Her breath started coming in quick, sharp gasps, her chest tightening.

She was having a panic attack.

'Raven? Raven!' The fear in Archer's voice pulled her out of the pit she was sinking into. He was crouched in front of her, squeezing her hands, looking up at her.

It was her fault. It was all her fault.

She hadn't realised she was saying it out loud until Archer spoke. 'It is *not* your fault.'

Suddenly the hot rage that had so often burned away the guilt and fear over the past few years rose up.

'Why the fuck didn't you notice this?' she stood up, almost knocking Archer back, and glared at Éabha. 'You're clairvoyant. You have *one* job. And you just didn't sense that our father is trapped in a house with that monster?'

Éabha stepped back, as though Raven had slapped her. The stab of guilt Raven felt was quickly engulfed by flames. It was easier to be angry, easier to lash out than face whatever was churning up inside of her.

'I didn't know for sure until now,' Éabha said. 'The Lady, she's so strong, she overpowers everything. Occasionally I'd have a sense that there was someone else there, but it was so sporadic, only right before moments where someone was in danger, that I thought … I thought I was imagining it.' Her eyes filled with tears and her voice started to shake. 'I was told my entire life that the things I see and feel were imaginary. I try not to doubt myself but … it's hard. I'm still learning all this. I'm doing my best, and I know it's not enough. I'm sorry.'

Archer stood up and went to her, laying a comforting hand on her arm. 'Éabha, you're doing more than enough.' He shot Raven an angry look.

She looked away, avoiding Davis and Fionn's faces. She didn't want to see what they were thinking either.

'The point is,' Éabha said, her face in a poised mask again with no sign of the hurt she must be feeling – *because of me*, Raven reminded herself – showing in her voice. 'It's almost Halloween. It's the best time to do the séance, the most likely time for success. Lizzie is in hospital. We need to do this now. So I have to be the one to lead it.'

'And what if we can't stand by and watch you put yourself in danger?' Davis asked in a low voice.

'We'll be there to protect her,' Archer interjected.

He was still hovering close to Éabha protectively. *It must be nice for him to have someone who actually lets him in,* a small bitter voice whispered to Raven.

'How?' Davis demanded, leaning forward in his chair. 'Do you even know how?'

'I'll – we'll – figure it out,' Archer said. 'And if we can't find a safe way to do it, we won't do it.'

Éabha made a small noise of protest in her throat. Archer turned to look at her, a burning gaze that made Raven feel like she was intruding. 'We do not risk a single member of this team. No matter what.'

Éabha nodded slowly. 'We'll find a safe way,' she said, wrenching her gaze away to look at the others. She paused. 'I don't expect any of you to come with me.'

'Of course we're coming with you,' Fionn said, looking startled at her suggestion.

'That goes without saying,' Davis added.

'We're not going to leave Dad,' Raven said in a low voice. 'Or you.'

It was the closest she could come to an apology, the one she already knew she needed to make. Why did she do this every time? She never learned. She'd done it to Archer, pushed him away for years. Then just as she started to mend things, the moment something else came up, the rage took over. Of course they'd all rally around Éabha, the sweet girl with the soft voice and kind eyes. Would they be so quick to stand by her, with her spiky rage and harsh words?

Though they hadn't given up on her yet.

'How do we do this?' Fionn asked.

'I have to pick up some clothes for Lizzie. I promised her I'd feed her cat too,' Éabha said. 'I can grab the books while I'm there.'

'Do you think you should practise or something first?' Davis asked.

Fionn snorted, 'On one of the other ghosts we have hanging around for training purposes?'

Davis glared at him. 'I just meant –'

'It's three days to Halloween, and the viewings start the week after the bank holiday,' Archer said. 'We're running out of time. We have to do this now.'

The others nodded slowly and heavily at Archer's statement, each of them aware of the enormity of their decision. Now that Pádraig was at risk too, it felt like the stakes had just been raised, and Raven couldn't shake the fear that they had a losing hand.

CHAPTER FORTY-NINE

ARCHER DROVE ÉABHA TO LIZZIE'S house after the meeting. He was uncharacteristically quiet on the drive, every part of him tense with a focus she'd never seen before. He was humming with it, a potent mix of determination and anticipation. While Raven had looked scared, Davis and Fionn nervous but resigned, Archer almost seemed excited.

Did he actually care about her, or was it what she could offer? A chance to face down the figure he blamed for everything in his life falling apart?

Éabha didn't want to feel disappointed about that, but she couldn't help it. She didn't think she had imagined the moments between them: the way he would gravitate towards her in a room. How, before she moved in, they'd stay up late messaging about books and TV shows. The way they sang along badly to the radio when they were in the car together, making up their own lyrics when they didn't know the words, laughing as they tried to outdo each other. How he always listened to her as she talked about what she worked on with Lizzie, what she had learned. How he confided in her, too.

Maybe she had read too much into those things, desperate to be seen by someone for who she was.

But he'd held her when she cried, offered her a home when she had none. He was someone she could be silly with, be herself. Around him she could drop the mask she so carefully tried to keep in place. She couldn't believe it was all from self-interest. That wasn't fair on him, who he'd shown himself to be.

She was still afraid though.

'You don't have to come in. You can stay here,' Éabha said quietly when he pulled up. It was the first time one of them had spoken on the twenty-minute drive. She saw him jump at the sound of her voice, jarred out of his reverie, and he turned to her.

'Of course I'll come with you,' he said, adding, 'If you want me to, that is.'

'I'd like that.'

The warmth in his answering smile couldn't be fake. The slow tingles spreading across her body in response definitely weren't.

They went up, Éabha unlocking the door with the keys Lizzie had given her. The first thing they did was go to Lizzie's meditation room. It was chaos. The bookshelf was still on the floor, its contents strewn everywhere. She couldn't look away from the pool of dried blood on the wooden floor. The lingering feeling of malice that she now recognised began to wrap itself around her. She wanted to turn and sprint from the room and never look back.

'I'll help you clean it before she gets home,' Archer said, following her line of sight. Éabha smiled gratefully at him before starting to search through the scattered books and debris on the floor. Eventually she found it, picking up the locket like it was radioactive and dropping it quickly into a pouch stuffed with the same herbs and crystals she had used to protect Cordelia. She tied the string at the top of it tightly.

'I'll go grab her things. Will you go through the office book-shelves for anything that looks useful?' Éabha said, pointing across the hall to Lizzie's study. 'The books in here are the client-friendly ones.'

She bounded out of the room and up the stairs, quickly gathering the items Lizzie had requested for her stay in the hospital. Pepper followed her, meowing and winding himself around her legs. She bent down, stroking him. 'Lizzie's had to go away for a while,' she told him. 'She'll be back soon.' She tried to keep her tone soothing. Pepper looked at her patronisingly, then turned and trotted away.

She returned downstairs, carrying a small leather holdall filled with Lizzie's clothes and went into the study to find the rest of the things on her list. In typical fashion, Lizzie had requested several work files so that she could continue to work on cases. Éabha was pretty sure people with head injuries shouldn't overly tax their brains, but she would let the nurses argue that point with Lizzie.

And hope they didn't find out who had brought her the work.

Archer was in the study, surveying the bookshelves, a small pile of books already beside him.

'It's such a contrast,' he laughed, as he turned to her and waved his arm at the bookshelves. One set was filled with large, intimidating legal tomes, books on feminism and documents from different organisations like Women's Aid and Free Safe Legal. The bookshelf beside it was crammed with volumes on all aspects of spirituality: meditation, reiki, crystals, tarot, mediumship, clairvoyancy, herbs, a whole host of topics that Éabha had barely begun to explore. A spike of fear jabbed through her. If Lizzie, with all her experience, had ended up in hospital, how could she do this?

Though Lizzie had said herself that she'd made mistakes. Told her what they were so that Éabha could learn from them.

And Éabha would not let Lizzie endanger herself again.

She stood beside Archer, allowing herself the comfort of standing that little bit closer to him under the guise of examining the bookshelves. A band of heat she knew was energy crackled between them. She wondered if he felt it too. He leaned across her, plucking a book from the shelf and turned to her.

'Do you think this looks good?'

He was close, so much in her space that part of her wanted to step away. His proximity was overwhelming, the good kind that made her want to lose herself in it. The warmth from his body. The smell of his shampoo. How, when he tilted his head to look at her, like now, his eyes were such a rich brown she felt she was melting into them. She tore her gaze away from his and looked at the book he was angling towards her.

'Yeah, that looks great.' Her voice caught slightly. She could see the smile hiding in the corners of his lips and took the book from him in a brisk movement, trying to break the tension. Her fingertips brushed his and static jolted through her. She yanked her hand away, the book coming with her, almost flying out of her hand. Stepping back, she placed it on the desk with the other books and flicked through them, just to keep some space between them for long enough for her treacherous heart to stop pounding.

'It looks like there's some good material here.' Her voice was steady, to her relief. She cocked her head thoughtfully. 'I'll take more of the protective herbs and crystals she gave me before. I can repay her afterwards.'

'That's a good idea,' Archer said.

He continued to scan the bookshelf, exuding calmness. A little too much of it. She was consciously trying to close herself to other people's energy, so she couldn't quite sense what he was feeling.

She didn't know if she wanted to or not.

CHAPTER FIFTY

IT TOOK THEM A LITTLE OVER half an hour to gather everything they needed for both the séance prep and Lizzie's hospital
stay. Despite still reeling from Éabha's latest revelation about his
father, Archer hadn't been able to help getting distracted by a long
metal cone balanced on a wooden block on top of the bookshelf.
When Éabha explained it was a spirit trumpet, an old tool used
by mediums and spiritualists in the Victorian era, ostensibly to
amplify spirit voices, he'd doubled over laughing and had taken
a while to calm down enough to resume their search. Every
now and then, he'd murmured 'spirit trumpet' to himself and
chuckled, Éabha looking over at him with a half-exasperated, half-
affectionate smile.

At least he'd hoped it was affectionate.

He'd given in to the temptation to flirt with her earlier, but
when she'd stepped away, he hadn't continued. He didn't want
to pressure her. He hoped the flush that rose in her cheeks when
he teased her was the good kind of flustered, but until he had a
clear sign that she liked him that way, he didn't want to overstep.
Besides, cleaning the blood from the wooden floor in Lizzie's
study hadn't exactly been an appropriate flirting opportunity,
though it had been mercifully easy enough to remove. After
feeding Pepper, promising him they would be back to check on
him tomorrow and receiving a condescending look as though to

say he did not require their assistance, they made their way back to the car, laden down with books and supplies.

Archer hung back as Éabha gave Lizzie's bag to a nurse. She looked relieved when she was told visiting hours were over. When they got back to the car, she settled into the passenger seat and sighed, the deep, weary sigh of someone who was exhausted but still had much to do.

'Time to hit the books, I guess,' she said.

'Davis texted to say they've ordered Thai,' Archer said, looking at his phone. 'We can sort through the books as we eat.'

Éabha's stomach rumbled. 'That sounds amazing,' she said earnestly, leaning back against the headrest and closing her eyes for a moment.

Archer couldn't help letting his eyes linger on her, at how her lips – always coated in a subtle pink – curved up, her long, loose curls falling back from her face. She opened her eyes and caught him staring.

'What?' she asked, raising an eyebrow.

Archer hesitated, then shook his head. 'Nothing.'

'In that case, can we go, please? I'm starving.'

'You're very demanding when you're hungry, you know,' Archer teased.

She shot him a mock-earnest glance. 'I just take my snacks seriously.'

'I've always thought you had excellent priorities.'

'It's one of my best qualities.'

He couldn't hold back a low, soft laugh. 'I can think of a few more.'

Something flashed in her eyes, her lips parting as though she was going to speak. She hesitated, then laughed too. 'Well, you're a generous person.'

He would give anything to know what she had been going to say.

'One day you'll see how amazing you are, Éabha McLoughlin. And if you don't, I'll show you.'

He heard her breath catch, and his heart jumped. Before she could think of a response, he turned the key in the ignition and drove out of the hospital car park. 'Let's get you home. I wouldn't want to stand between you and food.'

She laughed, leaning forward to turn on the radio.

'Onward to the snacks please, kind sir.'

'Of course, m'lady,' Archer said, tipping an imaginary hat at her. Music filled the car as they drove, and Archer couldn't help but notice the smile that lit her face most of the way home.

CHAPTER FIFTY-ONE

THEY SPENT THE NEXT THREE DAYS sprawled on the floor of the living room, abandoning the office which had quickly become cramped and uncomfortable with the six of them crammed into it as they pored over books, making notes. Raven had called in sick at work, feigning tonsillitis, and as she'd never taken a sick day or been pinged as a close contact even at the height of the pandemic, and had actively volunteered to work most holidays and weekends (to have an excuse not to visit home), they didn't doubt her.

Davis had set up the whiteboard in the centre of the room on the first day, Fionn teasing him mercilessly as he wrote an agenda and list of discussion points down the side until Davis threw a marker at him, Archer bellowing with laughter. Raven ignored their antics as she sat cross-legged on the floor, leaning against the edge of the couch. Cordelia had come down every day too, taking a sick day from work on Friday and claiming a couch where she lay on her stomach, flipping through books and occasionally leaning down to show Raven some passage she had found. Cordelia always checked with her before raising something with the rest of the group. It was strange seeing her uncertain.

'OK, so far I have: we should or shouldn't do it at night, we should hold hands for the duration, we don't need to hold hands, and a list of about eight different ways someone can end up possessed,' Cordelia said, frowning at the piece of paper she had scribbled on.

'Well, at least it's clear and concise,' Fionn replied absently, turning the page of the book in front of him.

Davis snorted, leaning back in his armchair and stretching his arms over his head, his long legs extended out in front of him.

'A lot of these have an emphasis on prayers, specifically Christian ones,' Raven mused.

'I wonder what my mother would say if she heard that,' Éabha said quietly from where she was curled in an armchair. She was almost speaking to herself.

'Is your mum very religious?' Cordelia asked.

Raven saw Archer stiffen slightly, looking at Éabha protectively out of the corner of his eye. The corner of Éabha's mouth rose up.

'"Very" would be an understatement.'

'Herbs-wise, these websites have some good suggestions. Except for the ones that keep saying white sage,' Archer cut in.

'Yeah, let's keep the cultural appropriation to a minimum for this,' Davis said.

Cordelia raised an eyebrow at him. 'I thought sage was super popular?'

'It is, but it's sacred to several Native American cultures,' Fionn said. 'Apparently, now that it's become popular among mainstream wellness and spiritual cultures, corporate brands have been buying it in such high quantities that it's often hard for indigenous people to get it for their sacred rituals.'

Cordelia pulled a face. 'OK, agreed, no white sage.'

'Cedar is a good alternative,' Éabha offered. 'It's traditionally been used in Europe for centuries. Also, I took a bunch from Lizzie's house.'

'Always one step ahead,' Davis said approvingly.

Raven noted how Éabha smiled at Davis, her face lighting up. She was still so thrilled over even the smallest praise. Sometimes Raven thought she could feel the doubt radiating from her. Of course, she hadn't helped with that, even if Éabha had been very gracious when Raven awkwardly apologised for losing her temper.

The others kept chatting, but Raven tuned them all out and turned back to the book in her lap. Having a task was helpful. It stopped her from worrying too much about what they were trying to do. The familiar smell of sandalwood floated around her as Cordelia leaned over her shoulder, her breath soft against her ear and neck.

Suddenly she couldn't concentrate for an entirely different reason.

'You haven't eaten today,' Cordelia said softly.

'I'm not overly hungry,' Raven murmured back. It was true. Her stomach was knotted so tightly that even the thought of food made acid start to rise in her throat.

'You need your strength. Even just a piece of toast,' Cordelia said.

'Maybe in a little while.'

'You won't be able to concentrate if you haven't eaten.'

'I said I'm fine.' She heard the snap in her voice and winced internally, turning her head to see Cordelia flinch at her tone.

'OK.' Cordelia moved away again, looking down at the book in front of her, her shiny back hair falling across her face like a wall between them.

'Cordelia, I –'

'Raven, what do you think?' Davis called over, gesturing at the whiteboard beside him, oblivious to the tension.

She could have sworn she saw Éabha shoot him a disapproving look. The girl missed nothing. Raven got to her feet and walked over to study the whiteboard, where Davis had started to write his agenda for the séance, or the 'Ghost Intervention' as Fionn had nicknamed it. Even though Cordelia's attention seemed to be on the book in front of her, Raven could feel the weight of her stare burning into her back.

At nine that night, they finally had their plan meticulously laid out on Davis's whiteboard in neat handwriting. It was Halloween the next day and Cordelia had got a call confirming that the estate agency team setting up the house for viewings would be starting that week. They were out of time. It was now or never.

Raven was putting some mugs in the dishwasher when Cordelia stepped into the kitchen, balancing a pile of plates expertly in her arms.

'The perks of being a child of restaurateurs,' she smiled tentatively as she took in Raven's arched eyebrows at the crockery stacked high in her grip.

'Impressive,' Raven said. She paused, then took a deep breath. 'I'm sorry. For snapping earlier. You were just looking out for me.'

'It's OK. I shouldn't have pushed.' Cordelia paused, setting the plates onto the countertop and turning to Raven. 'I just … I see how much this is affecting you and I'm sorry. For bringing this back into your life.'

Raven felt like she'd been punched in the stomach.

Guilt. That was why Cordelia cared so much. Not ... not what she had hoped for.

'We're professionals. It's our job,' she said, starting to place plates into the dishwasher, turning her back so that Cordelia couldn't see the disappointment in her face.

'But you only came back because –'

'I would've come back anyway,' Raven said. It didn't feel like a lie either. Cordelia had been the catalyst but, in truth, part of her had been longing to mend the broken bridge between her and Archer for a long time. She just hadn't been brave enough to do it without a push. 'It had nothing to do with you.'

She heard the harshness of the words, but couldn't bring herself to soften them.

'OK then,' Cordelia said, her voice hard. 'Good to know.'

She turned and strode from the room. Raven stood frozen by the dishwasher, a plate in her hands, her knuckles white as she gripped it.

So foolish of her to think there was any other reason Cordelia spent so much time with her. It wasn't fair of her to lash out, though. It wasn't Cordelia she was truly mad at: it was herself. For thinking anyone could see what a tangled mess she was and still want to be with her.

CHAPTER FIFTY-TWO

ÉABHA COULDN'T SLEEP. She knew she needed to be well rested, but she kept going over the plan in her head, worrying about the next day. Archer had made it clear that this was a team effort, which was comforting, but she still had to lead it. She was the one who'd be at fault if it all went horribly wrong. The sounds of the recording Archer had played for her echoed in her mind: screams, desperate heart-wrenching screams she barely recognised as Raven's voice as she watched her father slump to the ground. Any time she closed her eyes, she saw Lizzie in her hospital bed, asking her to promise she wouldn't do anything dangerous, and guilt made her snap them back open.

At about two o'clock she got out of bed and slipped down to the kitchen. She hoped one of Lizzie's soothing infusions of lavender, chamomile and peppermint might lull her to sleep. She stopped on the threshold. Archer was sitting at the kitchen table, silhouetted by the flickering light from three candles he'd lit, a pink hoodie on over his pyjama bottoms, hair dishevelled, hands cupped around a mug on the table in front of him. A song by Ludovico Einaudi that she recognised from him playing it constantly in the office was coming softly from his phone. He looked up, startled, then relaxed when he saw Éabha in the doorway.

'Sorry to intrude. I just wanted to make some tea.'

'You're grand,' he said.

She crossed over to flick the kettle on before turning back to look at him. She was painfully aware of her cartoon llama pyjamas, her creased dressing gown and frazzled hair from tossing and turning.

'Can't sleep either?'

He shook his head. 'I know I should rest, but I can't switch my brain off. I remembered Lizzie's tea and thought I might as well try that.'

'Great minds,' she laughed, toasting him with the empty mug she had just taken out of the cupboard. She'd thought it was a plain white one, but when she turned it she saw the *Ghostbusters* logo on it. She let out a delighted laugh.

'Raven gave that to me for my twelfth birthday,' Archer said fondly. 'It's my favourite mug.'

'Is it OK if I –'

'Of course.'

She leaned against the countertop, waiting for him to speak. The world outside the window was thick with darkness. It felt like secrets, like midnight confessions and quiet confidences. The kettle hissed beside her, building steam, and she was relieved she had automatically put her hearing aids in when she got up.

'I'm worried I'm asking too much of you. Of the team,' he said quietly, staring down at his mug. He looked younger, his face a mirror of how vulnerable he had looked that day by the river.

'It's not anything we're not willing to do.'

'But would you be doing it if I hadn't asked you to?'

'You're not giving us much credit here, Archer. We're all capable

342

of making up our own minds. And it's not like we won't call you out if we don't agree with you – look at the conversation you had with Davis the other day. We can walk away at any time. We're choosing to go with you.'

'Why?' He looked at her, eyes bleak. 'Why do you trust me? Don't you think it's selfish of me to ask you to risk yourself against a murderous ghost just to free my father?' He gave a sardonic chuckle. 'I sound ridiculous just saying that.'

'You're talking to the person who grew up having visions,' Éabha said. She put her hands on the edge of the countertop and pushed, hopping up to sit on the edge. 'You're not ridiculous. And you're not selfish.'

'How do you know?'

'Because a selfish person wouldn't worry about being selfish.'

'OK, Miss I-Have-an-Answer-for-Everything, how do you know that I'm not just asking you this to make you reassure me I'm not being selfish so that you don't think I am?' he asked, a small smile tugging at the corner of his lips.

She gaped at him. 'That makes no sense.'

'Not a lot does right now.'

'You do,' Éabha said, before she could stop herself. 'When I'm around you I feel … safe.'

The darkness made her bold. It was as though any words uttered during the night would stay there, safely hidden in the shadows. She swung her legs and cocked her head thoughtfully. 'I don't know why, but ever since I met you, I've known I could trust you.'

Archer was looking at her, his expression unreadable. The kettle had long since stopped boiling, but she didn't want to break the flow of conversation by making the tea. It felt like they were dancing, one of those old-fashioned ones from the period films her mum loved, where the dancers' hands hovered a hair's breadth from their partner's as they circled each other.

She wanted to find where this led. She was terrified to.

Archer got up from the table, coming over to her. He stopped in front of where she sat on the counter, a smile curving his lips. His fair hair gleamed in the glow from the candles and his face was all shadows and light.

'So that's what you're thinking when I catch you looking at me? How trustworthy I am?'

She blushed and tilted her chin defiantly, meeting his eyes.

'If you see me looking, doesn't that mean you're looking at me too?'

'Fair point.'

He was close now, so close that with anyone else she'd be leaning back to escape their invasion of her space. With him, it didn't feel close enough. Her knees rested on either side of his hips, his body hovering just inches from hers. It felt like a dream, the ones she woke up from hoping there was no way he could ever read her mind.

'So,' she said, nervously biting her lower lip. 'What are you thinking about when you're looking at me?'

He leaned in, his lips beside her ear, his warm breath making her shiver as he whispered, 'It's a secret.'

The darkness had unleashed something in them both. She'd never seen him like this. This, in the depths of night, with hearts pounding and lips close to skin, felt dangerous, as though they were teetering on a cliff's edge and if they plunged off it there would be no climbing back.

She wanted to fall.

'I'm good at keeping secrets,' she murmured.

He looked at her, his eyes drifting to her lips and back to her eyes. He swallowed hard.

'I'll tell you mine if you tell me yours.'

It was an invitation and a challenge. Behind the teasing tone his eyes shimmered with something else – a nervousness and a yearning that made her hopeful, truly hopeful that what she felt was not one-sided. She was tired of holding herself back, of being afraid to tell people who she was and what she wanted.

'I'm thinking about how much I want to kiss you.'

The words hung in the air between them.

Silence.

A heartbeat, then two, enough for fear to douse her like ice-cold water, make her want to shovel the words back into her mouth and flee, leaving the whole conversation in the darkness.

Then his lips were on hers and she couldn't think, icy fear driven away by flames. She wrapped her arms around his neck and he pulled her closer, holding her waist and kissing her with a fierceness that took her breath away. She opened her mouth, curling her fingers into his hair as his tongue softly teased hers. When he gently bit her bottom lip she gave a low moan, wrapping her legs around his waist to pull him closer. The two of them pressed tightly together as though any space between them was unbearable.

'Oh, sorry!'

They sprang apart, breathing heavily.

Davis stood in the doorway, wearing an expression that was half-amusement, half-contrition.

'Can't anyone in this house sleep tonight?' Archer asked, exasperated.

'I think I heard Fionn snoring in the guest room,' Davis offered.

'That's good.'

Éabha steadied her breath. Archer stepped back from the counter and part of her felt bereft at the sudden distance between them. Was he embarrassed Davis had caught them? Had he hoped to keep this – her – a secret?

'I should try to get some sleep,' she said, jumping off the edge of the counter. 'Good night.'

Archer opened his mouth as though to say something, then looked at Davis, his expression impenetrable. 'Night, Éabhs.'

'Sweet dreams,' Davis said, winking. He pressed his lips together tightly like he was trying holding back a laugh, but it didn't feel malicious.

It was only when she got into bed that she remembered she'd never made her tea. She wrapped her blankets around her, replaying the scene in the kitchen in her mind.

She fell asleep with the ghost of Archer's lips on hers.

CHAPTER FIFTY-THREE

IT WAS LATE AFTERNOON BEFORE Raven and Cordelia left Dublin for the séance, driving down roads starting to brim with eager trick-or-treaters in extravagant costumes, the sound of fireworks already filling the sky though it wasn't even dark yet. Cordelia had had to run an open viewing and Fionn had had work that day, so it was almost evening before they could gather.

Now Raven and Cordelia sat in the car outside the gates to Hyacinth House, waiting for the others to arrive. By unspoken agreement, they had not entered the driveway. The sun was starting to set, though the light had faded from the estate long before then anyway. Everything here looked as though the colour had been drained out of the surroundings. The leaves were less orange, the ivy a dull green instead of a vivid, vibrant sign of life. Raven sighed, propping one foot up on the dashboard, staring at the house.

It always led back here, didn't it? She'd been hiding from the past for so long and then, the moment she thought she was safe, it sucked her back in.

She'd once seen a sign on how to react if you were caught in a rip tide. It was on a surfing beach in Mayo, and she had memorised the infographic with its stick-figure illustrations, despite having no desire to get into the sea. She was very much a land creature. The instructions said not to fight against the water, as that would tire you out. To go with it, then try to swim parallel to the shore.

Hyacinth House had sucked her into its current. It was time to surrender to it.

'I'm sorry,' Cordelia said quietly. She had been uncharacteristically subdued on the drive down, which Raven had assumed was just nerves.

'For what?' Raven shifted to look at her.

Cordelia stared straight ahead at the house.

'For pulling you back into all of this. I didn't know what I would be opening up when I asked Archer to get involved. I didn't think it was real.'

Her eyes, like melted chocolate, met Raven's. Shadows fell across her face from the setting sun.

She'd never looked more beautiful.

'But it is, and I've dragged you into it, and I feel terrible. And it's selfish, but I know you'll never want to see me again after tonight, and I hate the thought of not getting to be around you any more.'

'Cordelia,' Raven interrupted her gently. Her heart was thudding in her chest, a painful, hopeful rhythm. She took her foot off the dashboard, shifting to face Cordelia so that there were only inches between them. It felt like a chasm. 'No matter what happens tonight, I want you to keep being a part of my life.' She laughed awkwardly, suddenly aware of how dramatic that sounded. 'I just mean … I'm glad I know you now.'

She didn't know who had moved, but the gap between them was now so small she could feel Cordelia's breath mingling with hers, their lips hovering so close together that they almost, achingly almost, touched. Cordelia's perfume engulfed her. This was another rip tide, one she wanted to surrender to no matter where it carried her.

'Can I kiss you?' she whispered, her heart thudding.

'Please,' Cordelia breathed, closing the infinitesimal space between them.

Cordelia's lips met hers and Raven was drowning. The dread that Hyacinth House exuded was washed away as she was swept into the moment. She pulled closer, her hands tangled in Cordelia's hair, Cordelia's arms wrapping around her torso, holding her tightly. If this was drowning, she would embrace it willingly.

The beep of a car horn made them pull apart. A cherry-red car sat behind them, with Archer, Davis, Fionn and Éabha in it.

'Really?' groaned Raven. 'Now he's on time?'

Cordelia laughed, a throaty sound that made Raven want to press her lips to Cordelia's again. She rested her forehead against Cordelia's, taking a few steadying breaths, then sat back into her seat. Cordelia turned the engine on.

'Ready?'

'Absolutely not. But drive on.'

'Clearly there's something in the air today,' Fionn said as they saw Cordelia and Raven spring apart in the car in front of them. Archer had already beeped the horn before he'd realised what they were interrupting. He glanced at Éabha in the rear-view mirror, trying not to smile at the pink hue that flushed her cheeks.

The boys had teased her and Archer all morning, as though they were fourteen-year-olds after a house party. She'd taken it good-naturedly, and Archer had made a point of pulling her aside before they left the house.

'About last night,' he'd said, starting to raise his hand to his hair then stopping himself. It was a constant habit, especially when he was nervous.

Her face had been completely impassive, and for a moment his heart had sunk, afraid that in the morning light she'd changed her mind about how she felt. He'd ploughed on anyway. He needed to actually say how he felt for once.

'I know it probably wasn't the best timing. But I want you to know how happy it made me.'

She'd stared at him a long moment, her lips slightly parted. He'd felt himself shifting awkwardly, his whole body tense, waiting for her response. For her to turn away. Instead she'd wrapped her arms around his neck and pressed her lips to his, as if she was trying to convey everything she felt in that kiss. He hoped the enthusiasm he'd kissed her back with showed he had understood.

Davis snorted, smiling slyly at Éabha.

'Nothing like the prospect of a séance with a murderous ghost to get everyone declaring their love for each other.'

'I love all of you,' Fionn said solemnly. 'But I have no desire to kiss any of you.'

'I'll try to contain myself then.'

'Lads, focus,' Archer said, hearing his exasperation echoed in his voice. 'Can we at least pretend to be professionals?'

Davis saluted. 'Sure thing, Boss. In fairness, this is a first for all of us.'

'Which is why we need to focus.'

'Archer. I promise you, we're taking this seriously.'

'I could quietly whimper instead if you prefer?' Fionn said helpfully. 'Because that's the other option.'

'Stick to the terrible jokes then,' Archer said, attempting to smile.

They fell silent as they followed Cordelia up the drive. The stone walls of Hyacinth House towered over them, dark and forbidding. The old house seemed to cast shadows that were longer than before. Logic would say it was the time of day, the time of year, a sign of the imminent onslaught of winter, but it was hard not to read more into it.

Did The Lady know why they were here?

What would she do about it?

Was he putting his team – his friends – in danger?

Fionn popped the boot and he, Davis, Raven and Cordelia began ferrying things up the stone steps. The easy banter that usually passed between them all was stifled by the looming presence of the house. Éabha took a step to go and help them, but Archer gently took her arm to hold her back.

'Are you sure you want to do this?' he asked, voice low.

'Of course,' Éabha said, raising her eyebrows in surprise.

'No one would judge you if you decided not to.' He needed to know he'd given her every opportunity to turn away. He needed to know it was her choice.

'Archer, I want to do this. There's been enough pain in this house. I want to help stop it.'

He shook his head, looking at her admiringly. 'You really are something, Éabha McLoughlin.'

'I hope it's a good something.'

'It is.' He wrapped his arms around her, pulling her in close, and after a moment she wove her arms around his waist, burying her head in his chest. He could feel her taking a few deep, slow breaths. She looked up at him and he smiled down at her before placing a gentle kiss on her forehead.

'Let's go talk to a ghost.'

CHAPTER FIFTY-FOUR

THEY MOVED SILENTLY THROUGH the long, gloomy halls, strewn with shadows. The staircase creaked under their feet and Éabha winced at every small sound. It was impossible to move in Hyacinth House without alerting the presence in there. The Lady had sunk her essence into the foundations, permeated the bricks. The walls, the floor, the tiny particles of dust that rose up as they crept quietly down the corridors, they were all infected with The Lady's presence. It was a house, but it was *her* too, an organism that they moved through, triggering an alert like the vibrations of a fly landing on a spider's web.

'This feels like the bit in a horror film where I would yell at the characters for being idiots,' Davis murmured.

Cordelia gave a high-pitched, nervous giggle, completely at odds with her usual throaty laugh.

'"Let's investigate ghosts," they said. "It'll be fun," they said,' Fionn muttered under his breath as they went into the bedroom beside the tower. He was carrying a camera and tripod, a bag filled with extra batteries and power packs slung over his back. 'Kinda makes you wish we were off trick-or-treating or something, right?' he asked, winking at Éabha when she looked over at him.

She smiled tightly back. Davis and Fionn were trying their best to keep the mood light, even though she could see their apprehension in the way they moved. Raven was paler than Éabha had ever seen her, but her eyes flashed with a steely determination.

Her hair was pulled back into an even tighter plait than usual and she was wearing heavy black boots, black jeans and a grey flannel shirt. It was like she'd put on armour. Cordelia had forgone her usual heels, but she was still wearing her immaculate red lipstick. Éabha had seen her apply it like a weapon before. It was her shield against whatever they were about to face.

Archer started placing LED candles around the room, Davis helping him. Fionn sorted through the equipment while Raven and Cordelia conferred in low voices, standing so close together that Éabha felt it was almost intrusive to look over at them, as though she was observing some intimate act that was not meant for her eyes. Their hands were just brushing against each other, Raven's head tilted up to look at Cordelia, Cordelia's hips angled so that the space between them was minimal.

Éabha had no task to do yet, and this allowed time for the doubts that had been knocking on the doors of her mind to sweep in. Could she do this? How could she look Archer in the eye knowing that his father was still trapped here, with *her*, and she hadn't saved him?

What would be the cost if she failed?

She didn't care what happened to her, but her friends, they mattered. She'd already formed a bond with them that knitted her closer to them than should have been possible after so short a time. The fierce protectiveness she felt towards them startled her. They were the first people to see her for who she was and accept her for it.

What would her parents think if they saw her now? If something happened to her, would they shake their heads and take it as proof that this gift of hers was 'wrong', that she herself was broken? She took deep breaths, in through her nose, counting and calming her mind. Lizzie had warned her about the dangers of an agitated mind, a heightened emotional state. She had paid the price for hers.

'Éabhs?' Archer said gently. She hadn't noticed him cross the room to stand beside her. 'You OK?'

She nodded, trying to smile reassuringly. 'Just thinking.'

'We're going to be with you the whole time,' he said.

She could feel his warmth, a bright spot in the ice-cold room. Tentatively, she brushed her fingers against his. 'I know. I trust you.'

He wove his fingers into hers, giving her hand a gentle squeeze.

'I think we're ready,' Davis said, surveying the room.

Archer and Davis had set the LED candles in a circle. They'd decided against real candles, worried about fire hazards and damaging the floor with wax. They hoped that the ring of salt and herbs Éabha would form around the team would at least protect the candles within the circle from being drained by The Lady if – when – she appeared.

The electricity had been reconnected in anticipation of preparing the house to be shown, so they were able to plug some of their equipment into the wall sockets. Fionn had brought extra cables and batteries, since The Lady had consistently drained the battery of any device nearby when she manifested. Two cameras were set up, one at either end of a diagonal axis, just outside the circle of candles.

'Do we really need so many candles?' Cordelia asked, wrinkling her nose. 'They make it look even creepier than it already was.'

'Sun's setting,' Davis said, nodding out the window. 'Want to sit here, on Halloween night, trying to contact The Lady as the light gradually fails?'

She looked at the shadows clinging to the corners of the room. 'Do we have any more?'

Davis laughed, the sound hushed and low, as Fionn started to dig through one of the backpacks, pulling out a few more candles. When he'd finished placing them, Éabha took a deep breath before saying, 'Everyone: get inside the circle.'

The others stepped in, forming a ring.

'Remember, once the circle is sealed, it mustn't be broken,' she warned.

It was probably the fiftieth time she'd said it, but no one pointed that out. Raven cringed as she spoke, and Éabha knew she was thinking of the video on the flash drive, of salt and candles scattering under her feet.

Éabha moved around the circle, placing protective crystals in between the candles, sprinkling water around the circumference before following it with a thick ring of salt. As she did, she felt the atmosphere in the room shift. The others became silent, their energy, which she gradually opened herself up to, fluctuating between nervous and determined. Finally, she pulled out the herbs she'd prepared, placing them into a burner in the centre of the circle. As their scent started to fill the room, the others watched her. Waiting, she realised, for her to take the lead. Taking another deep breath, she looked around at the five of them.

'Let's begin.'

She was proud and surprised that she managed to keep her voice steady.

CHAPTER FIFTY-FIVE

THEY SAT CROSS-LEGGED IN A CIRCLE inside the small ring of light, so close together that their knees almost brushed against each other. Raven could feel Cordelia to her right, Archer on her left. The smoke from the herbs in the burner in the centre of the circle rose lazily, tendrils wafting out to wrap around each of them. Raven could place only a couple – rosemary and cedar – the others unfamiliar but comforting. Éabha had adopted the poised mask she so often slipped into. The locket was on the floor in front of her, and Raven couldn't take her eyes off it.

'We'll begin by taking three deep breaths,' Éabha said, her voice low and calm.

Raven shut her eyes and obeyed. Her heart was thudding so hard she could feel the blood pumping in her wrists, her ears, a pulsing that moved through her.

'I invite you to take the hands of the people on either side of you,' Éabha said, her voice staying in the calm register she had started with.

Raven felt Cordelia's hand, warm and slightly slick with nerves, slide into hers. Archer's grip was strong, his long fingers wrapping around hers. For a moment they were children again, hands joined in a hotel corridor as they went to explore something they definitely shouldn't.

'I would like to welcome any guides or spirits who are here with our best interests at heart. We ask you to offer us your protection during our séance. If you would like to make yourselves known to us, I invite you to step forward now.'

The silence as Éabha paused was like being underwater, the air around them thickening. Raven's heart began to beat faster as she waited, nerves tingling. She could almost feel the emotions swirling around the room, each person's a distinct flame of light in the darkness that surrounded them in Hyacinth House. Then, there was another: a seventh presence. Was this part of the séance? Could everyone else feel it too? For a brief moment, she thought she felt a warm pressure on her shoulder, a comforting weight as though someone were resting a reassuring hand on her. She felt Archer's hand tighten in hers as well. Just as the sensation faded, a familiar scent washed over her. Peppermint.

A strangled sound crept from her throat. Everyone's eyes snapped to her. Across the circle, Davis looked at her with wide, sad eyes. He nodded just slightly, and she knew he smelled it too. He knew what it meant. She couldn't bring herself to look at Archer, even as he clung more tightly to her hand, his fingers trembling.

'I would invite any other guides or protectors who would like to make their presence known to step into the circle now,' Éabha said.

She sent Archer a tender look as she spoke. Her gaze then moved to Raven, blue eyes shimmering with the silent question. Raven gave a barely perceptible nod. She glanced at Archer and saw his face shining with tears. Her heart wrenched so fiercely it felt like it was being crumpled, then ripped in two. She squeezed his hand again, trying to put everything into that touch.

I am here, she told him silently.

She'd been gone for too long, but she was here now.

'We would like to invite the spirit of this house, The Lady of Hyacinth House, to join us in the circle. We ask that she mean us no harm, and promise we come in good faith, with open hearts. We wish only to talk and understand.'

They waited in silence, their ragged breathing the only noise. Raven's muscles grew tense. A low hiss of breath from beside her made her realise how tightly she was gripping Cordelia's hand, and she softened her fingers with an apologetic squeeze. Cordelia gently squeezed back. As she did, Raven felt it: the cold sweeping down the corridor, oozing into the room, filling it up with an aching chill. She could see gooseflesh sprouting on Davis and Fionn's arms, Cordelia's fingers starting to tremble in hers. The smell of peppermint faded, the feeling of her father's presence weakening, as though it was being slowly siphoned away.

'We ask you to speak to us if you mean us no harm,' Éabha said again.

Her voice was strained now. The calm tone was beginning to crack. The cold intensified, a huge, suffocating menace that clamped down around them. Suddenly the LED candles, the circle of salt, the herbs burning in the centre all seemed pathetic. Toys instead of shields, a child's attempt to protect itself. Like shutting your eyes and hoping the monster can't see you.

They'd made a terrible mistake coming here. Raven knew it, dread crawling into her bones, nerves prickling over her body like insects on a rotting corpse. A low knocking started on the wall by the door, growing steadily louder.

Closer.

Her hands twitched, almost involuntarily, and Archer tightened his grip, shooting her a wide-eyed warning look.

Don't break the circle, Éabha had warned them. It was the most important thing. The knocking stopped, and Raven felt a wave of relief. Then the cold, prowling sense of menace grew stronger. It was circling them, an invisible enemy looking for a weak spot, a way in through their protective measures.

Raven knew she was weak. She always had been. She'd break now and let the monster in and someone else would pay the price, just like all those years before. She was drained by the thought of it, energy leaking from her, limbs shaking, not from the cold but the inevitability of living with the consequences of her own failures.

'We ask you to join us in this circle. You may only cross in if you do not mean us any harm. We would like to speak with you,' Éabha intoned again.

Her eyes were wide and Raven could see her quaking, tremors spreading down her limbs.

'Join us, please,' she said again.

The words were fading into silence when it happened. One moment the room was empty. The next, a woman appeared directly behind Éabha, her face covered by a veil, her hands outstretched for Éabha's head. Archer lunged for Éabha to knock her out of the way of The Lady's grasping hands.

Pulling his hand from Raven's.

The LED candles flared and exploded, tiny plastic bulbs shattering and showering them with tiny cuts. Before they were plunged into darkness, Raven saw Archer's foot scrape over the circle of salt as he moved.

Breaking the circle.

Opening a gap.

A doorway.

Fionn's howl of 'ARCHER, NO!' came too late.

CHAPTER FIFTY-SIX

THEY WERE IN COMPLETE DARKNESS apart from the faint glow of the smouldering herbs between them. Raven fumbled in front of her for one of the emergency torches, hoping those batteries hadn't been drained too. Just as her trembling hands found the switch, she heard a long, low laugh.

It took her a moment to place Éabha's voice. It was her but utterly different, as though her vocal cords had been coated in something bitter.

'You'll never learn, will you?'

Raven clicked on the torch. A second, third and fourth beam joined it almost in unison, lighting up the scene in front of them. Archer was kneeling beside where Éabha was standing. One of his hands was outstretched, his face a mask of horror. Éabha surveyed them imperiously. Raven's mind tried to make sense of what was in front of her, but she couldn't. She knew she was looking at Éabha, but it wasn't her. Her eyes were narrowed and icy, her mouth skewed into a malicious sneer. Even the way she held herself was different, her straight-backed posture exuding superiority.

'Éabha?' Cordelia's voice was soft, hesitant.

'That's not Éabha,' Davis said, his face grim.

'Get out of her,' Archer said, his tone furious.

'No,' Éabha – not Éabha, The Lady using Éabha's voice – replied. 'A medium ought to have put better boundaries in place before she

362

played around with séances. And here two of you are, completely unprepared.

Two of you?

She sniffed derisively. 'Though I should have known from your father not to expect much.' A cruel smile spread across Éabha's face, an uncanny expression so at odds with her usual one that Raven felt ill. The Lady's next words only added to the urge to throw up on the floor. 'He has had his uses,' The Lady continued. 'His energy has been … delectable. It almost made me forgive his intrusion into my house. Almost.'

Had The Lady been feeding off their father for *five years*? What had he endured? She could see the horror she felt mirrored in Archer's face.

'You're dead. This is not your house any more.' Davis folded his arms and glared at the thing inhabiting Éabha's body as he spoke.

'This *is* my house,' The Lady snarled. It was jarring, seeing that vicious look sweep over Éabha's face. 'No one can take it from me. It is *mine*.'

'You're dead,' Fionn said, his voice calm enough that the shake in it was barely perceptible. 'You know that, don't you? Don't you want to … cross over? To wherever is next?'

They were floundering. Éabha was meant to lead the session and even though they'd all helped research and plan it, without her they had no idea what to do or say. There hadn't been an 'Éabha gets possessed' section on the whiteboard.

'This is my house. *Mine*,' she hissed.

'You can't stay here forever,' Fionn said evenly.

Éabha's fingers turned clawlike as she shrieked the words at him again.

'*This is my house!*'

'This isn't working,' Cordelia said, her face ashen.

'What have you done to Éabha?' Archer demanded.

Éabha's face smirked as she turned to him. 'Oh, she's in here. She's not very happy. Seems she also doesn't like people trespassing.'

'She is not a property, she is a *person*,' Archer growled, standing up. 'Get away from her.'

'Why would I do that, when this is so much more fun?' The Lady purred.

Archer took a step towards her and, quick as a striking asp, Éabha's arm extended, hitting into his chest and sending him flying to the back wall of the bedroom. It was far more force than Éabha could ever have exerted. Archer slumped to the ground and Davis bounded over to him. As he moved, Éabha-not-Éabha shot a glance at the ceiling. A beam cracked and fell. Davis dived out of the way, the wood catching his arm instead of his head. A sickening snap accompanied the impact and he let out a shout of pain, an agonised noise Raven had never heard him make before. Never wanted to hear again.

Éabha's face contorted, morphing from vicious glee to horror.

'She's using my energy,' she gasped. 'Knock me out.'

'What?' Cordelia said.

Éabha's face changed again. 'This is my house,' she sneered. 'And your friend is mine now. No one can take them from me.'

'The house will be sold,' Cordelia said firmly. She gestured slightly at Raven with her fingers, a gentle twitch in the direction of the timber that had landed nearby. 'New owners will move in. No matter what you do, that cycle will not change. This is not your house. Not any more.'

'You lie.' For a moment Éabha's eyes looked black, incandescent with rage.

'It's true,' Cordelia said firmly.

'It is,' Fionn echoed. He'd positioned himself to block The Lady's gaze from Davis, who was crouched beside Archer at the back of the room.

'It is not,' The Lady hissed.

Energy sizzled all around her, a static that filled the room. They heard a distinct pop and crackle from the walls, and smoke began to billow out of the plug sockets. Raven inched towards the wooden beam, her stomach roiling with nausea, her limbs heavy. She didn't think she could do it. But Éabha was in there. She saw Éabha's face suddenly change to desperation as she looked directly at Raven.

'Please,' she begged.

Then she was gone again, The Lady's expression snapping across her face as she fixed on Raven. Fionn lunged forward, reaching out to stop her and Éabha grabbed him, twisting his arm with a ferocity that made him scream. When she dropped him, his shoulder had been torn from its usual position, the arm swinging loosely. She turned back to Raven.

'No one will ever take this house from me,' she hissed. 'Even if I have to burn it to the ground.'

A jet of fire sprang from the smoking socket and flared across the centre of the room, engulfing the herb burner and the locket in crackling flames. Cordelia gave a horrified scream. Raven lunged for Éabha's body, only to be knocked back. She felt her ribcage crack, her breath coming in short painful gasps. Then The Lady was pinning her to the ground, Éabha's face warped with hatred.

'Your brother and your friends are going to die, just like your father did,' she sneered. 'Just like you will.'

She wrapped her hands around Raven's neck, squeezing. Raven tried to struggle, but she felt weak, exhausted, like her will to fight was ebbing from her. Confusion swept over her. The Lady leered down, pinning her to the floor, her hands still tight around Raven's throat.

'You still haven't realised I can use your energy, have you?'

Raven stopped struggling. Suddenly everything Éabha had told her about how spirits used mediums' energy aligned along with the fatigue she'd felt in the house, the sensations she'd picked up on. How Pádraig had had similar gifts.

'You truly didn't realise?' The smirk forming on Éabha's mouth was unlike any expression Raven had ever seen her make before.

It was as though the revelation had opened a door in Raven's mind. She could see The Lady's sharp, haughty features flickering under Éabha's face. She could see the two merging: The Lady's face getting stronger, Éabha's fading away. Then, behind her, an iridescent figure, his face concerned, his hands outstretched.

Her father.

His mouth moved and she could hear him. '*Use my energy. Fight her.*'

She could see it, a silvery, shimmering spiral reaching out from him, sinking into her chest. Her heart.

A rush of energy rose through her in a cascade, replacing

everything The Lady had taken. Her muscles strong again, Raven's arm reached out, searching along the ground until her grasping fingers touched the hard piece of wood. Her hand closed around it and, silently asking Éabha's forgiveness, she hit her with it. Éabha's hands slipped from her neck as she slumped to the side, unconscious. Cordelia and Fionn were there a moment later, Fionn coughing fiercely from the billowing smoke as he hoisted her to her feet.

Raven's whole body was racked with shooting pain, her legs wobbling under her, her vision blurry as she looked from where Cordelia was crouched over Éabha's motionless body to where her father had been. He was fainter now, but she could still see him, even through the dense smoke. He gestured urgently behind her and she whirled to see the thick flames that had spread across the room. There was no way through that barrier of fire, and Davis and Archer were on the other side of it. If she could have gotten enough air into her lungs, she would have started to scream.

CHAPTER FIFTY-SEVEN

ÉABHA CAME BACK INTO HERSELF to find that she was lying on the hard wooden floor, acrid smoke scorching her nostrils and coating her throat. Cordelia was leaning over her, the concern on her face melting into relief.

'You're back!' she cried out, smoothing Éabha's hair away from her face. 'You *are* Éabha, right?'

'Yes,' she croaked. Beside her, Fionn was supporting Raven, who was barely conscious and was coughing heavily. Smoke billowed around the room in a thick, choking cloud that made her eyes and throat sting. Fionn's other arm was at an awkward angle, his shoulder not where it should be. A vague flash told her how it happened and she shoved the horror down. She would deal with that later.

'Archer?' she yelled, scrambling to her feet. The room swayed as her vision narrowed, black spots dancing in front of her eyes. The deep breath she took in to steady herself only filled her lungs with more smoke, making her double over and cough heavily.

'He's unconscious and my arm is broken,' Davis called back. 'I can't carry him on my own.'

Éabha stared in dismay as the leaping flames between them rapidly grew higher, scorching heat burning the oxygen from the air. She could just make out Davis silhouetted through the flames, trying to pull Archer up.

'Get out of here,' Davis yelled. 'It's too dangerous.'

'Not without you,' Éabha called back, her voice cracking from the dryness of the air and the thought of leaving them behind that wall of flames. She turned back to the others. Behind them, she could see the figure of a man, slight with dark hair, who was looking from where Raven was leaning heavily on Fionn to the wall of flames trapping his son: Pádraig. He looked imploringly at her, the frustration he felt at not being able to help his children so strong it surged through her, even though his spirit itself was fading. She straightened her spine, quelling the panic threatening to overwhelm her.

'Get Fionn and Raven out of here,' she ordered Cordelia.

Cordelia shook her head. 'I'm not leaving you.'

'Fionn can't carry her on his own: you need to get them out,' Éabha said.

Cordelia nodded, eyes shining, and turned to go. Raven tried to refuse, her face white with pain and fear.

'I can't leave him,' she cried.

Cordelia took her other arm, looping it over her shoulder. 'We have to get you out of here.'

'Not without my brother. I can't leave him, not again.'

'I'm sorry,' Cordelia said, looking over at Fionn, and the two of them half-carried, half-dragged Raven from the room.

Éabha turned to look at the wall of flames.

'Get out of here, Éabha!' Davis yelled. As he did, a momentary gap in the flickering flames appeared and without hesitation she ran and jumped. Ravenous flames reached out to engulf her, biting at her dress, but she rolled to douse them as she hit the ground.

Archer was unconscious on the floor. She could see white poking out from the skin on Davis's arm and realised it was bone. Bile rose up in her throat.

'Can you take some of his weight on your good side?' she asked urgently.

Davis nodded, determined.

'We'll just have to move through it as quickly as possible.'

Davis pulled his jumper up over his mouth. Éabha grabbed a bottle from a bag beside him, dousing her cardigan in water before tying it around her face. The house was starting to creak and groan around them, like a dying animal. She crouched down and pulled one of Archer's arms over her shoulder, while Davis prepared to hoist him up on his other side. They heaved him up and looked at each other over where his body dangled between them. Davis's eyes reflected the determination she felt. And the fear. Before she could think about exactly what was going to happen, they staggered towards the fire, hauling Archer between them.

Greedy flames scorched her skin. Beside her, Davis cried out in pain, though neither of them baulked at their task. Her hearing aids grew agonisingly hot in her ears, and she ripped them out with her free hand, the plastic melting under her fingertips as she threw them to the floor. Everything was muffled now, her body was in agony, but all she could think about was the boy in her arms. Smoke obscured their vision as they emerged into the hallway, making her eyes stream. She paused to beat out the flames eating through Archer's clothing before trying to quench the worst of the ones on her, Davis doing the same on the other side. Her oxygen-starved lungs protested, her eyes weeping acid tears as they moved through the thick, choking billows of smoke. The fire pursued them as they limped towards the staircase, flames crawling along the walls and along the floor behind them so that they were trapped in an endless tunnel of flames. Her ankle was throbbing, her blistered skin screaming in pain, a cry she felt echoed in the house around her, the enraged howl of a dying monster from a nightmare.

Each step was slow, agonisingly slow. Her strength was almost gone, the toll of The Lady's invasion of her body and mind too steep. Panic started to overwhelm her as her feet slowed even more and she struggled to keep going. She was going to fall. She was going to drop him. They would not be able to outrun the flames, and it would be her fault. She felt rather than heard herself let out a choked sob.

Then, amidst the smell of burning hair and flesh, there was a waft of peppermint. A gentle touch on her shoulder, and a wellspring of cool energy boosting her, giving her the strength to keep going.

They lurched through flames that licked at their hair, their clothes. Then they were on the stairs, lungs bursting, Archer a dead weight in their arms, and then they were half-running, half-falling to the threshold, out the door, to where Cordelia was holding back a screaming Raven and Fionn was on his knees, struggling to get to his feet. Éabha stumbled, half-dropping, half-easing Archer to the ground, and collapsed. Hands thumped her, furious, heavy beats all over her body. She whimpered. Were Raven and Cordelia attacking her? What The Lady had said and done through her flashed into her mind. She deserved it, she deserved it all.

It took her a moment to realise that her clothes were on fire and they were putting out the flames with their bare hands.

Behind them, the house was fully consumed by a roaring inferno. The groans and cracks that filled the air as the house imploded, collapsing in on itself as the flames leaped skywards, were loud enough that she didn't need her hearing aids to make them out. Then, over the sound of destruction, she heard a long scream of fury. Her head snapped up to see a figure in the window of the bedroom beside the tower, a writhing shadow that disappeared in a final wail of rage and frustration. She looked at Raven, who was also staring up at the window. Her frightened eyes met Éabha's and, at Éabha's questioning look, she nodded. She had seen her too.

Éabha felt her leave. The air of foreboding that had always spilt from Hyacinth House was gone. She saw Raven stiffen, her face tight with grief and longing, and turned to see a faint figure on the gravel beside them. He smiled, looking from Éabha with gratitude to Raven with love. Éabha's tears continued to fall from her stinging eyes, the boost of energy he'd gifted her dwindling as she struggled to hold onto consciousness. She felt, rather than heard, the words 'Thank you' as her mind slipped into darkness.

CHAPTER FIFTY-EIGHT

IT WAS A BLEAK DECEMBER DAY, one where the sun struggled to break through the grey clouds even in the early afternoon, and the air filled your lungs with sharp needles. Éabha shivered, despite the fact that the heat in the car was already turned up to full blast. Archer glanced over at her, the pink welt on his cheek less vivid than before but still shining in the winter light. His hands tightened slightly on the wheel as he looked at her.

'You OK, Éabhs?'

'I'm fine.'

The lie felt thick on her tongue. This had happened a lot since The Lady had possessed her: random chills in warm rooms, dreams that felt like memories, memories that weren't hers. Recollections of the powerlessness of being in her body and unable to control it. Being filled by a sense of malice that shot through her. The Lady was gone, crossed over in the destruction of the house, but remnants had clung to her. Shadows lurking in the corners of her mind. Flashes of spite and vengeance and malice. Archer reached over and squeezed her hand, keeping his eyes on the road as he smoothly changed lanes.

'Have you spoken to Lizzie about it yet?'

'Not yet, but I will,' Éabha said.

That wasn't a lie. She'd tell Lizzie, eventually. Lizzie had been guiding her through some practices to help her heal from being possessed, but Éabha hadn't told her the extent to which she felt that stain clinging to her. Lizzie probably already knew, anyway; it was hard to hide anything from her, especially now that they lived together. Once it became clear that the rift between Éabha and her parents was not temporary, Lizzie had insisted that her niece move in with her.

'Allow me to make up for eighteen years of missed time,' Lizzie had said with a smile.

Éabha could have stayed at Archer's house but, after the fire, Emily had come back from her book tour and she, Archer and Raven had a lot to work through. It was one thing for Davis, who was practically a member of the family, to live there. Éabha would have felt like an intruder. Besides, between working together and now whatever this fledgling relationship between them was, living with Archer felt like too much, too soon.

Anyway, she *wanted* to live with Lizzie. She wanted to get to know her aunt, their relationship already part mentor–student, part friends. Lizzie spoke to her like an equal, like an adult. She saw her for who she was and encouraged her to flourish. In some ways, her house already felt more like a home than her parents' house ever had. She had a fleeting moment of treacherous guilt at that thought and her stomach heaved.

'It's going to be OK,' Archer said softly.

'Is it that obvious I'm freaking out?'

'Not at all. I just figured anyone in your position would be feeling a *little* apprehensive.'

Éabha snorted. She'd known her parents were stubborn, that they drew firm lines about what they approved of and what they didn't, but it had still hurt when she woke up in the hospital and they weren't there. It had taken her hours to ask the question, to give voice to the fragile hope that somehow, in the chaos of their team nearly dying, someone had forgotten to inform them.

The gentleness in Lizzie's voice as she told her they knew nearly broke her.

She'd cried herself to sleep that night, and many nights after. But the pain was starting to lessen, especially as she considered the people who did come to visit her during the days she'd spent waiting for the burns to begin to heal. Fionn, his arm in a sling and his voice even raspier than hers, sneaking her bags of Maltesers. Davis, his forearm in a cast already enthusiastically decorated by the others. Archer, first wheeled in from next door as they monitored his head injury, then limping in by himself. Raven and Cordelia, always arriving together, covered in bandages and trying not to be obvious that each of them was always aware of where the other was in the room at all times.

Archer pulled up outside her house. Her parents' house. She took a deep breath.

'You don't have to come in with me.'

'You're not doing this alone.'

'It's not going to be pleasant.'

'You jumped through a *wall of fire* for me. I can deal with your parents.'

She laughed, then leaned over and gave him a soft kiss. When she pulled back, he raised a hand to cradle her cheek, his thumb gently stroking her skin.

'You can do this,' he said.

She nodded. 'I can.'

She checked her reflection in the rear-view mirror, still taken by surprise by her new look. The fire had burnt so much of her long hair that she'd gotten a short pixie cut to even it out. It was a big change from the perfectly coiffed style she'd felt obliged to wear for so many years. It suited her.

Her mother's face as she opened the front door said she thought otherwise.

'Hi, Mum,' Éabha said. 'This is Archer. He's going to help me with my stuff.'

For a moment, her mother's gaze was approving as she took in Archer's tall frame, handsome face and clean-cut outfit. He was wearing grey jeans, a cobalt-blue jumper and his camel trench coat, and looked every bit the respectable young man she would have pushed Éabha towards. Then her eyes fell on the hand Archer was holding out to shake, on the deep blue nail varnish he had painted on the night before, and her mouth tightened. Éabha wanted to curl up in shame at her reaction.

Her mother took Archer's hand for the briefest of shakes, stopping just short of wiping her hand on her dress afterwards. Archer's affable smile never wavered.

'We'll go pack my stuff then,' Éabha said woodenly, after the silence lingered too long.

'I have a meeting at the church at three so don't delay.'

'We'll be long gone,' Éabha said coolly.

She went up the stairs to her room, Archer following. She shut the door behind them and leaned against it, shaking.

'I'm sorry about her,' she said in a low voice.

'You have nothing to apologise for.' Archer pulled her away from the door slightly, wrapping his arms around her and kissing the top of her head.

'If only my mother felt the same way.'

'If she doesn't see how lucky she is to have you as a daughter, that's her loss.'

Éabha sighed into his chest, her arms tight around him. She could feel his heart beating, and the steady thud soothed her. 'Thank you,' she mumbled into his jumper, then pulled back and looked around the room. 'Let's get packing, I guess.'

They gathered her things quickly, stuffing books and clothes into a suitcase, along with make-up, spare hearing-aid batteries and other things she had forgotten in the shock of her first departure. Luckily, she'd packed her spare hearing aids in her initial round of frantic packing, so Lizzie had been able to bring them to her in the hospital. They were an older, clunkier model that she'd kept when her parents had bought her a sleek, new upgraded version last year.

She found her painkillers on the bedside table, and lingered at the photo of her and her parents on holidays in the south of France that stood on top of it. Her fingers started to reach for it and then she sighed, turning away. She felt, rather than saw, the sympathetic look Archer gave her. She left everything she didn't absolutely need, nostalgia knotting her gut as she looked around at all the memories she was abandoning. But with them, she was also leaving the Éabha that lived in constant fear. The Éabha convinced that she was unwell, that she should be ashamed, that she was cursed. The lonely Éabha with no friends, afraid to let people close in case they saw who she really was and vanished from her life.

'Ready to go?' Archer asked.

'Yes,' she said emphatically. 'There's just one thing I need to do first.'

She found her mother sitting in the kitchen, the newspaper spread on the table in front of her.

'I'm all packed, Mum,' she said.

Archer hovered out in the hallway, close enough that she could feel his supportive presence, far enough away to let her do this on her own. She had rehearsed the speech in her head hundreds of times, never sure if she'd have the courage to actually say it. But now that she was here, she knew she needed to speak it into existence. Even if it achieved nothing, she needed to finally stand up for herself.

'I'm not the disappointment here,' Éabha said. She took a deep breath, squaring her shoulders. 'I know you like to think I am, but I'm not. You're my mother. I know that what happened in Hyacinth House was traumatising for you, but that doesn't give you the right to take it out on the people around you. The people that love you.'

Her mother looked up from the paper, her face inscrutable, and Éabha stared determinedly at her.

'I was scared, Mum. For years. And you and Dad made me think I had a mental illness, when all along you knew it was real. Love isn't only caring about someone when they behave the exact way you want them to. You could have helped me. And you chose not to.'

She could feel herself shaking, but her voice was steady. She held her head high and looked her mother in the eye, making sure she took in every word.

'Do you know how it felt to wake up in that hospital, after I nearly *died*, and find out that you knew I was there but weren't going to visit? Do you really hate who I am that much? I'm clairvoyant, not a serial killer. I help people. I can do good with this gift –' Her mother shifted slightly at the word. '– yes, *gift*, Mum, because that's what it is. It can be difficult and I still have a lot to figure out about it, but the one thing I do know is that I won't be ashamed of it. I want you in my life, but if you can't accept me for who I am, then I guess there's nothing I can do about it.'

Her voice cracked slightly. 'I love you, Mum. With all your flaws, and all the mistakes you've made, I love you, as you are. I wish you could do the same for me.'

Her mother sat silently. Éabha waited to see if she would say anything. Eventually she spoke.

'Is that all?'

'Yes.'

Éabha's heart felt like it was breaking in two.

'Goodbye, then.' Her mother looked back down at the newspaper.

'Tell Dad I said goodbye.'

Éabha turned and walked into the hallway. A single tear slipped down her face and she wiped it away determinedly, holding her chin up as she stepped to where Archer was waiting. He took her hand as they walked to the car. She got in and turned to look at the bags and boxes in the back seat, her life neatly packaged to start afresh, and then to him.

'Let's go home,' she said.

The others were waiting for them when they arrived back at the house, gathered together in the living room. Fionn waved from an armchair as they walked in, his arm out if its sling as of a day before. His lungs were holding up after all the smoke damage. Cordelia and Raven were chatting to him, Raven perched on the arm of his chair while Cordelia stood next to her, their fingers intertwined.

Raven was still coping with the revelation that she had some of the same gifts as Éabha. Lizzie was helping her but, after Hyacinth, Raven hadn't been able to access them. There was a wall in her mind, something blocking her. Lizzie had warned her that if she couldn't access her gifts, she wouldn't be able to control them, which could leave her vulnerable again in the future. The three of them would work on it together.

Davis smiled at them from where he was arranging champagne flutes on the wooden sideboard. The short-sleeved T-shirt he wore revealed a still-healing burn mark on the arm that wasn't encased in a cast, though it had been his legs that had suffered the most from the fire. At least, he'd pointed out cheerfully, he'd never been one for shorts anyway.

Looking around at all of them, still bearing the wounds of their encounter with The Lady, Éabha felt a stab of guilt. Despite what they'd told her, repeatedly, she still felt like it was her fault. She'd been possessed. She'd lost control. She still woke from nightmares of Archer and Davis behind a raging wall of fire, Fionn falling to the ground unable to breathe in the smoke, Raven and Cordelia reaching for each other as the building collapsed around them. The stain of The Lady being inside her had not washed away yet.

It was easier to push the feelings aside at times like this, though: when she was surrounded by the people she cared about. She curled up beside Archer on the couch, his arm slung comfortingly over her shoulders.

'Now that we're all here, shall we?' Cordelia asked, reaching for the bottle of what they'd nicknamed 'Lizzie's Winter Warmer', a fizzy infusion that Lizzie had concocted from winter berries and herbs in her garden. She popped the cork and poured it into the six glasses Davis had arranged, handing them out around the room.

'What will we toast?' Fionn asked.

'To family?' Raven suggested, looking at Archer with a smile. While the hurt from the past years hadn't magically disappeared, they were working through it together. Which was all Archer had ever wanted anyway.

'To not dying?' Davis suggested wryly.

'To not getting sued,' Cordelia added.

They laughed at that, the relief at the result of the inquiry by the insurance company still fully sinking in. There had been an investigation into the fire, of course, to find the cause. It had been a long month as they waited to find out if they would be held responsible for it. *They* knew they'd had nothing to do with it, but they also knew that 'it was the ghost' probably wasn't a defence heard much in court if they needed to fight an accusation of wrongdoing.

Luckily, it hadn't come to that. The inquiry ruled that the fire had been caused by an electrical fault. Not only would the sellers get insurance compensation, but the land could now be sold for a multitude of purposes as the conservation order was void. Cordelia had messaged the group chat with the news: the sellers were delighted.

'They're welcome,' Davis had said with a smirk, though the relief was tangible for all of them.

Cordelia wouldn't lose her job. She was already on the lookout for another, sick of the boys' club culture in Rafferty and Co., but she wanted to walk away on her own terms. The commission from the sale of the land wouldn't hurt either.

'To us,' Éabha said firmly.

Archer squeezed her closer to his side and she turned her head to smile at him before looking around the room.

'To us,' the others chorused: her colleagues, her friends, her family. They raised their glasses and she took a sip of her drink, the bubbles filling her with brimming anticipation.

Something was about to happen; a tingling in the air told her so.

Archer's phone rang. He left the room as he answered it, using his formal business phone voice. The others chatted away while he was gone, Davis filling Cordelia in on his latest paper, Fionn bickering good-naturedly with Raven about some art house film they'd gone to earlier in the week. The warmth in the room washed over her as she watched them, content.

Archer slipped back into the room.

'So, that newspaper article seems to have not completely damaged our reputation,' he grinned.

A national newspaper had picked up the story of Hyacinth House. Luckily, they had really leaned into the supernatural aspects of the tale and had talked about them as 'plucky paranormal investigators', not 'potential arsonists' (though that was a theory heavily posited in the comments section).

The others turned to look at him.

'Wait, does this mean ...?' Raven asked.

Archer sat down again beside Éabha on the couch, putting his arm back around her and kissing her on the top of her head before beaming at the others.

'How do you all feel about a haunted cruise ship?'

ACKNOWLEDGMENTS

I wrote this book while shielding during the first fifteen months of the pandemic, when I was feeling scared and lonely. So now, several years later, it's overwhelming to see the long list of people woven into the fabric of this tale.

My heartfelt thanks go to all the booksellers, bloggers and early readers of *What Walks These Halls* for your kind words and for shouting so loudly and enthusiastically about it. You're integral to getting books into readers' hands, and your support is such a gift. Louisa at Raven Books, for tracking down many obscure ghost-hunting research books and all our bookish chats.

To everyone at The O'Brien Press: I haven't met everyone yet so I can't list you all by name, but please know that the care and enthusiasm the entire team have put into *What Walks These Halls* means the world to me. Thank you to my wonderful editor, Paula Elmore, for supporting me through the editing process and helping to make *What Walks These Halls* the best possible book it could be, to Emma for the beautiful cover, Eoin for the proofread, Bex in production, Ruth and Chloe in marketing, the sales team (especially Aoife, for opening a door I never dreamed I'd walk through), Kunak in rights, and Ivan O'Brien for welcoming me into The O'Brien Press.

To my Twitter pals Clarey, Aislinn, Gabbie, and the 2023 Kidlit Group: thank you for your friendship and support. Jess and Lucy, my Chronic Coven, thank you for caring for me and cheering me on (and for all the cat photos).

Being a debut author can be nerve-wracking and I'm so grateful to my writery friends for being so kind about sharing their wisdom and encouragement, especially Deirdre Sullivan, Claire Hennessy and Helen Corcoran. Courtney Smyth, one of the earliest readers of *What Walks These Halls* back when it was still 'Ghost Book', it would not be what it is today without you.

Carrie, thank you for your pop culture knowledge, your friendship, and, for so many reasons, for the ghost story. Tanya, for your constant support and understanding the urge to flee into the forest. Stacy, for the years of dreaming over brunches and your unshakable belief in me and this book. Rebekah, my dear friend and fellow desk enthusiast, thank you for loving these characters so fiercely, and talking through endless plot dilemmas over hot chocolate. Brian, you've listened to me ramble about this book from Day One. Thank you for the playlists, and for patiently supporting me through so many moments of panic. I love you.

To my parents, Eamon and Margaret – Dad, I'm sorry I killed the father off. Mum, I promise that neither of the mums in this book is based on you. Thank you both for being there for me through years of illness, and all the years before too.

Sib, I will never stop feeling lucky to have you as both my best friend and my sister. Thanks for being as weird as I am.

I can't forget to say a big thank-you to my four-legged supporters: Bailey, who snored loudly behind me as I typed, and Coco Swift, who thinks the typing-to-pets ratio must always be skewed in her favour.

And finally, to you, dear reader: thank you for taking a chance on my little team of ghost-hunting misfits.